Also by Lucy Vine

Hot Mess
What Fresh Hell?
Are We Nearly There Yet?
Bad Choices
Seven Exes

Lucy Vine is a writer, editor and bestselling author of six novels. Her books have been translated into sixteen languages around the world, with *Hot Mess* optioned for a TV series in America. Her writing has appeared in the likes of *Grazia*, *Stylist*, *Heat*, *Fabulous*, *New*, *Now*, *Marie Claire*, *Cosmopolitan*, *Daily Telegraph*, *The Sun* and *Mirror*.

First published in Great Britain by Simon & Schuster UK Ltd, 2024

1 3 5 7 9 10 8 6 4 2

Simon & Schuster UK Ltd
1st Floor
222 Gray's Inn Road
London WC1X 8HB

Simon & Schuster: Celebrating 100 Years of Publishing in 2024

Simon & Schuster Australia, Sydney
Simon & Schuster India, New Delhi

www.simonandschuster.co.uk
www.simonandschuster.com.au
www.simonandschuster.co.in

A CIP catalogue record for this book
is available from the British Library

Paperback ISBN: 978-1-3985-1535-2
eBook ISBN: 978-1-3985-1536-9
Audio ISBN: 978-1-3985-1537-6

Typeset in Bembo by M Rules
Printed and Bound in the UK using 100% Renewable
Electricity at CPI Group (UK) Ltd

MIX
Paper | Supporting
responsible forestry
FSC® C171272

Lucy Vine

DATE WITH DESTINY

**SIMON &
SCHUSTER**

London · New York · Sydney · Toronto · New Delhi

Ginny's Six Predictions

Losses:
1. A heartbeat
2. An independence
3. A death

Gains:
1. A lifechanging trip
2. A person you thought I lost forever
3. Your Soulmate

CHAPTER ONE

The trouble with spending half your life with six psychic predictions hanging over your head is that your friends never let you forget about it.

'You *must* be thinking about them!' Myfanwy cries, struggling to be heard over the pumping music blasting out around us. 'Surely you're excited! Your birthday's in a week! You've been waiting *sixteen* years for this!'

'But it's silly!' I shout back. 'And it's not like they're nice predictions anyway. I don't *want* them to come true.'

She pouts. 'Some of them are nice. And,' she shrugs, 'if it's your destiny, babe, it's your destiny.'

A woman beside us turns around. 'Did you say my name?'

We regard her blankly for a few seconds. 'Are you called Destiny?' Myfanwy asks at last.

She nods.

'Oh,' I swallow awkwardly. 'Sorry. We weren't talking to you.' She turns away and Myfanwy gives me a knowing look.

'See, Ginny? Destiny is literally here on your doorstep. Are you going to ignore it?'

Destiny turns around again. 'Seriously, did you want something?'

'Um, no,' I reply. 'She did say your name again, but she's still not talking to you.' I glance desperately at Myfanwy. 'She's talking about, like, fate?'

Destiny frowns as Myfanwy inches closer. 'But while you're here, Destiny, don't you think my friend here should be listening to signs from the universe?'

Destiny waves her hand dismissively. 'Oh, I don't believe in that woo-woo guff.'

My best friend looks put out. 'But you're literally called . . . OK, never mind. Don't you think Ginny should at least be *open* to possibilities?' She turns back to me, arms wide, imploring. 'Go with destiny!'

Destiny frowns again. 'Sorry, I probably can't leave – though I'd love to.' She rolls her eyes. 'I'm on a truly crappy hen do right now and the stripper won't bugger off.' We glance past her at a huge man in his fifties, jerking his middle-aged body towards our easily confused new pal, Destiny. Seeing our interest, he whips his top off, revealing a waxing strip-shaped rash across his chest. He leers, flicking his nipple piercing.

'HEY, STRIPPER? PLEASE GET LOST!' Destiny shouts at him, enunciating as clearly as she can. He continues to dance on the spot, awkwardly thrusting his hips like he's channelling Channing Tatum. 'Ugh,' Destiny turns back to us. 'This is the worst.'

'We're on the same shit hen do actually,' Myfanwy grins. There's so many of us, it's hard to keep track.

Without warning, the stripper changes focus, now thrusting his hips towards Myfanwy and me as we exchange a look of pure horror.

'Oh my god, I'm free,' Destiny breathes out, before making a run for the loos, her final word reaching us on the sweat-wind: 'Byeeeeeeee!'

The stripper moves closer, the heat of his body invading our personal space as he smiles an easy smile.

'Another Celeste special,' Myfanwy observes after a moment. 'Who hires a stripper for a hen do anymore? Haven't we progressed as a society?' She shudders as I nod.

'I think that's probably why Celeste had to hire out most of this place – because the general public doesn't want to be reminded of things we thought were fun and cool in the noughties.'

She shudders again. 'The noughties were full of dirty secrets.'

We turn our backs on the desperately sad man. 'God, Myfe,' I breathe mostly to myself, wishing I was anywhere but here. 'My life is going to be so much easier when everyone I know is dead.' I regard the rest of the room with dark eyes.

Myfanwy tuts. 'You just officially reached peak introvert.' I glance over at her, feeling a pang of guilt at her wounded expression.

'Not you,' I say, reaching for her arm. It's sticky from the last round of shots we all did – the one that mostly ended up *over* the group rather than in them. 'Never you, Myfe.' She beams as I continue, 'I just meant this is genuinely the most horrendous hen do I've ever been on.'

'A horren do?' Myfanwy muses, fiddling with the sleeve on her slutty air-hostess outfit.

'Who even was that Destiny woman? And who're all these people? Who are those women over there?' I squint into the distance, where a tight-knit group on the dance floor are grinding against each other, while thirsty glass-collectors and the DJ watch with wide eyes and wide mouths, facial hair wet with perspiration. 'Do you know any of them?'

She swats at the stripper as he attempts to grind on her. 'I think they're women Celeste met through Instagram? They're all called, like, Ariana and Kendall.'

I snort, not sure how seriously to take her. Myfanwy is super clever and very dry, while I'm pretty dumb and a bit wet. Sometimes her jokes are lost on me.

'HEY STRIPPER!' Myfanwy shouts as he attempts another grind. 'LOOK!' She points over at the group of Kendalls and his eyes light up. He pants his thanks, flinging himself – and his waxing rash – in their direction.

'Poor Kendalls,' I murmur as Myfanwy leads us to a pair of tatty sofas in the corner. Collapsing in a heap, I glance towards the bar where Sonali, Toni and Diane are doing pink tequila shots. At least we know those three.

'Ugh, I'm so uncomfortable,' Myfanwy whines, pulling at her too-small skirt, digging into waist flesh. 'This costume is at least two sizes too small.' She sighs and I try not to smile.

Myfanwy is a few months into a new relationship with Sonali. She's completely head over heels, madly in love, and, as tends to happen, love has brought with it many cosy nights in — accompanied by many a takeaway. She's now a stone or so heavier than she was pre-relationship, a fact Celeste passive–aggressively chose to ignore when handing out the weekend's costumes.

But — stupid outfit aside — the extra layer of fat really suits Myfanwy. Actually, both the weight and the happiness suit her.

'I'm soooo sweaty!' My sister Toni lands beside us with a heavy thud. She's all legs and the air-hostess skirt is more of a fabric belt on her.

Sonali and Diane are two seconds behind her, sheeny and manic-eyed.

'Are you two being boring?' Sonali flops down beside Myfanwy, kissing her cheek tenderly. It's still a bit strange seeing them be so openly affectionate. I met them both back at university when I was eighteen. We were all purely friends for so long and it wasn't until a few months ago that they both admitted how they felt and started dating.

Myfanwy grins at her. 'We're hiding from strippers and Celeste.' She pauses. 'Plus, my legs are killing me after the indoor wall-climbing earlier.'

'Yeah, who thought that was a good idea right after cocktail making?' Diane asks dryly, pointedly scanning the room for the culprit. Celeste is over with the Kendalls, wild-armed, gesticulating as she shouts at the stripper. I laugh, immediately feeling bad because I know how much time and effort all this unnecessary nonsense required to organize.

'I can't believe she made us zipwire as well.' Sonali rolls her eyes as Toni leans forward, examining bruised shins.

'Maybe we should go zipwiring again for your birthday next week,' Myfanwy guffaws, her Welsh accent at its strongest when she's drunk.

I shudder. 'Please no!' I beg. 'Can my birthday present be that I'm allowed to stay at home and go to bed really early with a packet of biscuits?'

'Nope,' Sonali grins.

'I can't believe it's your thirty-second birthday,' Toni says in an awed voice, staring at me with huge eyes.

My little sister is a hundred years younger than me – by which I mean nine years. She's a whole different generation, and I know in her eyes I am ancient. Wizened with age. Close to death. That I must've done and seen and learned everything by now.

I don't know how to explain to her that the older you get, the younger and more inexperienced you feel.

Myfanwy regards me with a level of seriousness before saying quietly, 'Thirty-two. At last.'

She's talking about the predictions again.

Diane gasps, 'Oh my god, *of course*!'

'Thirty-two,' Sonali repeats reverentially as she and Diane regard each other. 'It feels like we've all been waiting for you to reach this age for, like, *ever*.' She pulls out her tiny tub of Vaseline.

I swallow hard. 'Nothing will happen,' I comment, uncertainty clear in my voice.

Toni looks between all of us now, eyes even wider with confusion. 'What are you guys talking about? Is this another in-joke? I feel left out.'

Diane strokes her arm reassuringly. 'We're talking about Ginny's six predictions,' she reminds her gently as Myfanwy takes over, bouncing in her seat.

'You know this story! How Ginny went to a funfair when she was sixteen and this fortune teller accosted her by the candy floss? She told Gin that in sixteen years she would have three huge losses and three huge gains.' She turns to me accusatorily. 'She's turning thirty-two at long last, and Ginny claims she hasn't been obsessing about it.'

'Definitely not as much as you.' I try to sound amused instead of freaked. 'But like I said – like I've said a *thousand* times – it was probably all rubbish anyway.'

'I'd completely forgotten!' Toni breathes out. 'The fortune teller and her six predictions!'

'It's silly.' I force an eye roll, trying to swallow.

I don't want to talk about this, I *really* don't. Because even though I don't really believe in any of that stuff – psychics, mediums, ghosts, astrology – these six predictions have ... *haunted* me. For half my life they've hung over everything I've done; every decision I've made.

I picture the fortune teller woman now; the way she flung

7

herself at me through the crowds, her large hair framed by the Ferris wheel. 'YOU!' she shouted at me, before launching into a confusing monologue about my future. The whole thing frightened the life out of teen-me and I wanted to pack it away in some mind-box forever.

But I met Myfanwy two years later, and she never let me.

She really believes in all that stuff. She's one of the smartest people I know: a science teacher with *two* degrees! From *two* universities! But in her spare time she visits psychics, faith healers, regression therapists, obsesses over her horoscopes, follows the movement of the moon, and attends Reiki classes.

'What were the six predictions again?' Toni comes closer, excited now. She hasn't heard me talk about this in years.

Myfanwy opens her mouth to answer and I cut her off. 'It doesn't matter because it's just a load of nonsense,' I insist, trying to add a note of finality to the conversation.

Myfe shrugs. 'Well, there's really only one that matters. There are five of medium importance and one you can't just ignore, Ginny.'

I picture myself at sixteen, standing in front of the fortune teller. Huge hair aside, she looked like anyone; not like the fortune tellers you picture in old movies. There was no head scarf, no big hoop earrings, no eye patch, no hook hand . . .

Actually, I might be getting mixed up with pirates.

Either way, I remember watching her face as she finished the reading; how she held my eyes as she gave me the last of the six predictions.

Myfanwy echoes her words now, holding my gaze in the same exact way.

'In sixteen years, you will meet your soulmate.'

The six of us are silent for a moment before Myfanwy glances up, her face falling. 'Uh-oh, incoming,' she hisses as a staggering drunk with a full-sized sick stain down the front of her air-hostess costume flops towards us from the dance floor.

'Where are your earrings, Ginny?' Celeste demands, zeroing in on me. She's too close to my face, her breath hot with the smell of vomit.

'Er . . .' I instinctively grab for my naked lobes as she moves in even closer.

'Where are they?' She's angry now and I frantically try to recall the point of the day when I removed the oversized aeroplane-themed jewellery.

'Oh,' the memory returns, 'God, sorry! The bloke made me take them off for the zipwire. I couldn't get my helmet on over them. They're in my coat pocket.'

Celeste's fury dissipates instantly and she plants a wet kiss on my cheek before wrapping me up in a stinky cuddle. I hold my breath. 'It's OK, I forgive you,' she slurs into my ear. 'Just go get them because your outfit looks silly without them.'

'Help,' I mouth at Myfanwy, trying not to gag into the tight hug.

'You all right, Celeste?' Myfanwy asks in her slowest, most condescending tone. Still holding onto me, Celeste turns her head to peer at Myfanwy, confusion across her face.

'Myfanwy?' she asks, squinting harder now. 'What are you doing here?'

Myfanwy snorts and gestures at her costume. She looks to me. I bite my lip, trying to extract myself from between Celeste's boobs. 'I mean,' she adds slowly, 'I *am* the bride's best friend.'

Celeste snorts. '*I'm* her best friend,' she retorts, turning to square up to Myfanwy.

'Nope,' Myfanwy answers.

Celeste spins back to me. Her eyes are wet as she grips me tight around my shoulders.

'Ginny, I *am* your best friend, aren't I, darling? I know I'm your mother, but we can be parent–daughter *and* best friends, can't we?'

'Um . . .' I am trapped, panic-glancing between Celeste and Myfanwy. My mother doesn't wait for an answer. 'You *have* enjoyed yourself on your hen do, haven't you, darling, Ginny?' Her eyes – blinking and wide – search mine, and I swallow hard as she continues, 'I know you said you didn't want a hen do and you specifically said you didn't want any of this, but you didn't *mean it*, did you? I know you didn't mean it. And you've had a wonderful time with all your lovely friends, haven't you?'

I don't even falter, trying not to glance around at all the strangers she's invited. 'Best time ever, Mum! I'm very grateful. It's all been so much . . . fun.' Behind Celeste, I spot Myfanwy covering her mouth, suppressing amusement or irritation. Probably both. I carry on regardless, well aware of my lines. 'It's been the best weekend of my life, Mum, thank you so much.'

Celeste nods, satisfied. 'I can't believe you're getting married in a few weeks,' she says now and I meet Myfanwy's eyes again. I can tell she's thinking about the predictions again – one in particular.

Because what's a person meant to do when they're destined to meet their soulmate at the age of thirty-two – but they're also getting married in a month?

CHAPTER TWO

'How close to the use-by date do you feel confident consuming a food substance?'

Daniel doesn't look up as I walk in, too busy examining the back of a bottle of Baileys. 'Like, obviously if it's milk or something, it's probably fine until day of and day after, too, right?' He holds the Baileys up to the light now, squinting as he tries to see into the black bottle. 'But when something has a two-year shelf life and you're down to the date wire, I'm more suspicious.'

'Your logic is flawed,' I mumble, throwing myself down onto the nearest sofa. 'If you have seven days to drink milk, one day over the date is a much bigger deal than one day and two years. It's basic maths.'

'Maths!' he makes a dismissive noise. 'Maths and logic have nothing to do with it – this is about *instinct*.' He glances over at me now, lowering the liqueur as he takes in my broken-ness.

'Welcome home,' he says, and though my eyes are now shut, I can hear the amusement in his voice. 'Fun weekend?'

'In parts,' I reply, trying to find some fun in there somewhere, in among the exhausting madness.

'Was, er, this *costume* part of things, or did you change into it on your way home, just for me?' Feeling him move closer, I crack an eye to find him perching on the settee arm, giving me a leery once-over with a wry smile.

I pick up the hem of my skirt; it's encrusted with an array of alluring stains. That one is grass, I think. That must be pink tequila. Ah, that one is definitely sick. All covered in a thick layer of edible glitter from the cupcake-making course we did this afternoon.

Answering with only a low groan, I roll towards him. He slides down onto the sofa cushions, pulling my fragile head into his lap and cradling it gently.

'Poor Ginny,' he murmurs, stroking my lank, greasy curls. The blow-dry Celeste made us all have on Friday – before activities began in earnest – now seems a million years ago.

'There is one thing that would make me feel better,' I say, my voice muffled by his jumper.

'A glass of almost-out-of-date Baileys that may or may not give us the shits, but we should definitely drink tonight in its entirety anyway?' he suggests.

'No, god, please no,' I groan.

'Oh, I know!' he tries again, his voice several octaves above hopeful: 'A blow-job?'

'Nice try.' I sit up now, trying not to laugh at his crestfallen face. 'What I really need – what would cure my hangover

13

and make up for the hellishness of this weekend – is a huge puppy cuddle.' I smile widely and he rolls his eyes.

'After the wedding,' he tells me for the hundredth time to my sigh.

I've been on a dog mission since we got engaged last year. I am sooo broody for a dog-baby. Every time we pass one on a walk, I start pulsing with longing. I just want to stroke a silky ear and play fetch. I've never felt such a ridiculous longing to throw a ball.

But Daniel says we need to wait. And I know he's right. We can't exactly have a carefree wedding and honeymoon in Madeira with a new pup at home.

'OK, fine,' I reply, kissing him lightly on the lips. 'I guess I'll have to settle for a Daniel hug instead.' He leans in, wrapping big arms around me. He smells like fabric softener.

I feel my eyelids droop as the exhaustion hits me like a wall. Physically, mentally, emotionally; all of the different ways to be tired, I am there.

I'm so jealous of extroverts, who get energized by interaction. I find parties, events and conversation so draining. I'm even depleted after a short exchange with the Tesco delivery driver about replacement items. A single night out requires at least two days of quiet to recover and recharge, never mind three days straight of socializing with women I don't know, when I'm meant to be the guest of honour.

'How was it really?' Daniel asks nicely. 'Did Celeste follow your instructions?'

I side-eye him and snort. 'Of course she didn't.' I reach

for his hand, squeezing it and enjoying his warmth. 'If she'd followed my instructions, I wouldn't have had a hen do at all. But in the end, it was the hen do to end all hen dos. It was like a hen do went on a really bad hen do, got food poisoning and threw up hen do all over the rest of the hen do. That's how *hen do* the weekend was. Everything that has ever happened on a hen do in the history of hen dos, happened on this hen do.'

'Willy straws?' he asks seriously.

'We got a fresh supply of them each morning,' I reply, matching his serious tone. 'Mine were personalized with both our initials, and so graphically realistic, there were veins on them.'

'I wasn't going to tell you . . .' he begins, looking sheepish. 'But Celeste actually asked me for a mould of my penis.'

'What?' I sit up straight, staring at him. 'You're not being serious?'

'I am,' he nods, suppressing a laugh. 'She wanted to use it in one of your activities. A kind of Mr and Mrs game, but with my willy, I guess?'

'Oh my god,' I breathe out, familial humiliation radiating. 'Did she use her three stages on you?'

He nods. 'Always. But I stood my ground.'

Celeste uses a three-stage technique to get what she wants from people, and it's usually incredibly effective. First, a question: 'Would you be interested in making a mould of your penis?' The second stage is all about guilt: 'You really *should* give me a mould of your penis, it would mean so much to Ginny and show her how much you love her.' Then comes that all-important third stage; if stage one and two haven't worked, she gives up all pretence that you have an option: 'You're doing a mould of your penis for me. I've sent you the kit and I'll be in your house at 7pm helping to fit it.'

'I'm really sorry,' I say, head in hands.

'I'm used to it,' he laughs. 'So it sounds like you've had a very wild weekend.'

'So wild,' my voice is muffled by fingers. 'Aggressively wild. Won't-take-no-for-an-answer wild. It was the party to end all parties. It was like Downing Street during lockdown.'

'It sounds like a lot.' Daniel bounds out of his seat with that boyish energy of his, grabbing me a glass of water.

I love that about him. I love his exuberance for life. He's always excited for the next adventure, the next party, the next fun thing. He's always making plans: plotting our next holiday, making lists for Christmas in August, talking about where we'll go travelling when we retire. It brings me out of myself and makes *me* more fun. I can't believe I get to marry him. Even after five years together, I still can't get over how lucky I feel.

'I wish we hadn't agreed to her paying for everything,' I sigh, shifting around to face him. 'It just means she thinks she's in charge.' I pause. 'And that she can keep changing things . . .'

He catches my tone, eyeing me warily. 'What do you mean – what has she changed now?'

I look down at the carpet, feeling ashamed. 'She told me

this morning she's amended the booking for a bigger room at the hotel – because she's invited an extra fifty people.'

'But we're already up to two hundred!' he cries. 'And we only know about twenty-five of them.'

'I knowwww,' I wail. 'I just don't know how to tell her to stop.'

He sighs heavily. 'Oh Gin, you're such a people pleaser.' I don't reply because this is a common refrain from Daniel. And Myfanwy actually. Because it's true, I know it is. I am a people pleaser. If we're being more specific, I'm mostly a *mother* pleaser.

But I just don't seem to have the mental equipment that other people possess. I see others – people like Myfanwy – drawing lines, setting their boundaries, saying no, explaining that they don't have time or don't want to do something – and I watch with open-mouthed awe. How is it possible? I go to say no or tell someone off and find myself staring at the wall or trying not to cry. I just can't face the awkwardness or the confrontation. I don't have the capacity. To be clear, it's not something I'm proud of. In fact, I feel very embarrassed about being such a child. But I can't seem to fix myself.

Until this wedding, it didn't matter that much. Daniel drew his life boundaries, I fitted mine around his, and it didn't impact our combined lives that much. But this last year, planning this huge, huge joint thing, it's become a Real Issue.

When we got engaged, we decided on a small wedding; nothing too flashy or expensive. We wanted an intimate ceremony to accommodate my introversion, followed by a cheesy disco in a nice venue. It would be a very average wedding, but full of details that made it *us*. Our colour choices, our table decorations; flowers Daniel and I chose. I work constantly around weddings at work, and I was so excited to plan my own for the first – and only! – time.

And at first everyone seemed pleased and happy to let us have our very normal, ordinary wedding.

At the beginning, Celeste said she just wanted to *help*. She asked to come along to view the venues or meet the officiants. Then, when I flinched at the prices, she offered to foot the bill. And once that happened . . . boy howdy, things changed so fast. She started amending bookings and adding random third cousins to the guest list. She would change our table plans without consulting us and booked a world-famous photographer who only does 'abstract' pictures. She cancelled our 'crappy' DJ and booked a jazz wedding band – and when I asked why, she claimed I'd once said I liked jazz. But I only said that when I was fifteen, because I was trying to impress Ian Pervis in GCSE Music.

And, like the blinkered, brainwashed fool I am, I didn't really notice she was taking over until it was too late to stop her. So now poor, sidestepped Daniel has been dragged into my people-pleasing by osmosis. He's trapped by my uselessness and it's not like he can tell off his future mother-in-law.

'It will all be fine,' he smiles brightly at me, reciting our mantra. 'Better than fine, it will be wonderful. We will ignore the hordes of people at our wedding we don't even know, and just focus on each other. When we're up there saying our vows, it'll just be about you and me, no one else. Trust me.'

I meet his eyes, still worried. 'Are you sure? It just feels like it's become this huge wedding monster that no one can tame.' I sigh. 'And it's not just Celeste, it's everyone.' I slump deeper into the sofa. 'Has getting engaged always meant you became, like, public property? I feel like I've been a museum exhibit this past year, opened up to the general population to view, comment on and review. *Two stars, very lacklustre, would not visit this bride exhibition again.* And every time I try to speak up or say what I want, I get shushed, like I'm ruining the experience for everyone else.' I pause. 'It's all just so intense, Daniel. I feel railroaded and bamboozled – and then pathetic for *letting* myself be railroaded and bamboozled. I'm a grown-up after all – shouldn't I be able to tell Celeste *no*?' I throw my hands up. 'The whole wedding is starting to feel like one big, bloated mess. Don't you just want to scream?'

'Sometimes,' he says agreeably, not looking the least like he wants to scream. He's better than me at all of this.

'Shall we just run away to Gretna Green or Vegas?' I suggest hopefully, only ten per cent joking.

'Our families would never forgive us,' he grins. 'Especially your mum.'

'I know,' I sigh dramatically, picking up the glass of water.

'Ooh, actually, can I have some of that?' he asks, grinning cheekily as I laugh and hand it over.

He downs it in one. 'Ugh, water!' He makes a face. 'Let's

have the dodgy Baileys, Ginny! Take our lives in our hands!' He jumps up with exuberance, grabbing the bottle. 'Let's drink this and then go meet Jimmy in the pub! The lads are all down there.'

I take a deep breath, steeling myself. I have the hangover from hell and would really like to sleep for, say, thirty or forty years, but I haven't seen Daniel in three days. I should make an effort. Even if it involves hanging out with his overly loud best mate, Jimmy.

'OK, I'm ready to risk it,' I say with determination. 'But I'm bagsie-ing the toilet now, so you'll have to take the bathtub if things get really bad!' I stand up, noticing what a state the flat is in. Tonight, I will be fun, and then tomorrow, I'll clean and tidy. Daniel has so many good qualities, but looking after himself is not one of them. But that works – *we work* – because I love looking after him. Plus, I need to do *something* to make up for my family; to make up for my flaws.

In the kitchen, I fetch glasses from the cupboards and he comes up behind me to wrap hot arms around me.

'Sorry to moan,' I begin, trying to shake the dread away. 'How was your weekend? Any willy straws involved?'

'Almost none,' he tucks his head between my shoulder and neck. 'I was mostly just chilling out.' He shrugs against me.

'Maxin'? Relaxin'? All cool?'

He nods. 'Shooting some b-ball outside of school.'

'Did a couple of guys, who were up to no good, start making trouble in your neighbourhood?'

'Exactly that,' he nods solemnly.

'OK,' I spin around, taking the bottle from his hands and sloshing suspicious liquid into glasses. 'Let's do this.' He laughs as we clink glasses.

I feel a rush of pride that I can make this gorgeous man happy. I will make him *so* happy, I know I can.

OK, so I'm not excited about the wedding itself, and the next hellish few weeks leading up to it, but if I can just survive it, Daniel and I will be married. And I *am* excited to marry him. We're going to be *married*! And I'm going to make him so happy.

That fortune teller didn't know what she was talking about.

CHAPTER THREE

Across the room, I catch my sister's eye and she gives me the signal.

Swallowing a sigh, I paste on my Helping Face.

A sleazy-looking guy is lounging across the counter as I approach, asking the same question she hears all the time: 'So is your dad's name "Tony"?' He gestures at the name tag on her left boob, making no attempt to hide the simultaneous leering.

'Er, no,' Toni replies, and only I can detect the bone-deep sigh in her voice.

'How *is* your relationship with your dad?' He leans even closer, trotting out a line he no doubt read in one of those disgusting pick-up advice books. The ones that teach idiotic men that women are all vulnerable, emotional, jealous hags with daddy issues.

And only *some* of us are like that.

'How are you getting along?' I ask in my best professional voice. 'Can I help at all?' Sleazo looks annoyed by the interruption but straightens up off the counter.

'No, no, I think Toni here has got it covered.' His eyes trail lazily across my breasts but, finding them underwhelming, he returns his gaze to Toni's more curvaceous chest. Instinctively I pull my hair from my shoulder to cover my nametag.

For some reason, men like this seem to feel they have a weird kind of power over you – like they think they own a little bit of you – when they've learned a personal detail like your name.

'Unfortunately, we need Toni in the back office,' I lie, directing myself at her. 'Your *boyfriend* Shawn is on the phone.' I see her tense shoulders relax by millimetres as I turn back to the customer. 'But I'm available if you'd like to see anything else, sir?'

He is undeterred. 'Weeeeell . . .' He huffs out his chest and I get a hit of Lynx Africa wafting off him. 'If Toni leaves for her *boyfriend* at this crucial moment, you're going to lose a sale here.' His tone is playful but it's clear he's a man used to getting his own way. 'I work in sales, too, see? And we all know building a relationship – a *bond* – with the customer is key.' He leers at Toni again. 'And *Toni* and I have bonded quite nicely. You wouldn't want to ruin that, would you?' He turns back to me, eyes swivelling across my chest as he tries to locate my nametag under all the hair. I feel a small catch of triumph as he frowns, failing. 'And I was planning on spending *big* today,' he adds teasingly. Behind him, I catch the tension returning to Toni's shoulders. 'What do men' – there is that assumption, always – 'spend on engagement rings these days?' he asks, the supercilious note still there in his voice. 'On average, two, three grand I'd guess, right?'

I suppress a sigh.

There are so many plus points to working for the family business, a luxury jewellery store, Celeste's Stones. But today seems to be mainly lows.

I demur, unwilling to admit he's in the right area. I wouldn't tell him, not even if he was actually a decent human being. Celeste says money is gauche; we're not even allowed price tags on our stock. She gets this sour look on her face when someone asks how much a certain ring or bracelet is. And, on the very rare occasion she's actually in store and working these days, she always hands over the payment part to me or Toni. Honestly, I think she'd rather let clients wander off with a £50k ring than actually go through the horrifying process of asking for money from them.

'And I was planning on spending upwards of £10k on a ring,' Sleazo continues. 'To be honest, Toni,' he still can't see my name and I swear in that moment to never cut my hair short again, 'I'm really only getting this,' he gestures now with a sneer at the array of rings behind glass, 'to stop the little lady from nagging so much.' Rolling his eyes, he does the puppet hand to represent his future wife daring to speak. 'She's seriously high maintenance but her dad's my boss, so what are you going to do?' He laughs like none of this is a problem.

But then, you'd be surprised how many men come in here to buy an engagement ring for their future wife and behave like this. Poor Toni often gets the brunt of it, being so young and so buxom. It's like a lot of men feel they have to pretend they're not *really* in love. Because being in love is a silly, emotional, *female* thing, of course. Many of our male clientele come in and do this little song and dance about being 'tied down' and how they've 'given in' on the marriage decision. It happens less than it did ten years ago, when I first started working here at the store, but I'm sad to say the male ego is still alive and repugnant.

I'm really glad Daniel's not like that.

'Excuse me,' a female voice behind me clears her throat and I turn away from Sleazo, abandoning my poor sister to her fate. *Sorry Toni, I tried,* I internally whisper as a young woman who can't be more than twenty-one waves anxiously at the rings. 'I'd love some advice on all this stuff.'

'Of course!' I say warmly. 'Anything in particular you're looking for?'

'Well, I want to buy a ring ...' she hedges and my smile gets wider.

The rings are my favourite area of the store. They're our speciality. We do a broad range of jewellery, but engagement rings account for probably three-quarters of our trade. And despite the many idiots we see in here, like that particular sleazo idiot still staring at my sister's boobs over there, I love, love, *love* my job. There's nothing like helping people with this huge, exciting moment in their life. Even if you're not a big, fat, hopeless romantic – which I am, for the record, despite everything I've seen about much of the male population – it would be impossible for anyone to work in a boutique jewellery store and *not* get sucked into the romance of it all. For every guy like Sleazo, there are five adorable, sweet couples who are head over heels, dribbling love out of their very pores and thrilled by the notion of promising the rest of their existence to each other.

Actually, I keep a secret list of my favourite proposal stories clients tell me – what they're planning or what they've done – and read them sometimes when I get yet another cynical sleazo in store. I'll definitely be pulling it out to read later.

'Absolutely,' I lead the young woman over to a nearby counter, a discrete distance from Sleazo. I don't want anything to ruin this exciting moment for her.

I give her a moment to review the gleaming gorgeousness, taking in the array of yellow, white, rose gold, platinum and palladium options. We have every type of gemstone here, from amethysts to sapphires, in every kind of setting. Her eyes scan across the vintage section now, lighting on one of my favourites: a yellow gold heirloom from the 1800s, with three deep blue and green opals surrounded by tiny diamonds. She won't be able to tell through the glass, but there's an inscription on the inside that reads: 9th November 1867. It makes me want to cry thinking about everything it must've been through and seen since that date.

'Is it a gift or a, er, special occasion?' I fish as the woman hops excitedly from foot to foot. Her eyes are lit up with excitement at the prospects before her.

I really want her to say she needs an engagement ring. She's too young to be getting married, obviously, but I *love* it when women propose.

Though, to be honest, most people who come in here on their own are just here to gawp at—

'So, like, oh my god, it must be sooo cool to work for Celeste Bretherton!' The young woman is no longer looking at our rings. Instead she's suddenly very close to my face, stage-whispering as she eyeballs a huge framed photo behind the counter. It's a promo shot from the third series of *Engage!*

In the poster, Celeste stands in a power pose, hands on hips. She's covered head-to-toe in sparkling diamonds, looking huge and Amazonian, glaring down into the camera at her feet, as an oncoming storm darkens the sky behind her. The tag line declares, '*Engage!* Returns for a new series on 8 Jan.'

Five years ago, my mum screen-tested for a brand-new streaming show called *Engage!*, where contestants with an eye for design create bespoke rings within a time limit. It was billed as *Great British Bake Off* meets *MasterChef* for jewellery fans, and right from the start, my mum was an obvious candidate for judge. By that point Celeste's Stones had already established itself as the newer, sexier Tiffany & Co., more modern than Cartier, more upmarket than Pandora. And with my mother as its face, the brand had acquired a huge cult following online, close to a million followers on Instagram, with people clamouring to watch her daily reels. She would describe, in her throatiest voice, all about her high-end, hand-curated stock; every item depicted in intimate, sexy detail. Every diamond was 'naked', every gleaming gem 'erotic'. She was accused of being the Nigella of jewellery and when she early-adopted TikTok ahead of the teenagers, there was no stopping producers piling through our door.

I smile, a little tightly. 'Yes, it's incredibly *cool* to work for your mum,' I add a small laugh, covering my disappointment. She's not really here for a ring; she's here to celebrity-spot my mother.

Her eyes land on me with astonishment. 'She's your *mum*?' She takes me in, disdain lighting her eyes at my obvious lack of star quality. 'Wow, that's amazing. Do you ever get to go on set?'

'I have done,' I nod. 'But it's probably not as exciting as you think. I watched a bit of filming, but mostly just sat around on the catering bus talking to crew.'

'Oh.' She's dissatisfied again.

'So,' I clear my throat, 'back to the rings . . .'

She looks caught out for a second, before smoothly replying. 'Sure, er, I need a ring for my . . . gran. She's turning sixty-five. But, er, actually I'm mostly just, y'know, *looking* today. Doing my market research, you get it.'

'Of course,' I reply smoothly.

We go through the rigmarole of discussing options before I leave her to wander around on her own. I know before I've walked two feet away, she's already WhatsApping her friends about the encounter. She went into Celeste's Stones and met *the* Celeste Bretherton's daughter! And she was lame!!!

That might be the biggest problem with this job. I don't really mind the sleazos or the cynical celeb-chasers. But I do mind my mother. Working for your mum would be bad enough but she's also the world's worst manager. She's a short-tempered, controlling, micro-manager who wants you to do everything for her but then will also redo it all because it wasn't exactly the way she would've done it.

It's what makes her such sensational telly, but, as her eldest daughter, I can tell you – Celeste Bretherton is A Lot.

And, oh god, speak of the mother-devil.

Celeste sweeps in through the back entrance, already booming out in that lusty voice of hers.

'Where's my darling birthday girl?' She yells this at me, even though I'm right in front of her. 'I need a cuddle, my darling!' She opens her arms wide and I glance around, embarrassed. The young woman with the fake gran is by the door, face white, eyes wide; her hands visibly shaking. Sleazo is watching with big eyes, too, Toni and her boobs momentarily forgotten.

There's no denying my mother has that celebrity thing. She *sparkles*. Which, yes is another one of *Engage!*'s tag lines, but it's also true. Celeste is effervescent in that undefinable way some women are. She's other-worldly, somehow. I think that's why I always think of her as Celeste, rather than Mum. I know it bothers her and I try my best to say Mum out loud. She says she doesn't mind being Celeste Bretherton to the world, but she wants us – her family – to see someone else underneath.

The trouble is, she so often forgets to leave the character

at the door. I guess, when the whole world sees you a certain way, how can you not be affected by that? I watch Celeste *perform* even for us, like we are her fans and viewers. It sometimes feels like I don't know the real person there, underneath all that Celeste Bretherton. Maybe it's easier; hiding. I wonder if my dad ever gets to know the real her?

The truth is, I don't even know how old she is. Her stage age is between forty and fifty-five but I think she must be closer to sixty, if not tipping over. But her skin is flawless. She loves all the non-surgical surgery and has weekly laser-y, sonic-y, Gwyneth-y facials that keep her looking tight and blank in an ageless way.

Myfanwy says the moment she turns forty, she's going to get everything Celeste has done. Personally, I've always said I wouldn't do it, but now I'm in my thirties – thirty-two today actually – I've started noticing certain upsetting changes. Things are happening around my face that are really starting to bother me. In my twenties, if I had a rough night or got ill, sure, I'd have awful eyebags and my face would sag a bit, but after a decent night's sleep, it would spring back to its usual self. That doesn't happen so easily now. The eyebags and sagging have just become part of my existence. I find myself looking in the mirror every day, whispering at my reflection *hopefully you'll look better tomorrow.*

Now I wish I hadn't said quite so publicly that I would never get anything done.

It's easy to say you'll age gracefully before you've really started ageing.

I allow myself to be enveloped in a Celeste hug, and it's a lot nicer than last week's hen-do sick one. The huge silk dress she's wearing – perfect for a red carpet, or apparently, a visit to the office on a Wednesday in late June – rustles around me.

'Toni! My darling!' she calls out now, releasing me from her grip. Across the room, my sister smiles tightly, 'I'm just with a client!' she says smoothly, gesturing at Sleazo, who is fully ignoring her now to stare at the vision of Celeste before him.

Celeste pouts. 'Toni is so unaffectionate, isn't she, Ginny?'

I murmur a vague dissent but my mother is already off on one.

'She's never going to get Shawn to marry her if she continues like that,' she declares, at a volume that Toni can clearly hear. 'She's so beautiful, but it's not enough, is it, darling? She needs to be an appealing prospect to a man or she'll end up alone and lonely, won't she?' Her questions rarely require an answer. Her viewers play drinking games during *Engage!*, taking a shot every time Celeste Bretherton asks a question and then answers it herself.

It's a shame I've not been invited to contribute to our conversation because actually I'd like to point out that Toni is one of the warmest, most open and affectionate people in my life, and Shawn doesn't deserve to be near her, never mind marry her; I really don't like her boyfriend choice. He's much older than her – more like my age – and has an arrogance I can't stand. He's always showing off and one-upping everyone in the room. Toni can do a thousand times better, but it's not my place to tell her that. She's only twenty-three; she has to figure out about dickheads on her own.

Toni and I weren't that close growing up, what with the nine-year age gap, but it's been the nicest thing ever, working with her at the store and getting to know her as an adult these last few years.

Celeste is still talking to me, slash herself. 'No hugs for her mummy, and meanwhiles Daddy's abandoned me again.' She pouts. 'He's back in Canada for another scouting trip.'

It cringes me out so hard that she says Mummy and Daddy. As of 6.02am today, I'm thirty-two! Plus *Daddy* sort of implies a very hands-on, papa bear-type figure. Whereas my dad is actually quite a sweet but distant, *barely around* presence. He does the stone sourcing for our business, and is constantly in faraway places on lengthy research and purchase trips. We've made such a big thing in the press about being conflict-free and ethical about our jewellery practices, so Mum and Dad decided many years ago that he had to be totally involved in that side of things. We can't afford to let a blood diamond through the net.

He's currently in Canada, which compared to his other regular destination – Australia – is just around the corner.

'Has Daniel got something nice planned tonight for your birthday?' Celeste regards me seriously and it takes a moment to realize this is one question I'm actually meant to answer.

I smile shyly. 'Oh, I don't know – I don't think so. To be honest, I think we'll keep things low key. It's not a special

birthday and we do have kind of a big party coming up . . .'
I give a short laugh.

'Don't you dare call the wedding of the century a *party*!'
Celeste looks horrified and I try not to flinch at *wedding of the century*.

'Well, anyway,' I shake off the fear, 'he's probably too distracted getting excited for his stag do this weekend to worry about birthday stuff. He's already started packing!' I laugh at his enthusiasm, remembering how I tripped over a large suitcase and two rucksacks in the hallway this morning. Daniel and his friends are only going for three days, but the man has packed enough for a month. He's always been more high maintenance than me; his stuff takes up 90 per cent of our bathroom cabinets.

'Oh darling, well, let me take you out for the evening then!' Celeste cries excitedly and I panic-backtrack.

'Um, right! Er, that's so nice of you, Mum, but actu-ally, now that I think about it, Daniel *did* tell me to keep the evening free, so maybe we're going out for dinner or something?' I lie unconvincingly, catching Toni's eye a few feet away.

'Hmm, OK,' she replies with more than a hint of sulk to her voice. 'As long as he's making a *proper* fuss of you. You're so special and beautiful, you deserve to be celebrated at every opportunity.'

This is the thing about my mum. She's controlling and annoying but I've never been in any doubt about how much she loves me. The need, like, *pulses* out of her in this cloying, aggressive way, spurting in every direction. It's part of why I struggle to tell her to back off, because I know it's mostly coming from a place of love. Dysfunctional, aggressive love, but still love. I think it's also this misguided idea she has that Toni and I are an extension of her. She assumes that everything she would want must be what I would also want. So of course I'd want an over-the-top hen do with fifty people I've never met, collectively doing an array of insane, boring or dangerous activities. And of course I'd want a wedding with 300 virtual strangers watching me walk down the aisle in a venue with 2,000-foot ceilings. And of course I'd want a birthday extravaganza on a random Wednesday evening.

Because it's what she'd want.

'Hey,' she smiles beatifically down at her Celeste's Stones brand watch. 'It's almost five, why don't you finish early and go home to Daniel? I'm sure he's got lots of wonderful presents for you.'

I grin, because he probably has. He's always been so fun and unpredictable when it comes to surprises.

As it turns out, even I couldn't have called just *how* unpredictable.

CHAPTER FOUR

All the lights are off when I arrive home and, as I pass through the hallway, I wonder for a moment if there might be some kind of surprise party waiting for me in the living room.

Surely Daniel knows me better than that? Hosting a party is in the area of worst nightmares for me. I shudder at the thought. Obviously the theory is to have fun, but I can't get away from all that horrible fear of no one turning up; the pressure of ensuring everyone is having a good time; the stress of potentially running out of drinks or food; the neighbours complaining; everyone leaving early and bitching about how crappy your house is, or how ugly your sofas are. I can't see the appeal whatsoever. Even *attending* parties means I need a lie down for three days afterwards. I was OK with planning a tiny wedding as a one-off, but since it has become this monstrosity of an event, I've been surviving by telling myself it's Celeste's party, not mine. And it kind of is.

Myfanwy describes me as a sociable introvert. Because the

weird thing is that I *do* enjoy meeting people and talking to them – and especially getting drunk with them. But afterwards I need a lot of recuperation and recharge time.

Thankfully, there is no surprise party in the living room, only more dimness, and I fumble for the overhead light.

'Dan?' I call out to an echoey flat, nervousness in my voice. Daniel works from home as a freelance copywriter, so he's almost always here when I get back. Has he been kidnapped? Murdered? Taken up jogging? I don't know which one would be worse.

I check my phone. No message from Daniel, only one from Myfanwy asking if I want to be involved in her and Sonali's summer solstice ceremony this weekend – followed by another message, sternly telling me to stop rolling my eyes.

I shoot Dan a text asking where he is, and then set about checking each room for killers, turning on lights everywhere I go and ignoring the stabs of guilt about the unaffordable electricity bill.

The flat secured, I pause, unsure what to do next. Usually I'd get into my pyjamas the moment I'm home, but what if Daniel has got something planned? Maybe I should be putting on more make-up, not taking it off.

I try ringing him but it goes to voicemail and I feel a strange gnawing in my stomach. Where is he? What if he's not OK?

He didn't mention anything about plans tonight when we said goodbye this morning. But I was in a rush and fielding lots of lovely WhatsApp messages wishing me a happy birth-day. Maybe I missed something.

Oh god, what if he told me to meet him somewhere and I was too distracted shooting off amusing gifs to friends?

I message him again and then retrace my steps around the flat, checking for a note on the fridge or by the door. Something jangles in my head as I pass through the hall-way – I'm missing something. The *hallway* is missing something.

The bags! That's it. Daniel's suitcase for Amsterdam. The stuff he'd prematurely packed for his stag do. They're gone. I quickstep through to our bedroom to check and they're not there either.

Did I get the plan wrong? Surely I'd remember if his stag do in Amsterdam started midweek, on a Wednesday. On my *birthday*.

No, we talked about it enough – he was definitely going on Friday afternoon.

The gnawing in my stomach is starting to get more intense. If he was injured or there was an emergency, he wouldn't have taken his suitcase. And he would've messaged me. The last WhatsApp he sent me was yesterday and it just asked me to please bring home bread.

Slowly, my hands shaking, I make my way over to his side of the wardrobe and when I open it, I find . . . nothing. Just empty hangers, dead moths and dust. His clothes are all gone. His shoes are gone. His cologne, deodorant, shaving equipment, his *stuff* is all gone.

I try to ring him again because this can't be what it looks like – it *isn't* what it looks like. There's no way, no chance. He wouldn't do this. There was no warning, no signs. We're getting married and we have an amazing, lovely life together.

There is still no answer and this time I leave a strangled message that sounds nothing like me.

'Why are all your clothes gone, Daniel? Where are you? I'm really confused, can you ring me back, please? Please, Dan.'

Then I change into my pyjamas, get into bed and stare blankly at the blackness of the turned-off TV for hours, waiting for my phone to light up.

It is almost midnight before he finally messages me back.

> Ginny, I'm sorry. I can't go through with the wedding. I just need some time, a bit of space to think. You were right, it is all too much. I can't do it.
> Dx

I drop my phone back on the bed as my hands go numb. I look around at the flat – at our flat – and feel its barrenness reverberate back at me. I glance down at his bedside table, empty of its usual mess. There are no used cups with its standard coffee line around the rim. No empty Twirl wrappers, no little pots of vitamins, no half-read biography about some sports star. The tiny things that make this flat our shared space are all gone. And so is Daniel.

The numbness travels through me as one thought loops around my brain again and again.

Happy birthday, Ginny.

CHAPTER FIVE

Getting dumped turns out to be a slow burn.

When I get to the store for work the morning after my birthday, Toni asks me how my evening was and I tell her it was nice but quiet. We're busy all day and I spend two solid hours with a couple who want a bespoke ring, fully designed and customized, but without any idea of what it should look like. I spend a while showing them options around the store and then refer them to the outside company we use for bespoke items.

They're sweet, I think, as I take their details, but I have a feeling it won't last. She's already got that ever-so-slight disdain for him. You can see it when he suggests something she doesn't like, or when he tries to kiss her. And once the contempt has set in with a relationship, from what I've seen, there's rarely any coming back.

Daniel and I don't have that. We're kind to each other, we look after each other, and we compromise. We're a healthy, functional, affectionate couple who are going to have a long and happy life together. There isn't any other option.

Days go by and I still don't tell anyone.

On Saturday, Myfanwy drags me to her summer solstice ceremony in her garden and I laugh as she lights a bonfire. I join in when she and Sonali sing weird nature-y songs. I even find some enthusiasm when she declares that next year we'll all take a trip to Stonehenge. I laugh even harder when she says we'll make our other uni friend Emily join us on the pilgrimage. Emily never comes to *anything* and is only a WhatsApp ghost on our uni group these days.

I want to cry a lot, but I don't because I don't want everyone to know. If they know, they might judge Daniel badly for doing this. I don't cry, not even as he contacts our wedding vendors and the emails start coming in.

> 'This is to confirm you've cancelled your flower order for 10th August. Unfortunately we are unable to refund your ...'

Blah blah. They all say the same kind of thing. We're not getting any of the money back. Not a penny.

And the only thing I feel is relief that Celeste is not cc'd into any of the messages.

Mostly, I don't cry because I know − *I know* − that everything is going to be OK. I know that this is just a blip. Daniel said in his message − his only response to the hundreds of messages I've bombarded him with − that he needed some time and space. He's just overwhelmed. Exactly like I was. How can I blame him for calling off the wedding when I pretty much said I wanted to do the same? This isn't about me and him – we're great together! We love each other! – this is about that stupid, awful, OTT wedding. Once we've cancelled it and dealt with everyone's anger and disappointment, we can get back to our lives. Maybe we'll sneak off to Gretna Green or our local registry office. But either way, we'll be happy and live a lovely long life together.

This is a blip and it's going to be fine. So why would I cry?

It is nearly two weeks before I am finally caught out.

UNI DICKS

Myfanwy
Er, weird question, Ginny, but how come Daniel's blocked me on Instagram?!

Sonali
Same question here! Is it a mistake? Is he that bad at social media?

Emily
I'm not on social media these days, guys! Sorry.

Ginny
Weird! Probably a mistake?

Myfanwy

Probably?! Ask him!!! Or shall I text him direct?

Ginny

Er, no, definitely don't do that. Look, it's not a huge deal and please don't overreact, but Daniel's taking a little space. We're going to postpone the wedding for now. Sorry to mess you all about! xx

Myfanwy

What?????????

Sonali

He's broken up with you?????

Myfanwy

The wedding's off????

Emily

Whoa, Ginny, I'm so sorry!!!

Myfanwy

I'm so confused. When did this happen?
I just saw Jimmy's pictures from the
stag do a couple of weeks ago?!

Emily

Who is Jimmy?

Sonali

@emily He's Daniel's best mate. They went to Amsterdam, right? Has this happened since then?

Ginny

Actually, it was a couple of weeks ago, just before the stag.

Myfanwy

AND HE STILL WENT ANYWAY?

Sonali

But he's all smiley in those pictures?! They're all drunk and happy and having a great time, cheersing the camera with their shit beers. THE ABSOLUTE FUCKERS.

Myfanwy

Right???! Everyone was commenting on it, saying, like, 'Congrats!' and 'Can't wait for the wedding!!!' The absolute barefaced HIDE on him.

Sonali

Even I commented something like that! Is that why he blocked us?

Sonali

Wait, wasn't that week your birthday???

Ginny

Um, yeah, it was around then. But it's just a blip, Daniel needs a minute, that's all. It'll be OK, it's just a small break.

Myfanwy

@ginny are you still in the flat or at your mum's? Come stay here with Sonali and me.

Sonali

Yes, a thousand times, yes. Stay here, don't stay in the flat on your own.

Sonali

Shall we have him killed? I know people.

Sonali

I lent that fucker my Point Horror collection only last month

Myfanwy

Are you on your way here yet? The sofa bed is up and ready for you.

It goes on like that for hours, with Sonali and Myfanwy veering between loving support and fury at Daniel. Emily stays quiet, probably worried she will be required to see me or offer proper friendship, but I much prefer her silence to the unnecessary sympathy from Sonali and Myfanwy.

Eventually, I put the group on mute and go to bed.

Unfortunately, muting and ignoring doesn't work.

Ten hours later, Myfanwy and Toni are on the doorstep of my flat, wearing sad, poor-Ginny faces and holding six tubs of ice cream.

'Er, this is nice of you,' I begin, unsure how to handle it. 'But I don't really fancy eating ice cream right now.' I check my watch. 'It's 8.35 in the morning and my sugar addiction doesn't usually kick in until after lunch.'

'But you've just been dumped,' Myfanwy blinks at me in shock. 'Of course you have to eat ice cream. And what are you doing dressed? You should be unwashed and stinky, awake all night funnelling ice cream on a drip.' She squints as she regards me closer. 'You look well rested, Ginny, what the fuck?'

I stand up taller. 'I haven't been dumped. He's just taking a bit of time. It's about the wedding; the mad, stupid wedding. It's not about me or our relationship.'

They exchange a look and Toni offers up a spoon.

I shake my head. 'Honestly, it's really thoughtful of you both, but I don't want it.' I shrug. 'I'm sorry, I hate not to lean into a cliché but I'm doing OK. I slept fine, I don't want ice cream. I'm not wailing into a pillow or screaming into Daniel's voicemail begging him to come back.' I don't mention the forty-odd voice-notes I have left for him; some of them admittedly a bit wail-y.

They glance at one another again and I try not to get cross.

'OK, you're fine.' Myfanwy rolls her eyes to let me know she's not buying it. 'But I'm missing my Reiki session this morning for you, so can we at least come in?'

I stand aside and Myfanwy barges past. For her part, Toni looks a little more cautious as she enters, squeezing my arm gingerly as she passes.

As we sit down in the living room, I try not to make eye contact with the many photos around the room. I don't want these two to catch me looking at all these happy memories and think I'm sad or mooning over Daniel. Because why would I be?

'Tea? Coffee? 9am wine?' I offer and then feel annoyed with myself. They might think I'm serious and it's a cry for help.

'Tea please,' Toni chirrups and then jumps up. 'I'll make it, you stay sitting, you need looking after!'

'I'm not sad!' I say, unable to disguise my exasperation. 'I can make tea! I was going to get out for a run in a bit, that's the only reason I'm in my gym clothes.'

Toni freezes, halfway to the kettle, unsure what to do. Myfanwy gives her the nod. 'Ignore her, make the tea,' she instructs. 'I'll have one, too.'

There is a moment of silence between us, as the kettle hisses into life. Toni is the first to speak.

'You really don't want to talk about it?'

I shake my head with determination.

'Don't you think maybe you should?' she asks nicely. 'Like,

47

oh my god, if Shawn dumped me or my fiancé had just left me before our wedding, I'd . . .'

'I'm fine!' I say again, trying to keep a lid on my emotions. I know they're just trying to be nice, but they don't understand what's happened. They think it's bigger and more horrible than it actually is.

'You know, being single could be fun!' Toni tries again. 'Mum will probably give you a hard time about meeting someone else right away, but being single seems great. You can do what you like, when you like. You can eat whatever you like and stretch out across the bed. You don't have to get someone else's sweat on you or share your dinner. You could travel or move somewhere exciting! You should have some fun.'

This hits me hard, like I've been slapped. 'I'm not single!' I can't keep the anger out of my tone. 'Why would you say something like that? I don't care if being single is fun or not, it's not, like, applicable to my situation.'

Toni reddens. 'Sorry,' she whispers and I immediately feel awful. I swallow.

'Sorry,' I say back, my chest still tight and suffocating from her words.

Toni smiles shyly, then her face falls as something occurs to her. 'Does Mum know yet?'

I shake my head, swallowing.

Myfanwy leans forward, placing a hand over mine. 'I'll tell her, and you're not to listen to her histrionics about it. This is about *you*.'

I'm unsure what to say. I want to say again that there's no reason to be comforting me like this. But I also really, really, *really* want her to deal with Celeste and the wedding stuff for me.

'Sonali wanted to come,' Myfanwy continues nicely. 'But I told her it would be too much.' She pauses before adding accusatorily, 'I thought you'd be really gutted and wouldn't want to see everyone. Maybe I should've made Sonali and Emily both come; we could've had a denial party.'

I sigh, imagining all four of them shouting about Daniel all at once in my small living room. I'm glad they didn't. I love them dearly, but Toni and Myfanwy looking at me with these sad eyes is bad enough. Actually, I note, Myfe is glaring at me.

'And don't think we haven't all noticed that you've muted us,' she says sternly.

I dip my head, feeling bad. But our WhatsApp group, Uni Dicks, is non-stop and intrusive enough on a good day, never mind when I'm going through something. It's exhausting having loving, caring friends.

I take a sip of the weak tea Toni's given me. I know they're just trying to help but I really want them to leave.

'You know what this is, don't you?' Myfanwy says suddenly.

'A small break so we can both think?' I offer and she tuts.

'No, this is the first of the fortune teller's predictions coming true.'

Toni gasps dramatically and I eyeball Myfanwy. 'Please don't,' I beg.

'Sorry but it is! The first of the six prophecies was a heartbreak.'

'My heart isn't broken,' I point out, my voice getting higher. 'Because this isn't a break-*up*, it's just a break.'

Myfanwy ignores me. 'There are three losses that come first, before the three gains, right?' She doesn't wait for confirmation. She knows the six predictions better than me by now. 'Up first is a heartbreak. That's what she said, isn't it? Number one is a heartbreak. This is very clearly the first prediction coming true.'

'No, it isn't,' I say in a level, steely voice.

Across from me, Toni looks anxious. 'He's called off your wedding. It's surely costing you thousands. You really think you can forgive that?'

I swallow hard. 'I have to accept that he's a real person who has feelings I have to try to understand. That's what a long-term relationship – a marriage – is all about. And at least he was honest. He needs more time – he needs *this* time – to get his head around it all. It's a lot. You know I was freaking out about the wedding, too. I had cold feet as well!'

Myfanwy looks annoyed. 'You didn't have cold feet about getting married, you had cold feet about the oversized event Celeste had foisted upon you.'

'Well, exactly. I'm sure that's how Daniel feels too.'

'You haven't heard from him?' Toni gives me a sympathy head tilt and it makes me want to scream that I don't need her pity. I'm fine. I'm fine because he's coming back and it will all work out fine. They don't get it and they won't get

50

it. But it doesn't matter what they think or say because *I* get it. I know what Daniel and I have. I know that he's not going to throw everything we have – five years together! – away. This isn't over, no matter what anyone says. They just don't understand yet, but they will. Give it a few weeks and everything will be back to normal. They'll see.

Daniel and I will be *fine*.

'Look, can we just change the subject?' I plead and Toni looks down in her lap, sadly. I know she's just trying to help but all I want is to be left alone to get through this *temporary* situation. 'Do either of you want any of that ice cream?' I gesture over the counter at the sweaty gifts they brought.

'Ohhhh,' Myfanwy sighs. 'Of course I do! I'd love some! I'd love some breakfast ice cream. Why do we only assign certain foods to the morning hours? Why am I not allowed pasta bake and ice cream at 8.50am?' She sighs again. 'But I have to be able to get into the next hideous air-hostess costume Celeste insists I wear.'

'For the record, I thought you looked gorgeous in that costume,' I comment and Toni nods enthusiastically.

'Beautiful!' she adds with enthusiasm, then her expression falters. 'I can't believe that was your hen do, Ginny, only a couple of weeks ago.' I scowl as she shuffles closer. 'Look, sorry, I know you don't want to talk about it,' she says in an urgent whisper. 'But are you going to be OK, working in a jewellery store that specializes in engagement rings, when you've just been, y'know ...' she glances at Myfanwy anxiously ' ... *jilted*?'

Myfanwy looks thoughtful. 'Maybe your work is something to do with that second prediction.' Before I can stop her, she is listing the predictions again. 'The first three are all losses, as we know. Firstly a heartbreak.' She does an air tick with her finger. 'You've had that—'

'Not a heartbreak,' I mutter but she ignores me.

'Second in the losses is "An independence".' Myfanwy frowns, adding, 'Whatever the hell that's meant to mean. It could be your work, maybe?' She looks to Toni. 'You think?'

'There's not much independence at work with Celeste around,' I interject moodily.

'Hmm, that's true,' Toni confirms as Myfanwy moves onto the next prediction – the third and final loss. We don't talk about this one very much because ... well, because it's too frightening. 'And after you lose your independence, there's going to be ...' She pales a little, glancing anxiously at Toni and me.

My sister finishes the third prediction for her in a whispered voice.

'A death.'

CHAPTER SIX

It takes another twenty-four days for the reality to finally hit me. To hit me that Daniel has broken up with me. To hit me that I'm not getting married. To hit me that my partner has gone. For real. That he's not coming back. That the life I had painted for myself in sweeping, technicolour, 4D high-def is never going to happen.

And unfortunately, it happens in the middle of an All Bar One on a Friday night.

I'm having cocktails with Myfanwy, Sonali and Toni. The first two are regaling us again with how much they secretly fancied each other all those years before they finally got together, while Toni frowns with bafflement that two people could like each other so much. I've never heard her speak with this kind of affection about Shawn.

As Myfanwy and Sonali get to the part we all know — because duh Toni and I were there — about when they first kissed at New Year's Eve, two men in their thirties approach.

I automatically look down at my drink, wondering like

I always do, whether it's worth eating the coffee beans decorating the top of my cocktail. I patiently await Myfanwy and Sonali's dismissal, but when there is silence, I look up, realizing with some shock that the two men are focusing their pervy energy in my direction. It's actually *me* who's getting hit on. This never happens.

The man nearest to me clears his throat and repeats himself, 'I said, "Can I get you another drink?"' He pauses, reviewing the cocktail before me. 'What's that, an expresso?'

'Espresso,' Sonali corrects him primly – she's the one we all cheated off at uni – and he takes it as an assent.

'Expresso coming right up!' He beams and turns away towards the bar, his friend slapping him on the back in that sad faux-alpha way.

'No! Er, sorry!' I shout after him. 'Sonali was . . . no, thank you! I have a fiancé! I can't have a drink!' But the noise of the crowd is too loud. I turn with terror to the group who share an odd look. 'I have to stop him buying the drink,' I say, stricken. 'I can't . . . I don't . . . what if Daniel . . .'

And with that, the truth hits me like a ton of bricks. Metaphorically, but also not: it literally feels like a huge pile of stone lands heavily on top of me all at once. And then those bricks keep coming; hitting me on the head, landing on my back, collapsing my chest. I can't breathe.

'Oh my god, I'm single,' I hear myself saying as if from down a long tunnel. 'Daniel's really gone, hasn't he?' I look for help between Toni, Sonali and Myfanwy but their faces are blurry. The weight of the bricks is crushing me and I fight for breath.

How have I been such an idiot? How have I been lying to myself so easily for all these weeks? He moved out. He cancelled our wedding. We've lost thousands of pounds – most of that my mother's money, though she hasn't said a word about it. I've heard almost nothing from him in all that time. He's ignored all my messages and calls, while I pretended that was *normal* and *fine*! This is not just some whim of his or some need for breathing space; he's broken up with me. He's ended things. After five years of love and friendship, it's truly over. He doesn't want to be my boyfriend anymore, let alone my husband. He doesn't want anything, except for me to leave him alone.

'Why haven't you got any ice cream?' I wail at Toni and Myfanwy's stricken faces. 'Don't you know I've been *dumped*? Where is the ice cream? And the booze? *Expresso martinis*? That's not break-up alcohol, I need tequila! Or wine at the very least!'

I vaguely catch Sonali murmuring, 'Espresso martinis,' because she can't let anything like that go, and I burst into full-on weeping. My friends encircle me, as people in the crowd around us turn to watch.

How have I been so blind? It was so clear; so undeniable. He left me weeks before our wedding without a word. Without a proper explanation, without discussion, with barely a text explanation.

It feels cruel. It feels *mean*. But that doesn't fit with the

Daniel I know, the man I was so close to for so long. The partner I wanted to spend the rest of my life with.

Maybe that's how I've been able to stay so long in denial, because none of it makes any sense. This person is not the person I knew.

'Shall we take you home?' Myfanwy whispers, her head touching mine.

'No,' I sob. 'I don't care if everyone sees me crying. Who cares what any of them think? I'm such an idiot. I'm *such* an idiot. Why didn't you tell me Daniel had dumped me?'

'We tried to . . .' Toni points out and I nod, tears still blurring my vision.

'I know you did,' I sigh. 'I'm sorry. I'm really sorry. I've been a nightmare. I can't believe I thought he'd come back. I can't believe I thought this was just a blip and wouldn't matter.' Myfe strokes my arm as I continue. 'How could he do this to me? How could he leave me like that? Out of nowhere? Without even an explanation?'

I am suddenly so angry. What kind of person could behave like that? Did I even know Daniel at all?

'I really don't know.' Myfanwy shakes her head, looking disgusted. 'And I'm so glad you're finally angry. It's such a horrible, horrible thing to do and you've been blaming yourself.' She shakes her head again and something in me still tugs defensively at her calling Daniel horrible.

'Am I really so disposable?' I whisper and Sonali makes an outraged noise. 'I feel so worthless,' I continue. 'How can someone say they love me and then throw me away so easily? I didn't know he was capable of that. I didn't know *any* human was capable of that. Even if he didn't love me anymore, he knows I'm not an evil person. I don't deserve this, I don't!' I throw my hands up, tears streaming down my face. 'I don't *get* it! I just don't understand! We were really happy. We were! I'm not just saying that, you guys. We laughed every single day. We were nice to each other. We never argued!'

'Never?' Myfanwy looks suspicious. 'What do you mean *never*?' she asks, adding dryly, 'Bullshit.'

I nod, the tears momentarily stopping. 'It's not, we didn't argue. I'm not just saying that. We really didn't!'

'But how?' Myfanwy looks even angrier. 'Even *I* argued with Daniel. Everyone's annoying sometimes.'

'Of course,' I nod again, slower this time. 'And obviously there were times when he bugged me a little bit, but it was never anything big enough that seemed worth falling out over. So I just let it go.'

'Everyone should argue,' Sonali points out, her voice slightly scolding. 'Avoiding conflict only leads to resentment.'

'Wait, you didn't even argue over wedding planning?' Toni is wide-eyed with shock. But she argues with Shawn all the time. Some people just don't like confrontation and can let things go; it's not weird.

I shake my head. 'Not really. We were stressed about it but we had a common enemy in Celeste. I just felt terrible he was being forced into WeddingCon.' I pause, considering this and letting the guilt flood back in, washing away my anger. 'This really is my fault. I should've stood up to Celeste,

I shouldn't have let her and all of the mess she brought get in our way.' I wipe my face with my coat sleeve then look between my friends, who all share the same unrecognizable expression. 'I know Daniel shouldn't have dealt with it the way he has, but I have to take some accountability.' I down the cocktail before me in one. 'Do you think, if I finally tell Celeste off and promise him he never has to deal with her again, that he'd come back? That we could make it work?'

There is a sad silence around the table that some part of me – some faraway part – understands. But I'm too far gone.

'Do you guys think there's someone else?' I say it in a quiet voice: the thing I've been thinking all along.

On the table before us, my phone lights up with a message and the name on it makes my vision swim with stars.

It's him. Daniel.

'Shit,' Sonali comments, sounding alarmed, while Toni gasps.

I pick it up, afraid and hopeful. Maybe it's taken Daniel all this time to realize he's completely fucked up. That he's sorry and wants to try again. I open WhatsApp and read his words slowly, terrified I will miss something or read it wrong in my current emotional state.

'Hey,' it begins, which feels like a bad start. With people you love and know inside out, you rarely start with a greeting. I take a deep breath, forcing myself to continue.

> Hey, I hope you're doing OK. Sorry to do this, but I can't carry on paying half the rent on the flat. We're nearly at the end of our contract, so I've just messaged the landlord to let him know. I'll carry on paying until then but we'll both have to be out by 29th August. Dx

I burst – back – into tears.

Myfanwy lifts the phone gently from my grasp and there is silence on the other side of the table as she passes it around and they all read his message.

It's over. It's really over. If I wasn't sure before, I really am now. And on top of everything, I now have to find somewhere new to live. How had that not occurred to me? The sadness of that might not be up on the same level as getting dumped, but it's very real and very painful. I love our flat. Our cosy, one-bed flat on the outer edges of London with its local 24-hour booze and biscuit shop across the road and friendly drug dealer, Kevin, two doors down. I love living there and I love my life there.

But there's absolutely no chance at all that I can afford the rent on my own.

Across the table Myfanwy whispers something and when I catch it, the reality hits me.

'*The loss of an independence . . .*'

Prediction number two.

I'm going to have to move back in with my mum. It's my only option. Toni lives with her, but she's only twenty-three. Living with your parents in your twenties is practically the only way to survive these days, but moving *back* when you're in your *thirties* is all kinds of humiliating. Plus, Toni doesn't seem to mind our mother's overbearing tendencies like I do. I feel suffocated and claustrophobic being around her at work, never mind in her house, in her vice-like clutches.

It's going to kill me.

Maybe I could afford a houseshare somewhere? Except I know Toni's been searching for something affordable in the London housing market for a year with no luck. Landlords are squeezing everyone out to make room for yet more Airbnbs. I know everyone probably assumes I can just ask Celeste for money. She's rich and famous, right? But she's always been clear that there would never be any handouts in our family. She's earned her money; we have to earn ours. She will help me if I ask – but only with my old room, not with cash.

I don't have any other options.

I'm single, jilted, about to be stuck living with my parents, and cursed by a fortune teller.

The wails come thicker and faster as everyone fusses over me.

'Should we call someone?' I hear Sonali murmur the question as Myfanwy replies quickly.

'Not Celeste.'

'I'll call Aunt Diane,' Toni says and I feel her moving away from the table. It makes me cry harder.

'Is she OK?' It's the guy from before and he's slopping an overflowing ex or espresso martini into my lap. The tears come even faster. 'What's the matter?' he asks. 'She on her period or something?'

'Fuck off,' Myfanwy snarls and I stop crying for a second.

'Do *you* want to marry me?' I implore him and he takes a tiny step back.

'Huh?'

I sit up straighter. 'Do you want to get married? I have, like, a whole wedding ready and planned for a week's time. We could make it work.' I take a big gulp of the drink he's just bought me as he watches with frightened eyes. 'I'm a really nice girlfriend, I swear! I do the washing-up and I take the bins out. I know how to bleed radiators and I can cook four different meals really, really well. OK, two of them are variations of the same cheese toastie but still.'

'Um,' his eyes dart back and forth, as he slowly backs away, crashing into several groups of people and not caring. I finally lose him in the crowd, as Myfanwy shuffles closer, encircling me with her arms.

'He seemed nice, didn't he?' I ask through shuddery sobs.

'Not really,' she says disagreeably. 'That *expresso* thing should've been an instant deal-breaker, and then the period comment should've been a leg breaker.'

'Oh right,' I nod, still crying. 'OK, fair enough. Well, what do I know about men? Clearly absolutely nothing. I thought Daniel was a nice guy who wouldn't pack up his belongings and leave me on my birthday three weeks before our wedding, while I was at work wondering which cheese toastie I might make us for dinner.'

Myfanwy holds me closer as I try to catch my breath.

'I just wish,' I realize I'm shaking, 'I just wish . . .'

'What? What do you wish?' Myfanwy asks kindly, stroking soggy, tear-soaked strands of hair away from my face.

'I just wish Kirstie and Phil were here to cuddle me,' I get the words out at last.

'The TV presenters?' She sounds confused.

'No . . .' I try to better form my thoughts into sentences. 'They were going to be our dogs. Mine and Daniel's. We were going to get two puppies and call them Kirstie and Phil. We thought that was really funny. Imagine running around the park throwing balls and shouting for them! KIRSTIE AND PHIL, DO YOU WANT A TREAT?' I'm vaguely aware of more people glancing over as I shout about my imaginary dogs. 'HEY KIRSTIE AND PHIL, DON'T POO OVER THERE! KIRSTIE AND PHIL, STOP SNIFFING THAT STRANGER'S CROTCH, IT'S RUDE!' I pause. 'But Daniel said we had to wait until after we got married and bought a place. I thought he was being sensible – usually I'm the boring one – but maybe he was already planning on leaving me, even then. He didn't want to get Kirstie and Phil because he didn't want to be with me. He didn't want dependents tying us together.'

Toni returns to our table, and Sonali makes room for my sister as she drags her stool round to join Myfanwy and me in our tight huddle. She's brought tissues and I wipe my face with them, trying not to think about the mascara mess my face must be right now. Sonali takes one too, dabbing at her own eyes.

'Diane's on her way,' she says quietly. 'She's going to drive you home, Gin.'

I nod, relieved. My Aunt Diane is the parental figure I need right now. I need to be mothered, but not by my mother.

'Do you think that man is OK?' I ask, embarrassment finally arriving. I glance around, noticing several of the bar's clientele are still watching the show. I nod awkwardly at a group of women nearby, who raise their glasses and nod back solemnly in solidarity. They're not judging – they recognize dumped.

'I'm sure he's fine.' Myfanwy waves her hand. 'He was an idiot, and you're allowed to stand up for yourself with idiots.'

'And at least you got a free expresso martini out of it,' Toni says cheerfully as Sonali and Myfanwy shoot her daggers.

'That's true,' I say, grabbing it and downing it in one – coffee beans and all.

Ginny's Six Predictions

Losses:
1. ~~A heartbeat~~
2. An independence
3. A death

Gains:
1. A lifechanging trip
2. A person you thought lost forever
3. Your Soulmate

Myfanwy loves sonali

Don't doodle on the predictions!!

Soz
xx

CHAPTER SEVEN

'Dude, you're a mess! This is wonderful!' Diane tells me plainly, as I stagger out of the bar and she throws her blazer around my slumped shoulders.

'I know,' I begin, before frowning. 'Wait, *wonderful*?' We make our way towards her ancient Volvo and Diane opens the passenger door for me to collapse inside. It swings open with a creak, revealing rust lining the door frame. Celeste tried to buy her a new car a few years ago but Diane says she doesn't want her sister's money.

They get on well most of the time, I think, but they're very different.

'It's a good thing!' Diane rushes around, climbing in and starting the engine. 'I just mean you've kind of been a bit of a cliché with the five stages of grief these last few weeks.'

'A cliché?' I cry, a little offended.

She gives me a quick smile as we pull out onto the main road. 'Is that anger you're feeling? Because that's exactly what we need to see. You've been stuck in denial for so long, I'm relieved to see you're moving out of it. Everyone gets caught up in denial – it's very tedious. You need to pass through anger, bargaining, depression, before you can finally find some acceptance about your break-up.'

'It wasn't denial,' I attempt weakly. 'It's just . . . I know he's . . . I know what we had.' I pause. 'And I got quite angry in the bar just now!' I consider the wailing carousel of emotions I swung through. 'Then I started bargaining with everyone.' I glance down at my hand. 'I was ready to sacrifice my mother if Daniel would come back to me.'

Diane side-eyes me. 'Like a blood sacrifice or the relationship?'

I shrug. 'Probably both.'

'I imagine Myfanwy was quite into that idea,' Diane muses. 'She's bound to have tried a blood sacrifice during one of her witchy phases *and* she can't stand Celeste.'

'Well, either way, I'm basically through the five stages and out the other side already. I'm fine.'

She snorts. 'Are you trying to rush your way through all the stages in one night? You can't force it, dude.'

'OK,' I say quietly, thinking about the stage that comes after bargaining: depression. Maybe I don't want to rush it after all – I really don't want to deal with that bit.

We drive in silence for a minute before Diane speaks again. 'You know, I dated a Daniel once.' She pauses and I hold my breath, waiting for her to continue.

Diane and I don't really talk about her love life. She's

one of the most open and loving people I know but she's also private about certain things. I've always told her everything about my life, but we have more of a mentor/ mentee relationship. Plus, it seems like she has everything sorted and together – why would she ever come to me for advice?

'He was great but . . .' She sighs. 'I don't know, they're a *lot*, y'know? Daniels. They need a lot of maintenance.' She pauses before adding oh-so casually: 'Plus, he made noises during sex that sounded like a bad Cher impression.' She checks her wing mirror. 'Whoaaaa,' she says in a deep, throaty voice, flicking her long hair. 'Whooooaaaaaaaaa.'

I cock my head. 'Is that meant to be Cher?'

She shoots me an amused look, pulling up at traffic lights. 'I told you it was a *bad* impression.' She smiles again, but this time it's a private, secret smile and I can see she's in her memories. After a moment she gives herself a shake. 'Anyway, my point is, it *can* work with a Daniel, where you're the supporting character in the relationship. It can be lovely, looking after someone and caring for them. And you, Ginny, are a very nurturing, kind soul who is very good at looking after people. You don't mind being the supporting character, but I'm just saying you don't *have* to be. You can be the star if you choose to be. You can even *both* be the stars in a relationship.'

I consider this. In theory I don't want to have a bit part in my own life. I don't want to be the side character in a relationship. But on the other hand, it sounds safer; easier in a lot of ways. Who's got the energy to be the Sandra Bullock of their own life? I think I'd rather be Sandra Bullock's friend.

I actually would *love* to be Sandra Bullock's friend; she seems like the best.

'And you know being single is *super* fun,' Diane continues, wiggling her eyebrows at me. My brain responds by replaying her Cher impression, the *whoaaaa* echoing around my head.

'That's what Toni said,' I tell her vaguely, noting the familiar streets whizzing past. We're nearly back at my flat. My home. The home I have to give up.

'Well,' Diane takes a deep breath. 'Toni wouldn't know, but I wish she would find out.' We look at each other pointedly, silently acknowledging our mutual unhappiness with Shawn.

'But really,' she says, 'being single is not just fun and exciting, it's also your chance to figure things out. To get to know yourself and like yourself. It'll give you a chance to work out what you want and what you need – and whether those two things are compatible.'

'Daniel is what I want and need,' I mutter in a low voice, staring down at the seatbelt pulled tight across my chest.

'OK,' Diane says amiably, before adding, 'but maybe that's not the only thing you want and need. Maybe this is your chance to think about your world and explore what makes you happy. Maybe there's more to life than marrying Daniel.'

'I know there is.' I feel defensive now, hearing the low-grade sarcasm in her voice. 'I'm not one of those women who think getting married is my entire reason for being.'

'You mean like Celeste?' Diane sighs. 'Look, I know you've got a sensible head on your shoulders, but you're not immune to what society – and your mum – tells you. I know that you settling down with someone means a lot to her and to nosy strangers. Believe me, I know!' she says pointedly, eyebrows practically in her hairline. 'As someone who has never married and is well past her societal sell-by date, I am well aware how difficult it is to resist all that and figure out what works for *you*. Sometimes the universe forces our hand in these things.'

'Now you sound like Myfanwy!' I complain. 'She won't leave me alone about these bloody six predictions. She's practically crowing about how Daniel dumping me is the first one coming true. And now I'm going to have to move out of my flat in a few weeks, she thinks it's the independence loss.'

'Maybe it is?' Diane shrugs. 'Have you considered maybe all the predictions, all the losses, are about this one thing?'

I glance at her, confused, then back at the car in front. 'What do you mean?'

She takes a moment, flicking her windscreen wash on. The road ahead of us briefly becomes blurry with water.

'I mean, maybe a heartbreak, an independence, a death – maybe it was all meant to be about this break-up with Daniel.'

'A *death*?' I ask, incredulous.

Beside me, Diane shrugs. 'Well, it is like a death, isn't it? You had someone in your life – intensely in your life! – and now they're gone. You're not even speaking, are you? He's completely gone, you've lost him. It's like he died.'

69

I keep my eyes tight on the road.

He's really gone.

'Have you thought about maybe trying to find her?' Diane glances over, her indicator ticking. 'Y'know, the fortune teller? The woman who lumbered you with this pre-ordained future? Might be worth trying. She could have answers. Even her having no answers might be a kind of answer for you.'

Her question takes me by surprise because the truth is I hadn't. It's never occurred to me. The fortune teller has been this ghostly supernatural figure from my past; in my mind she's barely a real person anymore.

I could find her. I have no idea how, but I could try? She might have information or questions or even more predictions. But what if I did find her? What if she was an obvious charlatan? Would that make me feel better or worse? And what if I found her and she was the real deal?

We pull up outside my flat.

'Want me to come in?' Diane offers, her voice soft and kind.

I shake my head. I'm so tired, so drained. I feel wrecked by the weight of everything that's happened – tonight and in the last month – and I need to think about everything she's said.

'I'm just going to head straight to bed,' I say, reaching for a hug. 'Thanks though, Diane, you're the best. And sorry for ruining your evening.'

'You haven't,' she replies into my hair. 'You tore me away from enjoying my post-takeaway heartburn in front of an episode of *Love Is Blind*.' She rubs her chest, her face screwed up.

I say goodnight and head inside, thinking about the searing, horrible, feeling in *my* chest, and if it's here to stay.

CHAPTER EIGHT

'Whatcha doing?' Toni bounces with too much exuberance into my shoulder and I wince slightly, dragging my eyes away from the screen, where I've been perving over the same old Instagram profile.

It's not Daniel's. Myfanwy's put me on a stalking ban – she blocked him *and* all his friends, which is so annoying. What am I supposed to do at 2am when I'm late-night-ordering a bottle of his aftershave from Amazon to spray on that side of the bed?

It's a brand's page: Walliams' Custom Designs. They're a bespoke ring designer I've been obsessed with for the past few months. As it stands, Celeste's Stones don't actually design anything in-house. We offer bespoke or personalized jewellery, but then we send it out to another company to sort. We're basically a middle man for the process, which doesn't really tie in with how I see the store, which is all about personal service. I've been thinking for ages that we should be trying to find a really talented ring-maker to bring on board.

It's something I've brought up with Celeste many times and she's always given me the brush-off. Until now.

'These are the guys coming in today,' I jab a finger at the Instagram page before me, pulling up their latest post to show Toni a ring design with intricate pearls encircling a rose gold band. She takes the iPad from me, flicking through Walliams' Custom Designs' posts, eyes wide.

'Wow, these are beautiful,' Toni breathes, swiping slowly from post to post.

'I know,' I grin, feeling proud. 'I found them a while back, aren't they great? They're London-based, same as us, but don't have much of a following yet.'

'They totally will though.' Her eyes finally leave the screen. 'Do you think they're any relation to David Walliams?'

I grimace. 'I hope not. But whoever they are, they're ridiculously talented.' I lean over to review the iPad again. 'Look at the shapes, Tone! And the materials! They're making some of the most creative and elegant stuff I've ever seen. It's absolute artistry!'

'Are we going to work with them?' she asks eagerly and I shrug like I'm not that invested either way. But the truth is, I'm *desperate* to work with them. When I showed Celeste their page, I was so worried she'd give me yet another brush-off. But even she had to admit they do stunning work and agreed to me setting up a meeting with the team to discuss collaborating. Plus, I think she took pity on me after everything that's been happening.

'Imagine if David Walliams walked in!' Toni snorts. 'Imagine if he's decided to diversify from kid's books into jewellery design.'

'It would be an interesting choice,' I comment distractedly. That name does set off alarm bells, but not because of a sleazy TV star.

Walliams. Or Williams. Ugh. One of the most common surnames in the Western world, and it also happens to be the most haunted for me. All my life, people called Williams have cropped up again and again, a karmic punishment for what happened between me and Flo all those years ago.

I picture Florence Williams now, visualizing her chubby face, giggling whenever I called her Mo Flo. We were best friends throughout primary and middle school; a solid, unassailable team, spending every lunchtime hiding at the bottom of the playground, playing with our Tamagotchis and writing in overflowing diaries about the people we fancied who literally didn't know we were alive.

Every time I meet a Williams, or a William, or indeed a tenuously named company called Walliams' Custom Designs, I feel the weight of guilt. I wouldn't even let Daniel call his thingy a willy.

Oh, Daniel.

It's been a few weeks since my breakdown in an All Bar One, and after my pep talk with Aunt Diane, I could really feel the depression stage threatening, especially when I finally packaged up the engagement ring Daniel had given me. I sent it to his mum and dad's house and, handing the parcel over at the post office, I came quite close to collapsing on the floor. But it was a family heirloom and I knew I couldn't keep it. I cried for two days straight after that, staring at my barren, empty hand and sobbing over old WhatsApp messages from him that mainly read stuff like, 'I've got a splinter, ughhh!' or, 'The bath mat has mould on it.' Focusing on work is the only thing getting me through right now, especially knowing I have to move out of the flat in just over a week. Borrowing some old stock and filling my fingers with other jewellery also helped. I don't miss my engagement ring quite as much when my hand is weighed down by beautiful trinkets.

Beside me, Toni throws the iPad down, breathless as she reaches for my shoulder. 'Oh my god oh my god oh my god, don't look, OK?' she hisses. 'Right? DON'T LOOK!'

'Don't look at what?' I stare down at the glass case before me feeling helpless. 'What am I not looking at?'

Toni grips my arm. I can feel finger-shaped bruises form-ing under her steel strength.

'It's that guy, *that guy*.' She's hissing in my ear. 'That guy just walked in!'

'What guy? Can I look up?' I murmur back.

'Oh my god! NO, DO NOT LOOK, GINNY!'

I sigh, feeling tired. I'm tired all the time these days. Misery takes it out of you. 'What guy?' I repeat.

'I can't remember his name but he's from that TV show, you know? That TV thing? Everybody watched it. You know?'

'Toni, can I please just have a look?' My neck is starting

to hurt, bent at its odd angle. 'It's surely more obvious something's happening when I'm literally staring down at the floor?'

'OK, fine.' Toni's grip doesn't loosen. 'But don't stare. Just a quick glance.'

That quick glance is enough to tell me the man who just walked into our store is one of the most devastatingly handsome people I've ever seen in my life. Tall, broad, covered in tattoos and utterly gorgeous. He definitely looks like a film or TV star, but I don't recognize him.

I turn sideways, picking up the iPad and pretending to look at it, so I can slyly watch him move slowly around the store, taking everything in. Hovering over my favourite section, TV star half smiles to himself, and beside me, Toni practically swoons.

'He's so hot, Jesus H. Christ,' she breathes. 'I can't believe the guy from that show is in *our* shop!'

'Is "H" a middle name?' I muse. 'Was it Jesus Howard Christ? Jesus Horatio? Or is it, like, Jesus Holy Christ?'

'Shushhhh!' Toni practically shouts, panting in my ear. 'He's looking over here!'

'Try to calm down, Tone,' I swallow a laugh. 'You have a boyfriend, remember? And we've had famous people in here before.'

I check my watch; the Walliams' Custom Designs people are due soon, so I need to stop sweating and check my lipstick before meeting this insanely talented group. I so desperately want to impress them. I've been polishing glass cases around the store all morning – something I know sounds like a euphemism, but isn't.

'Mainly our mum,' Toni pouts. 'Not really, *really* sexy famous people. Not *him*. Oh my god, should I go talk to him? Should I offer to help?'

'I mean, you *could* do your job, I guess?' I give her a half smile and she swallows hard, suddenly looking very young and vulnerable. I stroke her back. 'Is it too much?' I ask nicely. 'Shall I offer to help instead? I'll have to be quick though, I have this meeting.'

'No, it's fine, I can do it!' she says determinedly – and then her face crumbles. 'No, I can't.' She shakes her head. 'I'm sorry, you'll have to do it. I don't think I can . . . I mean he's too . . . he's just *glorious*, Ginny, look at him!'

She's right, he is.

I steel myself, straightening my blazer before making the approach.

'Hello, can I help at all?' My voice is a little high-pitched, but I'm proud a real, fully formed sentence managed to emerge from my mouth.

The TV star turns to face me, smiling the most dazzling of smiles, teeth white and straight. 'Hello!' His voice is deep and I realize he's older than I'd thought. Probably older than me – maybe mid-thirties? I would say he's too old for Toni, but Shawn isn't far off that . . .

'You must be Ginny?'

I blink, surprised. 'Oh? I mean, yes I am!' I say after a moment's confused silence.

'Zach Walliams.' He offers me his hand and I blink at it, baffled.

'Hi?' I say hesitantly, still confused. Was he in one of the Marvel movies?

His brow furrows. 'We have a meeting?' he adds after another long second.

'Oh my god!' The cloud clears. 'Of course! You're from Walliams' Custom Designs – I'm so sorry!'

He laughs lightly. 'Well, technically, I *am* Walliams' Custom Designs. I'm a one-man operation.'

'Wow.' I am genuinely awed. 'You do all that by yourself? That's really impressive.'

He blushes and it is so adorable I want to touch the pinkness of his cheeks.

Toni is suddenly at my arm, her breath short and hot. 'Hi!' she squeals. 'Can I just say I loved you in that show.'

Zach cocks his head, confusion lining that beautiful face. 'Show? What show?'

'That Netflix thing.' She sounds impatient. 'I can't remember the name, but I loved it so much! I got everyone I know to watch it. I even made my boyfriend—' She stops abruptly at this, paling. 'I mean, I don't have a boyfriend. Or, I kind of do, but y'know, it's very casual and—'

'Toni,' I warn in a low voice and she puts a hand to her mouth.

'Oh god, sorry. I *do* have a boyfriend really, I don't know why I said that! I feel terrible. Please don't tell Shawn I said that! We've been together for years! I'm sorry!'

'I won't tell him!' Zach reassures her. 'But I think you've got the wrong end of the stick. I'm not in any Netflix show—'

'Amazon Prime!' Toni shrieks. 'I meant Amazon Prime, I'm sorry!'

'No, no . . .' Zach looks even more concerned. 'I mean I'm not an actor at all – I never have been.' He pauses. 'Well, I was in a school pantomime when I was seven, but I froze up and started crying on stage. Never lived it down.' He smiles widely at me and I beam back, picturing this adorable little guy humiliating himself in front of a sea of judgy parents.

'No . . .' Toni is shaking her head. 'No, you're definitely that guy—' She stops short, a smile slowly creeping across her face. 'Ohhhh, right, OK, yeah, you're totally *not* him!' She winks at Zach. 'I get you! Totally understand. Our mum is famous, too, and it is so annoying being constantly pestered.'

'No, really!' Zach looks a bit panicked now. 'I promise it's not me! I'm a freelance designer.'

Toni winks again, leaning forward to lightly elbow him. 'No of course not! Nudge nudge, wink wink! I get it.' In a stage whisper she adds, 'But I really did love you on that Amazon Prime show.'

'Um, please ignore her, Zach!' I swallow hard, gesturing towards the back. 'Come on through to the office.'

He follows me across the store and I'm suddenly acutely aware of my butt. In the office I take a seat, finding the chair more uncomfortable than usual, as Toni hovers at the door.

'Can I get you a tea?' she offers Zach hopefully. 'Coffee?

Or something to eat? I read in that interview that you like M&S cookies – I can run out and get some for you?'

Zach shoots me an awkward look, before turning back to Toni. 'That's really nice, and I do actually love their cookies, but I swear to you, I'm not that actor.' He pauses. 'A coffee would be wonderful though, if that's possible.'

'Of course,' she winks slowly, backing out of the doorway. 'I hear you.'

Alone at last, I clear my throat. 'I'm really sorry about that. My sister, Toni, she's—'

He waves away my apology. 'She's lovely,' he says with warmth. 'It's flattering, I'm sure.' He pauses. 'Unless the actor she's thinking of is Steve Buscemi?'

I laugh. 'I think Steve Buscemi is quite charming-looking actually.'

He cocks his head, revealing a teasing half-smile that hides those white teeth. 'You do? Well, that's me told. Beauty is in the eye of the beholder, I guess.'

'I think you're safe though,' I tell him. 'Toni's only twenty-three – I'm not sure she would even know who Steve Buscemi is.'

'Gosh! Twenty-three . . .' He raises his eyebrows. 'What's that like?'

'No idea.' I relate to his bemusement. 'She's a lot younger than me, and sometimes it feels like we come from differ-ent planets.'

Toni arrives back with the coffee then, placing it down on the desk, along with a piece of paper and a pen.

'Thank you!' Zach says nicely, as Toni leans down, getting too close to his face.

'I know you're having a meeting,' she says in hushed tones, 'but when you're done, would you mind signing that for me? It's Toni with an I,' she gestures at the paper, slipping out of the room before he can respond.

Zach and I look at each other for a long moment and then – simultaneously – we burst out laughing.

'If I knew the name of this guy she thinks I am,' he says through amusement, 'I actually would sign this for her!'

'She clearly doesn't know his name either!' I am belly laughing now. 'You could sign whatever name you like! You could be Tom Cruise – why not!'

'Oh god no!' He looks horrified. 'Not him! I want to be someone cool!'

'Unfortunately, I'm not cool enough to know who's cool,' I shrug helplessly.

'Me neither,' he shakes his head, rubbing an eye.

The laughter trails off, and for a second we're left just smiling at one another in a strange moment of bonding.

I clear my throat at last. 'I guess we should get to business!'

'Right,' he nods, holding eye contact for a fraction too long. 'Business.'

I look down at my notepad, feeling a little awkward – a little *watched*.

'So then,' I cough again. 'Um, Zach, how did Walliams Custom Designs come about? Have you been designing jewellery long?' I try for job interview authority and immediately know I have fallen short. He takes a second to answer, and when he does, I find myself staring at his throat instead of his face.

'Well,' his Adam's apple bobs lightly, 'I set up the brand about eighteen months ago. Before then, I worked as a designer for a few years, making logos and marketing stuff for a very boring ad agency.' He smiles and I try to meet his eyes.

I know I have to be professional, but something about him is throwing me off. He's giving off distinctly *un*professional signals.

He continues, 'I started designing and creating jewellery on the side because I needed a creative outlet.' He pauses and I force myself to look up into his eyes. He is watching my mouth. 'Don't get me wrong, I enjoyed my job. I loved the creative side of it, but it was quite frustrating working for a bunch of sixty-something men who kept telling me to add more stars to everything.'

I laugh, feeling him studying me. 'I've never worked in a proper office – it sounds so grown up.'

He smiles, his big eyes blacker than before. 'You've always worked here?'

'Pretty much.' I glance past him at yet another poster of my mum snarling from the wall. 'A family business has its perks and its . . .' I trail off and he leans forward.

'Anti-perks?'

'I'm not sure that's a word,' I smirk.

'Well, I don't do words!' he replies expansively, waving at the store around him. 'I do jewellery!'

'Same,' I nod, reaching for my coffee. He does the same and for a moment there is silence as we both sip. I wonder if he's feeling as discombobulated as me.

The meeting goes so well. As we leave the office, I'm buzzing with possibilities. Celeste's Stones and Walliams' Custom Designs are officially going to collaborate for a trial period of four months up to Christmas. Zach will be signing up as a contractor on a freelance basis, coming into the store one day a week to sit down with clients and work with us on bespoke designs.

I'm honestly so excited – almost as excited as Toni, who bounds over.

'All good?' she asks with energy, searching my face, then Zach's.

'Very!' I nod as Zach hands her the piece of paper. She looks at it, squeals, then runs away.

'What did you write?' I ask, amused, and he twinkles.

'You'll have to find out . . .' he says mysteriously. I laugh at this, leading him to the door.

'Is it just the two of you? No more siblings?' He gestures in the direction Toni disappeared in.

I feel his eyes scanning my face.

'Yep,' I say, trying to make normal eye contact. 'I thought I was going to be an only child, but then along she came when I was nine. My mum decided it would be funny to name her Toni, middle name Celeste – after herself.' I wait for him to put this together but most people take a minute.

I explain. 'As in Toni C? As in Tonic? I'm Gin and she's Tonic?' I sigh. 'My mum thinks it's the most hilarious thing in the world.'

Zach's eyes widen and then he howls with laughter. 'I kind of agree with your mum! That's pretty epic.'

'The stupid thing is that Ginny isn't even my real name.' I shake my head, smiling. 'It's Jenny. I had a South African teacher at school who pronounced it *Ginny* and everyone thought that was better. Ginny stuck. I tried to go back to Jenny so many times, but only one person ever did as I asked – a school friend, Flo.' He frowns as I clear my throat, looking away. In that moment, my phone rings.

Ugh, it's Celeste.

'Sorry, one second, I'll just get rid of her,' I say in a whisper gesturing elaborately at my phone. He nods, looking distracted. I've kept him here too long.

'Ginny, darling? Are you there?' Celeste sounds odd and something like a stone hardens in my stomach.

'Mum? What's wrong?' I say and I can tell my face has whitened because Zach is suddenly looking at me intensely, eyebrows drawn together.

'Darling . . .' Celeste's voice wobbles and my hand tightens around the phone. 'Darling, it's your Aunt Diane . . . something's happened. They're not telling us much, but they said people should come.'

'*Come?* Diane? What? What do you mean? Come where?' My brain isn't processing the information.

'The hospital, darling, St Phillip's, come as fast as you

can, head for the A&E section, ask for us.' She pauses and I suddenly can't breathe.

'Did you hear me, Ginny darling?' She sounds impatient now. 'Come to St Phillip's. Bring Toni. Call me when you get here, OK?'

'Bring Toni? But the shop . . .'

'Close the shop.'

'Right, yes, of course.' I need more information, I need to ask more questions, but she's gone.

'What's happened?' Zach gets closer. 'Are you OK? What can I do?'

'It's my aunt . . .' I trail off. 'I need to get to the hospital, but I don't even know where St Phillip's is . . . I . . .'

'I do,' he nods decisively. 'I've got my car across the road – I'll drive you there. Shall I fetch your sister?'

I am unable to speak or think as he dashes off to get Toni.

I can't make this stranger drive us, can I? But the idea of getting an Uber right now, or worse, on the tube, trying to find an unknown place with my brain disconnected like this, feels impossible.

What's happened? Surely it can't be serious? Diane is so young and so healthy. She does yoga and runs and laughs a lot! People like that don't get really ill out of nowhere. Do they?

She has to be OK.

CHAPTER NINE

'It's a broken leg!' Diane laughs, pointing at the cast on the bed before her. 'It's so stupid, it's just my leg.'

'Thank god!' I shout, the relief flooding my body. Beside me, Zach reaches for my hand. 'It's OK,' I turn to face him.

'I know,' he smiles, squeezing the hand he's now holding as emotions zig-zag through me.

'Your aunt is fine,' a nurse smiles from across the room, as she approaches to adjust Diane's drip.

'It's a broken leg!' Celeste laughs and Diane is now laughing again, too.

'It's not funny, you guys,' I frown. 'I was really scared.' They continue to laugh, hysterically now, as another voice chips in from behind me.

'She's OK?' it says and I turn to find Daniel's familiar figure.

'Daniel!' I can't help the happiness in my voice. 'You came!'

'Of course I did!' His puppy energy is palpable, even in a yellowing hospital room. 'I had to be here for you.' He grins. 'I'm so glad Diane's all right. And I still love you. Will you marry me, Ginny?'

I frown. 'What? Are you serious?' I realize I'm still holding Zach's hand. Behind me, Celeste yells. 'Say yes! For god's sake, Ginny, say yes!' On the bed, Diane is still laughing and now there's another familiar person lying beside her. It's the fortune teller.

'Look who I found!' says Diane through uncontrollable giggles.

'Should I marry Daniel?' I ask the big-haired woman, who looks back at me blankly. I realize it's the nurse. The fortune teller was here, working as a nurse all along!

'Maybe!' she says. 'Or maybe Zach's your soulmate!'

I wake up with a start, disorientated and stiff. I've nodded off in my chair at work. I haven't been sleeping well lately, but this is still next-level unprofessional.

'Are you OK?' Thankfully, it's Toni who's woken me up. She's standing awkwardly in the doorway. 'Sorry Gin, I know you're knackered.' She pauses. 'It's just that Zach's here for your meeting.'

'Right!' My voice is croaky and I clear my throat, reaching for the glass of water on my desk. It's warm. 'I'm fine, I'll be there in two seconds. Sorry.'

'Don't say sorry,' she says quietly. Her eyebags are as deep and black as mine. 'The dream again?'

'Pretty much.' I give her a small shrug and she nods, disappearing back out to the store front. I quickly pull out my compact and swipe at black mascara flecks. I briefly wonder how long it's been since I bought a new mascara. This one is becoming increasingly flaky. Or maybe it's because my eyes are so swollen.

I sit for another minute, breathing deeply, steeling myself. I grip the edge of the desk, thinking about the dream. It's been waiting for me every night for two weeks and I feel like I'm starting to lose my mind.

Deep breaths, I tell myself, standing up and following Toni out.

'Hi!' I greet Zach from across the room with as much sincerity as I can muster. 'Nice to see you!'

He turns, smiling warmly, and raises a hand in a small greeting.

'Ginny,' he replies, approaching with some formality. For a second, I think he will hug me, but instead we awkwardly shake hands.

'Would you like a drink?' I keep my voice breezy, checking the wall clock. 'Our couple should be here any minute, but Toni can send them to join us in the back room.'

He nods. 'A coffee would be great, thank you.'

When I bring it through to the office, our clients are already in there, chatting animatedly to Zach. I feel strangely glad we won't be alone.

'The future Mr and Mrs Broom!' I greet them with delight. They came in a few days ago and were absolutely adorable. They're not yet engaged – hence the need for a ring designer at Celeste's Stones – but spent the whole time calling one another by their future married names. Maybe it should've been cheesy but I found it very sweet. It was a soothing, sweet balm on my anaesthetized wounds. And it felt better than the numbness of cold pain and grief.

I take a seat in front of the computer, diving straight into the conversation, my professional face firmly on. These two are doing everything together when it comes to the proposal. They're getting each other personalized rings, planning a special trip back to Ireland where Mr Broom is from, and then they're getting down on one knee for each other. It's lovely. We look through slides on Zach's iPad, discussing timeframes, and going over plans. The hour is through too quickly and Zach and I see them to the door, waving our goodbyes.

'You're so great with clients,' Zach beams, as the door shuts behind them. 'You really go above and beyond.'

'That's really nice,' I say, feeling far away. 'I'm so happy we've been able to get you on board. Everyone loves you. And your designs, of course. I think it's really going to make a big difference to our business.'

'Well it's definitely making a big difference to mine!' He gives a low laugh. 'I'm so grateful.'

I feel robotic, as I reply, 'I'm the grateful one!'

We head for the kitchen area in silence before he speaks again, this time in a softer voice.

'How have things been?' he asks and of course I knew this was coming. I hoped it wouldn't but I knew it would. It had to.

I nod, swallowing hard, using all my energy to stay focused on this moment.

Focus on work. I'm at work. Now is not the time for emotion.

'The funeral is next week,' I tell him, breathing carefully. 'Everything's been so delayed because of the autopsy and my mum's been in such a weird, detached state about everything, we just couldn't get her to sign anything off. Toni and I have had to do quite a lot.'

He gives me a short nod, understanding. 'I'm sorry, that's really rough.'

I sigh deeply into my cheeks, his kindness reaching in and through past my numbness. 'Life is shit sometimes, hey? But we'll get through it. I miss her a lot.' I pause to swallow the lump. 'A *lot*. But I just wish I could help my mum right now. Or see a hint of her normal self still in there. She's been so . . . silent.'

It's been two weeks since my lovely Aunt Diane died.

She was already slipping away when we got to the hospital that night. We left Zach in A&E reception with barely a thank you as Toni and I ran up and down corridors frantically looking for the right room, my stomach in the floor.

She wasn't conscious when we finally found it, but I still didn't understand how serious things were until I saw how white my mum's face was. I've never seen her that colour. She's usually *Strictly* dancer levels of orange.

Diane had a heart attack, the doctors explained. Which I'm still really, really struggling to understand. I stupidly thought only men had heart attacks.

Celeste said she'd been with Diane all week and she'd seemed OK. She'd been complaining recently about being tired and having indigestion, but that was all. That's *life,* isn't it? Nothing! It was nothing.

But the doctor said those are symptoms, and that women often experience heart attacks differently from men. All that stuff you hear shouted about – like pain in your left arm – doesn't even usually apply to women. Heartburn and some tiredness; that's like *every day* for a lot of people. How is anyone supposed to know to be worried?

The fourteen days since have felt blurry and out of focus. Nothing I do feels appropriate, but I do everything all the same. I go to work, I make food, I shower, I put the bins out, I debate with myself about putting the heating on because it's unseasonably cold, despite only being the beginning of September. I continue to cry over Daniel and the loss of that life we were going to have.

Everything feels disrespectful to Diane and wrong, but life has continued to go on.

I'm still kinda numb – in shock I guess – and I can't stop thinking about my mum. That afternoon in the hospital room, sitting in silence around Diane's prone body, I kept looking over at Toni and thinking what it would mean to lose her. How much of an impact, a *hole*, it would leave in my life. You don't lose *sisters*, I was thinking, waiting for Celeste to break down. But she didn't.

To be honest, and I feel mean saying it, but in my grief, I thought she would be in howling hysterics, bringing the whole show to her doorstep and wailing for the seats at the back to applaud. But, as Toni and I wept silently and held Diane's hand, Celeste just sort of shut down.

None of this horrible, painful time has been helped by the

fact that I still had to move. I called the landlord the morning after we lost Diane and begged for an extra week or two. I'm ashamed to say that I cried down the phone, and it wasn't even the grief, it was the humiliation of having to beg. But he was immovable. That husk of a human being had the gall to say my aunt dying wasn't his problem.

And so, with help from Sonali, Myfanwy and Toni, plus half-hearted WhatsApp well-wishes from Emily, we moved all my stuff back to my mother's house.

'If there's anything I can do . . .' Zach offers lamely, putting a hand on my shoulder.

'I appreciate it,' I tell him, meaning it. Toni and I have had to carry everything for the last couple of weeks. It feels nice to have someone ask how I'm doing. 'But what can anyone do?'

He doesn't answer, which makes me sad. I hoped he'd have an answer.

What *can* anyone do?

Ginny's Six Predictions

Losses:
1. ~~A heartbeat~~
2. ~~An independence~~
3. ~~A death~~ WTF is happening

Gains:
1. A life changing trip
2. A person you thought lost forever
3. Your Soulmate

Miss you Di

Minnie loves sonai

Don't look at the predictions!!

S ⚡
x x

♡ ♡

CHAPTER TEN

UNI DICKS GROUP

Myfanwy

Gin, what are you wearing for the funeral on Friday? What should Sonali and I wear? Is it the standard black or is it that modern funeral thing of wanting everyone to wear bright clothes and 'celebrate life'?

Sonali

She made that sound a lot more sarcastic than she meant it.

Myfanwy

I was being pretty sarcastic. Life is shit and this situation is shit, why do we have to celebrate it?

Ginny

I actually have no idea what to wear!

Emily

So sorry I can't make it!! Hope it goes well, will be thinking of you, Gin xxx

Ginny

I've tried to talk to Celeste about what she wants and what she thinks we should do, but I can't get through. It's like she's had a hard drive wipe and I don't know how to reboot her. It's freaking me out TBH.

Myfanwy

Hold on, I'm coming over xx

Myfanwy arrives at the house half an hour later and, on seeing her lovely, sweet face on my doorstep, it takes about three seconds for me to break down.

A woman standing on the pavement stares at me over the fence and I hide my face as Myfanwy half carries me up to my bedroom, where I weep in her arms for a while. When the tears eventually start to slow, she shifts underneath me, pulling something out of her top.

'Here.' She hands me a small, smooth purple stone. 'It's a crystal.'

I peer at her. 'Did you just take this out of your bra?'

'Yes,' she acknowledges impatiently. 'But now it's yours to carry in your bra.'

'Um ...' I rub a thumb along the palm-sized item.

'That's really kind and it's very pretty, but what exactly am I looking at?'

'It's an amethyst crystal,' she nods authoritatively. 'It's a good starter crystal for you. It's a soothing stone, really good for anxiety and sleep problems.' She stops and regards me closely, taking in my eyebags. 'You still having that dream?'

I nod slowly, staring down at the swirling patterns in the crystal. It really is very pretty. But it's also just a stone – isn't it?

'It will help,' Myfanwy nods. 'Just keep it close. It's also good for helping to align you with your higher purpose.'

'Which is?' I ask, genuinely intrigued.

'That's for you to work out,' she replies enigmatically.

I sigh. 'Right now I just want to help Mum. It would be hard enough living back here with him,' I gesture at R–Patz on the wall, 'and the usual Celeste hysteria, but this new Celeste is a zombie.'

'A vampire and a zombie,' Myfanwy observes dryly, before adding in a softer tone, 'And how do you feel? Y'know, about losing Diane?'

I look out the window. That woman is still standing out by the fence, looking up at the house. I sigh, turning back to Myfanwy. 'I keep thinking about the moment my phone rang. When Mum called to tell me to come to the hospital.' I swallow. 'I was just annoyed about being interrupted. I was flirting – *flirting*! – with some guy in the store and was about to fob Mum off.' Myfanwy reaches over to take my hand, as I continue, 'What if I made this happen? What if it's my fault somehow?'

'Of course it's not your fault, that's not how it works,'

she murmurs, then pauses. 'Who was the guy you were flirting with?'

I swallow. 'He's just ... just a someone. Nobody really.' I shrug lightly. 'His name's Zach Walliams, the jewellery designer I told you about? We're working together now at the store. He's been great.' I meet her eyes. 'I don't think I told you but he drove us to the hospital – Toni and me. And then he was still in reception when we were leaving, hours later. He said he just wanted to check I was OK.'

Myfanwy considers this. 'It sounds like he's into you.'

'No!' I am mortified – not by the idea that he could fancy me, but by the idea that I have painted a picture of him fancying me. The arrogance! 'No, Myfe, you don't understand. This man is the most beautiful creature I've ever seen in my life. He could not be any more out of my league if I was a tadpole in the pond, watching an eagle soar above me. He was just being nice. He's a good guy.'

There is silence and I look up to Myfanwy giving me a wry smile. 'You're an idiot, you know?' she says, amused. 'You're kind and fun and ridiculously beautiful. There's *no one* out of your league.' She pauses, thinking for a few seconds. 'What did he say?'

'Who, Zach? When?' I blink at her, my head all over the place.

'Yes, duh, Zach!' She waves her hand. 'This sexy jewellery designer who weirdly stayed in A&E for several hours waiting to see if you were all right – what did he say when you finally emerged?'

'Oh!' I settle back into a warm spot on the bed. 'He just sort of stared horrified at the whole grieving family around me and then stuttered, "Are you OK?"' I shrug. 'I said, "Not really, my aunt just died."'

'Heavy,' Myfanwy murmurs and I nod, feeling a bit guilty. I hadn't meant to make him feel bad. I spend my life tiptoeing around what to say in awkward moments, horrified that I might unintentionally upset someone with the wrong word or emphasis. I will literally lie in bed at night replaying something I'd said in casual conversation hours earlier, wracked with fear that the other person was somehow offended.

'He said he was really sorry and ran away.'

'That was it?' Myfanwy asks and I confirm, 'That was it.'

'But we've seen each other a few times since,' I add quickly. 'And it's not awkward. It's been nice actually. The customers love him and he's doing great work.'

'And the flirting?' Myfanwy side-smiles at me and I turn beetroot.

'No, there's definitely been no more of that,' I insist, even though I can't be sure. 'I can't be flirting with some guy with everything that's going on. Diane would be so offended.'

'I don't think she would.' Myfanwy's eyes are soft.

We sit in companionable silence for a few minutes, both thinking about Diane. When I was having a rough time at school in Year Eight – when I had no friends and Flo Williams had moved away – she used to come and pick me up at the end of the day in her crappy Volvo. She didn't say it out loud, but I know it was to save me having to walk home alone, surrounded by gangs of 13-year-olds who liked each other and hated me. In that ten-minute drive, she would ask me how my day was and I would get angry with her to cover up my own vulnerability. I would moan that we had to walk to the car, then moan about the car. All the way home she would ask me kind questions about my day and I would sullenly complain that I was too hot or else too cold.

I could've talked to her, instead of punishing her. I could've told her about the Art projects and the History essays — and how much I hated all of it. I could've told her about the bullies and the one that frightened me most, and how I lived in constant fear of being picked on. I could've told her how much I missed Flo and how I wished I could go back and undo what I did. I could've told her how I had no one to talk to. I could've told her how exhausting I found it all. I could've asked her how her day was going. I could've asked her about *her* life. I could've asked her about *my* life and how I was supposed to survive it. I could've enjoyed that small window of time Aunt Diane and I had together but instead I chose to sulk and hide myself.

I can feel the tears building again as Myfanwy begins to speak.

'I ...' Myfanwy stops there and I swipe at my wet face with the back of my hand.

'What?'

'No, never mind, it's nothing.' She shakes her head, looking embarrassed.

'No, say it.' I sit up straighter now, looking at her. 'You

can't just say "I" and then "never mind" – people aren't allowed to do that. It's a social etiquette rule: you have to say the thing you nearly said. Otherwise the person on the receiving end of this cruel act will start imagining all kinds of terrible possibilities.'

'Like what?'

'Like that you're dumping me as a friend because you've always really hated me and our whole friendship was a joke. Oh, and also Sonali and Emily also hate me and I was a pity-add to the Uni Dicks group.' I say all this with genuine fear because it has always been my secret belief about everyone in my life. 'Or maybe that you're dying, too, and this is our last chance to say goodbye.'

'It's not any of those things,' Myfanwy shakes her head. 'Although I think Emily probably does hates all of us. She would love to exit our WhatsApp group but it's too awkward.' I can see she is trying not to look amused as I fix her with my hardest, angriest stare.

'OK, fine! I'm sorry! I shouldn't have started the sentence but since I did . . .' She takes a deep breath. 'Can we talk about the three losses – the three bad things! – all coming true?'

I shake my head. 'I can't even think about it. It just makes me feel so selfish all the time,' I say quietly. 'My aunt died, my mum's a wreck, and all I keep thinking about is how everything in my life has fallen apart.'

'But that's OK!' Myfanwy says loudly. 'Because your life *has* fallen apart!'

'Oh, right, thanks,' I mutter.

'No, I mean it,' Myfanwy continues. 'Everything's a bit of a shitshow, isn't it? This time a few months ago, everything was sorted and now look at you!'

'Hmm.' I narrow my eyes. 'I'm not totally sure this is helping really, Myfe. I was more looking for some support?'

She rolls her eyes. 'Babe, I'm not going to, like, *gaslight* you by telling you everything is great, when—' She breaks off to wave around the room, gesturing at Robert Pattinson's poster on the wall. 'I mean *clearly* things are not good.'

I nod again, trying to gulp down more emotions.

'But!' She gets close to my face. 'We did know this was going to happen. You've known this mess was coming for sixteen years.' She pauses. 'OK, maybe we didn't know it would be *this* bad!' She waves again at the *Twilight* poster. 'But we knew you were going to have to deal with these three losses. And the good news is it means there are three *gains* on their way! Have you thought about that, huh?' I hadn't. Not really. She continues with enthusiasm. 'You know how Diane suggested you find the fortune teller?' She pauses briefly, wondering how I will react to the sound of my aunt's name. 'I've been trying to find her for you, but it turns out regional, travelling funfairs don't tend to have professional websites.'

'Weird that,' I murmur, feeling a rush of gratitude that Myfanwy has been trying to help.

'And since that seems to be a dead end, I was wondering if you wanted to try a different kind of psychic?' She beams excitedly. 'I go to this awesome woman who does tarot reading.' She looks excited. 'Or I could do you a reading myself. I bought this occult book and have been pulling a card for Sonali and me every day. It could answer some questions for you!'

I nod slowly, feeling too weak to fight her enthusiasm. Maybe it could be interesting? I don't have to believe in this stuff to be entertained. And it might be a nice distraction from my – what word did Myfe use? – *shitshow* of a life.

'OK,' I tell her thrilled face. 'OK then. Let's do it. It's not like things can get any worse, right?'

'Famous last words,' Myfanwy replies, biting back a smile.

CHAPTER ELEVEN

The following morning, I creep into the kitchen to find my mother standing at the sink staring out of the window.

That woman is out there again. The woman from yesterday who saw me crying with Myfe. She hovers for a minute by the fence, and then walks away quickly. There is something familiar about her.

'Hey,' I greet Celeste softly, not wanting to scare her. She doesn't move or react so I clear my throat. 'Hey!' I try again, a bit louder. Her head twitches a millimetre of acknowledgement in my direction. 'Are you OK?' I ask, moving towards the kettle.

She turns now, pasting on this weird, grimacey smile I've never seen before.

'Very well, thanks!' she says chirpily, like I'm a journalist harassing her on the red carpet about who made her dress and whether it's a sustainable brand.

She is a shadow of herself, which is funny because I've always thought of all of the rest of us as living in Celeste

Bretherton's shadow. My dad especially. He sometimes feels like an outsider in this family; this quiet man, so rarely here in the country. He even has a different surname – Lundin – while the rest of us are Brethertons. My mum not only insisted on keeping her name when they got married but also on her children taking that surname. She said she did all the hard work in bringing us into the world, so why should he get all the credit.

That was a different woman. I never thought I'd be missing her overbearing, difficult side, but now it's not there, I have to admit, I'm a bit frightened.

The front door bell goes and I open the door to find Sonali and Myfanwy, dressed in leggings and T-shirts, holding yoga mats.

'What . . . ?' I begin but Myfanwy cuts me off.

'We're going to a yoga class!' she announces. I glance back into the hallway to find Celeste looking off into the distance, pale and limp.

Down the stairs behind me, I hear Toni stomping down to join us.

'I've got a mat for you and Mum,' she chirrups, smiling excitedly. 'And what you're wearing is perfect.'

I glance down at my *Stranger Things* pyjamas and start to protest. 'I'm really not in the mood, you guys, and . . .'

Myfanwy waves her hand. 'No one is. That's when it's most important to do something. And exercise is the best something to do right now. It'll be good for you. My Reiki healer recommended this place.' Her tone is firm and final as she nods at Celeste. She means it'll be good for me – and for my mum.

I look again at Celeste, who is staring off into the distance, somewhere past my shoulder. She is barely there.

I go grab a jacket.

Twenty-five minutes later, rolling around on my mat as a shouty teacher at the front yells about being calm and controlled, I have to admit I'm feeling a little bit better. The endorphins are kicking in and it feels good and important to be surrounded by so many of the people I love best right now. This is heaven.

'This is hell,' Myfanwy mutters on my right and I snort. 'I should've made you all go to a spa or something.'

'I'm enjoying it,' Toni beams on my other side. 'It's inspiring me! I'm going to do Dry January and Veganuary next month.'

'But it's not January,' I point out, perplexed. 'Not even close.'

'Oh . . .' Toni looks baffled. 'I thought they were just internet terms. Are you only allowed to do it in January? That's a bummer, I really wanted to do it.'

'You know you could just not drink or—' I begin and Myfanwy puts out a hand to stop me.

'Don't explain.'

Now seated, the shouty teacher tells us to roll forward towards our toes. As my face arrives way too close to my bits, I hear my mum gasp.

She mutters something that sounds like but surely can't

be: 'She didn't even like yellow,' and then sits up straight, looking over at me fearfully.

'Huh?' I ask, untwisting myself.

'She didn't like yellow!' she says again and this time I'm sure.

Two mats down, Sonali leans over. 'Who didn't like yellow?' she hisses and Myfanwy shrugs.

'My sister!' Celeste looks at me, stricken.

Diane, she's talking about Diane.

'Diane didn't like yellow?' I try to keep my voice soft and understanding. Celeste shakes her head, looking down again into her lap.

'We've ordered yellow flowers for the funeral and I picked out this yellow dress for her to wear. I was thinking about how it was like sunshine – about how *she* was like sunshine – but I've just remembered her telling me once that she hated yellow. She said it always made her think of lemons and sick.' She looks up again and her face is bright red now. 'And lemons made her sick!'

At this moment, after weeks of waiting for this to happen, Celeste bursts into silent sobs. I scramble off my mat and over to hers, where I encircle her with my arms as we rock back and forth. She feels so fragile and small in my arms and I have to hold back tears of my own. From their mats, Toni, Sonali and Myfanwy all watch, eyes wide and sad. I nod at them to stay where they are. I don't want anything to distract Celeste from this moment. I think this is the first time she's cried – properly cried – and she needs it so badly. She needs to let it all out; she needs to fall apart; she needs to accept this horrible thing has happened. She needs to cry.

'I miss her so much,' Celeste whispers into my hair. 'She was so much better than me – so kind and fun. How could something like this happen? Why?'

As she asks this, a small voice from somewhere in me wonders briefly if the answer to Celeste's question is me. If it's my fault.

The prediction said there would be a death. Was this always going to happen or did it only happen because of me and this stupid – I don't know what to call it – *prophecy*? Should I have taken it all more seriously? Maybe if I'd warned everyone around me, they could've been more careful. Maybe Diane would've taken those symptoms more seriously; made it to the hospital before it even happened. What if I could've saved her?

The shouty teacher approaches, staring openly at my mum's tears. 'This is actually a very normal reaction in my classes,' she tells us smugly. 'People often cry out their inner turmoil. It just leaks out of them! My teachings are very cathartic and healing.'

Myfanwy snorts derisively at this but the teacher ignores her. She leans over, closer to my mum's tear-stained face and whispers, 'You're welcome.'

With that, Myfanwy lets out a defiant, unapologetic fart.

Sonali bursts out laughing as Celeste sits up straighter.

Myfanwy eyeballs the teacher. 'I bet that happens a lot in your classes too, right? It's a very normal reaction, isn't it? It felt very cathartic and healing.'

The woman looks disgusted as she stomps off back to the front of the class.

Myfanwy smirks as the rest of us – Celeste included – start to giggle uncontrollably.

'I don't understand people who don't think farts are funny,' Myfanwy says proudly. 'If you disapprove of farts, you're ruining so much joy for yourself. Like, we're all doing them and we're not going to stop just because Karen over there doesn't think they're funny. So you might as well enjoy them. That, or stop farting and literally die.' She does it again and this time it's even louder. 'Plus,' she tells us authoritatively, 'as a woman, farting – or any bodily function really – is a feminist act. A feminist statement. Men have had the monopoly on farting as a funny thing for far too long. It's high time women reclaimed fart jokes!'

At this, Celeste lets one rip herself and we all start laughing again as the room's occupants divide themselves between disgust and amusement. Through my watery, can't-stop-giggling eyes, I meet Celeste's. Her face is swollen from crying and there are mascara stains everywhere, but she no longer looks like a shadow. She has colour in her cheeks and sparkle in her eyes.

She looks like Celeste again.

CHAPTER TWELVE

There is just nothing *not* grim about a funeral; even when you try, like we have, to keep things lively. The florist has covered the place with beautiful, brightly coloured flowers – many of them yellow unfortunately – and photos of Diane in every pew, but it's all still very . . . funereal.

Churches may be beautiful but they're, let's face it, *grim*. This place is bones-cold, even on this summery day, and the priest must be a hundred years old. Which – no offence to all the centenarians out there – is also kinda grim. It's very . . . not Diane.

Beside me in the front pew, Celeste tuts, looking around at the full church.

'I just wish we'd had one conversation, one time, about what she would've wanted,' she comments sadly. 'We always seemed too young to talk about such awful things.' She pauses. 'I should've told everyone not to wear black, it's so cliché,' she tsks and I think back to this morning when she literally told me exactly what to wear, down to the earrings – and it was all black.

Celeste is very much back to herself since our cathartic yoga session a few days ago, and her mini-breakdown. Actually, she's been more *Celeste* than she's ever been before – which means out of control controlling. But I'm giving her some leeway given her only sister is in a box over there. The good thing is that she's got most of that Celeste shimmer back now. She's returned to the OTT, performing monster we know and mostly love.

'If it helps,' Myfanwy grins wickedly as we all turn to her, 'I'm wearing her favourite colour.' She undoes her coat, throwing it open to reveal a bright yellow sun dress. Celeste bursts out laughing.

'Thanks Myfe,' she beams. 'That does make me feel better. Diane always really loved you.' She sighs, still smiling. 'I should've had everyone wear yellow; it would've made her laugh a lot.'

'I think that's really inappropriate, actually, My-Fanny,' Shawn pipes up self-importantly from his place beside Toni. He's known Myfe for years now, but still aggressively gets her name wrong. Just one of the many things we appreciate about the guy.

'If it helps, I think everyone looks great,' Toni quickly jumps in as Myfanwy rolls her eyes. 'And Diane wouldn't care what people were wearing, she'd just be so touched by the turnout.'

We glance around at the packed room; the seats are all full, with mourners crowding into the aisle and jostling for space in the doorway. It's standing room only. I spot

Zach Walliams standing towards the back and feel my heart squeeze in my chest. It's so nice of him to come. Our eyes meet and we nod a greeting.

'Are you doing OK?' Myfanwy leans closer to take my hand and I drag my eyes away from Zach to smile at her gratefully.

'I am,' I tell her truthfully. I turn to the front where the coffin waits. It's so bizarre to think my Aunt Diane is in there. Is she here in other ways, too? Watching us?

'Do you believe in ghosts?' I ask curiously.

'Yes,' she nods with certainty.

Of course she does. She's so much more open than I am. Maybe I should be more open. Maybe I should try to believe in things.

'Do you think she's, like, *here*?' I ask in a whisper before hastily adding, 'I mean beyond being literally *there*.' I nod towards the coffin. Myfanwy swallows hard.

'I do actually,' she smiles softly. 'And I think she's loving seeing all these people who loved her.' She pauses. 'Speaking of turnout,' she murmurs, 'do you know if Daniel's coming?'

I look down and shake my head. 'I messaged him to let him know what had happened and mentioned the funeral details. He sent me a very kind reply, saying he was really sorry and how much he liked Diane — all that — but ignored any mention of the funeral.'

'Well, fuck him,' she says mildly. 'And PS you look amazing, I didn't even know you owned black earrings.'

111

'They're Celeste's,' I sigh, thinking again of this morning's battle. 'And thanks.'

'Maybe you should try and find a date here,' she comments drily, looking around the room with raised eyebrows. 'There are a surprising number of men here, and they're all pretty good-looking . . .'

I picture Zach all those rows back and suppress a snort. 'That would be super classy, wouldn't it? Trying to find a hook-up courtesy of my dead aunt. Imagine telling people about our adorable meet-cute!'

'But you should be on the lookout,' she reminds me. 'Remember that you're meant to be finding your soulmate this year.' When I look away, she adds, 'Three of the predictions have come true now – you have to start believing, surely?'

'Maybe,' I hedge.

She cocks her head. 'You're still up for trying the tarot reading, right?

I try not to pull a face. 'Sure,' I swallow, already dreading it. 'And I've got my stone.' I pat my pocket and she sniffs, irritated.

'Crystal,' she corrects me fondly. 'And I was thinking we could have a look at your birth chart or nakshatra. Maybe there's something in your stars to explain why you got singled out by that fortune teller. Maybe it was written in your future from minute one.'

'Er, sure, maybe,' I say, wondering what the hell a nakshatra is. I mean, I don't really know what a birth chart is either, but at least they're words I'm familiar with.

'And you never know,' Myfanwy shrugs. 'It could give you a clue about your incoming soulmate.' She elbows me gently.

'What are you two whispering about?' Celeste leans in.

'How Ginny's going to get laid today,' Myfanwy informs her casually. I swat her arm with a mild *hey*.

'Good idea!' my mother pronounces, looking around not at all discreetly. 'There are so many attractive men here. So what if they're a little older, age is just a number. I'll start making enquiries after the service.'

'*Please* don't!' I beg, mortified. 'Myfanwy was just joking around, honestly.' Celeste ignores me and I add beseechingly, 'Really, Mum, please promise me you won't! I'm really not ready for anything like that, *honestly*. I was supposed to be getting married last month! I haven't even cancelled the honeymoon in a few weeks. I have to get over Daniel and get my life straight before I start dating. Please don't start setting me up, promise?'

'Ugh!' Celeste throws up her beautifully manicured hands. 'That's so *boring* of you.' She turns away to talk to Shawn and Toni instead. Shawn glares at me and I look away. We're faux nice to each other but I've never had a good vibe from the guy. He's always so ... *performative*. I usually try to see the best in people and give them several chances, but he's had enough. I wish my sister could see that too.

Myfanwy looks at me curiously. 'Did you say you haven't cancelled your honeymoon? When were you meant to be flying? You were going to Madeira, right?'

I nod, thinking how beautiful and romantic it all looked when we booked the holiday. It's the final thing that needs sorting out from the wedding, but I haven't been able to face it.

She elbows me, leaning into my ear. 'You know you're due a life-changing trip, right?'

I stare at her, the words sinking in. She thinks I should go on my *honeymoon*? On my *own*?

Myfanwy leans back into my ear, 'What about—'

We're interrupted by a kerfuffle breaking out behind us, among the guests – *guests? Audience? Fans?* – and we turn en masse with curiosity. There are several men in a pew halfway back engaged in what looks like a heated argument. Faces are red, voices are raised, and I can see tension pulsing between them even from our position in the front row.

I glance at Celeste and she looks delighted. 'Oh my *god*,' she breathes out, thrilled.

Then one shoves another and the crowd draws away, horrified. A man falls backwards, sprawled across the floor, as another bloke steps back and throws a punch at the shover. It's mayhem for a minute and I lose sight of the action.

'What the hell is going on?' Myfanwy murmurs as our group moves into the aisle.

I can hear shouting, but there are now too many people in the way. I turn to the tallest of us.

'Toni,' I stage-whisper, 'are they literally fighting? What's happening?'

'Erm,' her head moves back and forth, following the

action. 'There seems to be four main guys involved, and then the rest of them are trying to get in between, to stop the fight, I think.' Next to her, Shawn tries to puff up to her height. 'I better get involved,' he says with genuine serious-ness, and Sonali covers a snort.

'Leave this to me, Celeste,' he says in a deep voice, step-ping forward.

'Don't, Shawny!' Toni calls after him. Her protests are quickly redundant as he can't get through the crowds. He returns sullen-faced back to our spot glowering at Myfanwy's smirk.

'What's happening now?' Sonali asks, as Toni's eyes remain riveted to a spot beyond heads blocking my way. 'Ooh, now the priest is getting involved!'

'YOU'RE A LIAR!' I hear one of the voices raised loud above the din.

'Uh-oh, the priest just slapped one of them,' Toni informs us.

'I could've slapped them,' Shawn pouts.

'Maybe we should, er, try to do something about this?' I suggest and Celeste sighs dramatically.

'Do we have to?' she whines, looking annoyed. 'I'm sure this whole thing was orchestrated by Diane; I think she's enjoying it immensely.'

'I'm sure she is,' I hedge. 'But I'm also worried we might have another death – if not one of the men fighting, then the very elderly priest.'

'Ugh, I *suppose* you're right,' she concedes, pulling herself up to her full height. 'Right!' She strides with determination into the crowd. Celeste is a foreboding presence, even when she isn't the grieving sibling of the deceased. And much to Shawn's fury, moments later, the room parts for her. At last, we can all see the four sulky, slightly damaged men at the heart of all this, standing in a line.

'Now WHAT was that all about?' Celeste has the tone of a furious headteacher, scolding naughty schoolboys.

'He's a LIAR,' one of them quickly snarls and I recognize the raised voice from the fight.

'HE is!' The rebuttal is livid.

'Shut up!' Celeste is having none of it. 'What are you all lying to each other about?'

There is a painful silence before Naughty Schoolboy Number One pipes back up. 'He says he's been dating Diane for three years.'

Oh! This is a surprise; I had no idea my aunt had a boyfriend. I wonder if he's the Cher impersonator.

'I *have*!' comes the reply from Naughty Schoolboy Number Two.

'You have *not*!' says Naughty Schoolboy Number One again. 'Because we've been together for a year and a half!'

There are audible gasps around the church as people take this in.

My mouth gapes at Toni in shock. Diane was cheating? She had two boyfriends? This is awful.

'BULLSHIT!' pronounces a new entry from Naughty Schoolboy Number Four who has stepped into the fray. 'She was with me for almost five years, there's no way she was dating either of you at the same time.'

'I've been with her for eleven months,' Naughty Schoolboy Number Three laments and they all start arguing again.

Jesus! Is this . . . this can't be true? Surely this isn't right? My lovely, sweet, fun, kind Aunt Diane had FOUR boyfriends?

Celeste looks taken aback, cutting off the bickering once again.

'You're saying that all of you were her boyfriends?' They collectively nod. 'And that none of you knew about the other?'

At this, they all look down at the floor.

'Do you have something to say?' Celeste prompts and Naughty Schoolboy Number One looks sulkier than before, if it were possible.

'I mean . . . she did say to me that it had to be an open relationship and that she was never going to be monogamous, but I didn't really take any notice!'

The three others slowly nod. 'She told me she was with other people, too,' admits Naughty Schoolboy Number Four, still sad.

'I guess she did say we could only see each other on Sundays because she had other boyfriends,' Naughty Schoolboy Number Two shrugs.

Celeste fixes them all with her steeliest of looks, the one she reserves for the most deluded of contestants on *Engage!*

'So what you're all saying,' she says slowly, 'is that Diane

117

was actually very honest with each and every one of you. But your sad little egos couldn't believe it?'

They glance sulkily at each other. One turns his chin up more defiantly than the others. 'I thought she loved me.'

'I'm sure she did.' Celeste's tone is a little kinder now. 'People love in different ways. And it sounds like she was completely, 100 per cent honest with you. And isn't that all we can ask of our loved ones? I'm sorry you've all been so wounded by this, but you should really have believed her when she told you who she was. She told you her truth and you decided to ignore it. We can't get angry with her now, can we?' She glances around at the crowd, a few of whom nod back at her, dazzled by her presence. Celeste turns back to the still-sulky Naughty Schoolboys. 'Now, do you understand we're at a *funeral*?' They nod at last and she adds, 'Do you want to stay and shut up, or fuck off?'

The congregation – *congregation*? *Flock*? *Churchgoers*? – take their seats, excitable whispers echoing around the room, and the battered priest slowly returns to his pulpit. Toni, Shawn, Sonali, Myfanwy, Celeste and I all file back into the front pew in shocked silence.

Wow wow wow. I can't believe it! My Aunt Diane was a polygamist! Or is that only the right term if she'd married them all? I know for a fact she would never have done that; she always said she didn't like the idea of marriage. Too many outdated traditions around the whole thing. I always assumed that meant she was single. I glance at the four glowering sulky guys, standing around looking increasingly embarrassed by their behaviour. They're all quite handsome and much younger than my aunt; she was clearly having a wonderful time with her singledom.

Maybe I should be more like Diane.

Not necessarily the multiple men thing because that seems like it would be too exhausting. Even dating one person is tiring; imagine having the headspace and extroversion to handle four! But I could be inspired by her enthusiasm for life. I could be like her. I could be open to more experiences. I glance over at Zach, who is smiling to himself as he moves back to position. He's *so* handsome. What if I could have a fun, no strings attached fling? Maybe it would actually help me get over Daniel. And I'm sure there was something there between us that first time we met. I could also try that stuff Myfanwy keeps going on about – the birth charts, the Reiki, that neck-salami thing she mentioned before. Perhaps I could even get into ghost hunting! Buy a Ouija board and belatedly ask Diane what the hell happened to my life and what I did to deserve any of it.

But maybe she'd be annoyed I'm making her death about me?

CHAPTER THIRTEEN

'How do you decide what sandwiches people want after watching a body burn?' Myfanwy asks bluntly as we hover over the buffet.

'We actually couldn't figure that out,' I admit, smiling wanly. 'I kept asking Toni what we should make, and Toni kept asking me back. Celeste was still too out of it to make a choice, so we just ended up ordering some platters from the supermarket.'

'Hmm.' Myfanwy picks a triangle up. 'Apparently M&S think mourners want prawn mayonnaise.'

A voice behind us makes us both turn. 'Did you see there was a vending machine in the crematorium?' It's Zach, eyebrows raised. 'For people who crave a KitKat in the waiting room.'

I sigh. 'I wish we'd bought some KitKats,' I admit, glancing back at the half-hearted trays of grey food we've provided for the wake.

After the funeral, we invited everyone to a nearby pub,

where we have an area reserved for eating lame sandwiches and consuming hot drinks. But no one is drinking the tea and coffee, and have instead hit the bar really quite hard.

'I'm Myfanwy.' My friend extends a hand for Zach to shake, and I turn my attention to introductions.

'God, sorry,' I say. 'Zach, this is my best friend. Myfe, this is Zach, of Walliams' Custom Designs who's working with Celeste's Stones.'

'Ohhhh,' Myfanwy says a bit embarrassingly. '*You're* Zach!' Her eyes trail up and down him and I swallow hard.

'I've told her how much we love your designs,' I say quickly. 'How talented you are.' I pause, ready to ferociously elbow Myfanwy if necessary.

'Right,' she says agreeably. 'Ginny says the customers are loving having you on board.'

Zach smiles widely. 'I love it more; it's been fantastic working with Gin and Tonic.'

Myfanwy shrieks at this and I laugh, embarrassed. I forgot I told him about our silly names. That was right before I got the call about Diane.

It already feels like a lifetime ago.

'Thanks so much for coming,' I say shyly. 'It's really good of you.'

'I wanted to,' he says simply. 'It was a lovely service. Which I know is a thing everyone always says, but it really was.' Zach pauses. 'I especially enjoyed the entertainment.' He nods towards the corner of the room where the four Naughty Schoolboys have shocked everyone by arriving together for the wake, and are currently hitting the shots hard, laughing and joking over their black eyes.

'That was a bit of a shocker, wasn't it!' Myfanwy says in an awed voice. 'I had no idea Aunt Diane was such a goer.'

'A goer?' Zach looks amused. 'I haven't heard that expression in a while. I feel like it's something my nan would've said.'

'I bet me and your nan would've had a lot in common,' Myfanwy says sombrely.

He laughs. 'Indeed.' He turns to me. 'I'm sorry, I didn't want to interrupt, I just wanted to say hi.'

'Hi,' I say shyly, feeling his eyes burn into my face.

'Hi,' he says back softly and the air around us thickens. After a moment, he clears his throat. 'Can I get you both a drink?' He nods at the bar.

'Vodka tonic, please,' Myfanwy grins and I nod.

'Same for me would be great, thanks.'

He heads for the bar as my friend leans into me. 'Phew,' she says once he's out of earshot. 'That was some fucking intense sexual chemistry there!'

'Nahhh,' I wave her away. 'He was just being nice.'

'Do we think he might be your soulmate?' She moves closer, shovelling in another prawn mayo sandwich.

'Oh stop it!' I cry. The idea of falling in love with anyone who isn't Daniel terrifies me.

'OK, I'll stop,' she says nicely. 'Let's talk instead about your life-changing trip.' She raises her eyebrows mischievously. 'We got interrupted when we were talking about you going on your honeymoon.'

I scowl at her. 'I think that's a terrible idea. Why would I want to go anywhere on my own right now, never mind on a trip that was supposed to be the most romantic week of my life?'

'Not on your own,' she shakes her head triumphantly. 'With me!'

'With you?' I repeat back to her dumbly.

She nods. 'After you mentioned it, I talked to Sonali and she agrees we should go. You and me.'

My heart leaps at this. A trip away from all of this. Escaping from the grief and the heartache with my favourite person in the universe . . .

But still. It would be my *honeymoon*. We'd have to stay in the romantic suite Daniel and I chose. We'd be surrounded by loved-up couples and romantic tourist spots.

Sensing my indecision, Myfanwy speaks quickly, 'Come on, Gin, you need this! It's your life-changing trip! Destiny has instructed you to take this holiday, and I can be there to supervise said destiny to ensure you listen.'

I narrow my eyes. 'Hmm, OK, but if I *choose* to go on a life-changing trip, doesn't that feel a bit like I'm making the predictions happen?'

'Don't overcomplicate this,' she waves her hand dismissively. 'Forget about the predictions for a minute, life-changing trip or not, you clearly need a break. You lost Daniel, you lost Diane, you moved back in with *your mum,* and we can't find the bloody psychic who started this whole thing – you need to get away. Let's just drop everything and

123

go. I checked the dates – it's during half term! This is meant to be. Please let me come! Otherwise that's me locked in with those awful dickhead children until fucking Christmas.'

'I thought you liked the kids at your school?'

She nods earnestly. 'I do! It doesn't mean they're not awful dickheads though. They're *children*, Ginny.'

'Girlieeeees!' Celeste arrives with her usual fanfare at the buffet table, gathering us both up in a too-tight cuddle. Upon release, she regards the food with distaste. 'What on earth were you and Toni thinking?' she sighs, appalled. 'You know I have a caterer on retainer.'

I meet Myfanwy's eyes, choosing not to point out that Celeste has been in a useless walking coma for the last few weeks. 'Sorry, Mum,' I say, swallowing down so many other answers – like, *No, I had no idea you had a caterer on retainer because that is not a thing.*

'Anyway, I'm having a lovely time, people are being so sweet!' She surveys the room, where she is the centre of attention, before returning her gaze to us. 'What's going on?' she suddenly looks suspicious. 'Were you talking about me?'

This is always her default assumption.

'No, Celeste!' Myfanwy eyerolls. 'We were talking about Ginny going on her honeymoon.' She pauses, then hastily adds, 'Without Daniel, obvs.'

Celeste gasps, then claps her hands delightedly. 'Oh of course! That's perfect. The whole thing's paid for anyway, you *must* go, and you *must* take your little sister.'

'Oh but, um . . .' I glance frantically at Myfe. I love Toni, but she's so young! The last thing I want is a Gen Z-er with me on this trip, wanting to go to nightclubs and, I don't know, environmental rallies??

Myfanwy jumps in smoothly. 'Actually, Celeste, we were thinking I'd go with Gin. Y'know, as her best friend, seeing her through this difficult time?'

'*I'm* her best friend,' my mother hisses before whipping around to face me. 'No, darling, you simply must take Toni. She's mourning Diane, too, and you can look after each other. I'd feel much safer knowing you were together.' Celeste and Myfanwy glare at one another.

I suddenly feel like a teenager again, with my mother insisting I take my baby sister along everywhere. But Celeste *did* pay for the honeymoon . . .

I'm about to give in – like I always do – when Myfanwy swoops in. 'Sadly, Celeste, it's too late,' she lies. 'We've actually just changed the booking into my name. They only let you change it once, so we're stuck, I'm afraid.'

Celeste's face is thunder, but she has no clue if this is true. All her – first-class – air travel is arranged via her agent or manager and their many PAs.

'Fine,' she flicks thick, blow-dried hair off her shoulder. 'I'll pay for Toni to come, too.' She turns on her heel. 'I'm texting the PAs right now. We can call in the summer workers to cover you at the store for a week.'

Myfanwy and I exchange a look.

OK . . . It could be fun? Myfanwy, me and Toni, on

a life-changing adventure together! We really do love Toni, and Celeste is right, she needs a holiday, too. If only from Shawn.

Zach arrives back with the drinks and Celeste is imme-diately *on* him, too close to his face, asking questions about the store and giggling at everything he says.

'I'm just going to get some air,' I say, making eye contact with Zach, who nods desperately.

'I'll come with you,' he says, extracting himself from Celeste's clutches.

Outside, the early autumn wind is biting and I wonder if he will offer me his jacket. That's a thing people do, isn't it? Maybe only in rom-coms.

The Naughty Schoolboys are nearby, finishing cigarettes, roaring over something about Diane. We watch them for a second before they head back inside.

'Do you think your aunt had more than just those four?' Zach asks. 'Like, maybe a few more of the attendees in the church were also conquests, but didn't want to get involved in the fight?'

'I'm sure you're right!' I snort. 'And maybe some didn't know when or where the funeral was. I bet Diane had at least fifty boyfriends.'

'It sounds exhausting!' he says, breathing out heavily.

'That's what I thought!' I exclaim, thinking how much we seem to have in common.

'Are you an introvert?' he smiles.

I nod, beaming back. 'I don't like to admit it to most

people though. I think there's this idea that introverts hate everyone and never want to go out—'

He dips his head eagerly, 'But that's not the case, is it? It's just that it drains us and we need a lot of time to recover afterwards.'

'Right! Exactly!'

We go in and order our drinks. As Zach pays, his arm brushes mine. His closeness is suddenly too intense, it makes me dizzy. I continue quickly, 'It's funny because my mum is the very *definition* of an extrovert.' I pause, picturing Celeste last night, posing for the Yodel delivery driver, like he was a pap, as he tried to get a shot of the parcel in our doorway. Meanwhile, when I'm waiting for a delivery, I hover by the front door in a state of anxiety, trying to remind my body that the fight or flight response is supposed to be about life or death, not for the times when I might need to sign for something.

'My family's the same,' he comments. 'Sometimes I feel like I don't really know where I come from.'

I suppress a shiver of recognition and watch him for a moment as he takes a sip of his drink. It's all too much.

'I just . . . I wanted to say how much I'm enjoying working with you,' he says suddenly, looking at me intensely.

Oh god. I've just realized I want to kiss him.

'Me too,' I smile nervously, everything feeling charged. 'I think it's really making a big difference to the brand. And the customers have been raving about your designs . . .' I trail off. Am I really going to kiss this man? At a *funeral*? No, of course not. That would be ludicrous and inappropriate and—

Yes? Oh god I think I am. I step a little closer, just an inch, but it changes everything between us. We're both suddenly breathing faster, my neck is hot, my stomach doing somersaults. He moves another inch and I suddenly know with certainty that it's going to happen. I'm going to kiss this gorgeous, film-star-handsome man at my dead Aunt Diane's funeral. My eyes start to close. I'm really going to—

'And I just want to say how great it is to be mates,' he says and I open my eyes. He has moved away and is looking at me with pity. 'I'm really happy to be *mates*,' he repeats. 'I think you're really brilliant as a friend.' Oh god oh god oh god.

I'm being rejected. Hard. This is so humiliating. There is no chance at all that he missed what I was about to do – what I was *trying* to do. I am a blundering idiot, how could I have thought he was interested? A man this good-looking? I'm a fool. I've been with Daniel so long, I don't know how to read signs anymore. Of *course* he doesn't like me. The embarrassment stings so hard.

'I'm just going to the loo,' I choke out and he grimaces but looks relieved.

'OK,' he replies lamely and I feel his flustered eyes on me, watching me flee.

I practically run to the loo, my face burning. The Naughty Schoolboys are in the corner, very drunk now, loudly talking through watery eyes about what a woman Diane was. 'Crap!' I shout, bumping into someone in the corridor. They reach out to steady me and I recognize a small scar across the hand from a particularly vicious bramble three years ago.

'No!' I breathe out hard, because before me, after more than two months of nothing . . . is Daniel.

CHAPTER FOURTEEN

'That's the death card.' The woman in front of me is staring down at what she's just turned over.

'I'VE ALREADY HAD MY DEATH QUOTA, THANK YOU.' I can't help that I'm shouting. No more death – *please* no more death.

'No, no,' she says kindly. 'That card just means that one phase of your life is over, and a new one is beginning.'

Daniel.

I glance up at Myfanwy, who looks unbearably smug. I still can't believe she managed to find a tarot reader in Madeira.

We've been here for four days now, and so far it's been exactly the lovely, relaxing trip I so badly needed. We've spent our days wandering around the little local town, relaxing by our hotel pool, and getting drunk on the island's namesake wine. Yesterday we took a two-hour boat trip to Porto Santo to visit the most gorgeous of beaches, where Myfanwy and Toni both got tanned, and I burnt my feet and knees.

OK, so the weather hasn't been totally ideal. It's been around 20 degrees every day, which would be fine by me – it is October now, after all – but apparently, back home, they're having an unseasonable heatwave.

We're all raging about it.

Today, Myfanwy's taken the lead, and after a long lunch at the hotel, we headed to Funchal, where we met up with this woman down by the lido.

She's watching me intently now as she prepares to turn over another card. I'm supposed to be focusing on my questions, what I want out of this reading, but there's a bird that keeps circling overhead and I'm convinced it's about to dive-bomb our whole group. Or maybe poop on us.

'This is a conduit for your innermost thoughts,' she reminds me now. 'There is no need to be nervous. You have to be open.' She turns over another card, from a different pile this time. 'Ah, you have the Here and Now card.' She points to the small images. 'There's an open door.' She looks at me. 'I feel that you are caught between the past and the future. One is not better than the other, but you're struggling to fully enjoy your life in the here and now. If you obsess over what's happened or what's to come, you can never live in the moment. I see you are stuck in your sadness; you must let go of what's happened and what *might* happen.'

I feel a lump in my throat.

'I'll try,' I whisper, trying not to cry.

'Amazing things are coming for you,' she tells me in a low voice. 'But only when they're meant to happen. There is an ebb and flow, and if you're in a low point, there's no point trying to rush through it. Don't push. Don't let expectations or fear make you take the wrong path.'

The wrong path.

I picture Daniel, standing there before me at the wake a few weeks ago. I re-feel all those weird bubbly feelings I felt seeing him. For the first full minute, neither of us said a word. We just stared at each other.

I couldn't really understand how he was there. I wondered if it was a coincidence — if he'd wandered into that very pub, into that very wake, at random, and simply happened into me.

He eventually spoke.

'I had to come,' he'd said, nerves jangling in his voice. 'I'm so sorry about Diane.'

He reached out for me then and I fell into his arms, crying for the first time that day. I hadn't cried as they brought in the coffin, I hadn't cried during the service, I hadn't cried during Celeste's eulogy, but in that moment outside the pub loos, everything hit me all at once. All that loss and all that sadness. I had sunk into his familiar arms, smelling his familiar smell, and sobbed for what felt like a really long time.

When we at last drew apart, I saw him properly: the man I'd loved, who had left me so abruptly and so horribly, but I couldn't feel any anger.

'Thanks for coming,' I'd said, wiping my face, embarrassed.

'I'm sorry I didn't make it to the service,' he said then, his eyes darting side to side. I understood immediately that he was trying to avoid my family – Celeste, probably, in particular. It wasn't a coincidence that he'd found me here by the loos, away from everyone else.

'Can we talk . . .' I began and he shook his head.

'I'm sorry, I can't stay.' He'd hopped from foot to foot, nervous energy bouncing off him. Full of beans, even on the darkest of days. 'I have, er, work,' he added and I recognized his excuse voice.

'Oh,' I nodded, hope draining out of me. He hadn't come to beg me to take him back. He hadn't even come to apologize.

Why *had* he come?

The woman before me continues speaking now, telling me about cards and cups, but I struggle to focus, thinking of Daniel and that bird above, closer now, ready to poo.

She's right, I feel so stuck. I know I shouldn't be obsessing over what has happened or what might happen, but how do you do that? How do you let go? How do you not fear what's to come? Especially when it feels like it's been laid out for me my whole life.

Minutes later, as we pay the woman and walk away, I turn back. 'Do you have any specific predictions for me?' I ask desperately. 'Do you have, like, six predictions or something?'

From her seat, the woman looks at me quizzically.

'That's not how it works!' Myfanwy hisses. 'Thanks again, Benediata!' she calls, hurrying me away.

We head back to the hotel in silence, each of us thinking about our own readings.

I have to admit, it was an interesting experience. She was interesting, the cards were interesting. And I believed in what she said. Or I believed that *she* believed in it. But god, how are you supposed to *know*?

'Did it help you feel any better about things?' Toni asks nicely.

I look out across the water as we walk.

'I don't know,' I tell her honestly, wondering to myself when the *life-changing* part of this trip is supposed to happen. And that's when the bird poos on me at last.

Fair enough, I think, and keep walking.

CHAPTER FIFTEEN

It's the last night of our holiday, and since nothing life-changing has happened, we've decided to get life-changingly drunk.

We are delighted and appalled in equal measure to find an Irish bar down the road from our hotel. So now we're drinking horrible Guinness in a horrible pub, full of horrible *Brits Abroad* shouting at one another about foreigners.

It at least makes me less homesick.

A group of lads in their twenties – also drunk – make their approach to our corner table.

'All right?' the leader smirks. 'Want a drink, ladies?'

'No thanks, kid,' Myfanwy slurs, struggling to be heard over the offensive music. 'We've got loads of drinks.'

It's true, we do. We decided to do our rounds all at once when we got here. And because the bar was busy, we all bought four drinks per person. We still have, like eleven warm pints on our table.

The twenty-something looks excited. 'Oh, you're an actual Irish!' he accuses Myfanwy, who rolls her eyes.

'No, I'm Welsh,' she says and he looks sceptical.

'Nah,' he shakes his head, glancing around at his ladz ladz ladz. 'Don't try and fool me, I know Welsh ain't real. You're Irish, that's an Irish accent!'

Toni leans in, more used to dealing with men of this age group. 'No really!' she smiles sweetly. 'Myfanwy's from Wales.'

The boy laughs. 'Babe, that is well cute, but I know you're just flirtin'. I did go to school y'know! I did my SATs and everything. So I *know* Wales is that mythical place in the ocean where the mermaids live.'

I frown. 'Are you confusing the animal whales with ... but how do you get to mermaids from ...'

Toni turns to Myfanwy. 'Is that true?'

Myfanwy smiles tightly. 'Yes, of course! I used to be a mermaid but then a sea witch, also from Wales, gave me legs and encouraged me to move to England where I would meet a prince and lots of micro-xenophobia.'

'Was the sea witch from SwanSEA?' I ask, trying not to laugh.

We both snort, while Toni looks surprised. '*Was* she?'

The boy and his ladz ladz ladz are getting impatient now. 'All right then,' their leader says. 'If you're really from Wales, say something in your foreign language.'

Myfanwy sighs. 'I can't speak Welsh.'

'No!' he rolls his eyes exaggeratedly, like she is dumb. 'I said say something in the Wales language.'

'Right,' Myfanwy says slowly. 'Sorry, the mer-language. Actually, they did send me to school to learn Wel– sorry, *Mer-glish*, but I've forgotten it all.' She pauses. 'Apart from the word coch, which means red. And I only remember that because it sounded like a naughty word.'

The boy looks awed. 'Wow,' he says. 'You really *are* from Wales!'

'Wow,' agrees Toni, staring in the same impressed way at Myfanwy, who is nodding sagely.

'I really am.'

'Anyway,' the boy says breezily. 'Speaking of which, does anyone fancy a shag? Asking for me or any of my bros.' He waves at the ladz ladz ladz, who are all smiling hopefully, apart from one who is distracted, picking something out of his teeth.

God! Dating hasn't gotten any better than it was in my twenties, then. I thought the new generation would be much better at all of this. I thought they'd be smoother and cooler, with fewer idiotic men embarrassing themselves in the vain hope of a fumble. Is this what the dating market looks like? Is this what I'm supposed to embrace? What I'm supposed to throw myself into for the next few years? Are these kinds of men my only option now I've lost Daniel?

Well, no bloody thank you. I will avoid the whole thing and eventually Daniel will come to his senses and marry me. That's it. Final word on the subject.

*

An hour later, I find myself snogging the boy.

His name is Matt and he's actually very sweet. Dumb as a rock, but he totally has depth. I found out he likes painting! Rooms and landscapes! And he has an old motorbike he's doing up with his dad. I don't ask how old his dad is because I have a feeling we'd be quite close to being peers. And the main thing I found out is that he is a great kisser and he really fancies me.

We pull apart at last in our dark corner, saliva all over the place; hands all over the place. 'I'll be back in a bit,' I gasp at him, staggering back towards Myfanwy and Toni and flopping down. 'I feel like a teenager!' I giggle happily.

'That might be because you were literally *feeling* a teenager?' Myfanwy points out, smiling widely.

'I know!' I swig from the nearest glass of alcohol. 'But it was great. I miss snogging. I haven't *just* snogged someone in so many years.'

'To snogging!' Toni waves her glass around, waiting to cheers and we oblige with our warm, horrible Guinness.

'Come dance with me!' Matt is suddenly at our table again, all wide-eyed pupils and horniness. I suspect he is on something, but he hasn't offered me any of it. I'm relieved and also offended.

'There isn't a dance floor,' I point out. 'This is a pub.'

'Who cares!' he grins excitedly.

'Maybe in a bit.' I wipe some sweat off my forehead. 'I'm just going to sit for a few minutes.' He looks sad and I add by way of explanation, 'I'm old, Matt.'

'Ah,' he nods, understanding now, and off he bounces towards the ladz ladz ladz.

His energy suddenly reminds me of Daniel and I'm hit with a crashing wave of sadness. It's followed quickly by guilt. Oh crap, I shouldn't have got so drunk, I'm going to start being boring and emotional now. Here it comes, I can't stop it . . .

'I really miss Daniel,' I slur, taking my companions by surprise.

'Where's this come from?' Myfanwy asks nicely, shuffling her chair around to me. 'I thought you were having fun! You had your tongue in someone at last!'

'It's the first person I've kissed since Daniel!' I say, realizing it's true. 'And this is our *honeymoon*. I shouldn't be kissing young boys. I should be kissing *him*.' I swallow, knowing everyone is sick of this chat. It's been *months*, everyone wants me to be over him by now, but I'm not. Seeing him at Diane's wake has thrown me back ten steps. I gulp down drunk tears as I continue, 'In some parallel universe, I'm sitting here in this bar with him, laughing at those ladz ladz ladz over there. We'd be holding hands and reliving memories from our wedding, saying it was the best day of our lives.' Toni strokes my shoulder nicely.

'It'll be OK,' she lies kindly.

'I just don't know what I'm meant to do,' I admit. 'That tarot woman said I have to stop obsessing over the past and the future, and live in the now, but most of the time my *now* feels really rubbish.'

'Oh, cheers!' Myfanwy says jokily.

'Sorry,' I say, biting my lip. 'I don't mean right now-now. Obviously I'm having a lovely holiday.'

'Why aren't you focusing on that then?' she asks. 'That's literally what living in the moment means. Enjoy where you are right here and right now. You're in a bar, having fun, snogging randoms like this is 2012.' Myfanwy pauses, something occurring to her. 'I've got an idea to distract you!' she says brightly. 'Maybe we should do a Ouija board! See if the spirit world can give us any answers.'

'Er, I don't think . . .' I begin and Toni looks between us, a little panicky.

'Shawn says Ouija boards are stupid and evil,' she says nervously.

I sit up straighter. I definitely don't want to be on the same side of history as Shawn. 'I think it's a great idea,' I say forcefully. 'Let's do it, Myfe!'

She goes to retrieve a pen and paper from the bar, while I consider what I should ask the spirit realm. What do I want? What do I want and what do I *need*?

I want to marry Daniel.

Scrap that.

I want to meet my *soulmate*, like the predictions promised. And if that happens to be Daniel, so be it.

What else?

I want to make Celeste's Stones even more amazing. I've been thinking about a concept recently that I really want to bring in as a new in-store service. I'd be an

140

engagement concierge, specifically helping people, not just with their rings, but with their proposals. It would be a really hands-on benefit to visiting the store. From what I've seen, people increasingly want that kind of next-level personal service.

I want to stop being a pushover. I want to be strong and brave, especially with Celeste. I want to be able to tell her what I really think and have her see me as an equal, instead of a silly little child. I have been too weak for too long. And I can't blame what's happened these last few months because I've been a coward my whole life. Look at what happened with Flo Williams back at school.

Myfanwy returns with paper and begins sketching, writing out yes and no at the top, adding letters and numbers below. 'Here we go,' she pronounces, flourishing the make-shift board. She places a small glass in the centre and instructs us to place two fingers each on the glass.

'Helloooooo, spirits!' Myfanwy says in a spooky voice. 'Can you hear us?'

Nothing happens and we all giggle.

'Maybe they're not here?' Toni says, nose crinkling. 'This Irish pub in Madeira might not appeal to ghosts.'

'Should we ask a question?' I whisper nervously.

'Erm,' Myfanwy considers this. 'Does Sonali miss me?' she asks with delight. The glass jerks, wrinkling the thin paper and stopping awkwardly.

'Oh my god!' Toni breathes, as we all regard each other with wide eyes.

'You moved it,' I accuse Myfanwy and she shakes her head. 'I didn't, I promise!'

Toni leans in to inspect the position of the glass. She frowns. 'It's stopped just under the C,' she says. 'What does that mean?'

Hazy with booze, I start singing 'Under The Sea' from *The Little Mermaid*, and Myfanwy gasps. 'That's definitely a message for me! Didn't we literally just decide earlier that I'm a mermaid from Wales? Under the sea!'

'That's SO weird!' Toni declares, but I pout. 'What does that tell you though? What does it *mean*?'

'Maybe I should go for a swim?' Myfanwy muses and I shake my head vehemently.

'If that's the message, it must be from a demon. We should not swim after eight pints of Guinness.'

Toni has lost interest. 'My turn. Will I marry Shawn?' She smiles eagerly and the glass shoots immediately over to no. 'Oh.' She observes the answer without much reaction.

'Do you *want* to marry Shawn?' I ask her carefully. She blinks at me with surprise.

'Of course?' she says with a definite question mark. 'I mean, I guess I do.' She pauses. 'Mum says he'd make a great husband and father, and I should be dropping hints about a proposal. She says three years is too long just to be dating.'

'But you're only *twenty-three*!' Myfanwy cries. We try not to comment too much on her relationship, but sometimes it's too much to resist.

'That's what I thought, but what do I know about love?'

Toni tinkles at this, failing to see the irony of her sentence. 'Plus,' she continues, 'I'm almost twenty-four! That's, like, *well* grown up.' She looks at us both anxiously, adding, 'Isn't it?'

God, I thought Gen Z were all supposed to be brimming over with certainty. They're supposed to know what they want and who they are. I thought they took no shit and were going to save us all from ourselves. Turns out they're as insecure and broken as the rest of us.

'Your turn.' Myfanwy nods at me encouragingly and I swallow.

'OK, um,' I pause. There are too many questions and I don't know if I want the answers. At last I settle on something important. 'Is Diane OK?'

Nothing happens for a few seconds, and then the glass moves slowly, more gracefully than before. It lands softly on *yes*.

'Shit, you guys, it's 3am!' Toni pronounces suddenly, leaping up out of her chair. 'We've got to be at the airport in a few hours!'

'Crap,' Myfe mutters, reaching for her drink and draining it.

My young paramour Matt bounds up as we gather our bags. 'You're not leaving, are you?'

'Yes, sorry!' I tell him. 'We're heading back to England today and—'

'Or,' Myfanwy interjects happily, 'under the sea, for some of us.'

Smiling at her, I continue. 'We have to go pack. Our taxi is picking us up in a few hours.' I pause. 'Also I'm super freaked out. We just did a Ouija board and it said some weird stuff.' Matt looks baffled and I explain nicely, 'A Ouija board is a kind of talking board where you can speak to ghosts.'

He nods. 'Oh, yeah, I know what a Ouija board is! My dad is a professor of neurology, he says it's all just the ideomotor response.'

I squint at him, 'Ideo ... what?!'

'It's a psychological phenomenon where a subject makes unconscious muscle movements. It's something a bit like a dissociative state. Lab studies have measured people moving the glass in a séance without having any idea they're doing it.'

The three of us gape at him as man-child Matt continues, 'Anyway, Ginny, d'you want my number or what? Be great to bang when you're back in England!'

I blink, taking all of this in as he rips off a piece of the Ouija board and scribbles down his number.

I don't look at it until we're in the taxi on our way to the airport two hours later. The number is there in big loopy handwriting, beside his name: Matt Williams.

Yet another Williams. Flo Williams, Zach Walliams, Matt Williams. What is the universe trying to tell me?

My head sags back into the headrest, as exhaustion over-whelms me. I feel surprisingly calm.

Maybe this didn't need to be a life-changing trip in a huge sense, because in a way it does feel like my life has shifted. Maybe that's all it means, that prediction – that it would be life-changing in a small way. Small changes can be just as important as big ones. Maybe I only need small shifts – several small, life-changing moments – to find my happiness. To get everything I want.

And maybe I should WhatsApp Matt Williams for a bang.

CHAPTER SIXTEEN

It's been a week since we got back from our kinda-life-changing trip, which means three months of living back at Celeste's house. And still – every day – I wake up baffled by where I am and how this could've happened.

Getting ready for work, I take it all in again, surveying my old bedroom, in my old bed with my old bedsheets; old curtains hanging from the windows, and surrounded on all sides by old teddy bears and a bookshelf full of old *Simpsons* DVDs.

I know I should change things up a bit. Like, at least take down that old *Twilight* poster of Robert Pattinson? But that would mean I *live* here. It would mean admitting defeat, conceding that I now really do co-habit with my mother in the house I grew up in.

And I can't do that.

So far it is definitely meeting – exceeding – all my worst expectations.

Celeste has been *on* me the whole time. She immediately assumed the old mother–child dynamic I was so eager

146

to escape at eighteen by running away to uni. She's been hovering around me ever since I moved back in — fussing, haranguing, asking at all hours if I need her to 'put on a wash'.

She follows me from room to room, telling me off for putting on the overhead light and leaving the sofa cushions at the wrong angle. Last night, when I announced I was going to bed, she chased me in here and I swear to god, she was *this close* to tucking me in. Every boundary I've spent the last fifteen years erecting is crumbling down around my ears.

I pull on a blouse, tucking it into my pencil skirt and smoothing out the creases with my hands. One nice thing about this situation, I think cheerfully to myself, is being able to commute to work with Toni!

I pad my way softly down the hall and knock lightly on Toni's door.

'You ready?' I ask, peering around the door.

'Yep!' She lays down her hairbrush, beaming at me and I step out of the way as she joins me on the landing.

'We're off,' Toni announces to Celeste as we pass the kitchen and she turns quickly, bouncing up from her seat.

'I'll take you! I'm going in today!' She grabs her car keys and Toni and I glance at each other in surprise. Celeste so rarely comes to the store, especially for opening hour! She is not really a morning person, a fact the studio have had to get used to around filming *Engage!* But maybe this is my chance to put those manifestations I made on the trip into practice. I've brought up my engagement concierge idea with Celeste a couple of times, but only in passing and she's given me the brush-off. If she's working in the store today, I can sit her down properly and talk her through my plan, I *know* she'd be excited. Christmas is coming up in a couple of months, which means an influx of clients looking for rings. If we can implement the service soon, it could be a huge boon for the business.

Zach's waiting in front of the store when we get there, pacing up and down a little impatiently. I feel myself turning red as we approach, thinking of the last time we saw each other at the wake. I've avoided him the last couple of times he's been due in the shop, rearranging my shifts so Toni could liaise with him instead. Then, of course, I was away on the trip with Myfe and Toni. All of it means, I realize now, that it's been a month since I've seen him. I also realize in a rush that the time apart has only increased my embarrassment.

'Hiya!' I call awkwardly and he turns, that actor smile spreading across his face. He opens his mouth to reply, then spots Toni and Celeste right behind me.

'Oh!' he says, his face falling. 'Hi, everyone.' He falters, gesturing behind him at the store. 'Sorry to be so early. I was going to get everyone a coffee and then forgot and ended up ... here ...' he finishes lamely and I breathe out. At least he seems as nervous and humiliated as me.

'We'll have to get you your own key!' Toni trills happily, completely oblivious, as she passes by, opening the front door and gesturing at him to head in.

Inside, he points towards the office and I nod, 'I'll be right behind you, one sec!'

My heart is pounding as I make us coffee. I know how he likes it now: black with two sugars. Just like a good *mate* would know. Heading in with the cups, I immediately understand coffee was a mistake; my hands are shaking but he pretends not to notice.

'Thanks!' he says faux-brightly.

'No problem!' I match his tone, dying inside. 'So, coming in this morning is lovely Joey Addiman.' Zach nods enthusiastically, picking up the bag at his feet.

'I've got the ring here. I hope he likes it.'

'I hope Hannah likes it!' I add, half laughing.

Joey met with us a couple of months ago, bringing in his great, great grandmother's engagement ring that he wanted reworked and personalized for his partner, Hannah. He didn't know exactly the look he wanted, so Zach and I talked him through options. Zach suggested adding some new feature stones to the design, and we discussed what would suit her personally, as well as her lifestyle. She works with her hands, as a private chef, which means some of the softer stones, like opals and turquoise, can get scratched or broken more easily than others. On the hardness scale, diamonds are the hardest material on earth, which is why they're so perfect for an engagement ring you wear every day.

Plus, they're so purty.

So he chose diamonds, but then we had to go through everything like cut, colour, clarity, and carat, plus the size of the band, with Zach working on mock-ups. Now the finished design is finally ready for collection.

Zach looks nervous so I reassure him. 'I'm sure they'll both love it. The designs you did were so beautiful.'

'It's a lot of pressure, especially when you're essentially melting down a family heirloom!' His voice jangles and he tries to laugh, but sighs instead. He looks up, staring at me with a serious expression on his face. 'Ginny, look, I really need—'

'Morning!' Joey greets us excitedly at the door.

'Joey!' I exclaim, leaping up to give him a hug. You get overfriendly when you've spent weeks talking about the biggest moment of someone's life.

'Is it ready?' the customer asks, nerves plain on his face.

'It sure is!' I beam, leading him to the counter.

We all grin at each other nervously as Zach reverently unpackages the box. Our mutual fear is plain on our faces and I hover anxiously as Joey stares at the finished product, the result of so much thought, care and love.

This is my favourite part – and also the scariest.

At last he breathes out heavily. 'It's stunning!' He looks up to meet my eyes – his are wide and damp. 'It's exactly what I wanted, I love it.' Beside me, I feel Zach exhale heavily. Joey pauses, his brow suddenly furrowed. 'Oh god, do you think Hannah will like it? She's shown me so many rings she likes over the years and this is definitely in the right area, but it's also so unique. Do you think she'll like it, you guys?'

'I really do,' I say as reassuringly and warmly as I can. 'I think she's going to love it.'

'I'm so thrilled you're happy,' Zach says with genuine delight and I grin over at him.

'He was so nervous,' I share teasingly.

'*You* were nervous!' he laughs at Zach. 'Think how nervous I've been!'

We all laugh now, full of relief.

'Are you popping the question soon?' I ask as I carefully replace the ring in the velvet box, admiring the satin lining as I close it, and begin the careful process of packaging it back up as beautifully as possible.

Joey is silent for a moment and I look up, concerned.

'I actually don't know,' he admits. 'I've been thinking so long and hard about the ring, I kind of forgot to make a decision about the proposal itself.' He bites his lip, looking worried again. 'I know I have to get down on one knee, right? Or is that a bit *done* now? My knees are a bit dodgy actually.' He glances down at his legs, his face paling. 'Should it be at home, with just the two of us, do you think? Or at a really big, fancy hotel? Or should it be in front of all her friends and family?' His words are coming thicker and faster as the panic takes hold. 'Or perhaps I should whisk her off abroad somewhere and do it on a beach? Or back to the place we had our first date? Or our first kiss? Or maybe that's all too cheesy and she'd rather do something fun? Has anyone ever proposed during a session of laser tag? Ughhhh!'

I rest a comforting — and hopefully *calming* — hand on his arm.

'Hey, it's OK!' I say nicely. 'You'll figure this out.'

'And where am I going to hide that,' he gestures wildly at the packaged-up ring on the counter, 'until I decide on this and arrange everything?!' He looks like he might cry and I fight the urge to hug him. 'It has to be *perfect*, y'know? This proposal has to be the most memorable, amazing moment of Hannah's life — it's what she deserves — and I have to get it right. I want her to cherish this and for us to tell our grandchildren about it one day. I want her to be *wowed*!'

'Right,' I nod decisively and grab both his shoulders. 'Joey, listen, you need to calm down and stop freaking out, OK?' He swallows tearfully, shutting up at last, as I nod authoritatively. 'Good. Now let's go sit down for another minute and talk this through.'

We spend the next hour going through his options. We talk about Hannah and what she likes and dislikes. We talk about how close she is to her friends and family. We talk about how she feels about surprise parties, cheesiness and romance. He paints a picture of this woman he loves so much, and by the end of the hour, it seems clear to both me and Zach that Hannah is one of those increasingly rare people who will want a public proposal.

We settle on a plan for a surprise party at a hotel they stayed at early on in their courtship for their first minibreak. It's where Joey said he loved her for the first time. Her friends will surprise her there for a huge celebratory party, where he will get down on his bad knee and propose. I am to hold onto the ring for him until everything is ready. Once it's all booked, I'm going to personally deliver the ring to the hotel, disguised in some way, and make sure the concierge knows to pass it along subtly to Joey – and *only* Joey – when they arrive.

He is so grateful for my help that by the end, he is inviting me to come to the proposal party. I'm completely elated, and wave him off, thinking about how this is a moment Joey and Hannah will remember forever. How amazing that I get to be a part of it. I haven't felt so buzzy and happy with my work in ages.

Zach and I wave Joey off at the door, both a bit drained – but happy.

'Wow,' Zach says quietly. 'That was really cool.'

'It was,' I say, turning to him, forgetting the awkwardness for a moment. He suddenly steps closer. 'Look, Ginny, about what I said at the wake.' He clears his throat. 'I really did mean it. About being friends, I mean. Do you think we could hang out as mates sometime? Away from the store?'

Oh fantastic. The rejection speech *again*. Just what I need.

'Totally!' I say, nodding too much. 'That would be totally, totally great! Totally.'

Celeste bounds in at this moment and I've never been so relieved to have her unprofessionalism around.

'Zach, darling!' She reaches to air-kiss him and he awkwardly obliges. 'How did it all go with the client? You two were with him for *ages*. I was starting to think you were up to no good!' She giggles flirtily as we both blush beetroot. 'Was he happy with your ring?'

At this Zach breaks out a genuine smile. 'I think he loved it!' He glances at me for reassurance and I nod. 'And Ginny was *amazing*. She basically ended up planning his whole proposal for him!' He laughs, then adds teasingly, 'She's a great engagement concierge, isn't she? You definitely need to make that a proper, official service you offer at Celeste's Stones.'

'A what?' Celeste frowns, peering at me.

'Um, that idea I've had?' I say nervously. 'I've, er, mentioned it to you a few times?' I swallow, steeling myself. 'Actually I was hoping to talk it over with you properly, if you have a few minutes now?'

She shrugs a yes and Zach gives me an encouraging thumbs-up. 'I'll leave you to talk. I'd better get off,' he says nicely, downing his half-drunk, cold coffee and heading to get his stuff.

'Thanks again,' I call out after him, relieved that at least some of the tension has gone. Maybe we could really be friends? Maybe it would be nice to have Zach as a friend.

As the store door shuts behind him, I take a deep breath. 'So, Mum,' I begin, 'this engagement concierge idea. I've really noticed an uptick in how much *more* our clients want from us. They don't just want a ring, they want help with the whole,' I wave my hand, 'deal. They want advice on the ideas, the planning, what to do, how to do it – they even want help with delivering the ring to the proposal venue!'

Before I can go any further Celeste turns on me. 'That was incredibly unprofessional,' she begins coldly.

'What?' I am startled. 'What was?'

'Talking about some silly little pet project with,' she waves her hand at the door, '*the help*.'

'The *help*?' I am horrified. 'You mean Zach? He's part of the team now and—'

'I don't care.' She looks furious. 'Things like this go through *me*. You are not to try and undermine me or go around me like that.'

'I, I, I didn't mean to,' I stutter. 'I've actually tried to talk to you about it before but you—'

She cuts me off again. 'I know and I thought I'd made it clear that I don't think it would work.' Her voice softens a little. 'Darling, it's sweet that you're trying to think of cute little things for the brand, but you need to leave this kind of big picture thing to me.'

'But ... but ...' I want to shout that bringing Zach on board was my idea and point at how successful it's been. I want to say *how dare* she talk down to me like this. I want to scream that I've been working here for ten years and I *know* this place! Better than her at this point, since she's so rarely here.

But I'm too blocked up. I feel clogged and choked by all the things I want to say.

She smiles now, her rage evaporating. 'We've actually got something rather exciting in the works for the brand. I've been talking to Daddy about it and it's time we told you girlies. Go grab Toni and I'll explain.'

I stand up, following her instructions though my whole body is numb with anger. I am so upset, so furious – mainly with myself. Why do I put up with this?

I beckon Toni into the office, still not able to find my words.

Once we're seated, Celeste regards her with sparkling eyes. 'Darlings! I have something big to discuss with you. I've been talking to Daddy—' I gag slightly at *Daddy* as she continues '—and we've decided to *expand*!' She looks between Toni and I. My surprise is mirrored on my sister's face. An expansion? What does that mean? 'We're going to start doing accessories!' Celeste continues, ablaze with excitement. 'And we want to open another store, followed – hopefully – by more later on. We want Celeste's Stones to take over the world!'

Toni claps, bouncing on the spot a little. 'That's brilliant, Mum!' she says and they hug happily. I paste on a smile, too, feeling wholly blindsided. She's been talking to Dad? Who's never in the country? Couldn't this discussion have included me?

And, *god,* accessories? What does that mean? Will it be in the new store or here? I'm not sure it's a good idea. We've always traded on being boutique; a unique, one-off store in Central London. People *travel* to visit us. Yes, for the Celeste Bretherton experience, but also for our personalized, individual service. We're a family business that can dedicate our time to clients. We genuinely care about what we're doing for them. If we expand, would we still be able to do that?

Celeste catches my expression. 'Darling,' she says breezily.

'Look, I know you've got your heart set on this little proposal butler thingy—'

'Engagement concierge,' I correct her weakly, wondering if *proposal butler* is better.

She waves her hand dismissively. 'I just can't really see it taking off.' My heart crashes into my stomach as she pulls a faux-sympathetic face. 'I haven't seen any evidence of our clients wanting that kind of service from us—'

You're never here to see it! I want to scream but don't.

'—and I just think it'll take you away from your real job. We'll be keeping you very busy with this new line and the new store. We're opening the new place in January and I want you running it. You won't have time for silly little extras like engagement concierging.' She giggles like it's nonsense and I swallow hard, feeling crushed.

'Right ...' I begin, trying to decide whether it's worth fighting my corner. I really thought I'd come up with something good – something our clients would be excited by! Maybe she's right that the demand isn't there. She does know what the people want, doesn't she? She's worked with the public long enough.

'*And*,' Celeste is still in presenting mode, 'we've already enlisted a *Love Island* star to help design our first range of accessories!' she smoothly changes the subject back. 'Daddy and I are thrilled!'

I nod, feeling overwhelmed. It's one thing having a reality star – my mother – as the face of our business, but at least she's seen as an expert in her field. Doesn't this dilute the brand?

I suppress a sigh, thinking about everything that's happened to me in the last few months; thinking of the multiple failures and rejections.

What do I know about anything? Why would I think I'd have anything decent to offer the business? I really thought the concierge service was a good idea, and it felt like a good way to carve out my own niche in the family business, away from my mother, while staying a part of a business I genuinely love.

I feel so locked in. Every time I try to move on with my life, I get blocked. I try to move on from Daniel and get rejected. I try to focus on work and Celeste slaps me down. I try to find the fortune teller so I can finally figure out if these predictions mean anything, and it's another dead end.

All I want to do now is go home – the home that isn't even my home – get into bed, and cry. I hate that life is supposed to go on.

CHAPTER SEVENTEEN

I spend the next two days in bed.

I tell everyone I'm feeling ill, and I just lie there, thinking about everything that's been happening and trying to ignore the world. I just want to be alone and embrace my solitary misery. But of course I can't even have that. Not when I'm living in Celeste Bretherton's house. She is in and out on a constant rotation, bringing me soup, plying me with Strepsils and/or Anadin Extra, asking me questions about how I'm feeling. It's endless and well meant, but all I want is peace.

It all feels like too much; it's overflowing and overwhelming. I feel like I am too soft and life is too hard. I revel in my grossness and stink; unshowered and unchanged.

And of course, that is when *he* turns up.

'Are you feeling well enough for a visitor?' Celeste asks from my bedroom doorway.

'Not really.' I don't even look up, flicking idly through my phone. I assume it's Myfanwy. She's already dropped off three tins of Roses and a carrier bag of Quality Streets. I suspect it's all Christmas leftovers from last year but I'll still eat them for sure. It's all very generous and kind, but I definitely don't need any more.

'I think you should see him,' Celeste needles and at that, I do look up.

'*Him?*'

'I'll send him in,' she grins excitedly. 'Brush your hair.'

I sit up, suddenly electrified. Which *him* could it be? I leap out of bed and grab the deodorant, spraying myself head to toe. Yanking a brush through my hair, I pull out more than I detangle, squeaking in pain, just in time for the man I was supposed to marry to enter my teen bedroom.

'Daniel,' I breathe out and for some reason my first feeling is . . . disappointment. I've wanted to see him so badly since the split – and in some ways even more since the funeral. I think maybe I'd imagined this moment so often, I thought it would be more dramatic than this. I thought it would be ground-breaking and earth-shattering. *More* than him just turning up in my bedroom, with me here in my pyjamas, the odour of Quality Street coming out of my pores, and a poster of Robert Pattinson still glowering balefully from the wall.

'Hi Ginny,' he says shyly and I blink back. Hearing him say my name feels so strange. But then, this whole thing is off-the-charts strange. He looks unfamiliar too. He's grown a beard in the month since Diane's funeral. I've never seen him with facial hair before. He's always been so clean-shaven, I wasn't sure he could even grow one.

'What are you ... what are you *doing* here?' I finally get out, suddenly so aware of my own filth.

He doesn't reply immediately, though I don't think I expected him to.

'Can I ...' he looks around the room for a chair and finds none available. Instead he gestures to the end of the bed, where Celeste has left a pile of folded-up clean washing. She wanted to put it away for me and I had to literally beg her not to. 'Can I sit down?'

I nod dumbly, shame at the state of everything radiating off me. He must think this is all about him; that all these months later I am still a shell – a wreck – from our break-up. And honestly, it's only, like, 80 per cent of why I'm a wreck.

He sits heavily and I do the same, the space between us on the bed suddenly very significant. We sit in silence for a full minute. I don't want to be the first to speak. I've already asked the only question I have.

I've had so many questions since he left me – *so many questions* – and I couldn't ask any of them at the funeral. It wasn't the right time, even if he'd been willing to stay more than six minutes. Those questions took over my life for weeks, filling up my brain and overflowing in every direction. Why did he do it? Why didn't he talk to me? How long had he been feeling this way? Why couldn't he tell me? Did he mean anything he ever said? Did he ever plan to marry me? Why did he leave like that? Was our whole relationship a sham? Was there someone else? Did I ever really know the real him? Where did he go when he left? What do his family and friends think? Do they blame me? Was it my fault? Was it Celeste's fault? Why why why why why why why why why why why why why why why why why why why why why why why why why why why why why why why why why why why why why why why why why.

It was the word of the day, week, month, for such a long time.

But, I realize suddenly, that voice has quietened down in recent weeks. Sure, I've still been sad, so very sad, about what happened, but the questions have dried up. And now I don't really want to ask Daniel any of them – or anything else.

At last he clears his throat.

'Firstly,' he begins, and I notice his hands are shaking a little. 'I need to say how sorry I am.'

A sort of numbness creeps over me as he speaks. Sorry. *Sorry.* I've wanted to hear that word from him, but I don't know how I feel about it now. It feels a bit nothingy, a bit hollow. It doesn't feel like enough.

'I know it's probably too little, too late,' he says now in a rush. 'I've wanted to say it so many times, I've wanted to *see* you so many times, and then when I came to the funeral, I ended up chickening out and running away.' He hangs his head. 'I'm sorry for that, too. I was scared of the conversation with you, but also terrified of seeing your family and how much they must all hate me.' He looks down at his hands. 'I kept wanting to message you. I'd start a text, but then I couldn't ever figure out what to say or how to put it.' He looks up at me now, his eyes beseeching, pleading with me to understand. I stay silent. He continues after a few seconds. 'But in the end, my cowardice wasn't enough to keep me away. I needed to see you.'

His words make my chest tighten. *Needed*?

'I've missed you so much, Gin,' he adds, looking at me in his familiar Daniel way. 'What I did was the worst thing I've ever done, to anyone, ever. I regret it so much.'

He regrets it? He wants to ... no, I can't even think it.

He moves closer on the bed. 'Please say you can find a way to forgive me?' I look away and he reaches for my hand, his voice now almost a whisper. 'I just got so, so, so scared. And I didn't see it coming, it hit me out of nowhere. We were planning the wedding and – hey, do you remember when you got back from the hen do and you were saying all that stuff about how out of hand everything had gotten? You said Celeste had expanded the guestlist again and you were just so exhausted and beaten down by it?'

I nod slowly and he nods too, encouraged by my agreement.

'See, I thought I was fine, even then. I laughed it off and cheered you up, and then I went off to get some work done.' He pauses. 'But I couldn't focus. What you said kept going around and around in my brain. I started getting more and more freaked out. And I was meant to be going on my stag do the next week and suddenly that was terrifying, too. I started packing and kept finding myself putting things I didn't need into my suitcase. My old teddy, mementoes, stuff I definitely didn't need for a weekend in Amsterdam.' His breath is coming out in ragged short bursts. 'And then, when you went to work that Wednesday, I found myself packing up the rest of it. I couldn't stop myself.' He sounds like he might cry. 'And then I left.' He throws his hands up in the air, like he was helpless in all of it.

And I feel sorry for him.

I don't feel angry, I feel sad. He's clearly genuinely devastated by all this. He hurt me so badly and made awful choices that made everything so much worse than they had to be. I want to be angry with him, but I don't have it in me, I just feel sad that all of this has happened. I feel sad that he *let* all of this happen when he didn't have to.

He looks at me now, waiting.

'Well, that's what I wanted to say,' he hesitates, still waiting for me to say something. 'I guess I better go,' he says limply after another minute.

'OK,' I reply simply. And then, because I cannot stop myself: 'I get it, I understand.'

He looks up at me with shining eyes. 'Really?'

'Really,' I say, trying to smile. In this moment, making him feel better, letting him off the hook – I hate myself. *I hate myself.*

Because I *don't* get it, I don't understand. I can see he is upset and I feel for him, but I still don't understand why and how he could do all that to me. He did all of this. He let all this awfulness happen, *knowing* what it would do to me. He ripped apart my life and my heart, and he put his own fears ahead of how much it would destroy me.

He could've talked to me, he could've been honest at any stage of this, and he chose not to be. He chose to be scared and cowardly instead of being honest, knowing full well how much worse it would make everything for me.

'Thank you, Gin.' His voice is full of emotion and I smile at him as nicely as I can.

I hate myself. I hate this! I hate that I'm still trying to make other people feel better in a moment like this; still putting their hurt ahead of my own. I am a pathetic loser.

I picture how Myfanwy would react in this moment. She would shout and scream and tell him the full extent of how much he'd hurt her. She'd order him out of the house and out of her life, calling him a bunch of cool rude names. She wouldn't feel sorry for him or pity him. She'd put her own pain ahead of his self-inflicted agonies.

But I can't.

I walk out with him to a seemingly empty hallway, but I know with absolute certainty that Celeste is within earshot. And probably eyeshot too. We stand together in silence, face-to-face at the top of the stairs and I think about *our* hallway, back in our old flat. Someone else will be living there by now. There will be another person or maybe another couple in there. They'll stand like this in that hallway, in what was once our hallway, talking about their day or kissing or arguing. Maybe they'll want to paint the walls, like we did. Maybe they'll have more imagination than us. We went with an ordinary, boring white. Cotton white, the tin said. But it was an ordinary boring, cotton white that we chose together.

'I wish . . .' he trails off, looking at me with intense longing.

He doesn't continue and I don't ask him what he wishes. If he wants to say what I think he wants to say, I'm not sure I can hear it.

Do I wish it too? Everything I've been through since he left me, everything I've done and realized – would I wish all of that away to go back?

A big part of me still wants him. Desperately. There's no denying I still love him. He's the same handsome and fun Daniel I wanted to be with forever. He still has an energy that can so easily brighten up a room. And getting back together would solve everything, wouldn't it? I could get out of Celeste's house and we could get a new flat. We'd get those two dogs, Kirstie and Phil. We could have the life I envisioned for myself, together.

We could have our lives back and forget about those six silly predictions that have taken over my life this year.

'Can we – can I . . .' He pauses, his eyes searching for mine. 'Can I see you again? Soon?' he pleads, taking my hands in his.

My hand crackles at the touch of his skin. There is so much warm, comforting familiarity there. I look up at him and for a moment I think he will kiss me.

It's too much and I take a step away, letting his hands drop away from mine.

'I need a bit more time, Daniel,' I say simply. I don't want to hurt him but I don't know if I can forgive him for any of it, never mind everything. I don't know if I could ever forget that he left me the way he did, right before the wedding, without a word. He hurt me so badly and left me to go through everything on my own. I don't know if we can get back to where we were, or anywhere near it.

'I understand,' he nods, hope still lighting his eyes. 'But I'll be in touch, if that's OK? Thank you so much for seeing me again.' He moves closer again and it sets something off in me, low down in my stomach. I really do want him to kiss me, I realize, so deeply disappointed in myself. I thought I had more strength of character than this. How can my body be so ready to forgive and forget everything he did, so easily? But it's not really *me* reacting, not my brain, not the me that gets the final say. Just because parts of my body still fancy and want Daniel, it doesn't matter. My head is in control, not my heart – or any other body parts.

I walk him to the door and close it on him as he turns for a hug. I know too well that my body parts might well win the day if we touch again.

CHAPTER EIGHTEEN

The door to the store jingles, snapping me out of my daydream.

I was thinking about the woman outside our house. I saw her again this morning. She was just standing out there, her top half visible above the wooden fence at the front. I watched her for a few minutes as she stood there, looking at the house. At one point she seemed to be looking directly into the kitchen where I was, so I hid.

Maybe she's a Celeste super fan? That's the most obvious explanation. I should probably warn Celeste. But there's another idea that's been playing around the corners of my mind, about who she could be. What if she's my prediction number five?

'Hi Micah!' I greet my customer warmly as they let themselves in, shivering from the late October winds outside. 'Your ring is ready!'

'Yay!' Micah replies, taking off their hat. 'I can't wait to see it.'

Micah ordered a simple but really stunning flush bezel solitaire with the most beautiful diamond at its centre. I've been waiting for them to collect it all week.

I pull out the box and do the reveal. Micah gasps and moves closer to inspect the result. 'It's beautiful!' they declare and I beam with pride. 'I can't believe you grew that diamond in a lab! Micah adds, breathless now as they reverently remove the ring from its silk-lined box.

'It's pretty mind-blowing, isn't it?' I agree.

We've been considering using lab-grown diamonds for a while now, and this was something like a test case. Even though we guarantee ethical practices when it comes to our mined stones, if we start using more lab-grown stones, it could free Dad up a bit more to be at home.

Anyway, Micah is an environmentalist and their partner Nicky works for a conservation charity, so it was especially important we got it right for this ring. As well as a lab-grown diamond, the band is made from recycled gold.

'I love it,' Micah gushes. 'Thank you *so* much for your help with it.' They look up, smiling. 'And with all your advice for the proposal. You've been such a lifesaver. I can't believe Nicky answered the phone when you called them the other day. And I *really* can't believe you were able to think on the spot like that! I'm useless at that kind of thing!'

'Ha!' I laugh at the memory and the fear that pooled in my stomach when I realized it wasn't Micah who had answered my call. I pretended to be ringing from their dentist with a reminder that it was time for a check-up.

'They weren't suspicious?' I double-check.

'Not at all!' Micah laughs. 'I'm so excited to propose – they're going to be so annoyed I got to do it first!' They laugh again and I join in.

'Let's hope Nicky's not *so* annoyed that they actually say no ...' I grin.

Micah grimaces. 'I hadn't thought of that. Fingers crossed!'

'I'm a million per cent certain it's going to be amazing,' I declare confidently. I swear, so much of this job is about cheerleading the proposer and supporting them through this process. It's yet another part of my role the job description definitely doesn't cover.

After helping Joey with his proposal a few weeks ago, I was more than ready when Micah came into the store wanting advice as well. It's really reinforced how many of our clients want this kind of help – I *know* I'm right about the engagement concierge idea. If only my mother would listen.

'Celeste is here!' My mother walks in literally announcing her own arrival.

'Oh my god,' Micah breathes out, way more impressed by this reality TV presenter than by the new engagement ring.

Celeste tinkles prettily as she sweeps around the room, pretending to review the stock, but really it's just because my mother's life is a catwalk.

'I can't believe Celeste Bretherton is here!' Micah says under their breath. 'I didn't think she *actually* worked here!'

'She rarely does,' I murmur but Micah is too starstruck to hear me.

'Would it be awkward to get an autograph?' Micah turns to me, looking desperate and excited.

'She'd love it,' I confirm and then call over. 'Mum? Come meet Micah.'

'Celeste Bretherton is your *mum*?' Micah looks horrified and enchanted all at once. 'I had no idea, oh my *god*.' I can see their brain whirring and whizzing through every interaction we've ever had with the benefit of this new information.

Celeste sweeps across the room, smiling widely and magnanimously at the fan awaiting her blessing.

'Mum, say hi to Micah,' I say and Celeste offers up a hand which – for a second – I honestly think Micah will kiss.

'It's *so amazing* to meet you!' they choke out, eyes welling up. 'I absolutely love *Engage!* My partner and I have watched every series, like, five times over.'

'Oh darling, thank you!' Celeste says in her 'Kind to Fans' Voice.

They exchange niceties for a few minutes before Celeste professionally extracts herself – but not before taking forty or fifty selfies with Micah.

A weepy Micah leaves at last, almost forgetting the ring they came in for, and I wish them luck with the proposal. They look at me blankly, Nicky clearly the last thing on their mind. This is the effect my mother has on people. It's part impressive, part exhausting.

On their way out, Micah nearly bowls Zach over.

'Celeste Bretherton is *in there*,' they stage-whisper in Zach's face and he nods seriously.

'Wow,' he deadpans, as Micah leaves. He turns to me. 'Ready?' I nod excitedly, grabbing my bag and coat.

'Good luck!' Toni shouts across the room as we head out, ready for our bona fide adventure.

This evening, my customer Joey Addiman is proposing to his partner Hannah, and Zach and I are heading to the hotel to drop off the engagement ring. Obviously it would've been easier for Joey to just collect it ahead of time – as we did point out – but he kept saying Hannah was suspicious and he couldn't risk having it at their flat. The plan is to be in reception as the couple check in, watching to make sure he collects it from our pre-arranged drop-off point. It's proper spy stuff.

'Ohhh,' I moan as we climb into Zach's car. 'I wish we'd bought two matching briefcases for the swap, like the spies have in the movies? That would've been *cool!*'

He nods. 'But then we would've needed a park bench to do the hand-off. And I didn't bring any sunglasses. You can't do a briefcase swap without a park bench and dark glasses.'

'Very true,' I agree seriously.

We pull up at the hotel and I find I'm more jumpy than I'd expected. 'Where are you going to park?' I ask anxiously and Zach glances over at me, amused. 'In the hotel car park, if that's acceptable?'

'But what if Hannah recognizes your car?' I worry out loud.

'That is a concern,' Zach nods sagely. 'If she'd ever met either of us or seen my car in her life.'

'Right, right!' I remember.

'But we could park several streets away?' he offers. 'On the

172

off chance she sees my car and decides to contact her many friends at MI5 . . .' He glances over. 'I'm just assuming this woman has MI5 contacts.'

'I'm sure she does,' I nod. 'Who doesn't?'

'And asks those contacts to trace my number plate. And then she might google me and see I'm a designer and then she might—'

'All right! All right,' I laugh. 'I get it, I'll calm down. Just keep your eye out for park benches and briefcases, OK?'

'OK,' he laughs, too, as we head into the foyer.

It's a beautiful old hotel. One of those that feels intimate, despite its high ceilings and low chandeliers. It's got the air of being freshly done and sleek, but also ancient and steeped in tradition. In other words, it's suuuuuper romantic.

Zach and I head towards reception, scanning the room. 'Where's the plant pot Joey wanted us to drop it into?' he frowns.

'Damn,' I mutter. 'He said it was right next to the desk, but there's nothing. They must've moved things around since his recce last week.'

'Crap!' I breathe hard, checking the huge clock that takes up half of one wall behind the check-in desks.

'It's fine,' Zach says soothingly. 'We're really early, we've got time to figure this out. Let's sit down.' He gestures at the bar area in the corner of the lobby and we head over.

'I don't think we can give it to the staff,' I say, heart in my stomach. 'I don't trust them – they'll just hand it over in front of Hannah.'

'Let's get a drink,' Zach ignores me, studying the cocktail menu. 'There's something here called a Fuzzy Navel.'

'Sounds horrendous,' I gag slightly. 'What's in it?'

'Peach Schnapps and orange juice.'

I make a face. 'Sounds like something I would've come up with as a teenager.'

Zach waves at the barman. 'Two Fuzzy Navels please!' I laugh at his excitement, then remember what we're here for.

'What should we do about Joey's ring?' I ask, my brow furrowed.

'Don't worry about that!' he waves his hand happily. 'We can see the entrance clearly from here. We'll find a way to hand it over once he gets here.'

Our drinks arrive and I take in his tattoo sleeve as he takes a sip. There's a bird flying through clouds, as a sun fights to break through. It's kind of hypnotizing.

'How many do you have?' I ask before I can help myself. He glances over and sees me studying his arm.

'About fifty.'

'That many?' I am amazed. 'Doesn't it hurt?'

'Not really,' he shrugs, then smiles. 'At least, that's what you're meant to say.' He laughs. 'Some of them *really* hurt. I have one on my armpit that *killed*. Even the tattoo artist told me to get it together.' He glances over, his eyes scanning me. 'Do you have any?'

'I have such a low pain threshold,' I admit, shaking my head. 'I'm too much of a wimp.'

'I don't believe that,' he says nicely.

I take a swig of my Fuzzy Navel and immediately regret it. It's sickly sweet.

'Yuck,' I declare and he nods.

'Disgusting, isn't it?' He takes a longer sip, smacking his lips joyfully.

'Did you design them all?' I ask, still fascinated. He nods, looking halfway between bashful and proud. 'They're beautiful,' I breathe, instinctively reaching to touch the bird on his arm, and then remembering myself. 'What else do you have?'

He looks down, thinking for a minute. 'There are a few more birds, a dragonfly, a lot of flowers. I've got sunflowers on my other arm.' He twists on his stool to show me the distinctive spiky petals covering his bicep. He flexes it and the sunflower moves like it's alive. 'I like nature,' he continues. 'Which I know is a bit middle-aged of me, but I've always loved being outside. So I have a lot of animals and wildlife. I have a butterfly on my sternum. They're supposed to symbolize transformation and growth. It reminds me to keep trying to be a better person.'

'Do you need to be a better person?' I ask teasingly and he regards me seriously.

'Of course.' His tone is serious. 'I think it's really important that we keep an eye on ourselves. It's too easy – especially as we get older – to decide we are who we are, and that people should just accept us. Obviously I'm not talking about physical flaws or stuff we can't change. I just mean, I've known a lot of people who refuse to ever be introspective. They say,

"I'm too old to change now, like it or lump it!" as some kind of excuse to be an arsehole! We can all change. None of us ever have to stop growing.'

'That's very wise,' I say quietly, thinking about the things I want to change about myself. 'I can't see any in colour, are there any?'

He pauses, before giving me a small smile. 'Just one.' I blush as he slowly lifts his shirt up. My breath catches in my chest as I glimpse toned muscle.

'Shit,' he drops the shirt and my stomach clenches with disappointment. 'It's them!' He gestures towards the door, where Joey has just walked in, a pretty woman at his side. Hannah! I'd almost forgotten why we're here. As they approach check-in, I see Joey's eyes widen with panic as he takes in a distinct lack of plants.

'Damn, what are we going to do?' Zach asks desperately.

'You were the one telling me not to worry!' I scold, downing my drink in one.

'That was before I realized how much there was to worry about.' He regards my empty glass admiringly. 'So ... any ideas?'

'I'm going to live in the moment,' I mutter to myself.

'Huh?' he frowns.

'Never mind,' I say breezily. 'Come with me!' I slip my hand into his and, channelling every spy movie I've ever seen, cross the foyer with confidence. 'Joey!' I call out happily when I get closer to the couple. He turns in surprise, paling almost indiscernibly when he sees me and Zach approach. 'Dude!' I add, 'I haven't seen you in forever! How are things?'

'Er, good,' he chokes out, no idea what I'm doing.

'You must be Hannah,' I say smiling, turning to her and offering my hand. 'Joey and I used to work together a million years ago. I'm Ginny, this is my husband, Zach.' Hannah smiles back politely. 'Well,' I say grandly. 'I won't interrupt, I can see you're checking in. I just wanted to say hi.' At this, I reach to give Joey a hug. 'So nice to see you! We should have a catch-up with all the old gang sometime.' He nods dumbly as I add brightly, 'Have a lovely time! It's a beautiful hotel, we've had a great time.' I glance at Zach who is watching me with a smile.

'We really have,' he agrees, still looking at me.

As we walk away, Zach squeezes my hand. 'What the hell just happened?' he hisses and I grin up at him.

'I put the ring in Joey's jacket pocket,' I explain. Zach snorts at this, sneaking a glance back at the soon-to-be-engaged pair. They're at the front desk now and Joey shoots us a look, subtly patting his pocket and giving a discreet thumbs-up. He is radiating excitement and relief.

Zach drops my hand as we leave the building, and I'm too buzzy with the thrill of our first experience as real, proper engagement spies to notice how cold my hand feels without it.

CHAPTER NINETEEN

'OH MY GOD, WHAT ARE YOU DOING?' I scream at
Toni from her bedroom doorway. She leaps away from the
mirror, guilt purple across her face.

She throws the offending scissors away onto her chest of
drawers. 'Nothing!' she shrieks as they clatter noisily.

'You're cutting your own fringe,' I accuse. 'We've been
through this, Toni – it's a terrible, terrible idea. Remember
that Christmas when you were seventeen? You couldn't leave
the house for two months.'

Her head hangs in shame. 'I remember.' She glances at
her reflection again and I move closer, inspecting her hair
for damage.

'I think it's OK,' I murmur. 'I got to you in time.'

Toni breathes out heavily. 'I knew it was a bad idea, I just
really wanted a new look for my birthday dinner. Taylor
Swift's fringe always looks so shiny and cool. I want to dress
for revenge like she does.'

I raise my eyebrows. 'Taylor's fringe is probably tended to by a team of well-paid hair stylists.'

Toni pouts. 'I just wanted a glow-up!'

'A *glow-up?*' I repeat back in astonishment. 'But . . . but you are so glowed up already, you glewed up years ago!'

'Is that a word?' She squints suspiciously at me in the mirror.

'Definitely,' I tell her confidently, perching on the edge of her bed. 'What's brought this on anyway?'

She shrugs, not making eye contact. 'I don't know. I just want to be sexy and mature.'

I'm flummoxed. 'You *are* sexy and mature,' I say, adding, 'I mean, gross at having to call you sexy but you're, y'know, beautiful! And who the hell rates maturity?'

She pouts. 'I don't feel it! I just . . .' She looks down. 'I've never really felt sexy.'

Shawn, I think to myself. If my beautiful little baby deer of a sister doesn't feel attractive, it's because her oblivious knobhead boyfriend is an oblivious knobhead.

I sigh, feeling helpless.

I am desperate for Toni to break the cycles of self-hatred. I don't want her to go through the same self-loathing spirals I've had to deal with my whole life. I want her to easily love who she is and feel strong enough to be the person she wants to be, vibrantly and without self-doubt.

'Honestly, you're gorgeous and lovely,' I tell her as sincerely as I can. 'And most importantly you're *kind*. That's the best thing to be.'

It's so easy to say these things to the people we love – to *see* their beauty and brilliance – but why is it so hard to internalize?

'OK,' she inhales deeply, standing straighter. 'So no fringe then?'

'At least not a bedroom fringe,' I tell her with a smile. 'Especially since it's time to go.'

When we arrive at dinner, everyone else is already seated. Flustered and a bit sweaty despite the freezing mid-November temperatures outside, I take my seat beside Myfanwy and Sonali. They are distracted ravaging the bread basket and for a moment I feel intensely lonely. Everyone here seems to be with someone. Myfanwy has Sonali, Toni has Shawn. OK, so Dad isn't here with Celeste, but the whole world is her plus one.

I'm suddenly struck by how much I miss having someone with me for things like this. How much I miss having *Daniel* at things like this.

He messaged me after his surprise visit a few weeks ago, apologizing again and asking if we could meet up for a drink when I'm ready.

And I want to see him, desperately. So what's standing in my way? Is it just pride? If so, that's got to be really dumb. I don't think anyone would judge me if I went back to him.

Maybe Myfanwy, she's quite judgemental. But she's also very *un*judgemental when you choose to ignore her judgement.

'You know what this is, don't you?' She leans over now,

interrupting my thoughts with a bread roll in hand, crumbs flying over me. 'We've been relegated to the *old people celebrations*.'

'The what?' I frown, absent-mindedly unfolding the cloth napkin from its nothing-like-a-swan fold and laying it across my lap.

Myfanwy gestures around the grand room, where we're having dinner in honour of Toni's twenty-fourth birthday. Celeste has hired a private space in a Michelin-starred restaurant to celebrate, and we're currently reviewing oversized menus with eye-wateringly expensive and eye-wateringly confusing courses.

'I mean, look at who's here.' Myfanwy nods again at the rest of the guests. Aside from birthday girl Toni and Shawn, it's just me, Myfanwy, Sonali, Celeste, several of my aunts and uncles, and my grandmother on my dad's side. There are literally none of Toni's young mates.

'Hmm,' I narrow my eyes.

'We're officially too old to be invited to Toni's proper, *fun* celebration,' Myfanwy adds. 'We've been lumped in with all the sixty-plusses!'

Sonali leans in. 'It's outrageous. We're far too young for a *dinner*. I'm appalled.'

'Do you really think?' I glance over at my sister. She's goo-goo-eyeing with Shawn, while on the other side of him sits my mother. Who is also goo-goo-eyeing him. 'Well that's embarrassing,' I comment and Myfanwy gives me a sideways look.

'The fact that we're too old to party with twenty-somethings, or the way Celeste is all over Shawn?'

'Both,' I grimace. 'To be fair, Celeste does do this. I'm having flashbacks to how she used to flirt with Daniel. She literally sat in his lap at my birthday last year.'

'Oh my god, I remember that!' Sonali snorts as Myfanwy adds, 'No wonder he left you at the altar.' She gives me another side eye. 'Too soon?'

'That will always be too soon,' I tell her.

I watch Shawn across the table and sigh. 'Do you really think Toni's happy with him?' I ask this in a low voice as he laughs in a sort of put-on way and throws an arm around Toni's shoulders, squashing her into him. There's always such an arrogance about him, as he reaches across people for the butter, still holding onto Toni who is forced to move with him. He spreads his roll now and chews on it lazily, smiling a little smugly as Celeste plagues him with questions. Then he – sin of all sins – reaches over Toni and *takes her bread roll*. Once he's got it, I see him ask her if it's OK, but that – to me – is even worse than not asking. He's already got it in his weirdly small, sweaty hands. He's already touching the bread roll. She's not going to say no now, is she? No one would.

'I'm going to ask her if there's a young people party we're not invited to,' Myfanwy leaps up.

'Don't ask her!' I pull her back down to the table, thinking of the vulnerable and slightly sad Toni I just confiscated scissors from. 'Leave her alone on her birthday. If she wants to have fun without us, she's allowed to! At least wait until the day after her birthday to make her feel guilty?'

'I think you should make her feel guilty now,' Sonali encourages, grinning.

'HEY!' Myfanwy shouts across the table. 'Toni, are you having a secret young people party for your birthday that we're not invited to?'

Toni looks surprised, still weighed down by Shawn's heavy arm across her. 'No, I promise! I swear, you'd be invited.' She shakes her head. 'No, I'm just having a low-key thing this year. I'm *twenty-four* now, you guys! I'm really too grown up and mature for silly nightclubs or bars!' She laughs in a way that is not like Toni at all, glancing up at her much older boyfriend like he might find this impressive. He smiles down at her benignly, signalling his approval. I suppress a shudder.

'Well, that's depressing,' Myfanwy sighs. 'I was hoping Toni had a fun-ner life than us.' The waiter arrives with our drinks, placing them down in the wrong order in front of us. Myfanwy reaches across me for hers before continuing. 'Anyway, don't worry, I have just the thing to get through this boring night.' She pulls out her phone, glancing over at Sonali and smiling broadly. 'We're going to find different ways to expand Ginny's spiritual thinking.'

I reluctantly shuffle closer as she pulls up Google.

'Shall we get you a moon reading?' she suggests, scanning the results. 'Or we could visit another psychic? Or a palm reader? Past life regression? Or, ooh!' she jabs at the screen.

'This woman is a soulmate sketch artist. We could see who we're meant to be looking out for. Or do you want to look at your nakshatra?'

She's mentioned that word before. I frown. 'My naked what?'

Sonali looks sombre as she explains. 'It's the idea that you can draw a line from where you were born – at the exact time of your birth – to the moon. The group of stars that line passes through is known as the nakshatra. It's like a star map for your life and it's very important for your astrological calculations.'

I blink at her. 'I don't think I need a star map, do I?' I hesitate. 'Would the moon reading help me with my period? I'm a week out and the hormonal anxiety rush is giving me heart palpitations.'

Myfanwy shakes her head. 'Nah.' She squints at the screen. 'Let's just keep things simple and find your birth chart.' She's already found the page she wants and Sonali and I lean closer to take in the website's introduction.

A birth chart tells you the position of the sun, moon and planets on the day you were born. The exact second you came into existence can determine your personalized chart.

'But what about twins?' I ask. 'Jessica and Elizabeth would have the same birth chart, those four minutes aside, but they're so different!'

'Don't bring *Sweet Valley High* into this.' Sonali pulls out her Vaseline for a fresh application on already shiny lips. 'That is sacred.'

Myfanwy sighs impatiently. 'When were you born, Gin?'

'I actually don't know the exact second I came into existence,' I admit, as Sonali waves her hand.

'It doesn't matter. Do you know the time without seconds?'

I nod, continuing to read.

Your astrology chart – or natal chart – contains powerful information about the energies you were exposed to at birth, allowing you a window into your soul's journey and revealing your strengths and weaknesses. We focus on scientific astrology—

I raise an eyebrow.

—to interpret the stars, allowing us to see the vibration you personally exude.

This can only be done authentically by people with experience and the appropriate certification.

'I wonder how easy it is to get certified,' I comment quietly taking in the next line.

Many people confuse birth charts with fortune telling, but it's very much not the same thing.

Oh, what? I wanted some more cool psychic stuff! If this website and the *birth chart* had come up with six predictions that were destined to happen during my thirty-second year, I *definitely* would've believed in them.

Myfanwy taps past the intro to the next page, where there are a series of questions.

'So, what day and time were you born?'

I glance at her, hurt. 'You don't know my birthday?'

She rolls her eyes. 'I'm just reading out what it says. I know it's . . . er, 22nd June?' She side-eyes Sonali, who nods discreetly.

'I was born at 6.02am,' I tell her proudly. I know this fact because Celeste likes to regale strangers with tales of arriving at the hospital just before six in the morning after only half an hour of labour – with my head literally crowning. The nurse had to cup Celeste's vulva, protecting my eager, slimy scalp, as they ran her down to a delivery room. I slithered out four minutes later.

Myfanwy scrolls down to more questions.

'Where were you born? And what's your relation-ship status?'

'Why does it need to know that?' I frown, adding dryly, 'Is there a *recently jilted* box to tick?'

'Do you think you need to have been specifically left at the altar to be classed as jilted?' Sonali muses.

'Nah,' Myfanwy answers. 'I'm pretty sure it just means suddenly rejected or cast off. Ginny was definitely discarded, ditched, dumped and deserted. She was *jilted*.'

'Amazing alliteration!' Sonali says admiringly.

'Thanks ever so, both of you,' I nod as Myfanwy continues with her questions.

'What is your favourite activity?'

'Is this just market research?' I squint at the screen, tapping my top choice: *reading a book*.

'Which of the four elements match your personality?'

Fire   **Water**   **Air**   **Earth**

'Shouldn't they be telling *me* that?' I ask Myfanwy, bafflement creeping in. She cocks her head, considering it. 'I haven't got the first idea.'

'Well, you're a Cancer – just – so you're a water sign. A *cardinal* water sign. You're represented by a crab.'

'So, I should put water?' I say anxiously, looking at Sonali for help. 'Am I watery?'

'Hmm, I don't know, you don't cry that much?' she says slowly, sounding as confused as me. 'And I've never thought of you as particularly sweaty. Do you take many baths?'

'I'm not that into baths,' I confess, feeling like I'm betraying a basic tenet of womanhood. We all like hot baths while eating yoghurt, right? I brighten, 'Oh, but I do like *drinking* water.'

'I think we might be losing focus . . .' Myfanwy sounds irritated.

'Sorry,' I shake my head. 'OK, shall we pick water? I don't think I relate much to earth, air or fire.' I pause. 'Though, I do like air quite a lot? I couldn't do much without it, could

I? And I don't like fires that burn down rainforests, but I *do* enjoy candles.'

Myfanwy loses patience. 'I've put water.' Her mouse hovers over the next confusing question.

Which signs do you get along with best? Choose only two options.

'I'm choosing Aquarius —' she clicks her own sign '— and Scorpio.' My sister's star sign.

We click through to the final page.

Your answers are being analyzed. We are calculating the position of the planets, the sun, and the moon, as your results are being prepared.

After another minute, a new page loads.

Congratulations, your birth chart is ready. It alone holds the secrets to who you really are and what awaits you.

Simply click below to pay £279.99.

Ugh. I glance nervously at Myfanwy and Sonali. I don't want to pay for this. Do I really need to know my *personality vibrations*? But maybe £300 is a good deal to discover what the planets are doing to my soul. I am dying to know what my destiny is telling me. Maybe I can borrow it from Toni for now or—

'Bugger that,' Myfanwy interrupts, shutting down the tab. 'You're not paying for this horseshit. Half of it wasn't even spelled correctly.'

It seems even Myfanwy has her limits with the woo–woo.

CHAPTER TWENTY

Shawn has promised to 'get us in' at a club after dinner.

Not a thing that has happened to me, since I was seventeen. And even then, I didn't *actually* want to get in to said club, I just didn't want to appear rude when offered. Therefore, I am horrified about this evening's turn of events.

Toni overheard Myfanwy moaning about all the 'old people' at dinner, and excitedly announced that Shawn was going to — and she kept using these words like we were going to a celebrity premiere — *get us in* to the opening of a fancy club in Central London. Myfanwy and Sonali tried to explain that none of us wanted to be 'got in', but then Toni said there could be free drinks and everyone immediately shut up.

So now we're here, outside this most special of all special clubs, which, from the outside at least, is mostly giving us hideous 1960s grey office block in Zone Six vibes. And the worst part of all is that Shawn hasn't even *got us in*; we've been in a queue for the last twenty-five minutes.

'Guess how much these trousers cost?' Shawn has made most of the conversation since we got here, and much of it has been in this kind of area.

Myfanwy sighs loudly, as Sonali impatiently asks, 'I thought you were *getting us in*? It's freezing out here.' She gestures at the unmoving snake of people ahead of us as Shawn indiscreetly rolls his eyes.

Toni removes her coat, handing it over to a grateful Sonali, who fixes Shawn with a stern look. 'You do know prolonged exposure to the cold can fuck up the brain?'

I gasp. 'Is that going to happen to us?'

She shrugs. 'Well, no. It's only mid-November and this is England, but if we end up standing out here all night, it's definitely a possibility.' She pauses. 'If we also removed all our clothes and it dropped about ten degrees. Either way, it's dangerous out here and Shawn promised to *get us in.*'

'I *am*,' he explains slowly, as though Sonali were a small child. 'This is the VIP queue. Believe me, babe, the other queue around the front is five times the length of this one. And even then, the place is so exclusive, they don't let *everyone* in from this line. I've called in many favours for you all. It's a good job I basically know everyone in London.' He nods smugly and Toni smiles eagerly up at him.

'That's amazing, Shawn, you're the best. Thank you so much!'

He bestows a kiss on her cheek and she beams even harder. 'So?' He looks around at the three of us.

'Right, yeah, um, thanks a lot, Shawn?' I offer, unsure

how much gratitude is required when we're standing in the rain without much movement.

'You're welcome,' he replies magnanimously. 'But I meant the trousers. How much do you think they cost?'

Myfanwy snorts a little at my side and I try not to look over at her. She's always getting me in trouble by making me laugh.

'Gosh, I don't know . . .' I begin, because I'm not totally sure what the rules of this game are. Plus, I'm not aware of how much men's trousers cost, nor do I – if I'm being completely honest – care. 'Erm, loads? Like £100?'

He looks at me with disdain. 'Way more.'

'A hundred and fifty?' offers Sonali, fiddling with her fringe in a handheld mirror as Toni watches enviously.

'More!' Shawn beams.

'Ten thousand,' Myfanwy says spitefully and he glowers at her from under his *Peaky Blinders* flat cap.

'Don't be ridiculous, My-Fanny,' he retorts, forever getting her name wrong. 'They were £250 and I had them customized with my initials on the underside of the inside leg.'

'Wow!' Toni and I say with differing levels of sincerity. Simultaneously, Myfanwy and Sonali mutter, 'Why?' which is luckily lost in the howls of wind around us.

'Here,' he reaches down, lifting up the hem of his trousers to reveal the initials *SC*.

'Why have you got Sean Combs' initials on your trousers?' Myfanwy asks curiously.

'Who's Sean Combs?' I ask.

'Puff Daddy,' Sonali explains.

'P Diddy,' Myfanwy corrects.

'I think he goes by both these days.' Sonali sounds defensive. 'Or indeed, just *Diddy*.'

'Are we sure SC isn't for Sean Connery?' Myfe jumps in, suppressing a smile. 'Or maybe Simon Cowell?'

'Or Steve Coogan?' I offer because I can't help myself.

'They're *Shawn's* initials!' Toni scolds lightly, then glances up at him. 'Right?'

'Obviously!' He looks irritated again. 'My name is Shawn Cochrane.'

'Shawn Cock Ring?' Myfanwy asks in the same innocent tone.

'*Cochrane!*' he raises his voice, his face going a little purplish, and Toni strokes a soothing arm along his jacket shoulder. His expression clears as he continues, 'I'm actually thinking of getting it as a tattoo.'

'You're thinking of getting a cock ring as a tattoo?' Myfanwy glances with pronounced confusion over at me and Sonali. I shake my head as a warning.

'No!' Shawn is livid.

'Oh, so you're getting Simon Cowell's initials tattooed on you?' she offers helpfully, as the purple hue of Shawn's face turns orange.

'MY initials!' he explodes. 'Why is this so hard for you to understand, My-Fanny?'

'Er, baby, is that a leg support you're wearing?' Toni searches desperately for a subject change. 'Are you OK?' She gestures back down at Shawn's still-exposed leg, where the edge of an orange band peeks out from beneath his personalized trousers.

Myfanwy gives him an exaggerated squint. 'Wait, you use a cock ring as a leg support?'

'No!' he howls, furious now and I feel bad for him. His basic bitchery is no match for Myfanwy's scathing wit. 'No!' he says again, breathing heavily as he tries to get a handle on his fury. He fingers the gold chain around his neck, taking a second. 'I have to wear it because of all the squash I play. I'm at the top of the third league at my club.' He glances down at Toni for reassurance that this is impressive and she rewards him with a huge smile. Though I'm not sure she even knows what squash is. The only thing I know about it is that lots of middle-aged white men play and they get really angry about the whole thing.

'He's really good at it.' Toni looks anxious. 'I mean, he's really good at *them*? Er, um . . . that?' Yeah, she has no idea what squash is. Shawn tuts sulkily and we all fall silent. He's run out of ways to impress us if we are not bowled over by expensive, personalized trousers and squash. What else *is* there?

In front of us, a group of hot women are talking loudly about what they would call their babies.

'I really like Sovereign,' one is saying in a lazy posh trawl. She has an eighties perm that somehow looks terrible and very cool all at once. I blame the curly girl method. 'They use that word on the news a lot when they're talking about the royal family and it feels really, I don't know, *regal* or something, yah?' The two others nod aggressively. The perm continues, 'Or I'm thinking something even more original, like, maybe Comma? The private tutor Mummy hired to get me into Oxford used to say that word a lot and Raphy was the cleverest person I ever met. I was so upset when Daddy sacked him. All he did was sleep with me and my sister – it was outrageously unfair.'

'I never know where to use commas,' says the shortest of the three conversationally, ignoring the statutory rape.

The second woman pipes up, 'A girl I know at the stables just called her baby Astrophel. Apparently it means *the star lover*!' She throws her long wavy hair back, showing off the largest, most garish earrings I've ever seen.

Perm snorts, 'It does not mean star lover!' She waves her hand dismissively and it's clear she is the leader. 'It's that comma thing you put in the air, yah? You know, like in *don't,* or *isn't*. Raphy spent weeks explaining about the astrophel. He only shut up about it after I gave him a blowie.'

The earrings woman scrunches her face up, clearly wondering whether this is worth challenging. 'I think that's an apostrophe actually,' she says quietly but loud enough to be met with a menacing stare.

'Well,' the shortest says quickly, 'I've decided on Harissa for my first child.'

Perm nods approvingly. 'That's very good.'

'Thanks,' she replies, delighted. 'I found it in a cookbook.'

I turn wide-eyed to Myfanwy and Sonali, who are struggling to keep it together.

'I really like Harissa, too,' Sonali says in a whisper. 'Especially on my chicken.'

'I'm going to call my firstborn Celeriac Puree,' I tell her in a low voice. 'Or maybe Tarte Tatin?'

'Gorgeous.' Myfanwy gives me an on-point chef's kiss before adding, 'I've been considering Remoulade for a girl and Emulsion for a boy.'

Sonali shuffles closer. 'How about Penny?' We cock our heads at her and she smirks, 'Penny Pasta.'

We hide mouths behind hands, trying to contain our joy.

'I can't really talk,' I say through giggles. 'I'm named after an alcoholic beverage.' As we all dissolve into more laughter, I turn to look for my accompanying mixer. But Toni and Shawn have stepped away and are now engaged in conversation with the posh food fans. Heated conversation.

'No,' he's saying with irritation. 'Shawn is actually an incredibly cool name! It's much better than Amadeus or Mazikeen!'

'Show them your trouser initials, baby,' Toni says helpfully, without a trace of mocking.

'Oh my gawwwwwd,' Perm says as he scrambles to pull up his hem again. 'You *don't* have *those* dreadful trews?' She turns to her cohorts. 'Annabellisey, Penelopicity, do you remember my awfers ex, Square? Remember how he used to wear those? Oh my gawd! I can't believe peeps are still wearing those!' She turns back to Shawn, who is horrified and purple again.

'YOU KNOW NOTHING ABOUT FASHION!' he shouts as the young women regard him with amusement.

'Why do I work for a premium fashion website then, *Shawn*?' Perm asks archly and he blusters.

'Probably because your daddy owns it!' he gets out at last, hit by a moment of clarity.

She pouts and then raises her voice. 'Just because he owns it doesn't mean I automatically got the job. I'm so sick of everyone accusing rich and famous people of helping their children also become rich and famous. Me and Brooklyn Beckham are so misunderstood. Daddy hasn't employed my little sister, so that proves it! And he won't even when she gets out of rehab.'

I glance over at Myfanwy and Sonali, who are both enjoying all this drama immensely. I want to remind her that the idiot man-child over there is my baby sister's boyfriend. A man she plans on *marrying*.

I glance over at Toni, who looks mortified and like she is close to tears. What is she *doing* with him? She's so lovely and kind and beautiful. She could have anyone; why is she settling for this absolute idiot? Is this really all that's on offer out there in the dating world? If so, I'm doomed. Maybe I *should* be trying to get back with Daniel.

On the other hand, is it purely love that's making me want to run back into his arms? Or is it the fear of ending up with only options like this guy in front of me, shouting at women half his age over what is cool and what is not cool.

No, I don't think it's just that. I really do miss Daniel. I ache for him. I miss the smell of him, the heaviness of his body next to me in bed, the way he'd grin and ruffle my hair when I brought him coffee in the morning.

I pull out my phone, rain drip-dripping onto the screen as people yell all around me. I find Daniel's last message and start to type . . .

'GINNY!' a new shouty voice finds me and I jump, throwing my phone back into my coat pocket. There is something I recognize about the . . .

Oh my god. It can't be.

The shouter bounds over to me in short leaps, a huge smile across his familiar features.

It's Mikey. Mikey Yates from a thousand years ago.

Mikey and I dated for a year when I was twenty-four. He was my first serious relationship.

I gasp out his name as he gathers me up in a huge bear hug.

Instantly, I think of one of the predictions. About someone coming back into my life. It couldn't be about him?

He pulls back, flashing the biggest row of white teeth. I'm sure his smile was never so bright and perfect? He looks great; all glossy and sheeny. His hair is just long enough to tuck behind an ear, and he does so now as he takes me in.

'Ginny Bretherton!' he says in an exhale as he smiles again. 'I can't believe it's you, this is so weird! Like fate or destiny!' The fortune teller's face flashes across my vision. He continues, oblivious, 'I came over to see what all the shouting was about.' He waves at Shawn and the tall women.

'Why is that purple old guy yelling at Trinny Woodall with a perm?'

My friends burst out laughing and I turn to them.

'Myfanwy, Sonali, do you guys remember Mikey?' There are looks of only vague recognition, so I add, 'My first serious boyfriend!' I say it lightly but Mikey turns to me with surprise.

'You were serious about me?' He throws an arm around my shoulder and squeezes me close. 'I was serious about you, but I didn't think anyone ever took me seriously.'

I giggle, embarrassed, and change tact. 'So, how are you? What are you up to these days? Apart from hunting through VIP queues for good times.'

'Oooh, VIP queue is it?' he says teasingly and his twinkly grey eyes make me feel a little faint. 'You always were too cool for me.'

'Stop it,' I lightly swat at him and catch Myfanwy's eyebrows shoot up. She's never seen me attempt to flirt. I'm not sure I have either. If this could even be classed as flirting.

'You were!' he insists, moving closer again. He cocks his head, looking at me and a tuft of too-long hair falls across his face. I visualize myself reaching up to push it away, like they do in the films.

'We should catch up properly,' I hear myself say, even though it cannot possibly be me. I'm not forward like that, I'm too much of a coward, but something about Mikey always made me feel braver. Maybe it was all the sex we used to have. It was *constant*.

'I'd bloody love that!' he says, grinning as we swap numbers. I grin back so hard my jaw hurts.

As he waves goodbye, after planting a soft kiss on my cheek that isn't so much a promise, as some kind of sexy swear, Myfanwy grabs me by the shoulders.

'You know what this is, don't you?' Her eyes are wild.

'It's Mikey?' I offer and she laughs maniacally.

'This is prediction number four, the person you thought lost forever.'

My brow furrows. 'I considered that, but I don't know . . .' Her grip on my shoulder loosens and she looks disappointed. 'I mean, he might be!' I try to offer hope. 'It's just that a part of me always thought I'd see Mikey again one day . . . We didn't end on bad terms, we were just young and always bickering.' I pause then smile brightly. 'But he could be my soulmate? This could be prediction number six instead of number four?'

At this Myfanwy throws back her head, laughing. '*That* guy?' she scoffs. 'He seems fun, but I doubt he's meant to be your soulmate. I remember now how all over the place he was ten years ago and he still has that same energy. You'd end up running around after him, cleaning up his messes like some kind of puppy. You're too much of a people pleaser and he's too much of a people dis-pleaser.' She turns to look again in the direction Mikey's walked off. 'Sexy though. I like his hair.' She pauses. 'No, he might be number four, but he's surely not number six.' She straightens up, regarding me seriously. 'And he could also be an excellent palate cleanser . . .'

'Palate cleanser?' I raise my eyebrows even though I'm very clear on the implication.

She shrugs. 'Y'know! Just shag him for a bit and see what happens. You *do* fancy him, don't you?'

I nod, because I can't deny that much. Mikey's hot in a confusing way. He wouldn't work in a picture – he's too sort of wonky and messy, even with his teeth fixed. But in motion, he becomes so attractive. He's, I dunno, *bewitching*. People always flocked around him when we were together. Like he was the hottest man in the room. I guess it doesn't help that he's also one of the funniest, cheekiest guys I've ever met.

Or maybe it's all just nostalgia. He takes me back to a time in my life before I had to worry about the cost-of-living crisis, or evil politicians, or climate-change guilt. Whatever it is, I *definitely* fancy him.

Myfanwy grins happily as she adds, 'It could also help you get Daniel out of your system.'

My heart thuds harder in my chest. I haven't told Myfanwy about Daniel's sudden reappearance in my life last month – or his follow-up messages. I don't really know why not. I think maybe I just wanted to figure out what I *want* to do about it before I hear from her what I should do. It's not that she wouldn't be supportive – she's the biggest cheerleader in the world about everything I do – but I also know she'd remind me of everything that's happened. Believe me when I say I definitely don't need reminding. It's all here, replaying in my head on a nightly circuit whenever I close my eyes to sleep.

'Maybe,' I shrug, thinking how fun it would be to spend some commitment-free time with Mikey. He was always such a laugh. It would be so nice to enjoy a bit of affection and some silliness without having to wonder if this is The One, or what he might be thinking, or where this is going.

Myfanwy brings her head closer to mine. 'Let's go after him,' she stage-whispers. 'We'll offer to take him for a drink, then Sonali and I can make an excuse and leave you guys to it. Come on! Let's get you laid!'

I make a face. 'What about those two?' I gesture at Toni and Shawn, who are now arguing with different people in the queue. 'Aren't we meant to be having a fancy VIP night in this exclusive celebrity hotspot?'

Sonali snorts. 'We haven't moved an inch along this queue for forty-five minutes! And those two,' she waves at Toni and Shawn, 'have barely noticed we're here. I think Shawn's really only interested in having an audience for his shit anecdotes.'

Myfanwy giggles. 'He really doesn't need human beings with ears, he needs smiley mannequins with working neck muscles that can nod.'

'It's a fair point,' I concede, feeling bad for my nodding, smiling sister. 'But oh no!' I gasp. 'I really wanted to know what baby names those women ended up deciding on!' I gesture sadly at the posh women ahead of us.

We all laugh as Myfanwy urges, 'Let's make a run for it!'

I dart towards Toni, kissing her breathlessly on the cheek and whispering a quick *sorry* in her ear. Her mouth hangs open as the whole lot of us turn and sprint out of that awful queue, away from the non-VIPs, away from my poor sister and her terrible boyfriend – and off to find my palate cleanser.

CHAPTER TWENTY-ONE

I wake up, groggy and confused by a different bed, different sheets, and a different kind of air in the room.

Where am I?

Flashes of the night before fight through the hangover fog and I gasp, remembering snogging Mikey. A lot. Like, a lot a lot. In the middle of a bar, in the middle of the street, in the middle of the tube carriage. People tutting, people tsking, people loudly telling us to *get a room*.

Oh god, I'm so embarrassed.

Am I at his house? Did we have sex?? And if so, where is he? I blearily scan the room and realize with relief that I know it – it's familiar. I'm not at home in my parents' house, but I am in a safe place. Myfanwy's flat.

I remember now. After abandoning the rubbish queue, we chased Mikey down the street. He was more than happy to go for a drink, and the four of us crashed from one bar to the next, while Mikey and I drunkenly pawed at each other.

I shudder with the thrill of it as I recall him asking me if

I'd come home with him and my having just enough where-withal to say no. I staggered home with Myfanwy and Sonali, where they installed me in their spare room.

There's a knock at the door, and I realize it's this noise that's woken me up.

'Hello?' my voice is unrecognizably hoarse as Myfanwy's face appears around the door.

'You're awake!' she says far too brightly.

'I think so . . .' I blink hazily at her as she enters, wearing Rudolph pyjamas.

'Is it Christmas?' I ask sincerely, honestly unable to fathom what's happening.

'Not for a few more weeks, but these are so cosy,' she says happily, picking up the covers and climbing into bed with me. 'We can't afford to have the heating on these days, so it's big, thick, flannel pyjamas for Sonali and me. In some ways it's terrible for our sex lives, but it's also quite fun rubbing up against one another in such friction-y material.'

'Good to know,' I reply mildly, realizing I myself am still fully clothed in last night's outfit.

'I made you a coffee but left it in the kitchen,' she says, tucking the duvet in around her. 'It's too far away now I'm back in bed,' she adds helplessly and I laugh.

'Thanks anyway.'

'Ugh.' Myfanwy covers her face. 'I keep getting flashbacks of you and Mikey being so disgusting last night.'

'Don't!' I squeak, humiliation burning through me, but also a fizz of excitement. 'I am so embarrassed. But,' I pause, feeling something else, too, 'I haven't done that in *so* long. Not since the last time I was with Mikey, probably. It was so much fun.'

'Well, yay!' Myfanwy declares. 'You have to see him again, without me and Sonali around, cock-blocking you. Time to get you shagged up.'

I check my phone, feeling a jolt of excitement at multiple notifications flashing from WhatsApp.

There are two messages from Mikey.

> I had the best time xx

Then:

> Can we hang out again this week?

And that's where the fun messages end. The rest are all from Celeste, each getting progressively more shrill.

> I know Toni's not coming home tonight, but I assume you are? Please let me know what time you'll be back so I know how long I'll be waiting up for.

> Ginny????

> Please can you reply and let me know where you are, I'm very worried.

> I've just spoken to Toni and she says you ran off into the night. I'm not sure that was very sensible. Do you need me to come and collect you from somewhere?

> WHERE ARE YOU????

And so it goes on.

I groan with guilt and Myfanwy leans over, reading the messages over my shoulder.

'For god's sake!' she huffs. But I feel genuinely terrible. I quickly type out a reply, telling her I'm safe and that I'm sosososososo sorry.

'You're a grown woman in your thirties!' Myfanwy says. 'You've been over here many times without having to check in with her!'

'But she probably stayed up all night waiting to hear from me!' I cry, horror-struck.

I watch as the blue tick instantly appears by my message to Celeste. My stomach flips as she comes *online* and my heart thumps as the dot–dot–dots start and stop several times.

'She made the choice to wait up for you,' Myfanwy points out. 'You didn't ask her to do that, did you? You're both adults and she's making a choice to obsess over your where-abouts. It's her trying to control you – *again!* You have to talk to her about this.'

'Oh god, I *can't*,' I wail. 'I know I'm pathetic, but she's so hard to talk to about things like this. She gets so angry and emotional.'

Myfanwy sighs. 'And she's allowed to have emotions and feel how she feels. But she's not allowed to pile all those emotions on you and use them as a way to bend you to her will. When she can't control you by literally telling you what to do, she tries to control you with her emotions.'

'I really don't think it's as cynical as all that,' I try weakly. 'I don't think she does any of it deliberately. She's just been ten times worse since Aunt Diane died. I think Diane was quite a grounding presence for her. And then with me moving in and being such a wreck, it's a weird time for her.'

Celeste's reply comes at last and it is as damning as I knew it would be.

A single, yellow thumbs-up.

The guilt in my stomach curdles into pure terror. Celeste is next-level furious and I am going to get it so hard when I get back there. I sink further into the bed, pulling the covers up around my ears.

Myfanwy switches on the TV and locates the latest episode of *Married at First Sight*.

We watch in silence while I pulse with dread.

I feel Myfanwy still beside me. She's preparing to speak. 'I wanted to get your advice on something,' she begins at last. I look up, waiting for her to continue. 'It's just . . .' She seems nervous all of a sudden. 'It's . . . I, well . . .' She clears her throat. 'I wanted to tell you, I'm going to propose to Sonali.'

'OH MY GOD!' I shout joyfully before I can stop myself, leaping up into a seated position before remembering Sonali is in the flat somewhere.

Myfanwy laughs, delightedly. 'I was worried you might be upset, after everything you've been through,' she begins and I burst into tears. She looks crestfallen.

'I swear I'm not crying because I'm upset!' I say through snot. 'This is all happiness, I swear to you!' I wipe at my eyes. 'This is just the *best* news. You two are so wonderful and kind to each other. Thank you for telling me.'

She breathes out, relief flooding her face. 'You're sure?'

I nod, pulling her back in for another hug. 'Really, really.' I pull away, drying my eyes. 'So what are you going to do? How are you going to do it? What's the plan?'

This is exactly what I need. A dose of my best friend's happiness. Seeing her so delirious with Sonali makes the world a better place. Nothing could take away from that; not even me getting left at the altar.

She throws herself back into the pillows. 'Argh! This is the difficult bit . . .' She looks up at me. 'And I was hoping you could help me with it. Could we talk through some ideas? You're so brilliant at this kind of thing, you'll help me come up with the perfect thing.'

Her compliments fill me with some indescribable emotion. It's the *nicest* feeling because I do actually feel like I can help her with this. I know I'm good at this! It's the best, loveliest thing, knowing I really can be of use with all this.

'Ooh, and you have to help me with a ring!' she says excitedly, as I nod, thrilled.

'Of course! You could work with Zach on something bespoke if you like? He's a genius.'

She wiggles her eyebrows at me. 'Ooh, Zach's a genius is he?'

'Shut up,' I laugh, swatting at her. 'Do you have a ring in mind already?'

Her shoulders lift. 'Well,' she begins, sitting back up and repositioning herself so she is cross-legged and facing me. 'Did you know Victoria Beckham apparently has, like, fifteen engagement rings?'

I raise my eyebrows. 'I didn't know that, but go ahead. Are we planning to outdo a former Spice Girl?'

Myfanwy smiles, 'Always! That's how I live my life. But it was more that I was thinking I might give Sonali several engagement rings. Maybe not fifteen! Maybe ten. One for each finger. Each one would represent the special moments throughout our relationship. Like, see, I could get a turquoise ring to signify our first holiday together, when we swam in this amazing blue water and I realized I loved her.'

I am trying not to cry. I'm trying really, really hard. 'That is totally beautiful,' I say in a quiet voice.

'They don't have to be expensive,' she says, embarrassed by my too-pure reaction. 'But maybe one of them will be. The final ring; the one she wears day to day.'

'That's perfect,' I reply, blinking fast. 'Because honestly turquoise stones are quite low on the density scale.' I switch into professional mode, trying to pull myself from an emotional edge. 'It means they're a bit soft to be used as an everyday ring.'

'Right,' Myfanwy nods, amused. 'I know you think

everyone should have diamonds, but I want to go through every option, OK? I'm going to work you hard.' She smirks.

'Fine by me!' I grin.

See, this engagement concierge thing surely has legs? So many people want help with their big moment. Maybe I should bring it back up with Celeste. But she was so anti the idea, and so caught up with her big expansion plan. She's had her *Love Island* stars in the store twice now, talking through their genuinely hideous range. I assumed the whole thing would be an email swapped between agents, but I think the lure of working directly with Celeste – with a potential cameo spot up for grabs on *Engage!* – is too big a pull for a reality star. We're also going to visit the new store in a couple of weeks. I'm dreading it.

'And then once you're married,' I sing in a posh voice. 'Of course, darling, you'll have to start thinking of names for your children. Have you considered iPhone as a name? Or iPad? They're very popular, I hear.'

Myfanwy nods. 'Actually darling, I've been thinking about Hero Styles, what do you think?'

'Oh darling, that's captivating. Is that Harry Styles' brother?'

'No darling, it's a headline on my new fashion blog.'

'Of course!'

We fall about laughing, as Myfanwy rewinds the parts of *Married at First Sight* we've talked over and then snuggles back into the bed to watch. But all we do is talk over it again.

I am just about to fall back to sleep, my hangover humming, when my phone beeps. I hope it's not Celeste again.

Sleepily I pick it up, registering the name and feeling adrenaline zig-zagging through my body.

It's Daniel.

CHAPTER TWENTY-TWO

Sometimes my brain feels like it's a washing machine. One of those fancy washing machines with like, fifteen settings that no one really understands or uses, like 'Sports' or 'Denim'. I mean what does any of that mean, really? What does a 'Sports' cycle do? Whatever, I think it's what's happening in my brain right now. My head is on some kind of confusing spin cycle where I know *something* is going on, but I couldn't tell you what. Someone has pushed the wrong button and every time I try to focus on my life and make some decisions, my brain starts a brand-new wash, with everything sloshing about in all directions. I don't know how long it'll go on for, how hot it's going to get in there, and whether anything of use is going to come out at the end of it.

It's been a week since Toni's birthday, when I 'reconnected' with Mikey. A week since Daniel texted *again* asking to meet up. A week since I pissed Celeste off more than ever before by staying out all night without telling her. She's barely spoken to me since, aside from a daily aggressive,

'WHAT TIME WILL YOU BE COMING HOME TONIGHT?' over our cereal. Followed by an even more aggressive threat to pick me up straight from the store when my shift ends. It means I've been too afraid to see Mikey again, never mind Daniel.

To be fair to Celeste, she is under a huge amount of pressure with the launch of this new range. The press release went out wide yesterday, and so far the few tweets about it have been vaguely positive. There is plenty of goodwill for my mother from fans and her celeb mates, but we await reaction from the media.

If I'm completely honest – and I feel awful saying it – I personally don't like what they've come up with. I think Celeste has been blinded by the yes folk around her who keep saying how great everything she does is, over and over. She's not doing what she's literally famous for, which is judging the items themselves – on their own merit.

But then, what do I know really? Taste is all subjective, and my mother has been in this business for a hell of a lot longer than I have.

Either way, it's not the best time to be dealing with a romantic crisis, coming at me from two sides. Daniel seems increasingly desperate to meet up, ignoring my requests for more time. Meanwhile, Mikey's texts are becoming increasingly flirtatious. I'm dying to see both of them, for very different reasons.

Oh my god, am I in a love triangle?? I am both horrified and delighted.

214

A voice breaks me out of my washing machine daydream. 'Let's go!' It's Zach and Celeste by the front door, waiting expectantly.

'Come on, darling!' Celeste says impatiently.

'Yep,' I say, trying to keep from sighing.

We're off to visit the new store across town, and I'm trying to stay positive. We're opening the first week of January, which is now only five weeks away, and I'm really, really trying to be excited. After all, it's a brand new adventure! Something totally new! A new commute, a new environment, new stock. And maybe it will be great; I'm getting to run the whole thing, after all. Maybe I'll be able to make it amazing!

And at least Zach's coming along today to metaphorically hold my hand if it's awful.

His contract with us technically ends at Christmas, but I know we're all hoping he'll stay on, maybe even in a more permanent capacity. He's got a meeting with Celeste about it next week and I know she'll be throwing all kinds of money at him. Which he totally deserves.

As we head for his car, Celeste rabbiting on about filming the new advert and how it went with our *Love Island* ambassador, I sneak a glance at Zach, taking in that strong movie star profile.

It feels like we've genuinely become friends in the last few weeks. For real, I mean. We laugh and joke, and gossip about Celeste. We've had a couple more spy missions, too, for our clients. It's always genuinely fun being around him and I look forward to the days he's in store. It's really nice having a male pal again. In my early to mid-twenties, I used to have loads of blokes as friends. But there is a thing that happens when they meet a partner, where they just . . . go. They disappear. And not in an initial love bubble way like everyone does. It's just like they no longer have *need* of you. They have filled their quota of oestrogen in their life. It made me very sad when I realized all my male friends had gone and weren't coming back. It made me feel a bit used.

I expect the same thing will happen with Zach when he meets someone.

I would say the one weird thing is that neither of us ever mention our love lives. Or, in my case, disastrous romantic bin-fire. But we've been working together for months now and at a certain point it's too late to suddenly go, 'So hey, do you even have a girlfriend? Boyfriend? Casual friend with benefits? Tinder addiction?'

He glances over at me now, raising his eyebrows as Celeste tells us about Photoshopping out the reality star's nipples, and I look away, embarrassed to be caught staring.

'I'm excited to see the place,' he says as we reach the car, climbing in and immediately blasting the heaters onto max.

'You will love it!' Celeste barks. It's an order, not a wish.

Zach nods. 'I'm sure it'll open us up to a whole new type of client.'

'Fingers crossed!' I agree, my heart sinking. I like the clients we have. But it's sweet that he's trying to be positive – it's very sexy.

I don't mean sexy. I mean platonically impressive.

I don't even fancy Zach anymore. I mean, you have to acknowledge his attractiveness because it's right there in front of you. It's undeniable. Like, you can't look at him and *not* immediately want to stroke his face.

But that doesn't mean I *fancy* him. I'm just stating facts: that he's insanely good-looking and talented, and I can't stand not touching him.

Facts not fancy.

He beams over at me. 'It's going to be great.'

It is not great.

The outside isn't too bad. It's a very edgy, colourful building in East London, but I had a feeling it would be, given the new direction Celeste seems intent on heading in. At least it has personality.

But the inside . . .

Barren is the word I would use to describe the aesthetic. It looks more like an Apple Store than a boutique family-run jewellery business. There are screens on every wall, and Celeste immediately grabs a remote control, blasting out the new advert. The *Love Island* star dances for us in a bikini, showing off an ugly scarf and gloves from the range. They did not do a good job with Photoshop because I keep making eye contact with her nipples.

'It's wonderful, isn't it!' Celeste shouts over the advert's pounding dance music.

Zach and I nod, dumbly.

'And the best thing,' Celeste shouts, 'is that there won't be any stock!' She looks so delighted at this best thing, which definitely sounds like the worst thing. She waves at a series of smaller screens dotted around the room. 'They're all interactive,' she explains as the *Love Island* star writhes around above us. 'So customers can review everything in one place and even design their own jewellery and accessories with a computer programme!' She grins at this and I glance nervously at Zach. He is crestfallen.

But surely, even if they can design their own thing on screen, we'd still need him? It's the difference between drawing a picture for yourself and having a professional artist do it.

I look around, horror pooling in my stomach. The advert looping on repeat is already giving me a headache. To me, this store — what Celeste has done with this store — makes *having* a store completely redundant. It's like we've opened a second shop just to show everyone how pointless having any shops are at all.

I should've spoken up. I should've been firmer when Celeste proposed all this. Is it too late?

'Anyway,' Celeste breezes happily. 'I've got to shoot. We're filming this afternoon, but you two stay here and get to know the space. I had a *very* expensive interior designer do all this.' She waves at the blank whiteness all around us.

We both suck in a breath as the door shuts behind her.

'Jesus,' I catch Zach muttering, all his positivity drained away. That's how I know it's bad.

I clear my throat, adopting a sunny American accent, 'Hi there! Welcome to the Genius Bar, would you like to drop off your laptop?'

It doesn't really break the tension but he laughs nicely.

'This is meant to be Celeste's Stones?!' he says with disbelief, taking in the room again with a level of dismay. 'It looks *nothing* like Celeste's Stones!'

'I know,' I say, my voice a mixture of sadness and embarrassment, like this is my fault.

'God,' he says, more under his breath now.

'There is no God here,' I say seriously. 'This is a place without soul.'

He laughs again, his smile back properly now. 'OK then,' he fixes me with a determined expression. 'Well, let's give it a bit.' He glances up at the screens, where the horrible advert repeats hellishly, over and over. 'We'll start by turning this shit off and get some music playing!'

I brighten. 'OK!' I find the remote Celeste has left on the counter and pull up YouTube.

'Girls Aloud!' he shouts, to my surprise, adding, 'Put on *Ten*, that's their best greatest hits album.'

'Big fan, are you?' I ask, amused and delighted. Because I *am* a big fan.

'Totally!' he says happily, taking my hand and leading me to the centre of the empty store. The screens around us show the five singers in orange stomping towards the camera and we copy the moves, strutting around the space. 'I love nineties and noughties girlbands,' he yells over the sounds of 'Something New'. 'The Spice Girls, B★Witched, TLC, Destiny's Child, obviously, Girls Aloud—'

'Obviously,' I snigger as we jump around the room in time with the music, singing tunelessly, getting the words all wrong.

'Very obviously,' he grins. 'And you know who were also a totally underrated girl band? The Saturdays. They rocked!'

'Oh yeah! My Aunt Diane had their album *Chasing Lights* stuck in the CD slot of her Volvo. We listened to it every day when she got me from school.'

He grins at this. 'Me and my mum and sister used to dance around the room like this to Girls Aloud after school. We would have huge raging arguments over which was the best member. Cheryl was my favourite, of course! We couldn't believe it when Ashley Cole cheated on her!' Zach suddenly looks furious. 'How could anyone do that? It's so—' He stops abruptly like he has just said too much. His eyes are flashing dark and haunted as he abruptly stops dancing and turns away. 'I'm just going to the loo,' he says shortly, his back to me, 'then I better get going. I've got a lot to get through.' He walks quickly away, leaving me to fumble with the controls, turning the music off and feeling weird.

What happened there? Did I embarrass myself?

No, there was something going on with him. He mentioned cheating? Did he . . . ? Has he . . . ?

It suddenly occurs to me that I really don't actually know that much about my new friend.

CHAPTER TWENTY-THREE

'Whaff hyme iz Shahi geckin har?'

Myfanwy scrunches up her face, trying to understand what I'm asking. 'Nope,' she shakes her head. 'No idea on that one.'

I finish applying my lipstick, popping the lid back on. 'Sorry,' I laugh. 'I said *what time is Sonali getting here?*'

Her face clears. 'Oh, she's meeting us there,' she replies. 'She's going straight from work.' She checks the small clock beside her bed. 'And we need to leave soon, so, quickly, I wanted to talk strategy for Project Proposal.'

'Yes!' I exclaim with excitement, picking up my eyeliner and squinting at my reflection in Myfanwy's mirror. Shall I risk it? I will inevitably end up with wholly uneven unsymmetrical flicks, but maybe that is my fate. The fortune teller didn't mention it, but it could be.

'Want me to do it?' Myfanwy offers, reading my mind, and I nod gratefully. She takes the eyeliner from me, pulling her best concentrating face as she begins carefully with my right eye.

'So I've made a list of important moments from our relationship,' she begins. 'There's that first moment I realized I
loved her on holiday – that one I already told you about –
then I've made a list of some others.' With one eye still shut,
I squint down at the piece of paper covered in Myfanwy's
handwriting scrawl. 'There's when we decided to live
together, then moving day when we hired a van, there's
that minibreak in Winchester, when we accidentally drove
to Windsor because I got confused with the Satnav. There's
that stupid day we laughed until we cried for literally hours
because a guy walked into a glass door in front of us . . .' She
stops for a second, looking annoyed. 'Can you stop blinking?
You're ruining the eyeliner!'

'Sorry!' I tell her. 'I can't help it, you're making me emotional with all this.' I scan the rest of her list, glancing over
at the photos around the mirror of these two together. So
many beautiful, silly, moving moments they've had together.

I wonder if I could make a list like this for me and Daniel?
And what would be on it?

'This is amazing, Myfe,' I say with emotion.

She switches eyes, suddenly looking shy. 'Thanks,' she
replies softly.

'Being a romantic really suits you,' I say, feeling so proud
of her. 'And – ooh! – I had a look on Etsy for you,' I continue
excitedly. 'There are so many fun kinds of rings you can get
made, they do basically everything! You could have a tiny
moving van as one ring!' I laugh and she joins in.

'That's amazing!' She pauses. 'Of course, I definitely also

want a proper ring from Celeste's Stones. I've already had a chat with Zach about it and he's drawing up some suggestions for me.'

'That's great,' I tell her, feeling all warm inside.

'Is Zach coming tonight?' she asks and I nod. She tuts at the movement but stands back after only a few more seconds.

'There!' she declares. I blink a few times, then turn to the mirror to review her efforts. The eyeliner is perfection. I take in the whole effect, head-to-toe, feeling pleased.

OK, so I moan about my mother a lot – a lot a lot – but there are some moments when having her around is oh-so useful.

'Beautiful,' I smile at Myfanwy. 'Thanks.'

Tonight, Toni and Shawn are throwing a Christmas party and we were told to dress up for the event in South London. I'm wearing the most incredible outfit, courtesy of Celeste's wardrobe. She gets sent so many free clothes, she barely even knows where to start with it all, and I found this dark blue jumpsuit with a feather trim around the sleeves. It's possibly totally absurd, but I looked at my reflection and felt absolutely gorgeous for the first time in ages.

'And what about Mikey?' Myfanwy asks. 'Is he coming?'

I look at my nails, freshly painted, already smudged and ruined. 'I think so. He said he'd definitely try to make it.' Myfanwy shakes her head. 'You two are really taking your time. You had such mad chemistry at Toni's birthday! But you haven't seen each other since. What gives, Gin? You urgently need a shag and he is perfect shag material.'

223

'Well, to be fair, he was away for a bit!' I explain, feeling a bit defensive. 'And with everything changing at the store, it's been really busy with work. We are opening a new shop in a couple of weeks,' I remind her. 'But we've been texting each other a lot. It's been very flirty.'

'You know,' she says dryly, 'a shag takes, what, like, an hour?'

I snort. 'Lesbian privilege. I think you mean, like, fifteen minutes, tops.'

She laughs. 'OK, fine but either way, you could've sorted this if you really wanted to.'

'I do really want to!' I insist. 'You don't know what it's like living in Celeste's house. She's been even more of a nightmare than usual, constantly asking what I'm doing and where I'm going.'

Myfanwy sighs. 'Just tell her you're staying at mine for the night.'

I raise an eyebrow. 'You haven't seen her lately. She'll want an itemized breakdown of our plan for the evening: what we're doing, where we're going and what time we'll be in bed. I wouldn't be surprised if she actually calls you to check up on me and confirm the plan.'

Myfanwy shakes her head in disgust. 'You really need to get out of there. She's out of control.'

'I know,' I give a slight nod, knowing I have limited options. It makes me think again of that option I might have. With Daniel. I sigh, picturing his face and thinking of his last text about meeting up. The text I decided to treat as maturely as possible, by completely ignoring it. 'And of course,' I add, thinking out loud, 'I still have to figure out what to do about Daniel.'

My heart thumps in my chest as I realize what I've said. I still haven't told Myfanwy anything about the situation. She turns to me, her brow furrowed, eyes narrowed.

'What do you mean? What do you have to figure out about Daniel?'

I stare down at my lap. 'He turned up at the house.'

'He *what*?' Her mouth drops partway open. 'Celeste's house? When? Oh my god, what did he *say*?' She leans closer, Project Proposal wholly forgotten.

I take a deep breath. 'It was right after we got back from Madeira. Like a week later,' I admit, shamefaced. 'And I'm so sorry I didn't say anything to you about it. It was, like, *too* big, y'know? I didn't know what to think and I needed to process it for a bit before I talked about it out loud.'

She nods slowly. 'OK, I understand,' she says, but I can see she is a little hurt. 'So? What did he say? Did he finally say sorry?'

'Yes,' I confirm, remembering his apology and the way he looked at me. 'And he hinted that maybe . . .'

'Oh my god,' she breathes, waiting for me to continue, but I can't. 'You think he wants to get back together?'

I nod slowly. 'I think so. Or maybe not, I don't know! He keeps messaging about wanting to see me and talk. I don't know what to think.'

Her eyes are wide. 'Wow,' she says in a whisper. 'This is

huge.' She gives the moment time to settle before continuing. 'But how did you feel when you saw him? How do you feel *now*? Are you angry or sad?'

I throw my hands up with exasperation. 'I honestly don't know! Both? Neither? One minute I think I hate him and will never forgive him; the next, I am physically aching for him. I want to cry with how much I still miss him and our life together. I know it's been six months, and I feel like I'm supposed to be totally over him by now, but I was so happy with Daniel, and I do still love him.' I sigh. 'But would I ever be able to trust him again? Would I ever be able to believe he wasn't going to do that to me again? Every time he went out or had a weekend away with work or friends, would I be thinking that he isn't coming back?'

Myfanwy doesn't answer and we fall silent.

At last I speak again. 'I just wish I had more answers. I wish I knew if those predictions were real and what they meant.'

'Of course they're real,' she frowns. 'And at least you've clearly had all your losses.' She ticks them off with her fingers. 'A heartbreak with Daniel, the death of your Aunt Diane, and losing your flat.' She looks up, smiling at me widely as if this is all good. 'Yay! So it's all gains from here on out!'

'And I've had my life-changing honeymoon trip,' I remind her. 'So it's just the last two left: someone I lost and my soulmate.' I hesitate. 'Do you think Mikey is the someone I thought lost? Or maybe he's my soulmate?'

Myfanwy sighs. 'It would really help if you could remember the fortune teller's wording. Did she say you'll *meet* your soulmate or *find* your soulmate?' She raises her eyebrows. 'Like, if it's *meet* we know that it probably isn't Mikey or Dan, because you already met. But *find* could mean that you already know them.'

I shrug sadly. 'I have no idea what words she used. It's all a bit hazy. I only remember that there were six predictions and that she had big hair.' Another thought occurs to me. 'On the other hand,' I feel my nose crinkling, 'Daniel is someone I'd thought lost forever and I already thought he was my soulmate. So maybe this was about proving that? What if all of this is a way for Daniel to prove himself as The One?'

'It'll take a lot of proving,' Myfanwy mutters.

'Argh! It's all too cryptic!' My voice is full of despair, as I put my face in my hands. 'I just wish I could speak to the fortune teller again and ask her to explain herself better. Or at least repeat everything she said the first time. There must be so many details I've forgotten.'

'These six predictions are a lot more specific than most people get!' Myfanwy points out and I pout.

'Yes, but they're still not clear enough. If these really are real, then she obviously knew more. There must be loads of extra info that she didn't share with me.'

Myfanwy looks thoughtful. 'I know we gave up looking for her, but maybe we should try again. She's got to be out there somewhere, right?' She regards me fearfully. 'Wait, how old was she? She won't have died, will she?'

I shake my head. 'No!' I pause. 'I mean, she could've died of a million other things, obviously, but not from old age. I'm not sure how old she was because everyone over twenty looks fifty when you're sixteen, but I'm pretty sure she couldn't have been much more than about forty-five.'

'Good!' Myfanwy's grin returns.

'But I know literally *nothing* about her!' I remind her desperately. 'I don't know what her name was, where she lives, nothing.'

'You remember what she looked like?' Myfanwy asks and I nod.

'Kinda,' I admit.

'Well then, we know *kinda* what she looks like, we know she's a psychic and that she travelled with that local fair. That place still visits the same park, so we start there. Who knows? Maybe she still does readings at the same fair?'

We stare at each other excitedly.

CHAPTER TWENTY-FOUR

We arrive early at the no-name bar, in a trendy area of Clapham. It's pretty upmarket and feels like Toni and Shawn have spent a fair bit of money on all of this.

'Fancy,' Sonali murmurs beside me, taking in the room.

'This is the perfect place for you to get some,' Myfanwy hisses in my ear.

It looks like we're the first to arrive, and we creep in, scanning the room for signs of life. 'Hellooo?' I call out awkwardly and a glamorous but nervous Toni appears from behind the bar.

'I can't find the Prosecco,' she says by way of a greeting. 'The manager said they'd leave out a bunch of glasses and the bottles so we could have trays of drinks for arrivals.'

'Don't worry,' I say as confidently as I can, throwing off my coat and joining her in her search. 'We'll sort it.'

She steps back, giving me a head to toe with wide eyes. 'Wow,' she says admiringly. 'One of Mum's? You look absolutely devastating. That is stunning, Gin. This is going to blow Mikey's socks off.'

'Thanks.' I suddenly feel a bit overdressed and embarrassed. Toni is wearing a lovely dress but there are no feathers. Why did I think feathers were a good idea? Nobody wears feathers! Will Mikey think I'm an absolute try-hard dolt?

Whatever, it's too late now and I focus instead on how genuinely excited I am to see him. Our texts have been ramping up over the last few days as we anticipated seeing each other again tonight. I can't wait to get my hands on him.

I've never been that great at one-night stands. Much as I wanted to enjoy them, I just couldn't. The one or two – OK three – I attempted in my early twenties always ended up being horribly awkward, uncomfortable encounters with men who ultimately just made me feel used, even though I kept telling myself *I* was using *them*. So I feel like Mikey is the perfect compromise. I don't want anything serious with him – at least I don't think I do – but he's a familiar, fun presence who knows my body and what I like. Or, at least, *some* of what I like. I have evolved since we last did it.

I take in Toni and beam. 'You look beautiful,' I tell her and she smiles back.

'It all looks fab,' Sonali tells her warmly, as Myfanwy glances around.

'Is Shawn here, too?'

She shakes her head. 'No, he's coming with his friends in a bit. I said I'd get everything ready.'

I catch a look between Sonali and Myfanwy but none of us say anything, busying ourselves instead with getting glasses out and onto trays. Guests start to arrive as we finish up and

Toni squeals with excitement as she runs off to greet friends I only know in passing.

I check the time. Mikey messaged on our way here to confirm the address, so he must be on his way by now. I feel my stomach flip at the prospect of seeing him and I pull out my compact to check for errant lipstick or mascara gloops. Over the mirror, Myfanwy and Sonali giggle over something as Sonali reapplies her Vaseline. She must get through *pots* of the stuff.

They both look so happy and excited, it makes my heart explode.

'Drink?' I turn to find Zach has arrived. His smile drops as he takes me in. 'Gosh, Ginny, you look . . .' He swallows. 'Very nice.'

'Thanks.' I feel silly suddenly. It's too much. 'You do, too,' I add sincerely. Because he does.

Myfanwy is at my shoulder.

'When is Mikey getting here?' she asks impatiently.

Zach narrows his eyes but says nothing. I suddenly feel awkward, like I've done something wrong.

'Um,' I hedge, still looking at Zach. 'I don't—'

A voice interrupts us. 'Did I hear my name?'

I spin around, nearly choking on my feathers. It's him. Mikey. And he looks amazing.

He greets Myfanwy and Sonali, hugging them both as they laugh about our last joint outing, remembering embarrassing moments of spilling drinks and dancing in the middle of bars with no music.

Then he turns to me.

He takes my hands in his, his eyes travelling up and down my body with a look I can only describe as *intense* approval.

'Ginny,' he says in a low voice, almost a growl, 'you look ridiculously sexy. Even better than the last time I saw you.' He pulls me close and I feel his breath hot on my ear.

I am acutely aware of Zach watching all of this. Pulling away, I clear my throat. 'Mikey, this is Zach.' Mikey turns to him with surprise, like he hadn't noticed the film star standing with us. 'All right mate?'

'Hi,' Zach replies shortly, and they shake hands.

'Zach works with us at Celeste's Stones,' I add hastily, like this will explain the tension. 'He's our bespoke ring designer.'

'Cool,' Mikey says dismissively, barely looking at him.

'I was just getting drinks,' Zach says, matching his tone. 'Can I get you one, Mick?'

'It's Mikey.' He corrects him smoothly, a crackle of testosterone in the air. 'And yeah, thanks mate. I'll have a lager.' He turns his back on Zach in an open display of disinterest and Myfanwy glances at me, eyes wide and sparkling. She loves drama.

'Now, let me have another look at you, you gorgeous thing . . .' Mikey grabs me, hands on my waist as Zach stalks off, his face thunder. 'I can't believe I'm finally seeing you,' he continues, pulling me nearer. 'I wish we were alone right now, you really have no idea.'

It sends a shiver through me as I smile into his cheek.

'We can be very alone later,' I murmur back and feel

232

myself redden, partly from the adrenaline, partly with embarrassment. 'I look forward to finding out what you would've done.'

He pulls away, staring at me with a small, longing smile.

I am definitely going to get some.

Three hours later and the problem with the party has revealed itself: it's *too* fancy. Toni's twenty-something pals are arriving, looking around with fear in their eyes, downing a drink and then leaving within thirty minutes. Considering Shawn's thirty-four, I'm surprised to note there are hardly any older people on the guestlist. In fact, I'd say me, Mikey, Zach, Myfanwy and Sonali are easily the oldest ones in the room. A fact we are trying hard not to care about as we forcibly enjoy ourselves, dancing around the room, swigging expensive shots from the bar and punching random helium balloons. Mikey and I have so far been incredibly restrained; dancing close but no cigar. By which I mean no kissing. We're at a grown-up party; you can't just snog in the middle of the room like it's a Year Nine Valentine's disco. Much as I'd like to.

The initial weirdness between Mikey and Zach seems to have – thankfully – eased up, with the pair bonding over the variety of lagers on offer.

'I'm off to the loo,' Mikey announces now and squeezes my hand, sending promising chills through me. Honestly, the sparks flying between us, it's like someone's handing out sparklers to teenagers and everyone forgot to do a fire safety notice. We're going to need a St John's Ambulance on standby if this keeps up. I watch Mikey's bum as he meanders across the room in the direction of the loos.

'Oh my god, he's so sexy, isn't he?' I murmur to Myfanwy, hypnotized.

'Sure, sure,' she says hurriedly. 'Listen, while he's gone . . .' I turn to give her my full attention but my brain is still full of Mikey butt images. 'I think I've found the funfair!'

'What?' The bum is gone, replaced by a blurry-edged image of our fortune teller. 'How? What?'

She nods excitedly. 'While you've been dance-flirting with Mikey and Zach—'

'I wasn't!' I try to protest but she waves my interruption away.

'—While you were toying with two blokes who are both clearly into you,' she doubles down, eyeballing me, 'I was googling a thousand different variations, trying to find a website or something – nothing doing, but then I finally found this random post on a Facebook page for a small town the funfair set up in after leaving London.' She gets taller as she speaks, her chest puffing out with pride at her detective skills. 'So then I clicked on their page and I'm pretty sure it's them! I've sent the guy who runs it a message.'

'Wow, you are amazing,' I tell her, blown away. 'This could be it then! We could be speaking to the fortune teller, like, *tomorrow*! She could tell me who my soulmate is and we could be settled down together by Christmas.' I breathe in slowly, trying to control the thumping in my chest.

Myfanwy grimaces. 'Hold your horses, mate. I don't think it'll be that quick. I don't think blokes who run travelling fun-fairs tend to be particularly quick at answering their Facebook messages. We might have to wait a bit to hear back.'

I nod, 'Right, sorry. I got carried away. I'll be patient. Thank you for doing all that, you are the absolute best.'

She smiles broadly. 'I know.'

Someone behind us clears their throat and I see Myfanwy's face change. The smile falls away as she pales with shock.

I quickly turn around, coming face to face with . . . Daniel.

'What the . . .' I run out of words.

He looks embarrassed but gives me a head-to-toe with wide eyes. 'Wow, Ginny, you look . . . just wow!'

I don't say anything, so Myfanwy does.

'What are you doing here, Daniel?' she says carefully. He visibly swallows hard, looking between us.

'Um, I wanted to talk to Ginny,' he turns to me, his eyes beseeching. 'Can we talk? Please? I know you said you wanted space and I'm really aware that you didn't reply to my last messages but . . . please?'

'How did you even know I was here?' I feel so bamboo-zled, so dazed, I don't know what to think. 'Did Toni invite you?' I glance over at my sister. She's oblivious, talking to Sonali and Zach, with Shawn glued to her side.

Daniel shakes his head. 'No, she tagged you all in on Instagram at this bar. I still follow her.'

Ugh, what? Who the hell *tags* everyone into a place or

venue on Instagram? Surely that function is only for celebrities who are getting their holiday for free.

'Right,' I say, still unsure what to make of his sudden arrival.

'Can we talk?' he asks again, stepping a little closer.

'Um . . .' I'm interrupted by Toni who has just spotted her never-was brother-in-law.

'Oh my GOD, Daniel!' she squeals, bursting into our small circle, Shawn close behind her. She throws herself into my ex-fiancé's arms before suddenly remembering everything that's happened and retreating, glancing at me guiltily. 'What are you doing here?' She echoes my question, before again looking over. 'Did you invite him? Are you guys . . . ?' She looks between us excitedly and I jump in, swallowing hard, 'No! No no no no no no!'

Daniel regards me sadly and everyone falls silent. The awkwardness reverberates between us, zinging from me to Daniel to Myfanwy to Toni to Shawn, and back again.

And it is just then, in the most horribly uncomfortable moment of my life, that Mikey rocks up.

'Wotcha!' he crows, throwing lazy arms around me and – oh god – Daniel. He quickly realizes his mistake. 'Oh sorry mate,' he unhooks himself and offers up a hand. 'I thought you were Zach. I'm Mikey.'

Daniel looks at the hand for a moment before taking it. 'Daniel,' he replies warily.

'Nice to meet you, Daniel,' Mikey says, tucking hair behind his ear, oblivious to the horror each of us is feeling.

'Are you one of Toni's mates?' Daniel looks down at the ground and Mikey glances around, frowning, finally sensing the mood. 'Or, er, one of Shawn's mates?' he adds, looking to Shawn anxiously.

'Er, no,' Shawn says, reaching into the group to offer his own hand to Daniel. 'Hi, we haven't met, I'm Shawn,' he nods.

'Hi,' comes the reply, but Daniel is now looking at me, and only me, his sad cow eyes penetrating my soul.

'Daniel is, um ...' I begin and Mikey raises his eyebrows at me. 'He's, er, he's ...' I can't. I don't know what to say. Honestly, I don't even really know how I'm supposed to describe him. Where to begin! He's my ex-boyfriend slash fiancé who I loved and adored for five years and thought I'd be with forever, until he moved out of our flat weeks before our wedding, ending our relationship without really telling me.

Would that cover it? But no, of course it wouldn't.

I would also have to point out that he's also the man who's suddenly back in my life months later, desperately sorry and wanting ... what? To get back together and forget everything that's happened – everything he did? And maybe I could add that I don't know how I feel or how much I still love him or whether I should get back with him or not. Should I also mention how much I desperately miss our old life and all the dogs we would've had and the future babies we could've brought up? But that I don't know if I can forgive or trust him?

Mikey looks nervous, glancing between us. 'Ha, don't tell

me,' he begins jokingly. 'You forgot you accidentally invited another date tonight!'

'Date?' Daniel chokes out, like he has been slapped. He looks to me for confirmation and it's now my turn to stare down at my feet.

Shawn clears his throat, reaching across the circle. 'Er, Daniel, mate, let's go get a drink while this lot chat. You can speak to Ginny later.'

I meet Shawn's eyes and nod, grateful, as he moves my shellshocked ex away towards the bar.

'Phew!' Mikey lets out a short laugh as everyone else breathes out. 'What was that all about? Talk about awkward!'

'Sorry,' I mutter, humiliation crushing me. 'That's Daniel, my ex. I had no idea he was planning on turning up tonight.'

'Oh shit.' Mikey covers his mouth with shock, his own casual words to Daniel hitting him in the face. 'God, I made that stupid joke about a date! I'm so sorry.'

'Humph,' Myfanwy grunts. 'I don't know what he's playing at showing up like this.' She turns to Toni. 'And I'm not sure what you're playing at either, tagging everyone into this place online. That kind of shit is a stalker's dream.'

'Daniel's not a stalker!' Toni scolds. She was always very fond of him. 'And I think it's romantic anyway! He's come back here to win Ginny's heart back.'

'It's not romantic!' Myfanwy rolls her eyes. 'Ginny has told him over and over to give her space. She couldn't have been clearer and he's chosen to ignore her wishes and put his own pain above hers – again!'

'But they never take no for an answer in the movies.' Toni blinks hard. 'Men are always turning up unexpectedly to win someone back!'

'Patriarchy horse shit probably paid for by the Harvey Weinsteins of the world,' Myfanwy declares. 'We brainwash young men into thinking persistence is romantic. Never take no for an answer! It's rape culture in an acceptable form.'

When Myfanwy gets going on rape culture, it's quite hard to move her off it, so I step in. 'Either way, it was really decent of Shawn to defuse the situation.' I direct this at Toni because it's probably the first almost-nice thing I've said about her boyfriend. I want her to know I see this other side to him. Maybe he's not so dreadful after all.

I realize suddenly that we've all gotten quite loud, and our voices all sound oddly echoey. Glancing around, it's clear why. Aside from Zach and Sonali chatting in a corner, plus Daniel and Shawn doing shots at the bar, the only people left at this party are me, Mikey, Toni and Myfanwy. Toni follows my gaze and her face falls as she takes in the remnants of her first real attempt at adulting.

'Oh,' she says sadly and Mikey slings an arm around her. 'Oh Tone, don't be sad. We're the best people anyway.' He whispers something in her ear and she giggles.

'Are you serious?' she asks and he nods, shooting me a mischievous look.

'What?' I ask, as Daniel and Shawn return from the

bar, both looking a little more relaxed – and cross-eyed from shots.

'Sorry about before, mate,' Mikey says to Daniel nicely. 'I have a plan to make up for it.' He gives him the same cheeky grin and I feel frustration rise. He raises his voice to get Sonali and Zach's attention. 'Guys! Over here!'

'What's going on?' I ask again, exasperated, as the room gathers together.

Mikey looks around the group. 'We are all going to go sit over there,' he points at a huddle of old sofas pushed together in the corner of the bar, 'and we're going to take some mushrooms.' He glances over his shoulder, checking the bartender isn't listening or watching. She's sitting down, bored, on her phone, ignoring the rest of the room. Mikey turns back to us, raises an eyebrow, and pulls out a couple of smallish plastic bags with brown contents.

'You're joking?' I am incredulous.

Mushrooms!

I've never done shrooms before. I don't think people even call them shrooms anymore, do they?

'I'm in,' Myfanwy says way too fast and I glance at her. She looks faux innocent and it's obvious she was already in on this plan. An excitable Toni looks to Shawn for a reaction.

He shrugs. 'No big deal – I've done it loads of times before. I'm up for it.'

'Me too,' Daniel surprises me by adding.

'Sonali? Zach?' I ask desperately. Zach looks as terrified as me but nods. An obviously thrilled Sonali is useless, too, declaring only, 'This is going to be epic.'

'Yes!' Mikey punches the air, as they turn to look at me, awaiting my response.

I mean, I don't really want to, but there is no chance I'm leaving this lot to do it without me. I'd rather die from the mushrooms than the FOMO.

I take each of them in: my friends, my family, two exes – oh, and Shawn – all here tonight, wanting to take drugs.

I take a deep breath. 'OK,' I say at last. 'Let's do it.'

CHAPTER TWENTY-FIVE

Nothing happens for ages, and then it does.

'Have the walls always been this bright?' I squint in confusion at the intensity of the surface in front of me. I give it a stroke. 'I'm sure it wasn't so, like, *neon* earlier?' I pause. 'Can the colour white actually *be* neon?' Everyone looks blank so I add, 'Maybe someone painted it since we arrived?'

The women all lean closer to inspect it, while Shawn, Zach, Mikey and Daniel all glance at each other, amused.

'Is this me *coming up*?' I ask anxiously and they nod.

'It'll be OK,' Daniel says nicely and I study his lovely face. He's so handsome.

'It really will,' adds Mikey, and now I'm looking at *his* lovely face. They're both so gorgeous, I don't know what to do with myself.

Having just stroked the wall, I resist an impulse to stroke both their faces. But I feel somehow sure that if I could touch them, I'd know which of them is my soulmate.

'Ooh, this is weird,' says Sonali, 'My bottom half is an octopus.'

'Lucky!' Myfanwy complains. 'So far, nothing's really happening for me. Should I take more?' She looks to Mikey, our resident expert, for an answer but Shawn interjects.

'Not a good idea, babe,' he shakes his head with authority and, even through the descending haze, I can see Myfanwy wants to laugh at his pomposity.

'I feel all giggly,' Toni says, nuzzling into Shawn. He smiles widely and encircles her with his arm.

'It's happening. I think I need to go for a walk,' Daniel announces, standing up suddenly. 'Ginny, is there any chance you want to come with me?'

'Sure,' I find myself saying, floating up to meet his hands, even though all I want to do is lie there staring at this cool neon white wall.

We wander over to the other side of the bar, where Daniel stares intently at a spot above my head. I wonder what he's seeing.

'This is weird,' he mutters, now staring at his own hands.

'But nice,' I either say or think. I'm not really sure my mouth is still attached to the rest of my body.

'So,' he takes a huge deep breath. 'Maybe this isn't the best time to talk; I know we're both high, but I've wanted to see you so badly.' He pauses and his eyes are saucers. And then teacups. And then saucers again. 'I want to talk to you about what happened and why and what next.'

That *what next*. Even floating above the conversation, I

feel those two words hard. Because, even in this strange, disconnected state, I'm pretty sure *what next* means: *are we getting back together*?

I try to focus, I try to pull myself back from the weird high, and focus on the issue. I need to answer these three questions for myself:

Do I want my life to be with Daniel?

Can I forgive him for what happened?

Can I ever trust him again?

If the answer is yes to all of them, then I need to get over any remaining pride that might be holding me back and give things another shot. Because we were happy, weren't we?

Question four: Were we really happy?

Daniel is still speaking. 'I need you to know that I really am sorry. You have no idea how much the guilt has been eating away at me over what I did.' He scuffs his shoes, kicking them against the floor. 'It's been pointed out to me over and over what a fucking twat I've been. Not just with the way I ended things, but the way I've been since.' He pauses. '*And* the way I was before. You did everything for me, you were always so kind and conciliatory. I was selfish, everything was always on my terms. I can see now it was always about what I wanted to do or where I wanted to go.' He swallows hard and I can see he is holding back emotion. 'But I'm changing, or I *want* to change, at least. I can see what kind of man I was – am – and I want to be better.' He takes my hand and I watch in wonder because it doesn't look anything like my hand. I consider that expression – when you know something like the back of your hand – and realize I don't know the back or the front of my hand at all. For that matter, which even is the front of your hand and which is the back?

Daniel's voice breaks through my reverie. 'I want to change, Gin, and I want ...' He trails off, trying to look at me, but I'm floating above myself.

Were we really happy? That fourth question keeps coming back to me. And now the other three don't seem to matter that much.

Were we really happy?

I watch the two of us from high up on the ceiling. We look so odd together from up here. Daniel is still holding onto my – Ginny's – hand and I am – she is – blank-faced and spacey.

Something in what he said a second ago is playing around the corners of my head. Everything was always on his terms. That is striking a chord.

I thought I was happy with him. I certainly told myself and everyone else we were really happy, but there's something ...

I look at myself, at Ginny, closely now, and through the layers of make-up I can see how tired she's been. How tired she was when she was with Daniel. Tired all the time. Because it was exhausting. She was exhausted, I was exhausted.

As an introvert, I was constantly pushing myself to accommodate his extroversion. I would run around trying to match his puppy energy, fixing the things he broke, picking up after him, trying to keep him entertained and amused.

I consider the night I came back from my hen do, and all I wanted was to go to bed with an M&S ready meal. Instead we drank nearly out of date Baileys and ended up in the pub.

It was constant emotional and physical labour, looking after him and the relationship. Plus, I never wanted to tell him off, or let him know what would make me happy because I was afraid he would find me boring.

Oh my god, I realize, I *like* being boring. All I want to do when I get home from work of an evening is lie around in my pyjamas watching mind-numbing telly and eating pasta, while I scroll through my phone and moan about people I don't like on Instagram.

I don't mind an evening out once a week – or y'know once a month, ideally – but Daniel wanted to *do things* all the time. If we had a night off, he would be bouncing off the walls, asking what we should do and messaging friends to meet up.

I was so tired all the time.

'Gin, I want to ask you something,' Daniel begins, his voice trembling, but I'm barely listening. I'm back in my body, which for the record, is now the shape and colour of a banana, and my stalk is leaning away from him.

I am so off my tits.

And oh god, now Zach's coming over.

'Have you met?' I ask in a weird voice. Daniel looks perturbed, then sighs.

'No,' he says, so I take his hand, and then Zach's hand.

'I'm a banana, you're both bananas,' I tell them both warmly.

'Right,' Daniel sighs, running out of patience. 'We'll finish this later. Maybe when we're both feeling a little less all over the place.'

I nod, knowing I need to tell him the truth. I need to explain the realisation I've had and what it means. Because I know now that we're not right for each other. These mad mushrooms have given me the clarity I need and now the right thing to do is to let him down gently. I need to tell Daniel he was right to end it and that we can't get back together. Not ever.

I mean, sure, he could've ended things in a better way, but I finally understand that we weren't right for each other and we never will be. He's not my soulmate; he's a nice, handsome soul drain.

He wanders off towards the bar and I watch the bartender leap out of her chair, pretending she wasn't on her phone the whole time.

Zach eyes me warily. 'Hi Ginny,' he says slowly, with trepidation. 'How are you feeling?'

'I'm amazing actually,' I tell him. 'How are you feeling?'

He leans in, giving me a small smile. 'Don't tell anyone but I didn't take any. I thought someone better stay sober in case anything went wrong.' He pauses. 'Are you sure you're OK? Your pupils are *huge*.'

I nod, trying to seem sober. 'I'm completely fine,' I reassure him, intent on not reacting as his eyebrows turn completely white. I don't want to alarm him, but his whole face is going white and saggy actually. Was Zach always eighty years old?

I thought he was quite a bit younger. Funny how wrong you can remember things, isn't it?

'Do you want some water?' he asks anxiously and I feel a rush of affection for him.

'I'm so glad we're friends, Zach,' I tell him and the old man grins. He's still quite handsome actually, for a very elderly person. I admire his wrinkles, they're so vivid and *real*. I keep going, 'Honestly, Zach, you're the *best*, and I love working with you. I hope you stay at the store forever.'

The old Zach looks a bit sad at this. 'Actually your mum's decided that we'll be parting ways after Christmas.' He stares down at the floor. 'I guess the expansion and new direction isn't very Walliams' Custom Designs.'

My mouth gapes open. Even through my messy haze, I feel the enormity of this.

'You're joking,' I say in a whisper. 'But . . . but . . . you've been so brilliant. And the clients love you! We've had such a surge in business because of you. This is . . . this is . . .' I trail off before finding the words in an explosion, 'so *STUPID!*'

'Oh, hey, don't worry,' Old Zach shrugs. 'It's OK, it's not the end of the world. It's been great for my CV, and my business account's gained five thousand new followers on Instagram thanks to your mum sharing my stories! I'm grateful really.'

God he's nice. This is so . . . *nice*. Celeste has screwed him over and he's still looking on the bright side.

'And,' he grins, 'I got to meet you. I hope we'll be able to keep hanging out? Now we won't be work colleagues anymore, we don't have to be so professional.'

This hits me hard. Is that why he's been keeping his distance? Because we worked together? I was so sure there was more between us and – oh god – the words are coming, the vomit overflows: 'Is that why you didn't want to kiss me?' I say in a rush, as the real Ginny inside me somewhere screams at me to stop. 'At Diane's funeral? Is that why you said you only wanted to be friends?'

He swallows, looking at the floor. 'No,' he says slowly. 'Um, there's a . . . this isn't really the time to talk. But there's . . . I . . .' He gulps again. 'Look, I do really like you, Gin, but I'm not looking for anything like that with you. It's not . . . I just . . . I don't think of you in that way but I'm really glad we can be pals.' He looks nervous and then adds, 'Sorry.'

Why are men always saying sorry to me? They're always discarding me and then saying sorry, like it makes up for everything. Why can't they try just *not* behaving badly in the first place and see how that goes? Why don't we – as a human race – just try being nice to each other and then we wouldn't have to keep saying sorry.

I realize I have solved all of humanity's worst problems and I spin around, looking for Myfanwy. She's the best person to tell that I've solved the world; she can implement my plan. She's always so organized and good at solving crises. Where is she? I keep turning, looking and looking.

Wait, what was my plan again?

The old man has his hands on my shoulders now. Have they been there the whole time? They feel warm and nice. What a warm and nice old man.

'You're warm and nice,' I tell him and he peers at me closely.

'Sorry,' he says again. 'But you were spinning round and round in circles, shouting "dizzy dinosaurs" and I was worried you were going to fall over.'

Was I? It sounds like a lot of fun; maybe I should do it again.

We are interrupted by a shouting person.

'HIYA!' It's Mikey! I remember Mikey, he's lovely. Much nicer than the other two men here who keep pretending to like me then rejecting me. Mikey is the only good one.

In fact, I think he must be my soulmate. I don't need to find the fortune teller after all. I need to tell Myfanwy this as well.

'I need to find my best friend,' I say loudly and Mikey jumps in the air.

'Oh my god, you can *talk*,' he says with amazement.

'Of course I can talk,' I declare, outraged. But doubt creeps in. Maybe this is the first time I've ever talked?

'You sound just like Ginny,' Mikey says now, moving closer and stroking my face. 'But you look like a beautiful unicorn.'

'I am a beautiful unicorn,' I say proudly, knowing for sure that I am. 'I like being a unicorn.'

'Just wait here, you two,' I instruct the old man and Mikey, remembering now that I need Myfanwy. 'Just wait, I need to gallop over to my friend.'

I leave them both and trot around the room, braying and

neighing as I go. I find Toni, sitting with Myfanwy and Sonali still on the sofas in the corner. It feels like years since I left them and I've learned so much about myself in that time. I've learned that I love Daniel but I'm not in love with him anymore. I've learned that we don't belong together. I've learned that Zach definitely isn't interested and he's sorry – and also that's he eighty or ninety years old. I've learned that human beings can be fixed, if we all just decide to be *nice*. And most importantly, I've learned that I am a unicorn, and isn't that just *wonderful*?

Myfanwy and Sonali are serene and peaceful, staring up at the ceiling with their hands intertwined. There is classical music playing on a phone between them. I slump down beside them and Toni. Toni snuggles into my side.

'Can I tell you something, Gin?' Her lovely voice floats through me. 'I think I might be asexual.' I try to focus because this feels important. 'I've never really felt ... attraction.'

'To Shawn?' I ask, turning to wrap my arm around her.

'To anyone,' she blinks. I search for the right words to reassure her; to let her know it's all OK because we're all unicorns, and unicorns are wonderful and precious.

'I—' She is asleep. I stroke her lovely face. 'Love you Toni,' I whisper, hoping I can always be a good big sister to her when she needs me. I close my eyes for a few minutes, letting the feelings and music wash over me. It's lovely. Then I remember.

'Myfanwy, I needed to tell you something,' I say and am

amazed again that I can talk. I must be an extra magical unicorn. 'I solved everything! These mushrooms are incredible, I get everything now, I know what the fortune teller wanted me to do. I know who my soulmate definitely isn't. I get it.' Myfanwy looks baffled by my words but *I know* I am making sense. I know it. 'This is big stuff,' I tell her with urgency. 'I've spent six months feeling confused and scared, but I don't anymore. I know who I am and I can be brave. I know how to fix my life!' I feel my eyes widen as it hits me. I understand the rest of it suddenly, too. I take a deep breath, gripping Myfanwy by the shoulders. 'Oh my god, Myfe, I get it now. I *get it*. The prediction! The honeymoon wasn't it – it's tonight.' She blinks with confusion. 'TONIGHT,' I shout in her face. 'This is my life-changing trip!'

CHAPTER TWENTY-SIX

The next morning, it takes approximately six minutes for me to remember my conversation with Zach and die a thousand deaths.

I cannot believe I said those things. OUT LOUD. To him! Having already been rejected by him a couple of months ago, I basically requested another rejection. I asked him for a confirmation! I pretty much begged him to explain that he doesn't fancy me.

Jesus Christ. I can never speak to him again.

And of course, I may not have to, I realize, remembering what he said about leaving the store. I'm in shock that Celeste has let him go. He's been such a great addition to the team; it makes no sense.

I groan as I roll over – thankfully in my own bed – and consider the rest of the evening. I'm surprised to find that, mortification aside, I still have the same clarity and certainty I felt last night. I still feel totally sure that it's over with Daniel.

And I remember that I am a unicorn.

The thing I have lost, sadly, is some of the bravery I felt about it all last night.

It all felt very easy and straightforward but this morning I don't have any clue on *how* to move forward with this new certainty. How do I tell Daniel I don't want to be with him anymore? What words do you use to cushion that? What time of day do you go for? What place do you meet that will make it better? Honestly, I'm kind of starting to understand why he just packed his bag and ran away. Sadly, I don't think I really have that option. Not when I have a sister who constantly tags me into places online.

I moan again slightly.

Someone moans back and I jump a little as a shape moves at the bottom of the bed. It takes a moment for the memory to come back to me. Myfanwy stayed over.

Another shape shifts on the sofa bed. Oh yes, so did Sonali.

'Morning,' I say sleepily.

After my life-changing revelation last night about Daniel, not to mention my humiliating encounter with Zach, I wasn't exactly my horniest self for Mikey. We all came down pretty fast and decided to call it a night, with Mikey running off sharpish. So, after all my careful pre-planning to get some, we did not sleep together. We didn't even kiss, actually.

'How are we feeling?' Myfanwy says in a yawn, stretching out to the ceiling. Thankfully, it's not neon white or moving, I note. I was slightly concerned that could be my new normal.

'Not too bad,' Sonali yawns back and I nod blearily.

'Surprisingly good,' I confirm. 'Maybe drugs are the way to go from here on out.'

'I can't see any problem with that,' Myfanwy comments dryly.

'God,' Sonali sighs. 'Last night was a bit dramatic.'

Myfanwy fists her eye, picking at a stubborn bit of sleepy dust before fixing her gaze on me. 'I can't believe you had three men there fighting over you.'

I shake my head vehemently, then regret it. I'm a little fragile.

'If anything, I was fighting for their attention, Myfe.' I throw my face into a pillow. 'I threw myself at Zach.'

'At *Zach*?' Myfanwy looks amused. 'Well, I saw that coming a mile off. But I thought you were just mates now? Didn't he tell you at Diane's wake that he just wanted to be friends?'

Muffled by the pillow, I reply, 'He did, but after all the shrooms, I decided it would be a good idea to check.'

'No one says *shrooms*.' Sonali sounds bored.

'Ooh.' Myfanwy's tone is impressed. 'That's very *men* of you, Gin. Refusing to take no for an answer. How embarrassing.'

'Yes, thank you for that,' I tell her into the pillow. I sigh now, sitting up. 'And Mikey ran off at the end, so I don't think he's very interested either.'

'I think that was Shawn's fault actually,' Sonali comments and I narrow my eyes at her.

'What do you mean?'

She raises her eyebrows. 'Didn't you see them having that argument?'

Shaking my head, I sit up straighter. 'What? Are you serious? Why is that man always getting into fights with strangers!'

'He's an arse,' Myfanwy comments dryly. 'What is Toni doing with him?'

'I really don't know.' I feel intensely sad suddenly. I think about our conversation last night. Will she remember what she said about being asexual? Should I bring it up with her or let her come to me when she's ready? 'I thought Gen Z were all supposed to be badasses who take no shit and know exactly who they are. But Tone seems to be quite insecure and unsure about everything. She can do so much better than Shawn.'

'Never mind doing better!' Sonali raises her voice, outraged. 'She's in her early twenties! She should be single AF and out there having loads of fun and random sex.'

'Hold on,' I whisper, standing up and reaching for my dressing gown. I press my ear to the wall, listening for any noise. 'It's OK, I'm pretty sure she stayed at his.'

We fall silent, considering our collective baby sister.

'You know she mentioned the possibility of them getting engaged,' I say in a quiet voice. 'On the honeymoon trip.' Myfanwy nods slowly as Sonali looks aghast.

'She can't!' she wails as Myfanwy shakes her head in agreement.

'I think you should talk to her about him,' she tells me and I nod. I'd come to the same conclusion. Usually my rule is never to get involved in other people's relationships but I honestly can't believe she's happy with Shawn.

'I think I have to,' I swallow, before looking up. 'Unless one of you wants to do it for me?' I smile and they both laugh scornfully. Myfanwy reaches across me for my phone on the bedside table.

'Message her now before you lose your nerve.'

'I don't have any nerve!' I cry, horrified by this suggestion. 'And I don't know what to say! I'm not ready.'

Myfanwy rolls her eyes. 'Just say you need to talk.'

Sighing, I accept my phone and begin typing.

> Hey Tone, can we talk?

Written down, it is too stark. Too direct. I try something else.

> Hey love, how are you feeling this morning?
> Thank you guys so much for putting on such a fun
> night. I hear Shawn and Mikey had a falling out?
> Maybe we should have a chat about it if you're
> around in the next couple of days? Xxxxxx

I don't press send, instead throwing my phone on the bed in frustration. 'Ughhh, I don't think I can do it!' I say in despair. 'It's too awkward and she's going to be so annoyed about me interfering.'

Myfanwy gently retrieves my phone from a squashed pillow. 'I know you don't like confrontation, Gin,' she says gently. 'But this is really important. Toni is important to all of us and we can't just do nothing. She might marry this idiot!'

'It's funny, isn't it,' Sonali begins. 'I feel like we all watched her grow up. She was so young when we first met her.'

'She must've been – what? – like eight? Nine?' Myfanwy chips in affectionately. 'So young.'

'She was really mature and serious, even then,' I say fondly. 'Not like me at that age. I was a pathetic, snivelling little idiot, so scared of everyone around me. So scared of being noticed but also so horrified no one ever did. I have a lot of regrets about the way I acted back then.'

'God, school was just a nightmare for everyone, wasn't it?' Sonali remarks thoughtfully.

'Secondary school was even worse,' I comment, thinking again about that miserable time. 'I was so relieved to get to university and meet you lot. Although, in hindsight, eighteen was really young, too! We felt like grown-ups, but from here, it feels like we were still babies. We knew nothing at all.'

Myfanwy smiles. 'I'm not sure we know anything now, in our thirties.'

'True,' I grin back. 'But we've reached an age where we have to at least pretend.'

Sonali nods. 'I may not know much, but I feel pretty confident that Toni's dating a wrong 'un. And we have to at least try to make her see that.'

'Poor Mikey,' Myfanwy sighs. 'He brought us such a fun party game.'

'You mean the mushrooms?' I confirm and she nods.

'And then he got viciously attacked by an absolute dickhead.'

'I'll message him later and see if he's OK,' I reassure her.

'Never mind messaging *him*,' Sonali scolds. 'Message Toni. We have to look after our little sister.'

I sigh. 'OK, fine.' I retype my previous draft, adding a few more smiley faces and kisses. Her reply comes fast. And I suddenly remember that I needn't have worried because we were brought up by the same mother. We are both intense people pleasers . . .

> Of course!! I'll be back later. Love you xxxxx

'Phew!' I say, leaning back into the pillows as Sonali and Myfanwy read her reply.

'Apart from Shawn's antics, last night was pretty great, wasn't it?' Sonali says now, smiling impishly at Myfanwy, who grins back.

'I really feel like I figured a lot of things out,' I say, remembering again how clear my thinking was. So many things that seemed impossible to decide when I was sober just seemed obvious all of a sudden. 'It's such a relief finally knowing how I feel about Daniel.' I laugh. 'I still can't believe he turned up like that! So weird that he saw me tagged in the bar on Instagram and just showed up.'

'But prediction number four is *definitely* ticked off now,' Myfanwy says excitably.

'Hmm, maybe . . .' I hedge.

Sonali sighs as Myfanwy makes a frustrated noise. 'Ugh, Gin! When are you going to accept that the predictions are real? It's all coming true! That psychic fortune teller was for real!'

'Sometimes I believe,' I whisper, feeling ganged up on. 'Sometimes it seems definitely real, but it's just . . . mad. It just seems so stupid to believe. I hate the idea that people will think I'm stupid. I feel stupid all the time as it is.'

'Same,' Sonali says sadly. 'I think a lot of people do.'

'Maybe once we've found the fortune teller . . .' I tell her seriously, 'and I've heard it all from her again, maybe I'll fully believe. Maybe . . .'

CHAPTER TWENTY-SEVEN

I unfold the tiny tissue that came with my cocktail. Then I refold it again. Then I use it to mop up the liquid ring left by the glass on the table. I pick up my drink and take a sip. It leaves another wet ring on the table so this time I use the napkin to dry the bottom of the glass, too.

Oh god, I'm super nervous.

'Hiya.' At the sound of the greeting, I look up. Mikey's handsome face smiles back nervously. He looks as scared as me.

This is our first attempt at a sort-of *date*. Our last two meetings have both been fairly spontaneous and random, with all sorts of people around us acting as a buffer.

I thought for sure he'd want nothing more to do with me after he and Shawn fell out the other night. I was so embarrassed and was composing a huge apology text the next day, when the doorbell rang and there were flowers on my doorstep from Mikey, with a note asking me to meet him.

Sonali kept winking at me about that final prediction.

That soulmate one. But that's her, not me! I am definitely not thinking like that right now. It's all too soon after Daniel. I mean, I have only *just* realized I don't want to get back with him! I haven't even told him that fact yet!

Actually, I haven't heard from him since the party; I don't think he much liked seeing me with Mikey.

Or Zach for that matter.

I stand up and Mikey hugs me, holding on for a fraction of a second too long as I melt into him. God, he smells *lovely*. I want to stay there in his arms all evening but he eventually pulls away.

'You look stunning,' he says appreciatively, and then leans in to kiss me on the cheek. My whole body reacts.

'Let's get you a drink!' I say, my breath shallow as I try not to make it too obvious what an effect he has on me.

'Sit down, I'll get it,' he smiles and I do so with relief. My legs are all wobbly.

He's gone a while, trying to get served at the heaving bar. It's Christmas in a week and London is out in force with office dos, mistletoe wielded in every direction as a weapon. There are groups of people in suits all around me wearing Santa hats, and at least a dozen more in awful festive jumpers. Tinsel and fairy lights have lit up the city, but I find I'm dreading the whole thing. I feel unprepared for the year to end.

In part, because in January I officially start at the new store.

Mikey returns at last with drinks for us both and sits heavily.

'I'm so sorry about the other night,' he begins anxiously, searching my face.

'Don't say sorry!' I cry, outraged that he feels so bad. 'Shawn seems to start arguments wherever he goes.' I shake my head. 'To be honest, I don't even know what it was about.'

Mikey's shoulders relax a little, but his voice is still worried. 'It was so stupid, just me trying to be funny. He takes everything so seriously.' He pauses. 'You know what I'm like, don't you? You know it was just a joke?'

'Yes, of course.'

'Whatever he says, I was just messing about, being silly.'

'I get it.' I try to sound reassuring but feel a bit uneasy. He seems so concerned. I don't remember Mikey being so bothered by what other people thought before. Was there more to it?

'It's just . . .' he begins, looking down at his drink. 'It's just that I *really* like you.'

Oh.

He takes a deep breath. 'I don't want some stupid comment Shawn might make a big deal over to ruin what we could have. I *really* like you.'

I can feel myself smiling, hard. He likes me.

'I like you, too,' I tell him shyly. 'Please don't worry about Shawn – I'm going to talk to Toni about him. She really can do so much better.'

He grins, tucking hair behind his ear and taking my hand as we change the subject.

Conversation flows easily as we cover work, friends, the ridiculous things we saw while on mushrooms, the times we had in our early twenties when we last dated. It's lovely and easy. It always is with Mikey.

I get drunk quickly on the cocktails and his compliments, so when he moves his chair closer to kiss me, I kiss him back hungrily. I don't care who's watching.

'Come home with me,' he pulls back, speaking with urgency, almost panting. I nod, unable to speak as we gather our coats and run outside. He's ordered an Uber within seconds and the Ford Mondeo pulls up only two minutes later. We climb in, laughing and touching.

As we move off, my phone buzzes. Glancing at it, my stomach turns over at the sight of Toni's name.

I still haven't spoken to her about Shawn. Or seen her, for that matter. She said she'd be back at Celeste's that same day, but there was no sign of her. I messaged her again yesterday and she said she'd be back today, but she still wasn't back by the time I left a few hours ago.

> Hey, where are you? I'm home xxxxx

Of course she is. The first time I'm out for the night, she's back.

> Sorry, I'm out with Mikey. You around tomoz? Xxxxx

Her reply is instant.

> You're still seeing Mikey? After what happened? xx

Wow, only two kisses, she is *furious*. Furious about what? Hmm, I guess Shawn will have his side of the story, which will be that Mikey was horrible and cruel. Of course Toni's taken Shawn's side.

Maybe Mikey was meaner than he let on?

I glance over at him now, on the other side of the car, looking out at the passing London landscape lit up by festive lights, while holding tightly to my hand between us.

No way. We've already seen so much evidence of Shawn's awfulness, and his tendency to massively overreact and start fights.

I suddenly feel cross. Toni's trying to tell me who I should and shouldn't be seeing, while she's dating one of the worst men on Planet Earth! She's my little sister – she should be listening to *me*. I shouldn't have to listen to her!

I reply, feeling Myfanwy's strength in my fingers.

> Yes, of course. We can talk about it tomorrow but Shawn should really apologize. Mikey was joking. I don't want to upset you, sorry. Xx

OK, it's probably not very Myfanwy in its tone, but that's as strong as I'm capable of being, even after five cocktails.

My heart pounds as she replies fast. I don't want to look.

> I'm not upset, Gin, but that's not what happened. Can you come home so we can talk? I think you should hear Shawn out. He's here with me xx

Ugh, Shawn's there with her. I re-read the message, my brow furrowing. What does that mean? So he doesn't think Mikey was joking? Obviously he doesn't, otherwise he wouldn't have reacted so badly. But that doesn't mean Mikey was at fault.

She messages again.

Please xxxxxxxxxxx

I let go of Mikey's hand, suddenly feeling intensely cold and unsexy. He glances over at me in surprise.

'You OK?' he says, registering my face. I shake my head.

'I've just had a bit of an argument with my sister on text.'

'Oh shit.' He shuffles as close as the seatbelt will allow. 'I'm sorry, that's horrible. Do you want to talk about it?'

See? He's *so nice*. Maybe I should just ignore Toni's message, try to forget it and go have an amazing night with Mikey. I can deal with the fallout of Shawn's crap tomorrow.

I re-read her last message.

Please xxxxxxxxxxx

I sigh heavily. 'I'm really sorry, Mikey, but do you mind if I head home? I need to talk to her and I won't be able to have fun tonight with that weighing on me.'

His face falls but he recovers quickly. 'Yeah, of course.' He pauses. 'Are you sure though? I could really cheer you up, y'know? Take your mind off it, and she'll still be around tomorrow?' He smiles cheekily and I giggle.

'It's tempting, but I don't think I'd be able to give you my full attention.' I smile bashfully. 'And I really want to. Can we pick this up later in the week?'

'Sure,' he smiles sadly, before leaning forward to redirect our driver.

Minutes later I'm outside my mum's house and he leaps out to hug me goodbye. 'Wow,' he says, taking in the tall Edwardian building surrounded by elegant fencing. 'Your mum's house is amazing.'

I nod, embarrassed. It is beautiful, but it's not my home. I would do almost anything to be living somewhere else, in my own space.

'I'll message you tomorrow,' I promise as I chastely kiss him on the cheek and hurry inside. Time to face the music. And Shawn. Ugh.

CHAPTER TWENTY-EIGHT

I walk into the house feeling head-to-toe dread. I hate confrontation. And I mean *I hate* confrontation. Toni and I argued as kids, but with our age gap, it wasn't ever really that much. She only got annoying just as I was heading off to university. And since then, we've just been pals.

I hate that we're about to have a fight. And I really hate that it's about men we're dating.

I am so coiled and ready for Toni that I'm taken by surprise when I enter the kitchen and find Celeste sitting at the kitchen table, a large brandy in front of her.

'Oh, it's you, Mum!' I say in shock and she cocks her head.

'Is it so horrifying to find your mother in her own kitchen?' she says with mock-hurt. 'I should be more surprised to see *you*. I thought you were staying out at Myfanwy's tonight?'

'Change of plan,' I say conversationally, listening out for sounds of life in the rest of the house.

'What was the change of plan?' she demands and I try not to sigh out loud. 'You *were* with Myfanwy, weren't you?'

'Er yes,' I hedge. I hate lying, but no way was I going to tell her I had a date with my ex-boyfriend, Mikey. She'd have my wedding rearranged in ten minutes flat. 'Myfanwy decided she wanted a romantic night in with Sonali,' I explain, avoiding eye contact.

'Hmm,' she says, but the usually lengthy interrogation ends there.

'Are you OK?' I ask, looking at her closer. She looks tired and sad. Her sparkle isn't quite so bright.

She shrugs. 'The media hates the new range.' She says it casually but I hear the wobble in her voice.

'Oh no,' I say, taking a seat at the table across from her. 'What have they said?'

She throws a newspaper on the table between us and I pick it up, scanning an article that talks about Celeste jumping on a bandwagon nobody wants to ride. How she's trying to attract the young and all she's doing is alienating her customer base. There is a lot about how hideous the items themselves are, too, but a lot of it seems to be a personal attack on Celeste's ego. Bizarrely, the piece is right next to a brightly illustrated Q&A with the *Love Island* star who's fronting the range, talking about her exes and which couples she's rooting for on the latest series. It comes with a credit underneath explaining where and how you can order Celeste's 'exciting' new range.

I tut. 'That's horrible. I'm really sorry, Mum.' I pause. 'But this is just one idiot's opinion!'

She shakes her head. 'All the papers say the same sort of

thing. That I've let fame go to my head and think I can do no wrong.'

I'm silent for a moment. 'I'm sorry.'

She looks up and smiles wanly. 'The bloggers and the influencers are all posting nice things though!' she says brightly before adding, 'But that might be because we gave them all endless freebies and even paid a few of them.'

'I'm sure they wouldn't write it if they didn't mean it though,' I say fiercely.

'That's true,' she says, looking a bit happier. 'And they haven't seen the new store yet! I'm sure they'll come around when they see it. This is going to take us to the next level.'

'But,' I begin carefully, not wishing to kick her when she's so very down, 'what's wrong with our current level? We are so bespoke and curated. That's why our clients love us. We can spend hours with them, talking them through what they want, making sure they have something that will be adored and treasured and handed down from parent to child to grandchild, forever.' I spread my hands wide. 'I love our store and I think what we do is amazing. It doesn't need to be more mainstream or reality show-friendly, does it? That's why I thought the engagement concierge idea—'

She doesn't let me finish. 'Oh, for goodness *sake*,' she says. 'Will you stop going on about that? I've told you no, let it go!'

'Sorry,' I say in a whisper, feeling stupid and crushed.

'Never mind,' she says breezily, her anger already forgotten. 'You better get to bed, it's late.'

I creep upstairs, spotting the light under Toni's door. I

could just sneak past, couldn't I? I could go to bed and nurse
my latest Celeste wound. I could deal with this conversation
in the morning. I could hide until Shawn goes home and
then speak to Toni on her own. After all, it's hardly fair that
it's going to be two on one anyway, is it?

I sigh and knock on her door.

A worried Toni opens it seconds later, her face sagging
with relief when she sees it's me.

'Ginny!' she says with such joy that I forget for a moment
that we're mid-pseudo-argument. She pulls me in for a hug
and behind her I spot Shawn, perched on the bed, looking
sulky. 'I'm so glad you came home, thank you!'

Her warmth knocks me completely off my stride. I'd come
in here ready to defend myself and Mikey, but instead I find
myself apologizing and nearly crying.

'Guys,' I say emotionally, 'I'm sorry your special night got
ruined, I'm really sorry. Mikey didn't mean it – he was just
joking, I'm so sorry, Shawn, he didn't want to upset you. Are
we OK? I'm really sorry.'

Toni takes my hand and leads me to the bed. 'Sit down,
Gin,' she says nicely, but it feels too intimate to sit between
them on the bed, so I select a beanbag and sit across from them.

'You have nothing to be sorry about,' Toni says earnestly.
'You've done nothing at all.' She nudges Shawn beside her,
who looks sullen.

I wait, a little confused by what's happening here.

After some resentful seconds, Shawn uncrosses his defensive arms and finally makes eye contact with me.

'What did Mikey say happened?' he asks and I can tell he is trying.

I shrug lightly. 'That he made a stupid joke and you over-reacted.' I look away, embarrassed. 'He's sorry. He was just drunk, or high, or whatever. It wasn't very nice, I'm sorry.'

Shawn takes a moment. 'He's got a girlfriend,' he says at last and my stomach falls through the floor. 'We were chatting about being the new members of the Bretherton clan and what an, er, *interesting* family you are.' He takes a deep breath, looking a bit guilty. 'Mikey clearly thought me and him were buddy–buddy – the outsiders of the group – because he then decided to tell me about the woman, Janine, who he lives with and has been with for two years.'

I can't move. 'Wait, *what*?' I shake my head, trying to order my thoughts. Mikey has a girlfriend? But he can't. He wouldn't *do* that. Would he?

Shawn looks furious. 'He was boasting about how he was going to bed the famous Celeste Bretherton's daughter again and tell all his mates about it. All while Janine was none the wiser.'

This can't be true, surely. I would've been able to tell? He said he really liked me. I look between Toni and Shawn again, shaking my head for the fiftieth time.

Am I just supposed to believe all this? It seems absolutely insane. Surely Mikey would never do that? He would never be that cunning or calculated. He wouldn't *use* me like that.

'Gin, are you OK?' Toni's voice is soft.

No way. It cannot be true. He wouldn't do that.

That would be next-level evil. Next-level arseholery. There's no way.

I look at Shawn.

Mikey has been nothing but lovely to me. Nothing but sweet and adorable and kind and brilliant. He's showered me with affection and compliments – he even sent me flowers! Meanwhile, all I've seen of Shawn is crappy mean-spirited spite and jealousy. He's petty and small and unkind. Plus, I've actually technically known Mikey for, like, ten years! Of those two people who am I going to believe?

Shawn looks back at me, pre-wounded, ready for me to accuse him of lying. Ready to attack, ready to shout and scream and tell me how much his ugly shoes cost.

And I believe him.

Fuck. I hate myself but I believe him.

Which means Mikey is a complete and utter – *complete and utter* – bollock-headed bastard of the worst order. And I'm SO done with him.

CHAPTER TWENTY-NINE

The next morning, Myfanwy is on my doorstep with ice cream.

'Déjà vu,' I mutter, thinking of the aftermath of my break-up with Daniel, as she pushes past me and up to my bedroom. I thought things were bad at that point, but the bad has just piled on top of bad since.

'Toni told me,' Myfanwy says, flopping onto the bed, lobbing Ben & Jerry's at me. 'Mikey is a piece of shit scumbag. He's completely undone all the calm I felt after I went to Reiki yesterday. What are we going to do to destroy him?'

I shake my head, feeling defeated, and place the ice cream on my dresser. 'Nothing.'

She blinks. 'What do you mean, nothing? He tried to get you into bed, with a poor unaware girlfriend at home! He's a pig and needs telling off.'

'What's the point?' I say listlessly.

She narrows her eyes. 'What's the *point*? The point is to make sure he knows he's hurt you.'

'He was going to take me back to his,' I comment distractedly. 'Last night. We were in a taxi heading back to his flat.
She must've been away. But how disgusting is that?' I furrow
my brow, thinking about how he must've carefully hidden
away her things before our date. I picture him stowing away
any photos of the two of them, concealing her toothbrush,
hiding her shower gel. The deception itself is disgusting, but
that level of effort somehow makes it worse. I can't understand, it just doesn't make any *sense*.

I try to believe people are inherently good, I really do.
I have always wanted to see the best; I believe people are
a product of where they've come from and mostly deserve
pity when they mess up. Because how else do you get
through the day?

Am I really this stupid? This naïve?

I thought I knew Mikey. He knew me before Mum was on
TV. We dated for, like a year, and it was good . . . wasn't it?

But I thought everything with Daniel was perfect. I am
an unreliable narrator of my own life. I look back at things
with rose-tinted specs and with too much hope.

I try to remember my time with Mikey again now with
clear eyes. My early twenties seem so long ago, so fuzzy. I was
a different Ginny and yet, when I recall specific moments,
I'm looking at everything with the same eyes; the same brain.

I remember laughing a lot with him. About stupid stuff
and serious stuff. I remember having loads of fun. I remember
going to clubs and dancing until the early hours. I remember
constantly drinking and constantly eating pizzas.

Lucy Vine

But some of the bad stuff comes back now, too. There was fun, yes, but also lots of arguments, now that I think about it. He was flaky, not showing up to dates when he said he would, not texting me back, always commenting flirtily on Instagram photos of women he said were just mates. But we were all so young and immature back then, none of it seemed like red flags.

Oh god, I bet he was a cheat back then, too.

I feel like such a fool.

'He is gross,' Myfanwy wrinkles her nose. 'And we have to do something. I'm too angry to figure out any option beyond murdering him in cold blood right now.' I stay silent, feeling detached, so she continues. 'Obviously we can't really kill him. But could we just kidnap him for a bit? It would barely be a crime! We don't have to tie him up or anything, just lock him in a basement or something for a week or two. A month tops.'

I smile weakly. 'He would deserve it.'

She looks at me impatiently. 'You're going to at least let him have it, right? Tell him he's a fucking louse and you hope he gets syphilis?' Her face lights up with an idea. 'Maybe we should contact the girlfriend on social media, or something? She deserves to know.'

I slowly shake my head, feeling far away from this conversation, from this room, from Myfanwy. 'I can't,' I tell her simply.

She stands up, looking infuriated now. 'What do you mean, you *can't*, Ginny? You can't just let him get away with this.'

276

'What's the point in confronting him?' I say, feeling desperate. 'He'll just laugh at me, then saunter off into the night and do it to someone else.'

'He might not!' she says with frustration. 'It could actually get through to him that he's been a dick and that he needs to change. If he hears it enough, from enough people, he might try and work on himself. You could be the final voice that pushes him to be a better person. But even if it doesn't have any impact, don't you want to tell him how much he's hurt you?'

I look at the floor, feeling too broken for this. 'Could I not just take to my bed and eat ice cream?' I ask, looking longingly at the tub she's brought. I sigh, continuing, 'I know you want me to be strong, Myfe, but what's the point? It's all fate, isn't it? Isn't that what you believe in? What's the point in trying to be better or trying to take control when it's all preordained? I've been cursed with these predictions, which are determined to ruin my life, and they have. So well done, fortune teller! It's all fucked. Everything I've tried to make work, every time I've tried to move on has blown up in my face. I might as well accept it.'

There is a long silence between us before Myfanwy speaks at last in a quiet voice. 'I'm getting a bit sick of this actually.'

'Sick of what?' I blink.

'Sick of you blaming the predictions for everything,' she spits. 'One minute you're complaining about this *curse*, as if it's responsible for every life choice you've ever made. And then the next minute you're saying you don't even believe in it. So, which is it, Ginny?' She narrows her eyes at me, waiting for a response. But I have none. She continues, looking furious, 'You have to start taking responsibility for things. You ignored your problems with Daniel, and then pretended the break-up hadn't even happened. Then when he saunters back into your life with barely an apology you just, like, *giggle* and tell him not to worry. You even let him hang out with us at Toni's birthday and do mushrooms with us! What the fuck was that! You don't even want to get back with him – you just can't stand the idea of upsetting him or making him accountable for behaving badly. And now you're letting Mikey do the same thing!' She's on one now, picking up the pace. 'And the situation with your mum is the worst part! You've let Celeste steamroll you for *years* on end and then you're upset at being flattened again! You let her control you and refuse to stand up to her. You couldn't even tell her you think the new store is shit when it's been your life's work!'

'I've tried—' I begin but Myfanwy raises her voice.

'Stop justifying it!' she cries. 'Do you understand how miserable and – I'll just say it – *boring* it is to watch you constantly self-sabotage with your people pleasing? It's not like you hate your job and don't care – you *love* it. It's something you really care about and you'll still let someone destroy it rather than actually standing up and telling Celeste *no*.' She is breathing hard as I stand there, in shock. I feel like I've been slapped. 'I'm sick of it,' she says again. 'And until you start taking ownership of your own life, and fighting back instead of letting this shit beat you down, I don't want to hear about it anymore.'

'I'll shut up about everything then, shall I?' I say, trembling with anger. 'I'll just not mention what a catastrophe my life has turned into.'

Myfanwy is purple as she shouts her reply in my face, 'Yes, actually! Fuck it! Just shut up going on and on about how awful things are for you if you're not willing to do anything to make it any better! I've had enough of it. There's only so much I can push you, Ginny, if you're not willing to take any responsibility. Ever!'

For a moment we stare at each other, both breathing hard, both livid. After another second, she storms out of the room, leaving me alone, listening to the sound of her furiously stomping down the stairs, the front door slamming seconds later. I sit heavily on the bed.

That's it then. Everything's fucked.

CHAPTER THIRTY

It takes me about four hours of tossing and turning to finally fall asleep that night. And when I do, my Aunt Diane is there waiting for me.

She's sitting on the end of my bed, like she used to when I was a teenager and she smiles in the same way.

'Hello you,' she says in the same voice as ever.

'Hiya,' I reply like it's nothing. I want to move, I want to hug her, but I am frozen in my bed. 'How come you're here?' I say and she smiles again.

'Do you want me to go?'

'*No*,' I tell her forcefully. 'I really need you. I don't think I've ever needed you this much, and you're not here.'

'Sorry,' she pouts. 'But I am here.'

'You're not really though, are you?' I take her in. She looks real. The end of the bed sinks down as if a real, live person were sitting there. She's got eyebags and stray flyaway hairs around her ponytail. It *is* Aunt Diane.

She doesn't answer and I swallow hard, my throat dry and sore. 'Everything's gone wrong,' I tell her weakly. 'Daniel dumped me, you died.' I pause. 'You know a bunch of guys had a fight over you at your funeral?'

She nods happily. 'Yeah, I saw, that was hilarious. I'm a hot mess even when dead.'

I smile. 'Celeste loved it, too. You and her are quite similar sometimes.' I take a deep breath. 'Mum's being a nightmare and destroying the family business we built up together. I got used by a cheating idiot, I scared off a new friend, Zach, by being a sex pest. And now Myfanwy's upset with me, on top of everything.'

'It's been difficult for you,' she acknowledges and I drink in her sympathy. It's all I wanted from Myfanwy. All I needed was a little support.

I cock my head, remembering the holiday. 'Were you there when we did the Ouija board in Madeira? I tried to talk to you,' I ask, and she nods, smiling.

'I saw you snogging that young man, too.'

'Embarrassing,' I acknowledge, looking away.

'You should've called him,' she tells me. 'You deserve to have more fun. I don't know why you give yourself such a hard time about the big life stuff. You need to just enjoy the silly little bits in between.'

'That's sort of what the tarot reader said,' I tell her. 'But she did it with pictures.'

'I think you're old enough to follow what I'm saying without a visual aid,' she says wryly, arching an eyebrow. 'I know

281

it hasn't been an easy year for you, Ginny my love, but it's been an important one.'

'Has it?' I say desperately. 'It hasn't felt important, it's felt wretched.'

'I know.' She reaches out a hand that looks solid and I want so badly to take it but I still can't move. 'But think about it. You were about to marry Daniel, which you now realize would've been a mistake. You wouldn't have been happy with him in the end. Even the situation with Mikey was helpful. You got to put that relationship to bed, without taking him to bed – and realize he wasn't a good guy. And I think having to move in here, with Celeste, might be the universe trying to force you to confront your issues with her.'

'What about Myfanwy?' I whine. 'Why did I need her to have a go at me like that?'

Diane sighs. 'Wow, you really are feeling sorry for yourself.' She tuts. 'Myfanwy loves you dearly, and she wants the best for you. That's all her outburst was about. She has been your shield from the real world a lot over the years, and she's probably been hoping you would build one of your own.'

'Oh,' I say, trying not to cry. I look at her, wondering if I'll ever see her again. 'But what about losing you? That wasn't important, that was just horrible.'

She laughs. 'That's true. But it's also just life. Things happen and you're allowed to be sad about them, but you can't let it dictate what happens next. You get to make choices – not about everything, it's true. But you can choose how you react to things, you can *choose* to be brave and strong.' She pauses. 'And being strong doesn't mean you can't ask for help, by the way. Oftentimes asking for help is the biggest show of bravery there is. Nobody should have to go through difficult times alone, if they don't want to. And I know it feels like it right now, but you're not alone.' I nod, looking down as she continues, 'In some ways I think losing me might've been necessary for you. If Myfanwy has been your shield in life, I was Celeste's. I kept her grounded in some ways, and protected you and Toni from the worst of her impulses.'

'She's been so much worse since you've been gone,' I nod emphatically.

'I know,' she grimaces apologetically. 'But you're a grown-up, Gin. You can tell her to back off. You can tell her she's wrong. You can even tell her to fuck off occasionally.' She grins mischievously, 'I certainly did.' She shuffles closer and the duvet lightly bounces and musses around her. 'You have to learn to stand up for yourself, my love. Focus on what makes *you* happy. Your friends, your work, Toni. It's time to stop obsessing over those predictions, especially that last one. A soulmate can be anything you want it to be.' She pauses, leaning in closer so I can see the pores on her nose and the mole on her cheek. 'Ginny, this will come as a shock to someone brought up and brainwashed by Celeste Bretherton, but I'm telling you, you can be your own soulmate.'

She takes my hand and I can feel the warmth of her fingers as she intertwines them with mine.

'And Merry Christmas,' she says lightly.

I snort, realizing it's Christmas Eve tomorrow. 'Oh yeah! And there's a ghost in my bedroom. I guess that makes this *A Christmas Carol?*'

'Which would make you Ebenezer Scrooge?' she enquires, eyes wide.

We both laugh, still holding hands. I close my eyes for a minute, thinking about what she's said – all that Diane wisdom and kindness – and after a few seconds, I fall asleep. But even asleep, I can still feel the weight of her hand on mine.

CHAPTER THIRTY-ONE

I'm crying when I wake up and my hand feels cold. I lie there in my bed for a few minutes, trying to make sense of everything. It all felt so vivid and real, was that really Diane? Or, more likely, am I going mad?

I head downstairs to make myself a coffee. I feel groggy and weird. Confused and low as I try to process the last few days. I put the kettle on and glance out of the window.

It's her. That woman. She's standing on the other side of our fence like she always does, looking up at the house. Looking up at my bedroom window. At the room she used to visit and play in when we were kids.

It's *her*, I know it's her. It's prediction number five: my Ghost of Christmas Past.

Something in me loosens and I find myself running for the front door. I'm in *Twilight* pyjamas, mug still in hand, but I don't care.

'Flo?' I shout as I fling the door open. I run towards the woman, 'FLO?'

She turns away, walking fast in the opposite direction, but I'm faster. 'FLO WILLIAMS?' I shout again. 'Don't go! I want to talk. Please can we talk?'

I catch up with her breathlessly and she turns around, surprise all over her face. She's walking a dog, I realize.

'Er, hi?' she says, part scared, part confused. 'Were you shouting at me? Did you say Flo? I'm not Flo, sorry. My name's Sonia Adam-Cash, I live round the corner.'

'God, sorry, I . . .' I fumble my words and glance down at the dog again. 'But I've seen you outside my house.' I wave at the building behind me. 'So many times now! Just standing there, looking in. I thought you were . . . I thought you were my old friend Flo Williams . . .'

I'm aware I sound like I've completely lost it.

The woman grimaces. 'Um, sorry.' She gestures at her dog. 'I walk Humphrey here along this road every day. He likes to poo on the pavement right there.' She points at the spot outside our house. The spot where she's always standing.

'But you . . .' I pull out my trump card. 'I've seen you duck down when I look out. Trying to hide!'

She looks at me askance. 'I mean, I've never *tried to hide*. I guess what you were seeing was me picking up the poo. I promise, I wasn't looking in your house, I was just day-dreaming while he pooed. He's quite old and slow with his constitutionals these days.' She shrugs as Humphrey the dog looks up at me, panting happily, tongue out.

Oh god. I could never see her bottom half because the fence blocked it. I never saw the dog pooing, just a woman – who actually doesn't look familiar at all up close – standing there outside my house for a few minutes every day.

'Um, I . . . I'm sorry.' I swallow hard, very aware of my pyjamas. What must she think? This mad woman accosting her like this about her daily dog walk. 'I'm really sorry.' I start to babble, wanting her to understand, needing to explain. 'I got dumped by my fiancé this year, and then my aunt died and I lost my flat.' I glance back at the house. 'I had to move in with my mum who is a total nightmare. Then I got rejected by this guy who looks like a film star.' I swallow. 'Or maybe a TV star, Toni still can't remember. Then I thought I'd met my soulmate in an ex and it turned out he was a total knobhead cheater who had a girlfriend.' The woman's eyes get wider and she's staring at me bug-eyed. Humphrey looks more sympathetic and I fight the urge to throw myself onto him for a cuddle. 'And now it looks like my ex-fiancé wants to get back together but I've realized I don't love him anymore and I don't know how to tell him that after five years together. And now I've fallen out with my best friend, too.' The lump in my throat threatens to turn into hot tears. 'She says I'm letting all this stuff happen *to* me and not taking any ownership. She thinks I need to stand up for myself and tell people off when they hurt me, and I know she's right. My aunt – the dead one – told me so last night. And then I thought my old best friend, Flo – my *first* best friend – was here and my life was literally *A Christmas Carol*.' I wave in the woman's direction. 'I've had so many signs from the universe that I should try and make up with her – I've met so many people called Williams, or variations of it, especially this year, and I thought maybe she was coming here to my childhood home, trying to work up the courage to knock and see me. I thought she wanted to be friends again and forgive me, but you're a stranger and I'm very clearly freaking you out. But you don't get it – it's these six predictions I got when I was sixteen and they've ruined my life.'

I finish abruptly and she gapes for a second, before finally speaking, 'Er, yeah, getting dumped is rough,' she says at last and I try not to laugh at the one thing she's pulled out of all of that nonsense.

'Thanks, Sonia,' I nod.

'Er, I better get Humphrey home . . .' she says awkwardly and I nod.

'Yeah! Cool, cool, cool! I totally have stuff to do as well.' I shake my head. 'Got to fix my life, y'know? Got to be braver and tell people what I think!' I laugh maniacally and she edges away backwards, yanking at the lead. I point a thumb back at the house, shout *bye* and walk – trot – back inside.

I have a feeling Sonia will be taking a different route on her dog walks with Humphrey from here on out.

CHAPTER THIRTY-TWO

Of course it's not as easy as realizing I've been a fool and sorting myself out overnight.

For the next two weeks, I am on autopilot. It's busy at Celeste's Stones with the Christmas rush and prepping for the new store. Christmas Day comes and goes with minimal fuss and only one text – slash guilt-trip – from Daniel. Toni, Celeste and I exchange presents at home and no one mentions Myfanwy or Daniel or Mikey or Zach – or any other relationships I've managed to mess up lately.

I fully indulge in the self-pity and self-loathing; arriving home from work each evening to stare at my reflection. I call myself names – all kinds of horrible names – and it makes me feel better to begin with. I'm feeding that dark place in my soul that believes I am the worst of the worst. That rat part of me wants to hear the horribleness, the meanness leaking out of me and into me. But after a few days, the catharsis of spite and rage against myself wears off and I feel at last the raw painful wound underneath.

I think about Diane and her kindness. I think about how much she loved me. I think about how much Toni loves me. About how much Celeste loves me – in her own way. I think about how much my dad loves me, wherever he is in the world right now. I think about how much Myfanwy and Sonali love me. Usually. Even Daniel loves me, I think, which, yes, is a problem, but it's also nice to be loved, right? I remember how unbelievably lucky I am to have all these people in my life.

As the world celebrates another New Year, I stand in front of the mirror and try saying kind words. I tell my reflection that I am a nice person. That I try to do my best. I tell myself things I think Diane would say to me, or Myfanwy, when she liked me.

I tell myself that I am capable of change; of being stronger and braver. Of not obsessing over the wrong things or taking bad behaviour lying down.

After all, Myfanwy is right, of course she is. Why should I shield Mikey from hearing that he's hurt me? Why should I protect Daniel from my pain? Why am I lying to my mother about this terrible expansion plan? Even if she doesn't listen, I deserve to be heard. As much as anyone, I deserve to have my opinions and my voice listened to.

And it turns out, saying kind things to yourself, while horribly uncomfortable, also *works*. I feel better. I feel happier. I like myself more. Because words are powerful.

I remember Diane said something like that to me once. She told me when I'm anxious or nervous, I should try smiling. Smiling tricks your brain into thinking everything is fine and good. It makes your body relax and release happy hormones. I think there's something in that when it comes to how we speak to ourselves. If we're lovely to ourselves, we can trick our brains into believing the loveliness and liking who we are that bit more.

And I don't care if it's a trick because I wake up late that Saturday morning in early January, the sun bursting through the outline of my curtains, and I feel . . . joyful. Happy and calm. They are unfamiliar emotions after so many roller-coaster months of pain and loss and ups and downs.

I know what I have to do and I feel like I have the strength to do it at last. Or, at least, I *will* have the strength, once I've got my best friend back by my side.

CHAPTER THIRTY-THREE

Myfanwy doesn't answer my call and for a minute my heart is seized with the fear that I'm too late. What if she's really had enough of my weakness and cowardice? What if this silence has proved to her that I'm not worth being her friend?

A big part of me wants to lie down and accept this. But that's the old Ginny and we like the new purposeful Ginny.

The answer, I decide, is to *show* Myfanwy that I'm capable of change. I pull Mikey's last message out of my archive and re-read it. He'd sent it the morning after I ditched him in the taxi after our date.

> How's your day going? Did you make up with your sister? x

It was slightly more subdued than any of his previous messages and it was clear he was hedging his bets; hoping I might buy the line he'd emphasized so aggressively on the date: that

he was kidding about all of it and he really, really liked me.
At the time I furiously archived him, feeling white hot rage.
But it's time to reply.

I start typing.

> Hey hey, Happy New Year! OMG so sorry for the delay,
> I've had the maddest couple of weeks with Christmas/
> NYE and the new store launching. My mum's had me
> running around non-stop. Hope you've had a lovely one
> with your family? All good with Toni – Shawn came up
> with some laughable rubbish about your argument, but
> everyone knows he's a liar. So anyway, is it too late to
> pick up where we left off? Do you fancy meeting at my
> house tonight at 7pm? G xx

I slightly vomit in my mouth at this. Especially when Mikey
wastes no time in replying.

> There's an offer I can't refuse!!! I'm getting
> in the shower right now (stop picturing me
> naked, you minx). Be with you at 7pm xx

The mouth sick is back. I can't believe how repulsive this
man is to me now. I screengrab the exchange and send it
to Myfanwy.

Whether she comes or not, I'm going to confront Mikey
and tell him exactly how he's made me feel. I don't care if
he calls me a bitch or laughs in my face. I don't care if it

doesn't change how he treats women in the future, he still deserves to hear how it's made me feel. *I* deserve for him to hear it.

At 6.45pm, the front door goes and I feel my heart in my chest.

Is it Mikey or Myfanwy?

It's neither.

'Shawn?' I blink in surprise and he pulls a face at my expression.

'Well, excuuuuse me,' he says, barrelling past me and into the hallway. 'Clearly you were hoping for someone else.' He glances around. 'Is Toni upstairs?'

'Oh, right, yes, I think so,' I tell him, distracted. I hadn't prepared myself to deal with Shawn's angry energy.

'I'm here!' Toni sings from the top of the stairs, coming down to greet Shawn. She takes me in. 'You look lovely! Going out?'

'No, actually.' I debate explaining. On the one hand, I'd love to have Toni with me for this. If Myfanwy needs to see me being brave, my little sister needs me to *model* bravery for her. On the other hand, Shawn's here, ugh. Either way though, they deserve a warning, since they're here. I gulp. 'Um, Mikey's on his way over.'

They both explode, shouting at me over each other calling him various names and asking what I'm thinking.

'I know!' I try to be heard over the exasperated din. 'I'm not giving him another chance or anything!' They finally shut up, so I continue, 'I've tricked him into coming over here so I can confront him about his behaviour.' I pause, puffing out my chest. 'I'm being strong!'

From behind me, my favourite voice in the world pipes up. 'It's about bloody time.'

'Myfe!' I whirl around on my heel, taking in my lovely friend's lovely face. 'You came.'

'Too right,' she snorts. 'That screengrab was beyond tantalizing.'

'Thank you,' I say, my bottom lip wobbling.

Sonali trails in right behind Myfanwy, shutting the door behind her. 'Oh, Gin, don't start crying, we're here for fun!'

'Sonali,' I say joyfully as she gathers me up into a big hug. 'I'm so happy to see you both.'

'Same,' Sonali says into my hair. 'Myfe's been a right fucking misery the last couple of weeks. I kept telling her to message you but she said you needed some time to get your head together and figure things out.'

I pull away. 'She was right,' I admit, glancing at my best friend. 'She's always bloody right – it's annoying.' Sonali nods, rolling her eyes.

Myfanwy looks delighted by this. 'Right, where do you want us?' She looks around. 'I assume he'll be here any minute.'

At this, the doorbell goes and I glance around at Myfanwy, Sonali, Toni and Shawn's expectant faces.

'Let's do this,' I say, with grim determination, suddenly not the least bit afraid. I open the door to find a grinning Mikey on the step. The grin fades as he glimpses the group gathered around me, and for a second I think he will make a run for it. Instead, his face crumples in on itself.

'I'm sorry, I'm really fucking sorry,' he whispers hoarsely. 'I know I shouldn't do it but I can't help myself. Please don't tell Janine. Please, I'm really sorry.'

He looks genuinely contrite, broken down by his own stupid male ego.

But instead of comforting him and saying it's all OK – which every awkward, introverted instinct is telling me to do – I pull myself up to my full height.

'You're a cheating prick,' I tell him, as he hangs his head. 'It's despicable and I can't believe I nearly slept with you. I deserve better and so does your girlfriend.'

He's silent for a minute. 'I know,' he admits in a low voice. 'I'm sorry.'

'I don't accept,' I say with feeling. 'Have you done it before? To Janine, I mean. Have you cheated on her before?' He answers this by staring at the ground. 'I guess that's a yes.' I sigh with disgust. 'Well, you're going to tell her, Mikey.'

He looks up at this, horror on his face. 'No, I can't! She—'

'—deserves to know,' I finish for him. 'And she deserves to dump your egomaniac necrotizing arse in the bin where you belong.' His eyes are wild, thinking this over, trying to find a solution.

Myfanwy leans in. 'I'll be checking your Instagram and Twitter and Facebook, and if it looks like you haven't told her in the next week, I'll be messaging her.'

Shawn steps forward. 'And you can try blocking all of us, but we'll just keep popping up with new accounts.'

Sonali pulls out her phone. 'Look at that, Janine's account is public on Instagram, and now I follow her!'

The inevitability hits Mikey and he nods sullenly. 'Fine, I'll tell her.' His bravado mask comes up and he rolls his eyes exaggeratedly. 'Jeez, you're making such a big deal over all of it. It was just a bit of fun.'

'No, *this* was a bit of fun!' I say, smiling widely. 'Now, off you fuck, you cheating knobhead. And please do lose my number forever, won't you?' I slam the door in his face and turn around to my cheering audience. 'Drink?' I suggest, laughing as they all cheer even louder.

'You were amazing!' Shawn says admiringly as we collapse on the sofa with wine. It's the first time he's given any indication that he likes me. 'You did so well!'

'Thanks!' I declare happily. 'That felt really good.' I glance over at him. 'And seriously, Shawn, thanks for telling me about the cheating.'

He puffs out his chest, looking thrilled. 'Of course. You're my sister.'

'Thanks,' I say, surprised by the warmth between us. I actually quite like this side of him. Underneath the vanity and ego and monstrous toxic masculinity, I suspect he's got a decent heart. He was horrified by what Mikey was doing, and he called him out on it. And he backed me up hard out there in the hallway. Maybe he's not such a bad dude after all.

Who would've thought the one guy in all of this who's turning out to be an OK person would be *Shawn*?

Or maybe my benchmark these days is just really, *really* low.

Myfanwy flops down next to me, swigging wine. 'Hey, you really were brilliant back there, Gin, scolding that knobber. I know you don't like confrontation, but you're really good at it!' She laughs and I join in.

'I want you to know that I've heard you; I listened to everything you said,' I promise with sincerity. 'I know you were completely spot on about all of it and I'm determined to be better. I'm working on pleasing myself instead of other people.' I grin and she pulls me in for a cuddle.

'It's only because I want you to be happy,' she tells me, sounding a little bit emotional.

'I know that,' I reassure her. 'And I'm sorry I've been such a broken record about these six predictions.'

'Maybe stop thinking about them as a curse, and instead as a gift?' she suggests, and it reminds me of my visit from Aunt Diane.

'I'm trying,' I nod. 'And I'm going to get control of my life. I'm going to speak to Celeste.'

Myfanwy raises an eyebrow. 'Wow.'

'I want to give the new store a few more weeks,' I explain. 'It's open now, so it's too late to stop it. Plus, she is technically my boss . . .' I pull an awkward face. 'So, I'm going to give the expansion my best try. I'm going to sell the crap out of these hideous new accessories.' Myfanwy snorts at this. 'But if it's not working out, I'm going to be so brave, Myfe, you'll see. I'm going to talk to her about her, er, flaws she might have ...'

'By *flaws*, I assume you mean her refusal to respect any of your boundaries?' Myfanwy giggles and I nod.

'I do indeed mean that. But I at least owe her my best efforts for now on this expansion plan. I want the company to succeed.'

'That's fair enough,' Myfanwy nods. 'And in the meantime, I have an update you are not going to believe.'

I sit up straighter, checking furtively around the room for Sonali. 'About Project Proposal?' I ask in a whisper and she shakes her head.

'Nope! And can I just say, for the record, that it's been *killing* me holding onto this info when we weren't speaking.' I turn to face her, leaning an elbow on the edge of the sofa.

'It killed me too—' I begin but she shushes me.

'I don't mean because I missed you.' She rolls her eyes. 'I *suppose* I missed you.' She grins. 'But I wanted to tell you: the funfair guy finally got back to me!'

'No way, my god!' I gasp, almost spilling wine across my lap.

Myfanwy mirrors my excitement. 'It turns out the fortune teller woman travelled with them for quite a few years but she left a while back ...'

'Oh.' I'm disappointed, but not surprised. Myfanwy gives me a cheeky grin and I realize there is more.

'He told me that the reason she left was that she got *discovered*. She now does readings on a random small fry, local

299

network in East Anglia. She does her psychic readings for an audience now.' I audibly gasp and her smile gets wider. 'That's not even the best bit,' she continues, looking mischievous. 'Guess what her name is?' I feel my brow furrow as Myfanwy bursts out laughing. 'She's called Crystal.' She pauses dramatically, adding: 'Crystal Ball.'

CHAPTER THIRTY-FOUR

'This couple came in the new store the other day – she's pregnant,' I begin, staring blindly at the TV screen in front of us. 'They were called Clive and Irene and said they want to name their kid after both of them.'

Beside me, I feel Myfanwy cock her head. 'Hmm, so that would make it . . .'

We say it at the same time: ' . . . Chlorine!'

She laughs. 'That can't be true – you're making that up,' she says through giggles.

'I swear!' I say, glancing briefly away from the captivating, familiar woman on screen. 'The new store really does attract some, er, interesting people. They're all too cool to breathe the same air as the rest of us.'

'I think Sonali and I will call our daughter Charlotte,' Myfanwy announces, throwing a piece of popcorn in the vague direction of her mouth.

I frown. It's a nice name, but not really in the spirit of our hilariously stupid baby names chat.

She glances over at me, grinning. There's a piece of popcorn sticking to her cheek. 'She'll be named after my favourite type of potato – I think that's really meaningful.'

'Oh phew,' I laugh. 'It was a joke; I thought for a moment you were telling me you guys were actually pregnant.' She doesn't answer and I sideways look over at her again. Oh my god, she's *not*?

'Sorry, what?' Her eyes are glued to the telly. 'I wasn't listening.' She furrows her brows, 'Did you just ask me if I'm *pregnant*? Ew! Gross, no!' She rolls her eyes. 'I think you'd know if we were planning to start a family; it's a bit of a different experience to hetero-pregnancies, you know?'

'Of course,' I mumble, feeling stupid and privileged. She turns her attention back to the TV screen, pointing at the shimmering star up there. 'She is *amazing*! Did you hear what she just said to that guy?'

I return my gaze to the woman in question: Crystal Ball.

It took us some time and some serious deep diving into local TV programming, but last week we managed to locate my life-changing psychic's show. We had to subscribe and download an app onto Myfanwy's TV, and the whole thing keeps crashing, but all the trouble is so worth it. Crystal is an absolute joy.

I watch her now, completely enthralled.

Crystal has her eyes shut as she awaits inspiration, holding the energy of the room with ease. A quivering young man in the front row awaits his future, and at last her eyes fly open and she shrieks, her huge, untamed red hair flailing in the studio wind.

Her hair is phenomenal, I note. It looks slightly like she's wearing a wig on top of another wig but that only adds to the fabulous. The colour is fire orange and moving, like something is alive in there, moving uncomfortably under the top wig beneath heavy studio lights. The orangey effect extends to her skin, which is Tan mom-deep and glistening. Her whole head has the vibe of a lit candle wick, flickering and moving, dimming and brightening.

'I've had a vision!' she hollers now, enormous hoop earrings swaying from her poor earlobe; slightly elongated from prolonged abuse. She gets close to the young man's face and he is *so pale* beside her intense colouring. 'YOU! I can see it – she is coming back to you,' Crystal hisses at him accusatorily.

'She is?' he brightens enormously, some pinkness returning at last to his cheeks. 'That's the best news, thank you so much, Crystal!' He is gushing now. 'Do you know if that means she's forgiven me for sleeping with her mum and—' Crystal doesn't wait for his follow-up question, moving away and up the audience's middle aisle.

'YOU!' She points at a woman in her seventies with audacious purple lipstick, sitting dead centre of the row. 'You,' she says again in a softer tone, getting a faraway look in her eye. 'You have lost people ...' Crystal reaches across other audience members, squishing them without a care. 'And I'm sorry, my love, but you will lose more. There will be an illness, but that won't be the end, though you might think it. There is time for another adventure. Another great love is coming for you.' The woman gasps excitedly and the elderly man beside her looks put out. Crystal turns away from her and towards the camera.

It's like she's looking straight at me.

'There's something else,' she says, eyes narrowing. 'Something new. Some*one* new watching.'

Beside me, Myfanwy gasps. 'She means us!'

'She probably gets a notification when someone new downloads the app,' I mutter, a feeling creeping over me. 'We probably just doubled their viewer subscription.'

'No way,' Myfanwy moves away from me and closer to the TV. 'She's talking to us – to *you*.'

On the screen, Crystal looks dazed and far away, but still addresses the camera. 'You need something from me. You have questions. Tell me your questions, concentrate, I can hear you.' Myfanwy makes a choking noise but I am trans-fixed, staring into Crystal's deep, eerily green eyes.

They're probably coloured contacts.

'Talk back to her!' Myfanwy whispers intensely.

'What?' I scoff. 'Don't be silly.'

'I'm not being silly,' Myfanwy glares at me. 'She's the real deal and she's talking to you. Talk to her.'

Sulkily, I begin in a quiet voice. 'I just want to know more about these predictions you made for me when I was sixteen.'

On the telly, Crystal frowns. 'You're not being clear enough; I can't make you out. Focus, I want to help you.'

'OK,' I clear my throat, feeling intensely silly and

embarrassed. 'I want to know what the point of it all was, what was I supposed to learn? Was it all to make me a stronger person?' I pause. 'And where's my soulmate? It's been such a bunch of dead ends this last seven months.'

Crystal closes her eyes on the screen for a moment and when she opens them, her face is clear and serene. Even the oversized hair and earrings have stopped moving. 'I hear you,' she says at last. 'And I have answers.' She smiles. 'But that's all we have time for today. Goodbye for now, everyone.'

The camera pans away, across an awed-looking audience as a voiceover guy tells us this was the last episode of the current series — but we can apply to be in the audience of the next, by emailing or calling this very expensive number. Does that mean it wasn't live? She can't have been talking to me if it wasn't live.

Beside me Myfanwy scrambles for her phone, noting down the details.

'You want to go on the show?' I ask and she shakes her head. 'No.' She stops, looking up at me. 'I mean *obviously yes*. But I'm writing this down so that we can speak to the studio, see if Crystal Ball does private sessions or if she'd be willing to speak to us on the phone.' I nod, feeling very strange. It really did seem like she was speaking to us — or to *me*. What if she really could hear me across the airwaves somehow? What if she really can see into my future?

I switch off the TV and turn to Myfanwy. 'Right, enough spooky stuff, tell me exactly what the plan is for Project Proposal.'

She nods, looking thrilled. 'I've decided on a date!' As I gasp, she adds, 'The third of March.'

'Oh my god,' I breathe. 'Sonali's birthday! Of course! But that's only five weeks away. How many of the ten rings have you got so far?'

'Six,' she confirms and I squeal. I've only helped her source half of those.

Myfanwy grins, glowing with excitement. 'I've decided to throw her a party, and I'll get down on one knee there.'

'Oh, right! Wow!' I am surprised and a little bit unsure about this. Myfanwy obviously knows her best, but I have also known Sonali for a long time. She's not someone who would really like a public proposal, I don't think. She loves a party but for something intensely personal and romantic like this, I really think she'd want privacy.

'It's a good idea, right?' she looks at me eagerly. 'We're such a close-knit group, I think she'd be excited to share the moment with you all.'

'Hmm,' I say, trying to think of a way of framing my thoughts. 'I think . . .' I chicken out. 'I think it sounds lovely!' I swallow hard.

I might've found some bravery in telling Mikey off a couple of weeks ago, but I'm still working on the courage when it comes to talking to loved ones about difficult subjects.

'Great,' she beams. 'I've made some notes about the speech. I'm going to talk her through all those moments I loved her best, when I knew I wanted to be with her forever, then produce the real ring.'

'Has Zach finished it?' I ask, trying to keep my voice neutral. Although Zach's not working at Celeste's Stones anymore, he's been designing Myfanwy's ring in his capacity as a freelancer. We've provided the – hugely discounted – stones and metal though.

I haven't heard from Zach since Toni and Shawn's Christmas party. I still burn with the humiliation, thinking about throwing myself at him like that. But it's more than that: I'm professionally embarrassed, too. I'm the one who brought him on and I made all those big promises about working together – and then Celeste binned him off after only a few short months.

I find myself really missing his company in the quieter moments – of which there are *loads* at the new store. It's dead most days, with just the hideous noise of that dreadful advert playing above my head eight hours a day.

I think about how much we laughed together, and how kind he was. He was nice to be around. And I could use some of his positivity at the new store, watching it fail from the inside out.

Myfanwy reaches across to her bedside table, pulling out a small ring box from under piles of drawer junk. She opens it reverentially and we both blink at the dazzling jewellery inside.

Zach has done an incredible job.

It's very traditional and Myfanwy has gone for a diamond, which I'm delighted about – nothing beats a diamond in my opinion. It's a white gold band, with a majestic, Round

Brilliant cut diamond – I'd estimate just under a carat, maybe 0.86 – mounted with four tall, round claws and nestled between infinity-shaped shoulder diamonds. The smaller stones are set in a double row with mirroring curves that gleam like magic.

'It's perfect,' I breathe out, awed, as Myfanwy's phone buzzes.

'Jesus,' she mutters, looking at the screen. 'It's *Daniel*.'

'What?' I am baffled. 'Why is he texting you?'

She shrugs and opens the message.

I've not heard a lot from him since our life-changing trip on shrooms, when he found me on a date with another man.

To be honest, I've been hoping he'd got the message without me having to talk to him. Except now here he is, messaging my best friend.

Myfanwy reads it out loud.

> Hey Myfanwy, sorry to bother you. I wondered if I could ask your advice about Ginny? Is she still seeing that guy Mikey? I really want to talk to her about how I feel, but I'm also aware how badly I've treated her and don't want to interfere or wreck things if she's happy. Do you think I should just leave her alone now? Would really appreciate your advice. Daniel x

'Fuck.' Myfanwy's eyebrows shoot up and she's looking at me with alarm. 'Is Daniel . . . *growing up*? This is quite a mature message, isn't it? Actually putting your feelings ahead of his? Has he ever done that before?'

I give her a reproachful look before remembering I'd kind of come to the same conclusion about our relationship.

She's right – this doesn't really sound like that Daniel. Like *my* Daniel. The Daniel I dated for five years would never have worried about whether it was going to upset me to turn up or message again. Even the Daniel from a month ago apparently wasn't concerned about how it would affect me when he showed up at that bar trying to make some kind of heartfelt confession.

'I should probably talk to him,' I say hesitantly. 'I mean . . . I should, shouldn't I? If he's making an effort to think about my feelings, I should do the same for him.'

There is a question in my voice and Myfanwy begins with the same uncertainty in hers. 'I know you'd decided you definitely don't want to get back with Daniel,' she searches my face. 'But would it change anything for you if *he'd* changed? If this Daniel who is putting you first and wants you to be happy is a Daniel who tells you he's still in love with you and wants to give things another go, would you consider it?'

I am floored by this question.

And how can I answer it? If this really is a different Daniel, then how can I know how I'd feel? I know I don't want to be in that relationship we were in before. I know I don't want to be with *that* man. But what if it's a different relationship – a different man – he's offering?

I shake my head, dismissing the question. 'People don't change, not really,' I say with a surety I don't feel. 'Or maybe they do for a while but then they change back.'

Myfanwy smirks. 'I don't know, you seem quite different lately.'

I shake my head again, harder this time. 'No, I don't want to get back with Daniel, and I'm going to text him, arrange a coffee, and tell him that straight. He deserves to know where he stands and I'm being more direct with people this year.'

'Good girl!' Myfanwy says with enthusiasm. 'Speaking of that,' she continues conversationally. 'Have you decided not to talk to Toni about Shawn after all?'

'Ugh!' I say now, throwing my hands up. 'The thing is, I don't know if he's all *that* bad these days. Maybe he's growing up?'

'I thought people didn't change?' Myfanwy parrots my words and I shoot her a look.

'Admit it though, Myfe, he was pretty great with the Mikey stuff, wasn't he?' I sigh. 'I know he's gross and super annoying. But just because he chews with his mouth open and doesn't cover up when he coughs, does that mean he shouldn't be with Toni?'

Myfanwy pulls a disgusted face. 'But what about the age gap? Or the fact that he still explodes over the smallest thing?'

I nod. 'I know, I know. He's incredibly fragile and ego-driven, but I think he wants to be better. He was talking the other day about having three big brothers and a really overbearing alpha dad. I think he's just another sad product of the male surroundings he was brought up in.' Myfanwy looks like she will argue this some more so I put a hand on her arm. 'Ultimately, I'm still not happy about any of it, but I can only support Toni in her decisions. She's a grown-up and I can't force her to see what an idiot he is,' I say simply and her mouth closes. 'I think we have to respect her choices.' She rolls her eyes, but I know she agrees.

CHAPTER THIRTY-FIVE

Celeste is having a selfie with a security guard.

Oh and now with the man and woman on reception.

Now some guy with a lanyard who was on his way out is asking for one.

Several others now crowd around my mother with their selfie requests, and Celeste beams her exquisiteness into a thousand cameras as basically every single person in this building queues up, pointing and whispering.

It must be such a weird, exhausting life.

Selfie acquired, the lanyard man approaches Myfanwy and I, where we sit, quiet and unnoticed in the corner, just how we like it. 'Are you here to see Ms Ball?' he murmurs discreetly, and we nod excitedly.

As *if* we're getting to meet Crystal Ball! As if! Even if she didn't happen to be the fortune teller that changed my life sixteen years ago and predicted this whole bananas year, she's also *Crystal Ball,* the legend that we've been obsessively binge-watching on TV and YouTube.

Last week, Celeste happened upon us in the living room watching back-episodes of the show and, after hearing how much we love Crystal, she made exactly one phone call to her agent. Within an hour, we had a personal meeting arranged with Ms Ball for today. For now! It's another absurd and brilliant perk of my mother being my mother. I didn't tell her Crystal Ball happens to be the fortune teller I met when I was a teenager. I didn't know how she'd react and I didn't want to chance it.

As we pass by Celeste and her beloved fans, Myfanwy assumes the role of bad guy PA, tearing her away as she loudly protests and promises to reply to every Instagram DM. We follow the lanyard guy through turnstiles and long winding corridors, staring in wonder at picture after picture on the walls of local celebrities. We pass a long trophy case and I pause briefly, almost losing lanyard guy as I admire an array of awards I've never heard of.

I catch up with the group as we arrive outside a door. On the front is her name:

Crystal Ball.

I briefly wonder if I can ask to see her passport. It can't be her real name? Not the one she was born with anyway. But maybe she had it legally changed. If she *were* actually born with it, that's some next-level nominative determinism. Move over Phil McCann reporting on a petrol crisis.

Lanyard guy knocks efficiently and piles in without waiting. We follow him inside, to find Crystal posing elegantly – and very deliberately – on a long velvet chaise. In front of her is a low table full of fruits, nuts and crisps. It makes my stomach rumble.

Our psychic leaps up, a long skirt flapping around her ankles as she comes towards us.

For a moment I think she is moving towards me; sensing it's *me* who needs her. She knows that I'm the one who came for her, who requires her powers once again.

But no, of course it's not me. Not when I've brought a bona fide celebrity with me. She throws herself at Celeste, lavishing her with compliments.

'Celeste Bretherton, I am an enormous fan of yours! I watch every episode of *Engage!* Without fail. I cried buckets over the season finale, but Trisha really deserved the bejewelled crown, she was so talented, and *so relatable*.' She waves behind her at a desk in the corner. 'You've even inspired me to try my hand at a spot of jewellery making.'

Celeste makes that 'incredibly interested' face she uses with contestants on the show. The one viewers have recreated over and over in memes all over the internet.

'How wonderful!' she claps her hands, towering over Crystal. 'You must show me, my darling.' She pauses, remembering her lines when it comes to a fellow TV star, even one as small-fry as Crystal. 'And of course, I am a huge fan of yours, too. You are *dazzling* on the screen, my darling.'

Celeste has never watched a single minute of the show, despite our haranguing.

Crystal pales. 'I'm honoured,' she says humbly. 'And if you ever need someone with my skills on *Engage!*, I am more than available. I could do a five-minute segment at the end of each episode, revealing who is going to falter or win the following week.'

Celeste nods emphatically. 'That could be an interesting angle!' she lies. 'I shall have a discussion with my producer, darling, and get in touch.'

I clear my throat awkwardly, knowing she won't get in touch. Celeste uses the opportunity to redirect the conversation.

'Darling Chryssy,' she begins informally and Crystal colours with joy. This is the magic of Celeste; she can be as fake as anything but still make people feel special. Crystal thinks they're now friends, as does, almost certainly, everyone out in reception who got a picture with her. 'This is my beautiful daughter, Ginny, and her friend Myfanwy.'

Crystal turns her attention towards us, adopting her own professional Fan Face. 'Hello Ginny, hello Myfanwy,' she says in a softer tone, one I recognize from her show when she's starting a reading with someone. She shouts YOU at them, and then goes into this hypnotizing voice that reels you in.

'Hi Crystal,' Myfanwy squeaks, while I can only grin stupidly. 'We really, really, really love you,' she continues and I manage a nod. 'You're the best. That reading you gave that guy the other day, the one who was shagging his boss? It was amazing! I can't believe she's going to get pregnant and he's going to set fire to his office building. That is just so . . . *cool.*' She finishes breathlessly and I stare dumbly at this woman, trying to cling onto the real reason we've come here today.

Crystal smiles benignly as, behind her, Celeste looks put out. Neither of us have ever reacted to *her* like this. 'Thank you, girls,' Crystal says in her soft voice. 'I'm glad to have brought you some insight.' She turns to look fully at me, taking me in, and for a moment I think she will remember me. I want her to so desperately. I want her to prove herself; I want her to show me everything she said back then was real. I want her to be the real deal. I want to believe. *I do believe.*

She opens her mouth, still looking at me intensely. 'Ginny,' she begins slowly, 'can you,' she leans closer, 'put in a good word for me with your mum?' she tinkles, throwing a glance back at Celeste.

I swallow hard.

She doesn't remember me.

'Of course,' I choke out words at last. 'She'd be lucky to have you!' Over her shoulder, I see Celeste roll her eyes. I take a deep breath. 'Crystal, I know it was a long time ago, but we've actually met before.'

She cocks her head, curious but not alarmed. 'We have?'

I nod slowly. 'When I was a teenager, I went to a funfair, where you were working . . .'

She looks a little embarrassed. 'Oh my goodness, that was a different life!' she exclaims, turning to glance at Celeste for a reaction, but she's too busy staring at me, eyebrows knitted with confusion, to care about this woman's shameful past as a fairground fortune teller. I feel a pang of guilt for not telling Celeste the truth, but plough on regardless.

'You gave me six predictions for my future,' I tell her quickly. 'And loads of them have come true! But I need to . . . I need to know . . .' I trail off. What do I need? What do I need to know? What am I asking for?

Crystal looks at me closely. 'You, know, Ginny, you *do* look familiar. And I remember . . .' She stares off into the distance, her eyes glazing over. 'I remember those predictions. I can see! I can see it all. Your path is clear.'

My heart leaps with excitement. She can see! She can see what's going to happen on my path. She can tell me everything's going to be OK. 'What?' I ask eagerly. 'What can you see? What's going to happen?'

Her eyes return to normal and she smiles nicely.

'Ginny, this is my work.'

'Huh?' I glance nervously between Crystal and Myfanwy, who looks as confused as me.

Crystal's smile gets wider. 'I mean, Ginny, that I do personal readings and I do the show, but we're not currently on camera and you're not a member of my TV audience.'

'Of course!' I say quickly. 'Can I schedule a personal reading then?'

'Sure!' she says brightly. 'It costs £15,000.'

'Oh.' I feel myself deflate. 'I see.'

Crystal places a kind hand on my arm, barely disguising a glance back at Celeste. 'But I can offer you a ten per cent discount as you're the daughter of my special friend, Celeste Bretherton!' She puffs up, proud of her generosity, and I smile weakly.

317

'That's great,' I swallow hard, knowing there's no way in the world. 'I'll, er, I'll be in touch.'

'It was so wonderful to meet you all,' she says magnanimously, handing me a crisp white business card. 'Would you girls like a selfie?' Myfanwy yelps a delighted affirmative and the three of us crowd in front of her phone. I try to smile as the flash goes but I feel a little disappointed. Actually, more than that: I'm crushed, deflated. Of *course* she charges. What did I think was going to happen? That she'd sit me down and spell everything out for free? Even back then at the funfair, she charged me a fiver. And with the way inflation's been going, a price increase of £14,995 seems about right.

As we leave, filing back out the way we came, at lanyard guy's heels, Celeste is silent. But the moment we exit the building – twenty-five more selfies later – she explodes.

'Why didn't you tell me she was your fortune teller?' she growls. 'Why did you lie? You *tricked* me into arranging all this!' I cower, feeling terrible. I should've told her, I should've explained. Celeste paces back and forth angrily, before jabbing a finger back towards the building. 'That woman was the one you met when you were young? You should've told me! Why are you hiding things from me?! You *keep* hiding things! What have I done to deserve this? You're always shutting me out! You're always lying! You don't seem to like me or want me around. You let me stay up all night worrying about you and wondering where you are—'

'Mum, that happened once.' I try to find the firmness in my tone. 'And I'm really sorry again—'

She interrupts furiously. 'You never tell me where you're going or what you're doing! You can't wait to get out of the house every day! What's so terrible about me that you want to escape so much?'

Myfanwy takes a small, protective step forward, still acting as my shield. 'Celeste,' she starts in a warning voice. 'You're not being fair.'

'It's none of your business!' Celeste looks even angrier. 'You stay out of it!'

Myfanwy turns to me calmly. 'Gin, do you want to come stay at mine and Sonali's for a while? This is not a healthy situation.'

Celeste turns white at this. 'How *dare* you?' she shouts and a couple of people in the street look over. 'You have no right! You're always interfering, Myfanwy, always trying to get between Ginny and me! You want to steal her from me!'

'A person can't be *stolen*, Celeste,' Myfanwy starts to redden. 'Ginny doesn't belong to you! She doesn't owe you anything. She's an adult, her own person! You want to control her and it's not OK!'

I feel myself starting to shake. I hate this so much. They both love me, they both want to protect me, and they're both talking for me.

'Please stop!' I get out at last. 'Please, both of you. I don't want you to argue.' I turn to Celeste, speaking calmly, 'Mum, I should've been honest with you about Crystal, I'm sorry. And we need to talk properly about everything, but not right now, in the middle of the street.' Now I turn to

Myfanwy. 'Myfanwy, thank you for the offer, but I can't live with you guys. You're just about to—' I stop myself saying the obvious: that they're about to get engaged. Project Proposal is still a couple of weeks away and Celeste has no idea. 'You're, er, a couple and I don't want to live with a couple of lovebirds!' I try to make my tone playful, to lighten the mood as they both stare at the ground. I sigh. 'Please, you guys? Let's not argue?'

Celeste nods at last. 'I'm sorry for losing my temper with you both,' she says quietly and Myfanwy takes a deep breath. 'I'm sorry too – I shouldn't get involved.' She glances at me a little reproachfully and her message is clear: she shouldn't *have* to get involved, because it's time – after everything I've said and promised – that I should be more honest with my own mother. And I will. But not today.

We return to the car in silence, my whole body vibrating with misery.

Finding the fortune teller was a bust, my mum is furious with me, and I'm still no closer to finding a soulmate.

I pick up my phone, flicking to the camera roll. At least I got a selfie with Crystal Ball.

CHAPTER THIRTY-SIX

Obviously I don't want to see or speak to or even hear about Mikey's existence ever again, but I'll be honest, so far this party would be way more fun with a few of his magic mushrooms.

We're an hour into Sonali's birthday party, the event Myfanwy has thrown together as a proposal cover, and it's not really *happening* yet. People are awkwardly milling about in corners barely speaking, the music is too low and the bartender keeps disappearing, so the booze isn't flowing like it should.

The trouble is, Myfanwy is too nervous. She's usually really on top of things like this, making sure everyone's having fun, turning the tunes up and ordering shots at the top of her voice so everyone gets involved.

Instead, she's sitting in a corner, looking beautiful but pale and sweaty.

I stride across the room to join her. 'You have to calm down,' I tell her out of the side of my mouth, worried someone might be watching.

'I'm trying,' she hisses. 'I'm just so scared. What if she says no?'

I shake my head. 'Of *course* she won't. She's going to be so happy.' I feel a pang. *Is* she going to be happy about a public proposal like this though? I hope Myfanwy knows what she's doing. I swallow hard.

I've been feeling so conflicted about Myfanwy's proposal plan. I've talked myself in and out of telling her not to do it so many times, and then it was suddenly too late. But I think I'm doing the right thing by not saying anything – it's not my place to tell Myfanwy how she should propose. She and Sonali are in love, Myfanwy knows what her girlfriend would want, she knows her best.

She looks around. 'Well, I can't do it if this party doesn't improve,' she says sadly. 'It's terrible so far. There aren't enough people here!' She looks at me anxiously. 'Do you think more people will turn up? You invited loads of extra people, right?'

I regard her with bafflement. She knows literally everyone I know. Our friends are the same people. Suddenly she pales, looking behind me in the distance. 'Oh,' she says quickly. 'I forget to mention someone I did invite!' I turn in slow motion as she continues, sounding panicked. 'I asked Zach to come and I meant to tell you, I'm really sorry. But he designed the ring for me, I couldn't *not* invite him to the proposal party!'

'It's fine!' I choke out, watching in slow motion as he approaches across the room. 'Of course you invited him.'

He's just some guy, I remind myself. Just some random dude I worked with for a few months. He's just a hot man who I stupidly convinced myself – briefly! – was my soulmate. I force myself to laugh at my own ludicrous vulnerability back then. I only decided he was my soulmate because I was sad and lonely after my break-up with Daniel. I was looking for an instant soulmate jigsaw piece to fill the hole, so everything could just go back to how it was.

But I'm really glad now that I didn't fill that hole right away. Being single for all these months has forced me to spend some time with myself. And I've decided I mostly like what's going on here, inside me. Sure, I have many things I need to work on, but that's good, too. Sometimes you need to be on your own to figure all that out.

Zach smiles as he closes the gap between us and we reach in wrong directions for an awkward hug.

'Whoops!' I cackle horribly as we crash into one another.

'Ginny!' he says with apparently genuine happiness. 'It's so nice to see you.' He turns to Myfanwy, greeting her with warmth. 'Myfe!' he says, hugging her in a normal way. I feel a pang of jealousy that they have connected in the last few months without me around.

'Great!' I shout. 'Yes! I mean great seeing, erm, you,' the nerves are crushing my windpipe. I step back, taking him in. He's as absurdly handsome as ever. He's wearing a shirt that hasn't been ironed very well – a part of the collar is crumpled and bending the wrong way. I fight the urge to reach over and straighten it.

'I'm going to go practice my speech,' Myfanwy says after a moment, looking between us carefully. 'I need to settle my nerves! Do you guys want a drink or anything?' I shake my head dumbly, nodding at the huge double gin in my hand, as Zach requests a lager. With Myfanwy gone, he steps closer, an urgency to his tone. 'It really is nice to see you, Gin,' he clears his throat. 'I'm sorry I haven't been in touch since Christmas. I—'

'No, no!' I cut off his apologies. Please god, I don't want another rejection speech. 'I totally understand! How's work been?'

He is silent for a moment, and I can tell he is mulling over what to say next.

'It's really good,' he says at last. 'Of course, I miss working for Celeste's Stones, but I made a lot of new connections and the clients I met there have been very kind. I've had a lot of recommendations come through and I'm keeping very busy.'

'I'm so glad!' I say with genuine feeling. I've been carrying a lot of guilt over what happened.

'Look, I have to explain something,' he begins and I turn quickly towards the bar.

'I better help Myfanwy!' I get out in a strangled voice, making a run for it. I find her in a corner with Toni, both giggling.

'Ooh, saw you with Zach over there,' Toni says, wiggling her eyebrows at me suggestively.

I groan. 'Don't!' I warn.

She cocks her head. 'You're not interested? I can't believe that. He's so gorgeous and sweet!'

'Er, I'm not interested in getting *rejected* again,' I roll my eyes.

'What?' She looks utterly baffled. I guess I never told her about how I came on to Zach – *twice*. 'But,' she frowns, 'he totally fancies you.'

I laugh. 'I promise you, he *doesn't*, Tone. Believe me, I've double checked. He just wants to be friends.' I sigh. 'And not even that really anymore, I don't think.'

'You're wrong,' Toni tells me stridently. 'Have you forgotten about the note?'

It's my turn to be confused. '*What?*' I glance at Myfanwy who looks as befuddled as me.

'Toni,' she shakes her head. 'What are you talking about?'

My sister tuts. 'I've told you this, I've *definitely* told you this.'

'What note?' Myfanwy shrieks.

'You know . . .' Toni laughs and then she pales as a thought strikes her. She looks at me, 'You *do* know, right? I definitely . . . I did . . . oh my god, didn't I?' I shake my head slowly and she covers her mouth. 'I was so sure we'd talked about it, Gin, I'm really sorry—'

Myfanwy screams it this time. 'WHAT NOTE, TONI?'

'Right . . .' She wets her lips, looking a bit frightened. 'The first time we met Zach was in the store, remember?' She looks to me for confirmation and I nod impatiently. 'And I thought he was that actor guy, you know the one from that

325

Amazon Prime show?' She giggles now. 'I was so sure he was! He's got that kind of look, you know? That bone structure and that—' Myfanwy looks like she will strangle her and Toni gets the hint. 'Um, anyway, I asked for his autograph and he handed the bit of paper back to me as he was leaving.' She swallows as we both stare at her, utterly hooked. We've never been this interested in one of Toni's stories before. 'He wrote his name, but also a message,' Toni pauses. 'He wrote, *Hi Toni, sorry I'm not your TV star, but can you please tell your sister that I think she's the most beautiful woman I've ever seen and I'd like to take her on a date. Love Zach x.*'

My mouth drops open and I look at Myfanwy. Her mouth is also wide open.

I remember the piece of paper now. The way Toni took it from Zach, squealed and ran off with such delight. I thought he'd just signed it with some A-lister's name to give her a kick. 'But . . .' I don't think I've ever been this flummoxed, 'Why didn't you give it to me right away?'

Toni looks down at her hands. 'Well, we got the call about Diane being in hospital literally, like, two minutes later and it completely went out of my head.' She shrugs. 'I'm really sorry, it was such a horrible time, I forgot all about it. But if you'd ever mentioned liking him . . .' she trails off. 'You always seemed so keen to emphasize that you were just mates. Then there was Mikey, and Daniel was back . . . I figured you just didn't like Zach and I didn't want to embarrass him.'

'This is . . . so . . . *much*,' I say quietly.

Zach wanted to go out with me.

'But he kept rejecting you,' Myfanwy frowns. 'What the hell is up with that?'

I stand up, surprising Myfanwy and Toni. I have to find Zach. I think I'm about to humiliate myself with him for a third time but I don't care. I'm brave now and I need to understand what happened. I need to know why he changed his mind and what it means. I want to know what I did that so repulsed him.

I spot him by the bar and stalk over.

'Hello, you,' he greets me with a smile before catching my expression. 'Er, are you OK?'

'Can I talk to you?' I am determined, taking him by the arm and leading him out into the hallway away from the music. Once we're alone, I stare him down, face-to-face, no escape. After a few seconds, I speak. 'Toni just told me about the note.'

Confusion clouds his face, 'The note . . . ?' What I mean suddenly hits him and he looks away, reddening. 'Oh,' he adds in a low voice. 'That must be confusing after all this time.'

'What happened?' I ask, feeling helpless. 'What did I do wrong?'

He takes a deep breath. 'OK,' he begins, faltering over his words. 'OK, right, I should explain. You should know. The truth is,' his turn to swallow hard, 'Gin, we know each other.' *What.* He takes in my blank expression and nods. 'I mean, we knew each other from . . . before. And I know you don't remember. I didn't remember at first either. It only clicked when we were leaving after that very first meeting.'

'How?' I interrupt urgently. 'What are you talking about? When . . . who . . . what?'

'Primary school,' he says simply, breathing in deeply. 'I was a couple of years above you. But you were best friends with my little sister . . .'

It all floods back. Flo. Florence Williams. She had a big brother, of course she did. Not that I ever dared look him in the face back then; I was too shy. No wonder I didn't recognize Zach.

He continues, 'As I was leaving the store, just after giving your sister that note, you told me your real name was Jenny, and that your school friend Flo was the only person who called you that. It clicked. Jenny Bretherton. My little sister's best friend. The one who . . . well.' He finishes lamely and we both stare down.

I understand now.

No wonder.

Florence and I were best friends in Year Four, Five and Six at primary school. But when we went to secondary school it all changed. We met a new girl, Mindy, who joined our twosome with enthusiasm. She had so much more confidence than either of us and soon the trio had a leader. But after a few months, things changed again. She kept trying to separate us, always trying to keep us apart. She 'forgot' to invite Flo to things, she told me secrets I wasn't allowed to share with my best friend. She was mean about Flo and I swallowed hard and nodded. And when Flo got upset – when she stood up for herself – Mindy turned on her. And I was too pathetic and cowardly to say a word. I didn't want Mindy to start on me, too, so I just started avoiding poor Flo. I hid from them both, ignoring Flo's phone calls and messages while Mindy's bullying got worse and worse. Eventually Flo's parents moved her and her brother away and I never heard from her again. I never made any other friends at school and spent my days alone, hiding from Mindy and desperately wishing I could just grow up and escape. I've felt unbelievably awful about it ever since.

'But you're *Walliams*, with an a,' I say desperately. 'Flo was just a normal Williams, wasn't she?'

Zach sighs. 'It's just branding. Williams is too easy to lose on Google. So I decided to be Walliams' Custom Designs. It worked for David Walliams, right?'

'Was he a Williams first then?' I'm aware this is off topic.

He nods slowly. 'To be honest, I thought you'd have seen my real name spelled on my invoices.'

'I never looked at them,' I say vaguely. 'I just forwarded them to the accountant.'

'Right,' he replies quietly and we share another long silence. 'Flo was so devastated by what happened back then,' he begins and I nod. 'I knew immediately that there was no way I could date you. Not ever. She'd never forgive me.' He looks sad. 'And of course, I would've told you who I was then, but you got that awful call about your aunt and I had to get you guys to the hospital.' He pauses. 'I nearly told you again, that day we visited the new store and were dancing to Girls Aloud.' He looks down at his right wrist. There are letters there he didn't mention that day we talked about the rest of his tattoos. One of them is F, I now realize. He continues, 'I used to dance with Flo to that same song.' Ah. So that weird moment between us wasn't about Cheryl Cole getting cheated on, it was about Flo.

'I get it, and I'm so sorry,' I breathe, trying to take all of this in as moments from the last six months all fall into place. 'God, you must hate me. I think about what happened with Flo a lot. It's been a huge regret for me, my entire adult life. Flo was my only friend back then and I betrayed her. I let her down. I've always felt terrible and wondered where she ended up.' I pause anxiously, remembering Sonia, the dog walker I accosted not so long ago. 'How is she?' I continue carefully. 'Is Flo OK?'

'She is,' he nods carefully. 'She's doing great. She's a doctor, actually. I don't see a lot of her, she's so busy, but she's happy.'

'She's really OK?' My body floods with relief.

'That school we moved to was brilliant,' he half smiles. 'No psycho Mindy types! She made friends, did well in her exams. She's married now, two kids.'

'That's so good to hear,' I say tearfully.

'And I also realized that you were, like, eleven, twelve years old back then!' he laughs. 'You were just a kid; I can't blame you for what those bullies did to my sister.'

'You *can* blame me for abandoning my friend though,' I

330

reply, hanging my head. 'I was such a coward. I was so scared of Mindy.' I gulp. 'I ran away and hid from her – and from Flo. I'm really ashamed of it. Honestly, I regret it so much.' I pause, looking around the bare hallway. 'We talk about abusive, controlling relationships in adults, but I sometimes think the way Mindy manipulated us . . .' I shrug. 'I don't know.' I look up, adding hastily, 'And I'm not trying to shift the blame. I was *awful*. I can't believe the way I treated Flo. The truth is, I've been a coward my whole adult life. I've never stood up to people the way I should.' I meet his gaze. 'But I'm working on it.'

He smiles. 'It's all history,' he says, looking lighter. 'And it turned out so much better with us being just friends! I loved working with you, we made a great team – short-lived as it was!' His words hang between us. Better as friends. 'We better get back in there!' he says now, brightly. 'We don't want to miss Myfanwy's big moment!' He throws a brotherly arm around my shoulder. 'Come on, mate!' The certainty hits me square in the chest that he will never again think of me as – how did he put it in the note? – the most beautiful woman he'd ever seen. He's been clear how he feels, and – you know what? – that's finally, really OK with me.

I sabotaged any chance we might've had twenty years ago, when I hurt his little sister.

CHAPTER THIRTY-SEVEN

When we return, Myfanwy eyes the pair of us warily, but at least she's now looking distinctly less sweaty. The drama between Zach and I has given her a welcome distraction from the proposal.

'All right?' she says carefully and we both nod a lot. She looks annoyed – she's *dying* to know what's happened.

'Myfe!' Toni bounces back up to us, fresh from the bar, with Shawn and future bride Sonali in tow. 'No offence, but why is this party so . . . ?' She waves discontentedly at the room, before Shawn finishes her sentence:

'Why is it so boring?' he pouts.

Zach looks embarrassed. 'It's not *that* bad,' he says nicely, making it worse.

'Are you guys bitching about my birthday party?' Sonali sips from a glass of water in her hand as she turns on Myfanwy accusatorily. 'Why did you make me have a party?' she wails. 'I hate this, it's too much pressure! No one is enjoying themselves and Toni just handed me this *water*.'

Toni looks ashamed. 'It's not my fault!' she says. 'I asked the barman for a vodka tonic. He disappeared for ten minutes, then handed me that water. I thought it was better than nothing.'

'I'll go get you a proper drink, Sonali,' Zach offers nicely and Myfanwy stands up suddenly, her back straight, her face determined. 'No, Zach, I'll do it,' she says, fixing the barman with a steely glare. 'I can't let this happen. This is going to be a good party if it's the last thing I do.'

Everyone cheers and Sonali perks up as Myfanwy stomps over to the bartender. We watch in awe as she tells him off, arms waving. Her sweat has turned to an Amazonian glisten and she looks like some kind of warrior as the shamefaced bartender nods. Within moments, he lines up an enormous queue of shots along the bar, and Myfanwy turns to us triumphantly, gesturing at the lot of us to come drink.

'Let's do this!' she shouts, the energy back in her voice. Our eyes meet as we all pile over to the bar shouting across each other. I meet Myfanwy's eyes and she smiles with a trembling lip.

Two hours later, and there's no longer any doubt that this party is a *party*. People are dancing and laughing. There is a high-five contest going on across the dancefloor, while someone else does the splits and takes a shot as the room cheers. I'm so proud of my friend for turning things around. Myfanwy bounces over to me, tray in hand. 'Here,' she instructs, offering it up and I accept a purple-coloured shot, downing it in one. It's sour as anything and I grimace.

'This is the best party ever,' I tell her, grinning, and she beams back.

'Do you think I should do it now?' She bites her lip nervously. 'I don't want to do it right at the end; I want us to be able to celebrate with everyone after she says yes.' She snorts, adding, '*If* she says yes.'

I laugh and then grab her hands excitedly. 'Yes! Do it now if this feels right. I can't believe you're about to,' I glance around furtively, checking no one is listening before adding in a whisper, '*propose*. This is so huge, I'm so happy for you, Myfe. You deserve this so much.' I swallow down the big emotional lump in my throat but both our eyes are shining. 'Go go!' I urge her and she laughs, a little hysterically.

She takes a deep breath and turns to the room, her eyes searching for Sonali. We spot her doing a cartwheel as part of a dance-off with Zach and Toni.

'There she is,' Myfanwy murmurs. 'I'll just get the music turned down a bit and then—' As if by magic, the music turns off altogether and we look at each other in surprise. Is Alexa listening? Did she do it for us?

'Can I get everyone's attention?' A loud male voice shouts over the room and we all turn in shock towards . . . Shawn. He's at the bar, holding a glass of champagne and looking nervous.

'What the hell?' Myfanwy mutters, echoing my thoughts.

With the room's attention all on him, Shawn clears his

throat. 'Can I get Toni up here?' He scans the room, finding her, a deer in headlights, arms in the air mid-cartwheel. 'There she is,' Shawn says happily. 'Baby, can you come up here?' She slowly walks over with wide, nervous eyes.

'What's going on?' she mouths at me as she passes and I shrug.

'Toni,' Shawn begins excitedly as she reaches him. 'Don't panic, this isn't a marriage proposal!' He laughs long and hard as the room relaxes. He continues, delighted with himself, 'Har-har, don't worry − I'd never propose at a *party*.' His voice scathing, he looks around at the room. 'And especially not at a party *like this!*' I glance sideways at Myfanwy, whose face is a colour I've never seen. Somewhere between purple and greeny orange? Across the room, Shawn also spots her. 'No offence to your party, My-Fanny, eh? I know you've gone to a lot of trouble and it's a great do, if you like that kind of thing! It's just not exactly an event a person with any class would propose at, is it?' He laughs again, before turning back to Toni and taking her hands. 'Babe, you know how I think you're the best I could get?' He turns back to the room and winks. 'You should see her butt!' Low groans echo around the room and Toni titters, clearly embarrassed. Shawn continues, oblivious to the negative reaction. 'So I wanted to ask you in front of your mates and your sister,' he nods at me like I'm in on this, whatever this *is*, 'whether you would do me the great honour of agreeing to live with me?' Toni's mouth gapes open, as do most mouths around the room. None of us thought this was going to last. Or we *hoped* it wouldn't. Shawn might have grown on me somewhat in recent weeks, but *this?*

'Wow.' Toni finds her voice at last, repeating in a trembly tone, *'Wow.'*

'I know it's a surprise,' Shawn says, beaming at her. 'But I've been looking at rentals and I think we'd be great as roommates!'

'Wow!' she says again and he pulls her in for a hug. From inside his cuddle, I hear Toni squeak about being *thrilled*.

Toni's going to live with him. She's going to live with a boy. This is huge. I . . .

Oh my god, Myfanwy! Her proposal. For a moment, I'd forgotten. I forgot what should've been happening. But the terribleness is written all over her face.

Shawn has completely and utterly ruined her big moment. There's no chance at all she can propose now. Even if he hadn't slated the idea of anyone popping the question tonight, there's literally no thunder left, he's stolen it all.

'I'm so sorry!' I whisper urgently as Myfanwy blinks hard. 'Shall we go to the loo?'

She nods, swallowing hard as she tries not to cry.

No one notices us slipping away, as the party – Sonali included – all crowd around the star of the show, Toni, shouting their congratulations at her as she beams at the fuss. It should've been Sonali at the centre there, showing off all her mad, stupid, sweet, beautiful rings.

In the loo, Myfanwy lets go, bursting into tears.

'Well, that's that fucked,' she declares through snot.

'It's not fucked!' I protest, looking through the cubicles for toilet roll. There are only wads of paper on the soaked floor, so I offer her my sleeve.

'What am I going to do?' she wails. 'It's all ruined.'

I stroke her hair. 'It's not ruined, Myfe, you just need to come up with a new plan for when to do it.'

She harumphs. 'I can't exactly throw another big party for her, can I?' Her voice is exasperated as she cries into her hand.

I take in my best friend, crying in a loo over what should be a magical night for her and Sonali. And I make a decision.

'Actually, Myfe, I think this is a good thing,' I say decisively, and she sniffs loudly, looking up at me with eyes narrowed.

'What?'

I stand up a little straighter. 'I should've said something before, but I don't know if proposing in front of everyone is the right thing.'

She stares at me. 'But that was the plan. We agreed.'

I cock my head. 'I know, but I don't know if Sonali is really a public proposal kind of person . . .'

'*What?*' Myfanwy says again, looking outraged. 'But you said it was a good idea!'

'I didn't want to interfere,' I say lamely.

'It wouldn't have been interfering!' Myfanwy cries. 'You were part of Project Proposal from the start. I literally *asked you* to interfere. Not just as a best friend, but as a bloody expert in proposals! It's basically your day job to help people like me! I wanted you to tell me if I was doing anything stupid because I knew I was too close to the whole thing to see it clearly! That's why I wanted you on board, to let me know if I was going in the wrong direction!' She sighs. 'So you think I should ask her one-on-one, in private?'

I nod sheepishly. 'I really do. I think that would mean a lot more to her.'

She sighs again. 'Is the rest of it wrong, too?'

'Oh my god, *no!*' I tell her hurriedly. 'The rest is perfect and wonderful and I know Sonali will completely love it. Every one of those stories and rings are exactly right. But I do think she would prefer it if it was just the two of you. Much as I'd love to watch.'

She considers this, letting my words sink in. After a minute, she gives me a small smile. 'I could record it?' she offers, and I think about this. I'm the professional, after all – *the expert* – and she wants my genuine opinion.

'Yeah,' I nod, considering Sonali's reaction to this. 'I think she'd like that. She'd like to have a record of it. And I definitely would like to see that record.'

'The only question left now then,' she sighs, 'is *when* to do it.'

We're about to start brainstorming when Toni appears at the door. She looks out of breath, eyes widening as she spots me.

'Daniel's here,' she says.

'Fuck,' I say, because who the hell *forgets* that they invited their ex-fiancé to a party?

CHAPTER THIRTY-EIGHT

'You invited Daniel?' Myfanwy is shaking her head, her mouth gaping at this news. 'I knew you'd been texting a bit, but have you been seeing each other again?'

I shake my head. 'No, not at all. Not since that mushrooms night.' I grimace, remembering again how weird that was. 'He's mentioned wanting to talk a couple of times, but he's also been quite good about not putting pressure on me.' I pause. 'I don't know why I haven't had The Chat with him yet . . .' I shrug. 'My only excuse is that he does genuinely seem quite different these days. I thought maybe it would actually be quite nice to see him and catch up here. One-on-one seemed a bit too intense; this way there's no pressure.'

Myfanwy watches me carefully. 'What about Zach?'

I smile, feeling clear about him for the first time since we met. 'We're just mates. Honestly, Myfe. We talked things through and I'll tell you all about it another time, but we really are just friends. I'm happy about it, too.'

Myfanwy raises her eyebrows. 'OK.' She pauses. 'You better get out there then.'

Daniel has his back to me as I make a slow approach, standing at the bar, talking to the now-attentive bartender.

I know he will be ordering a lager, even though he prefers a white wine spritzer. He is afraid of men thinking he is not like them. That he is too flamboyant and energetic for other men. It always made me sad, seeing the way he would tamp down his boyish girlishness when he was around his friends.

Daniel turns and I am surprised to see that I'm wrong. He is holding a white wine spritzer after all.

God, maybe he really has changed.

'Ginny!' His joy at seeing me is genuine and with one arm he gathers me up in a hug. I find my face next to the wine, the smell making me want one.

'Hi Daniel,' I say happily. 'It's really good to see you.' I am surprised again to find that I mean it. I thought I'd have a strange and confusing set of feelings when I next saw him.

But it is only one feeling, a very straightforward feeling, and I identify it easily.

'You too,' he beams, waving back towards the bar. 'Can I get you a drink?' I nod and we stand side by side as I order, 'What he's having.'

'You'll never believe it,' I say, turning to him. 'Shawn did a big announcement thingy – him and Toni are moving in together!'

'Wow.' Daniel's eyes widen. 'How do you feel about that?'

'Well,' I say carefully, ignoring the obvious shock and confusion. 'She seems very happy so we're all happy *for* her.'

'Got it,' he nods, message received. He looks down, acknowledging my dress and smiles widely. 'You look great, Gin! Is that another special from Celeste's wardrobe?'

'It never even made it as far as the wardrobe,' I confide. 'It came straight from the Evri delivery driver to my body. It may be hell most of the time, but there are occasional benefits to being a 32-year-old woman living with her mother.'

He nods, looking a little shamefaced. After all, he is the reason I'm there.

But I find I don't mind – I don't blame him.

I've forgiven him, I realize. Properly this time.

I don't think I could feel the way I'm feeling towards him now if I hadn't fully let it go.

'Shall we dance?' I smile, grabbing his hand and leading him towards the dancefloor.

He obligingly starts bouncing around to the Taylor Swift song blasting over the speakers. I forgot what an adorably goofy dancer he is. It was always another thing he worried about doing in public, but he shows no signs of embarrassment or reticence now. We make eye contact as he does the robot dance, and both burst out laughing.

As the song segues smoothly from one to another, he leans a little closer, still dance-bouncing.

'Hey, I'm sorry about everything that's happened these last nine months,' he yells in the direction of my ear. I wave the apology away.

'Don't worry about it,' I say dismissively. He stops bouncing, suddenly looking very serious. He regards me for a moment and then grabs my hand, leading me away from the dancing to some chairs in a quieter corner. He sits me down and takes a seat opposite, still giving me the same serious look.

Oh god, he's going to say it. We're finally going to have The Chat.

And I'm ready now. I know what I need to say.

'You have to stop dismissing my apology,' he begins, eyebrows knitted together. 'You've done it every time I've said sorry and I need you to really hear me.'

I mirror his serious expression. 'But I already accepted your apology that first day you came to see me – months ago, when you showed up at my mum's house out of nowhere. You said sorry and I said it was OK.'

He shakes his head. 'I know you did, and I was so relieved at first. But it took me about four seconds to realize you obviously didn't mean it.' He sounds frustrated. 'I could see you were doing your usual thing of letting me off the hook.' He pauses. 'You forget I *know* you. You were always forgiving me too easily when I didn't deserve it.' He takes a deep shuddery breath. 'I did something unforgivably awful to you. The way I ended things . . . the way I just left without a word. That was the lowest I've ever sunk. It was the worst thing I've maybe ever done to another person, and then to cut you off with barely a word . . .' He stops, his breathing ragged as he tries to keep it together. 'And to do it to *you* of all people . . .' He looks down at his lap and I wait patiently for him to get his emotions in check. 'I would understand if you could never forgive me but I want you to *really hear* how sorry I am and how terrible I've felt. I've talked to my friends a lot in the last few months and a couple of the best of them gave me a proper reality check. I heard some home truths about my immaturity level. I've spent a lot of my adult life being incredibly selfish and blinkered. I put myself first all the time, always looking for the next big adventure without considering you in any of it. It was always about me and I can see that now. I've been doing a lot of work on myself and trying to be better. Honestly, I barely recognize that awful childish idiot guy from last June who did that terrible thing to you.' He looks at me, adding quickly, 'Not that I'm trying to shift the blame! I deserve every bit of it and if you never wanted to see me again, I'd more than get it.'

I smile warmly, fully feeling every word he's said. After a moment, I reach across and take his hand.

'I forgive you, Daniel,' I tell him simply. 'I really do.' I pause. 'I admit, you're right, I hadn't back then – it was too soon. I had to fully process what had happened and *feel* it. I had to be on my own for a while and figure things out. I had to miss you and hate you for a while, but I really am OK with what happened now. I promise. It was bad, but I'm over it.'

'Really?' His eyes look overly bright and shiny. 'You honestly feel that way?'

I nod and take a deep breath. It's time to tell him how I feel.

'Listen, Daniel, I'm so sorry, but I don't love you. Not anymore. I don't think we should get back together. I don't want to hurt you and I've realized tonight how much I care for you — as a friend. But I know for sure that it's not more than that. I really have forgiven you, I promise you that, but I don't think we could ever work together, not really. I'm too much of an introvert for you. You need someone fun and full of life and energy. I don't have the right components for you.' I pause. 'And you don't have the right ones for me. I don't want us to get back together — I hope that's OK.'

He blinks a few times.

'Huh?' he says at last, dumbly.

'I'm really sorry,' I say again, feeling awful. I hope he's not going to cry.

'Oh Ginny, no!' He looks mortified. 'Did you think I was hassling you all this time to get back together? I'm such an idiot, of *course* you would've thought that! I just wanted to say sorry properly, even if you couldn't forgive me.' He grimaces before adding sheepishly, 'I'm so relieved you have forgiven me, but it sounds like I should say sorry again. I really didn't mean to make you think I wanted to give our relationship another go. I just regret so much the way I acted and wanted to be sure you knew it was my fault.' He cocks his head at me. 'You always had a bit of a tendency for blaming yourself for things, so I was worried you thought it was something *you'd* done. And it wasn't! You were the best girlfriend, always so thoughtful and kind.' He takes a deep breath. 'For ages after I left, I couldn't understand why I'd done it. Everyone around me kept saying how good we were together. My mate Jimmy would hound me with whys every time I saw him – we had the shittest time in Amsterdam because he wouldn't let up! He kept going on about how lovely you are and how we never seemed to argue.' He sighs and I think back to those miserable, sleepless nights looking through Jimmy's Instagram pictures from that trip, thinking how happy and carefree Daniel looked. 'But,' he begins again, 'I realized that was kinda the problem. Um . . .' he hesitates. 'Not you being lovely, but us never arguing. I've realized in this past year that I'm also a people pleaser.' He meets my eyes and smiles sheepishly. 'While you've been focusing on our clashing introverted and extroverted natures, I've been considering those traits we share that are *too* similar! I know I gave you a hard time sometimes about your people pleasing, but I've realized I was doing it too. I bounced around, saying yes to every invitation, saying yes to all the work, saying yes to the people I love.' He frowns. 'Saying yes to getting married. I never wanted to be a disappointment. But I was so focused on making sure everyone else was happy, including you, that I didn't stop to realize I wasn't happy.' He gulps. 'Sometimes everything can *seem* perfect. It can be the life you thought you wanted for yourself – what everyone around you thinks you should have – but it still doesn't feel right.'

I nod. He made himself unhappy, trying to make me happy. Just like I was doing. How stupid. Why is it so hard for people to be honest with each other – with *themselves?* And why does it seem to be so much harder with the people closest to us?

I sit back in my chair. *And* he doesn't want to get back together! I was so sure. I've been so bloody worried about telling him I didn't want to be with him! I feel like such an idiot.

'Hold on . . .' I begin, unable to fully move the subject on just yet. 'But you seemed so jealous that night, when you met Mikey. When we all did mushrooms?'

He shrugs, a bit uncomfortable. 'Well yeah, I didn't really *love* that, I'll admit it. I might be sure we're broken up for the right reasons and be OK with it, but it's still hard for me to see you with someone else!' He pauses. 'But to be honest, I was more jealous of that ridiculously good-looking other dude.' He narrows his eyes in the direction of Zach, across the room dancing. 'Zach, was it? I know he was only there for a few minutes but I could see right away how much you fancied each other.' He laughs. 'Even through my mushroom haze.' He leans in, a small smile playing on his lips. 'I noticed he's here tonight – are you seeing him?'

'Zach?' I am shocked by this. 'No, no, it wasn't like that, it *isn't* like that! We're just friends.' Why do I have to keep saying this to people? It's so depressing that people can't accept a man and a woman can be just friends.

'Right!' Daniel snorts. There is silence for a second before he smiles shyly. 'So . . . you think you and me can be friends? For real?'

I smile back. 'I think it's worth a try.'

'In that case,' he leaps up, reaching for my hands, 'let's get back on that dancefloor. I have a lot more awful dancing to show you!'

CHAPTER THIRTY-NINE

It is so weird how a person can look so much exactly the same, while also being completely transformed.

In my mind, Flo Williams has been this tiny, fragile victim for so long, I can't quite comprehend this fully adult woman with so much confidence and a sarcastic sense of humour can be the same person. And yet, there's that nose. There's that same fringe that she flicks away with the same small hand with chewed nails. She laughs now, and it's that same bloody giggle she had aged nine.

'And do you remember Mr Johnson who taught us for a term in Year Four?' She throws her head back laughing, her mid-length hair swishing around her shoulders in the wind.

'I do,' I nod happily. 'And how Martin Mantle told everyone what "Johnson" meant, and nobody could answer, "Here, Mr Johnson," during the register without sniggering.'

'Yes!' Flo grins. 'And then everyone got convinced

Mr Johnson was having an affair with the school secretary, Mrs Grain, because someone saw them talking at breaktime.'

'And Martin Mantle kept telling everyone Mr Johnson was giving Mrs Grain his Johnson.'

'Even though,' Flo muses, 'in hindsight, I'm pretty sure Mrs Grain was about forty years older than Mr Johnson.'

'I still think they were at it, and I'm sure Martin Mantle would agree with me, whatever he's doing now,' I comment dryly. Flo laughs that familiar laugh, as a dog bounds up with a stick in its mouth. She accepts the gift, lobbing it back out onto the field. We watch in silence as it runs about in the open air with pure joy.

My old school friend and I have been sitting on this park bench near Flo's house for thirty minutes already, and so far, we've managed to avoid the reason we're here. Instead, we've been reliving silly memories from primary school. The time before.

'I guess,' Flo begins hesitantly, 'I guess everyone was getting picked on or teased in some way or another. Even the teachers.' She lets this hang, as I stare at my hands.

'I'm so sorry, Flo,' I say at last in a quiet voice. 'I'm really, really sorry. For all of it. You have no idea how much I regret what happened. What I did.'

She sighs, wrapping her coat around herself as the wind picks up around us.

'I know, Gin.'

I wait, barely breathing, and at last, she turns slightly to me.

'I'll be honest, I was really angry with you back then. *Really* angry. I was madder with you than that cow, Mindy.'

'I get it,' I nod. 'I was, too.'

Despite that, she keeps going. 'You were my best friend.' There is pain in her voice. 'And you just disappeared.' I stay silent, knowing this is important for her to say. 'I struggled to trust people when I got to the new school; I thought they'd abandon me, too. I felt like I'd lost everything.'

I don't say that I felt the same way.

Flo audibly swallows, before continuing. 'But Mum made me meet with a counsellor, and she was great. I worked through it. She helped me understand that you were just protecting yourself. That you were just as scared and lonely as me.' I give a small nod, trying not to cry, as she adds, 'It took me some time, but I realized that being angry was just hurting me. It was self-destructive.' She pauses. 'I forgave you. I *do* forgive you. We were just kids.'

The tightness in my chest loosens.

'Thank you,' I say at last.

She smiles. 'I better get these idiots home.' She waves at her dogs, calling them in. I nod again, not trusting myself to speak. All this guilt – years of it poisoning a part of me – has lifted. My heart feels light and grateful.

I've accomplished prediction number five – the person I thought lost forever.

As we say our goodbyes, she gets this weird little smile on her face.

350

'My brother really liked you, you know?'

'Zach?' I reply dumbly, feeling strange about how often people bring him up around me. She rolls her eyes, laughing and flicking her fringe again.

'He kept on at me for weeks about meeting up with you and talking things through.' She pauses. 'Like I said, I'd forgiven you a long time ago, but I also didn't want anything to do with you, obvs.' She shrugs an apology and I nod a *fair enough*. 'But he kept saying what a great person you are now and emphasizing how much people change after the age of twelve.' She frowns, amused. 'I get the impression he thinks you're a bit wonderful.'

'He does?' I reply, confused.

'Don't worry,' she adds quickly. 'He's over it now, he's not going to ask you out. He knows you're taken.'

'Taken?' I say, shocked. 'I'm not taken. I'm single!'

She hooks the lead onto the dogs' harnesses, barely glancing up. 'Oh?' she says disinterestedly. 'He said you were in a relationship.'

As I walk away, I can't stop thinking about her words.

Was Zach just trying to reassure Flo? Make sure she knew he wasn't interested in her traitor former friend?

It's not like I can ask him. I've made a move *three* times now. I can't ask him yet again why he doesn't like me.

And either way, like Flo said, he's over it now. Too much has happened. It all got so complicated: exes hanging around, lying cheats, me on mushrooms claiming to be a unicorn.

It would've scared anyone off. Never mind the weird extra layers of history I have with his family.

I get it. I understand. It's not going to happen.

It's time to let it go.

CHAPTER FORTY

HOW DID IT GO?????????????????

It's been an hour since I sent the message. I should've heard something by now. A horrible feeling is creeping over me. What if Sonali said no? There's no way, is there? She wouldn't have said no — it can't be that.

So why haven't I heard?

I should've added more question marks. Hold on.

??????????????????????????????
????????????????????????

Nothing. Myfanwy's not been online and I remain unread. I'm sure they're probably just too busy yay-ing and probably having lovely celebratory sex or something. But Myfe promised me she'd take a two-second loo break after the proposal to let me know how it went. And she hasn't.

Oh god, this is too tense. I need to distract myself. I stare at the store door, willing a customer with a complicated ring-related question to walk through.

For the first time in ages, I'm back in the original store, working here instead of the new location, covering for Toni who's flat-hunting – and it is so nice. I feel like I've come home.

Celeste hasn't said much, but I think she's finally realizing the accessories range and expansion were a mistake. I know the new place has been making no money at all, despite my best efforts. The trouble is, so few people come in, and those that do would always take one look around at the empty white walls, and leave again.

But I don't understand Myfanwy not messaging me with the biggest news of her life! *AAARGH!*

Celeste sweeps in from the back office. She's been making a big effort to be in store lately. I have a feeling it's on the advice of her team as the internet continues to mock her failing expansion. Admittedly, her presence has brought some celebrity oglers in, but they don't tend to buy stuff.

On cue, two customers walk through the door and I stand to attention. I can tell right away that these two are just window-shopping and won't want to be bothered.

'Can I help at all?' Celeste shrieks across the room and when the couple look up, I realize that – for the first time in my living memory – recognition doesn't light up in their eyes.

They don't know who she is!

'No thanks,' the man mutters and I see the woman glance at the door, already planning an exit.

Celeste takes no notice, sweeping over and waving in my direction. 'My darling Ginny here will help you, she's an expert in our entire, personally curated range.' They look blank as I awkwardly shuffle towards them, feeling like a child in the playground being forced to play with the new kid. 'No reality star accessories in here,' Celeste twinkles, choosing not to notice their discomfort. 'Just hand-selected, tasteful items from our family-run business.' She gives me a tiny shove, and I land at their feet.

'Was there, er, something specific you were looking for?' I enquire politely, knowing full well they will be out of here in moments.

'Not really,' the man mumbles. 'Just looking . . .'

'We have to get going actually, we . . .' The woman gestures towards the door, and I step back, giving her space.

'Of course,' I say as warmly as possible. I clock her body language, relaxing as she realizes there won't be a hard sell. 'Oh wow, *that's* stunning!' Her eye catches something in one of the cases and she moves towards it. 'Look, Gerry!' She waves the man over and he reluctantly joins her, glancing longingly at the door again. 'My grandmother always wore something just like that!' She beams at me, adding unnecessarily, 'My grandmother on my mother's side. Maisie was her name – she was so glamorous! We used to go over for Sunday lunch and Grandma would always be dressed to the nines! She wore a brooch exactly like that!' She jabs smeary fingers at the glass case. 'I was always obsessed with it. My sisters and I used to fight over who would get it when she died, but then my aunt swooped in and nabbed it. I think one of my cousins has probably sold it off by now.' She gives me a dark look. 'Bunch of money-grabbers, that side of the family. One of them went to prison, you know?' She nods pointedly at me like I should be horrified. 'I think it was for a pyramid scheme thing but *still*.'

'This is a piece from our vintage selection,' I tell her nicely, vaguely aware that another customer has arrived behind us. Toni's off today, viewing flats with Shawn, so it's just me and Celeste. God, she might actually have to serve someone herself – *imagine*. 'Would you like to have a proper look?' I offer and the woman nods, almost salivating. I unlock the case and tenderly retrieve the brooch, holding it carefully with a handkerchief. Laying it gingerly on the case, the woman leans in, nose practically touching the brooch.

'It's beautiful!' she breathes.

It is actually. It's a Victorian art-deco 15 carat gold bird brooch. Two swallows made from seed pearl face one another mid-flight. They look like they might crash into each other but that's what I like about it. We're all mid-flight, trying not to crash into each other, aren't we?

'Can I touch it?' the woman asks respectfully and I nod.

'Of course!'

She picks it up and sighs happily. 'It really is exactly like Grandma's,' she tells Gerry, who stands just behind, hopping from foot to foot. He looks like a man who knew he shouldn't have come into an expensive jewellery store without a plan. 'Is it mad to get it? I really love it!' She turns to Gerry, with a look I've seen on many-a-face over the years. She is in love.

'I don't think it's a good idea!' Gerry says in a panic and I discreetly move away, giving them a moment to fight it out.

As I do so, I spot a familiar face talking to Celeste. It's Joey! The customer I helped with a proposal to his partner Hannah a few months ago. How lovely to see him again.

Except ... I study their body language for a second, suddenly feeling a little concerned. He looks very intense, talking in animated tones to my mother, who in turn, wears a serious expression.

What could he be saying? Not complaining, surely? I worked so hard to make sure he had the most amazing experience buying his engagement ring and helping him plan the ultimate proposal, Zach and I even personally dropping off the ring at the hotel! My heart starts beating too fast.

'We want it!' The oversharing woman and poor Gerry are back, argument won and lost.

I escort them to the pay point, carefully wrap up the brooch in tissue paper, placing it in its original antique box, all the while trying not to side-eye the conversation taking place across the room.

What could they be talking about?

A bead of cold sweat runs down the middle of my back as I take payment and listen to the woman talk about how she's going to wear the brooch every day and how that will show Shona from across the road who thinks she's so amazing with her great aunt's pin. She's still talking to Gerry about 'that bitch' Shona as I wave them off.

Not wanting to seem too worried, I give Celeste and Joey another few seconds before casually making my way across to them. Somehow I don't scream *WHAT ARE YOU TALKING ABOUT?* Which, I'm sure everyone would agree, shows an incredible level of self-control.

'Joey!' I greet him warmly, my delight at seeing him genuine. Unless he's complaining about me. 'So wonderful to see you.'

'Hi Ginny!' he grins and I can immediately see everything is fine. He's not angry or upset with me. There is only joy radiating from him. 'I was just passing and popped in to say hi and another huge thank you for everything you did. My *fiancée* – love saying that! – said I had to come in and' – he pauses, trying to remember – 'give you, er, *mad props*.' He hesitates again. 'I think that was what she said. She's American, did I mention that? Sometimes I don't under-stand a word.' He laughs. 'But then she says the same about me. She still looks at me in horror and bafflement when I say I'm knackered.' He smiles brightly at Celeste. 'We're like chalk and cheese – which is another saying she doesn't understand – but it works. We're so happy.' He gives me a pointed look. 'And a lot of that recent happiness is down to you, Ginny.' He nods at Celeste. 'I was just telling your mum how incredibly helpful you've been. You need to be better at boasting at work, Ginny! She had no idea how much you'd been involved in every step of the proposal.' He shakes his head in wonder at Celeste. 'Honestly, she was invaluable, talking me through everything, talking me down a few times when I was really freaking out. She and the designer Zach even came to the hotel undercover to deliver the ring! Never mind selling me a ring, Ginny's been like an emotional support worker!'

I blush a deep red and shake my head instinctively. 'Stop it! You did the hard part! I'm just so glad it went well and you're happy.'

We beam at each other happily for another moment before he notices the clock on the wall.

'Whoops, I'm late, better get going!' He reaches to give me a hug and, unprofessional as it probably is, I hug him back, my whole body vibrating with pride and osmosis-love.

As the door shuts behind him, I turn to find Celeste looking at me with wonder.

'You—' she begins but the bell at the door sounds again, distracting us.

I scream when I see who it is.

'MYFANWY! SONALI!' I leap elk-like across the store to sweep them up in my arms. I don't need to hear what happened. If Joey was radiating happiness, these two are *uranium* blissful. The three of us cuddle for a minute, laughing then crying.

Behind us, Celeste sounds bewildered. 'What's going on?' she calls and the three of us pull apart, drying faces on sleeves. Sonali laughs and throws her hands up. Every single finger has a different ring, each with a silly, romantic,

Lucy Vine

gorgeous meaning behind it. And right there, in the midst of them, is the beautiful, classic Celeste's Stones – Walliams's collaboration ring.

Celeste gasps and joins us, grabbing Sonali's hands roughly to inspect each one. 'This is absurd!' she says in an awed voice, as we all giggle.

'I'm assuming it was a yes then?' I grin and Myfanwy nods, unable to speak just yet.

Sonali finds the words faster. 'It was so romantic, Ginny, I can't even tell you.' She gasps. 'Actually I don't need to tell you, do I? Myfe told me how much you helped her.' She side-eyes her new fiancée. '*And* she told me that you stopped her doing it in front of a bunch of people. God, *thank you so much*. I'm really relieved she didn't do that. It was so much more special with just the two of us.'

Myfanwy and I smile at each other as I feel Celeste's eyes on me.

'Tell me everything!' I demand, though Myfanwy and I had gone through every detail, minute by minute, over and over, beforehand. I can see from Myfe's face that it all went according to plan.

'So we met up for what I thought was a very quick lunch break for me, since Myfe's on Easter half term,' Sonali begins excitedly. 'But instead of heading to grab a coffee outside my office, Myfe had a car ready. An *Uber Black,* if you can believe that outrageous spending. I'm like, "Where the hell are we going? Babe, you know I only have half an hour!" And she's like, "Actually babe, you have the rest of the day off. I've arranged it with your boss because I have a surprise for you." And I know it sounds stupid but I honestly *never* thought it could be this. I thought maybe she had a late birthday present for me. I was just excited I had the afternoon off!'

She laughs, looking over with adoring eyes at Myfanwy, who at last manages to speak. 'So I took her back to ours, where I'd laid out a blanket and plates. Seconds later – honestly the timing was absolutely perfect, Gin – the door went and it was our takeaway!'

'She'd got my favourite food!' Sonali squeaks.

Myfanwy snorts. 'We both know we're shit at cooking but I wanted it to be a special lunch.'

'I was so happy – it was the nicest burger I've ever had from there!'

Myfanwy shrugs. 'Well, I did tell them it was a proposal lunch, so they'd better make sure it was good.'

'No wonder they were so on time at your door!' Celeste comments beside me, delighting in the story.

'So then, I went behind the sofa and pulled out this tray of boxes—'

'I couldn't even speak when I saw them,' Sonali interjects breathlessly. 'I suddenly knew this was a big moment.'

Myfanwy smiles misty-eyed as she continues in a low voice. 'And she opened them one by one, as I said my speech, explaining each memory that each ring represented.'

'I was crying from about four words in!' Sonali rolls her eyes at herself.

'And we finished with that one.' Myfanwy nods at Sonali's ring finger and Sonali brandishes it.

'We sourced the stones and metal, but Zach designed it,' I tell Celeste as an aside and she nods, her eyes faraway and her chin trembling with emotion.

'And you said yes right away?' Celeste confirms eagerly.

'Of course!' Sonali laughs, as if it's the silliest question in the world. Which it is of course. Who wouldn't marry Myfanwy?

'And we're not done yet,' my best friend says suddenly.

'We're not?' Sonali looks at Myfanwy in surprise.

'Nope!' Myfe is *loving* this. 'And we better get going because we're now off to do an escape room—'

'OH MY GOD!' Sonali shrieks, because she loooooves escape rooms.

'And then I've booked us in at The Shard for the evening!' Sonali screams even louder at this because she's wanted to go up The Shard for literally years. 'And we're meeting both our parents there to celebrate together.' At this, Sonali tries to howl with joy, but it turns into big, gulpy, happy tears instead.

'That is just so perfect,' she finally gets out in a whisper.

'And I didn't tell you earlier,' Myfanwy adds tearfully, 'but you also have tomorrow off work, too, so you can get really, really drunk tonight.'

'Oh my god,' Sonali is finished. 'I love you so much, I can't wait to marry you.'

They leave, both sobbing and joyful after many more happy hugs, and I head to the bathroom to clean myself up.

When I return, Celeste calls to me from the office where she is sitting, staring at the computer screen.

'I haven't checked our Facebook page in years,' she comments, not looking away from the screen. 'And wow . . .' She lets out a low whistle. 'The reviews for our in-store service are just . . .' She looks up at last, staring at me like she's seeing me for the first time. 'They're just off the charts brilliant. There are so many long, rambling, embarrassingly gushy posts about how wonderful our personal service is. And they almost all name *you*. Every one of them. I started wondering after that man – what was his name?'

'Joey,' I fill in, something beginning to creep over me.

'When Joey came in and said all those things. And then Myfanwy said you helped her plan everything for her proposal, too. You have a real talent for helping people find not just the right ring, but the right way to present it.'

'Well,' I begin eagerly. 'That's why I suggested that engagement concierge idea ages ago. It's pretty much what I do already, and so many people love it and need it. I think our customers would really enjoy it.'

She looks thoughtful and I jump on the opportunity to push her – to push *myself*.

'I *know* it could work,' I say firmly. 'It already is working! What's the harm in giving it a try? I could write up a mission statement and some wording for the website. We could do a soft launch to trial it; we don't even have to publicize it initially. Just give it a chance. Give *me* a chance, Mum.'

She stares at me for a few seconds. 'It could work,' she says at last. 'But I think it's too soon after the accessories disaster.' She sighs. 'I'm shutting the second store and I've ended our arrangement with the reality star. We need to let things settle down for a while, then I'll maybe talk to my publicist about the engagement concierge concept.'

I give her the smallest of nods. It's a no. So much for advocating for myself.

Reading my mind, she adds, 'It's not a no.'

But of course it is.

At least it's a nicer no this time.

CHAPTER FORTY-ONE

I arrive home later that night, floating on air. It makes me so happy, knowing that Myfanwy and Sonali are off at The Shard right now, enjoying a glass of champagne with their families as they celebrate the biggest decision of their lives.

Or possibly they're still locked in somewhere? I've never done an escape room – do they let you out if you don't find the solution?

'Ughhhh,' I hear Toni yell from upstairs and I take the steps two at a time to get to her.

'What's up?' I ask anxiously, poking my head round the bedroom door.

'You're home!' She sounds startled, closing her laptop, where the source of her frustration lies.

'I heard you groan,' I explain, adding, 'Quite loudly and not in a fun way.'

'I'm just annoyed,' she says. 'I thought finding a flat with two incomes would be easy, but I've spent days trawling through SpareRoom and there's just nothing really affordable.'

'Bummer,' I say non-committally.

She sighs as I sit beside her on the bed. 'The trouble is that I have to pay most of the rent and the whole deposit for now, and there's just nothing I can afford.'

I am careful with my question. 'Why do you have to pay most of the rent?'

'Oh,' she says dismissively. 'It's just until Shawn's stand-up comedy career takes off. Or his band. Either way.'

I take this in, picturing Shawn performing on stage. Nothing hotter than a man over thirty who still thinks he can 'make it' in showbiz.

'But . . .' I continue even more carefully. 'He has a normal job as well, doesn't he? Does it not pay very well?'

'It pays OK,' she says evenly. 'But, like he explained, he has to use most of his money to fund the comedy and the music. Once one of those come off, obviously he'll be loaded and at that point he said he'll pay half the rent.'

It just gets worse and worse.

'Does he think you earn loads of money or something?' I ask, genuinely interested in how he can justify this.

She shrugs, reddening a little. 'We haven't really talked about money, but he has mentioned a few times how our family is clearly loaded.'

'But Celeste doesn't give us any of it! It's *her* money!' I say, unable to stop myself. 'Our wages at the store aren't even that great, and I haven't had a pay rise in two years.'

'Me neither,' she shakes her head. 'I suppose she does let us live here without paying rent, and I've been trying to save up. I've got enough for our deposit, which is handy because Shawn doesn't have any savings.'

'It may be rent-free, but there's a price to pay,' I mutter darkly.

Toni looks thoughtful and I realize I have to say something more. Things have been a bit better between Shawn and I in recent weeks, but even if he's not head to toe awful – maybe just head to shins – does he really belong with my baby sister?

'Hey, Tone,' I begin and she looks up. 'You know I think Shawn is . . . great.' I swallow hard. 'But . . . but . . . listen, are you *sure* about moving in together?' I continue quickly before she can say anything. 'It's just that you're still so young and it sounds like he might not be, er, financially set up to get a place with you right now. Maybe you could wait a little bit longer? See how things go?' I swallow. 'And I know this is absolutely none of my business, but are you sure about him? He is quite a, er, *character* and he seems to get angry a lot. Plus, there's the age gap . . .' I quickly add, 'But if you tell me he's wonderful to you and you're blissfully happy with him then I promise I'll shut up and never say another word!' I finish a little breathlessly, anxiously waiting for a reaction.

She is silent and I think for a second she is angry with me.

After another moment, she reaches across to her laptop, pulling it closer and lifting its lid. Instead of SpareRoom. com on the screen, it is open tab after open tab with Google search results. Toni has apparently asked the internet the following questions:

- Should you live with a boyfriend you hate?
- Do I have to live with my boyfriend?
- How do I tell my boyfriend I don't actually like him as a human being?
- Is it normal to find your boyfriend completely repulsive?

'Wait, what?' I ask, staring at the computer. I re-read the different questions three more times to check I'm not misinterpreting anything, then I look up at my sister.

'I'm *desperate* not to live with him!' she says anxiously. 'I couldn't believe it when he asked me in front of everyone like that at Sonali's birthday party! It was so humiliating and I could hardly say no or give him the brush-off, could I? Not that he'd listen.' Her face darkens. 'He never listens. He tells me all these tedious stories of work and the band, then when I try to tell him something about my day, he picks up his phone and completely ignores me. I think I'm just a receptacle for his speeches.'

'That's not . . . great,' I admit, alarmed.

'I hate him,' she adds damningly.

'That's definitely not great,' I say in a stronger tone.

'Oh well,' she shrugs and I regard her closer. 'What other options do I have? I have to move in with him.'

'What? No!' I soften my tone. 'You need to break up with him, Tone,' I tell her gently and she laughs in surprise – then looks panicked.

'But having someone I hate is better than having no one,

isn't it? I have a plus one for things. I have someone to pose with on Instagram.' She pauses, before adding softly, 'And you stayed with Daniel for years.' I frown.

'I thought I was happy though,' I protest weakly. 'You're not happy.'

'Sometimes I'm happy,' she insists. 'And it's better than people feeling sorry for me on my own.'

I am outraged. 'I never felt sorry for you!' I tell her and she smiles nicely.

'Mum did.'

'You've been speaking to Celeste about Shawn?'

She nods. 'Yes, and she's been reminding me how important it is to focus on the bigger picture – that someone wants to be with me! I have to stop being so shallow, always overexamining the annoying little things. She said I'll soon learn to ignore them or learn to like them. She said I need to give it a go.'

Oh my god, the absolute brainwashing. It's horrendous!

I realize suddenly that it's something we've grown up around; the idea that being single meant being some kind of failure. Mum has always pushed us to stick out our shitty relationships because it was better – as far as she was concerned – than being on your own. Toni is so brainwashed.

And so am I, a small voice inside reminds me.

I tried to leap straight from my relationship with Daniel into something with Zach. Then I tried to get straight into something with Mikey. And now? I think guiltily about the pathetic way I've been hanging around my phone since I saw

Flo, hoping Zach might get in touch.

I need to retrain my brain. Being single isn't something fearful and bad. Look at Diane! She loved it and chose it. My mum might be afraid of it, but she spends most of her life alone and does great. Being single should be brilliant and empowering. When I've allowed myself those times on my own, it's been such a joy. Especially as an introvert. I've loved nothing more than shutting myself away of an evening; eating what I want, watching what I want, seeing my friends when I want, playing stupid games on my phone without judgement. I've got to know myself better and I realize I like me. It's been great being single, so why do I keep resisting it?

I have to persuade Toni being single is not some kind of disease.

And Celeste.

'Why didn't you speak to me about all of this?' I ask Toni thickly.

She looks sad. 'I don't know . . . I didn't want you to think badly of Shawn. You seemed to like him so much. I didn't want to upset you.'

'I . . .' I'm so shocked I stand up. Vaguely embarrassed at the drama of my reaction, I sit back down. 'You think I *like* him?' I ask faintly.

'Of course,' she laughs. 'You guys are like besties. Shawn says he knows you better than I do these days.'

I swallow hard. 'Er, Toni, I guess he's grown on me a bit – he was helpful around MikeyGate – but otherwise' – how do I phrase this? —'I'm not that much of a fan.'

'You're not?' she says, her eyebrows drawing together.

'I'm *really* not,' I emphasize perhaps a little too strongly.

'Oh thank GOD,' she shouts, her shoulders sagging. 'Because I don't just hate him, I *really* hate him. I was so worried you'd be upset with me!'

'I kind of hate him, too!' I tell her and she bursts out laughing, then frowns.

'Do you know he has flatmates?' She suddenly looks disgusted. 'He talks constantly about how much money he makes, but lives with five students! He shares a bathroom with five hairy 18-year-olds. I know I shouldn't judge someone for not being able to afford a flat because lord knows, it sure looks like I'll never be able to, and I live with my *mother* for god's sake. But he goes on and on about how much money he has and is constantly getting his clothes personalized, meanwhile he goes back to this hovel to hang out with a bunch of teenagers who smirk at each other whenever he says anything. It's mortifying!' She laughs again, relishing the horror of it. 'Of course, that big money talk dried up once we started talking about flats. Suddenly *I'm* going to have to cover it all!' She takes a deep breath, preparing herself for yet another rant. 'And Jesus, Ginny, you should *see* his stand-up comedy! It's so unfunny, I can't stand it. It's mainly him riffing about how un-PC he is, which he thinks makes him edgy or something. And I know I'm stupid and don't get jokes, but I find it gross and offensive. He said one gay guy *one time* a few years ago told him he was funny, and that means he's allowed to say anything he likes about any subject. Yeugh.' She visibly shudders. 'And he always steals my bread roll when we're out to eat. Oh! And the last time we went out for dinner he asked if I'd pay half, and I said yes of course because I always have, and then he pulled out a 2-for-1 voucher. Which means I paid for my half so he could get his *for free*. He's *awful*.'

'Yeugh!' I echo her guttural noise. 'Toni, please dump him!'

She looks anxious. 'You really think I can?'

'Of course!' I sigh. 'Tone, were you really miserable when you were single?'

She considers my question, thinking back. 'No,' she admits at last, shaking her head. 'Not at all, actually. I loved having time to myself. I really love having my own space as well. I quite enjoyed dating and playing the field, and it didn't bother me that the dates never went anywhere. I liked going home to my own life and doing whatever I wanted.'

'Then don't think about it anymore!' I instruct, shouting the next part as joyfully as I can: 'DUMP HIM!!!'

She laughs hard and shouts back, 'I AM GOING TO DUMP SHAWN!'

It is as we both fall about laughing that we notice a towering figure in the doorway.

Celeste. And her face is absolute *thunder*.

Oh, shit.

CHAPTER FORTY-TWO

She's gone from the doorway before we can say anything.

I cower further into Toni's bed as we listen to Celeste stomp furiously down the stairs. Shit, shit, shit. I search for a way to fix things. And then I stop myself.

Why is she so angry? Because Toni wants to break up with Shawn? And I encouraged that? Something in me snaps. I've had enough.

She has no right to tell us who we can or can't date. She has no right to scare Toni into staying in a rubbish relationship with an idiot. How dare she? She can't control us anymore. We're *adults*.

I turn to Toni, 'Don't let that reaction get to you, Tone. You're making the right decision.' I fix her with a deathly, determined stare. 'Dump Shawn,' I say sternly. 'Today. Immediately. And don't be swayed when he tries to talk you out of it. You said it yourself, he doesn't listen, so *make* him listen. Be happy again, be single.'

Quaking a little, she nods. Then, like she's taking herself in hand, she stops looking frightened, adopting my same determined expression, and nods again much more convincingly.

I kiss her on the cheek. 'I'm going to confront our mother,' I tell her, feeling a thrill in my stomach of terror, excitement and – a new one – bravery.

'Good luck,' she whispers in awe.

I follow Celeste down the stairs, stomping down each step in much the same overly loud, angry way.

I find her in the kitchen, slamming things out of the dishwasher in a fury.

'What was that?' I demand, voice loud and strong.

She spins around, zeroing her terrifying laser eyes on me. 'You've told her to dump Shawn!' she half yells, waving her hand in the direction of the stairs. 'This is her chance for real happiness and you're sabotaging it! You know she listens to you – she looks up to you, she always has – and you're encouraging her to make the biggest mistake of her life!' She pauses angrily. 'Why can't you let her be happy?'

The snap I felt upstairs goes again, but this time it's more like a large break. I am *livid*. I want happiness for my sister and everyone I love more than anything. How *dare* she say I'm trying to hurt Toni!

'How can you say that?' I shout and she looks winded. I've never shouted at my mother before. I've never done much more than minimal sulking around her. 'I love Toni and I'm trying to make *sure* she's happy. That moron Shawn isn't making her happy – he was *never* going to make her happy.'

'She'll be much happier with him than on her own,'

Celeste yells back. 'Look at you! You're miserable single! And you've sabotaged your chance to get back with Daniel after everything I did to help—' She stops, looking caught out.

I screw up my face, breathing hard. 'What did you do?'

'I just got an obstacle out of the way,' she says almost nonchalantly.

My confusion wins over my fury. 'What obstacle – what are you talking about?'

'Zach,' she shrugs. 'After Toni told me about the note, I realized that's what was stopping you reuniting with Daniel and being *happy*. So I let him go.' She continues breezily. 'It was a shame because he was bringing in a lot of custom and everyone seemed very pleased. But we can get someone else when everything with the expansion settles down.'

I feel white-hot spikes of rage needling me. She's been manipulating me? Messing with Zach's career?

'You sacked Zach because of me?' My voice is even but the fury is evident because Celeste almost looks a little afraid.

'It was for your own good, darling,' she swallows. 'It was clear Daniel wanted to make a go of it after he turned up here out of the blue, and then showing up at Toni's Christmas party like that! You just needed that push – you needed me to clear the path of weeds for you. And if you weren't so obstinate, you'd be back together by now, with your life back on track.'

There is so much wrong with this, I don't know where to start.

'I was never getting back with Daniel!' I explode. 'And

you had no right doing that to Zach! How *dare* you interfere with my life like this? How DARE you?' I try to calm down and then think better of it. 'For the record, *Celeste*, Daniel didn't want to get back with me, I didn't want to get back with him, and Zach was – is – my friend. That's all there is to it. And I am *happy* on my own. Yes, it took me a while because break-ups are hard, but I *like* being single. These last few months have been great – I like discovering who I am and being my own person. And Toni will, too.' I inhale a big raggedy breath. 'But you don't really care about our happiness, do you, Celeste? As long as we're going along with what you want us to do. As long as you can control us both. All you want is for us both to fit into *your* definition of happy!' I am *steaming*. I can't remember ever being this angry. 'We're both grown-ups and yes, we're living in your house, but that doesn't mean you get to make decisions for us or that you get to know every single thing about our lives. You don't get to control us!' I run out of things to shout, breathing hard.

Celeste says nothing, too stunned to reply.

After a moment, her shoulders slump and she pulls out a chair to sit at the table.

I remain standing, panting as the anger drains out of me. Eventually I sit down beside her. I am surprised to find that I don't feel guilty. I'm glad I said all of that.

After a few minutes, she speaks, in a quiet voice. 'You're right,' she acknowledges. 'I know I'm too overbearing and controlling sometimes. Diane used to say the same thing.' She falters, trying to keep a lid on her emotions. 'I'm just so . . .

lonely and I don't want that for you two. I don't want you to be on your own and frightened like I am. I lash out, I know, but it's because I want the best possible lives for you.' She takes a deep breath. 'I did the wrong thing with Zach. And I've done the wrong thing by you both.' She smiles a wobbly, watery smile at me. 'I'm glad you're stronger than me.'

I nod, understanding. 'Have you ever thought about maybe ... talking to someone?' I suggest and she barks out a laugh.

'Oh darling, I work in showbiz – I've been in therapy for *years*.' She pauses, taking my question more seriously. 'To be honest, I've been thinking about maybe finding someone else. This woman I see is a celebrity therapist, she sees *everyone*.' She winks and there is a little more of the Celeste I know. 'And I mean *everyone*. I think I worry too much about what she thinks of me. I want her to like me, to be impressed by me, so I don't end up telling her things I know I should.'

'Hmm,' I grimace. 'That doesn't sound like the most effective form of therapy really.'

'No,' she concedes. 'I will ask my PA to get a list of other options together. A few who don't specialize in stars but in actual mental health.'

I laugh humourlessly. 'Good idea.'

She smiles again weakly, sniffly and shiny-cheeked from threatening tears, but they don't come yet. 'Do you forgive me?'

I open my mouth to say yes, but pull myself back. I'm not letting people off the hook anymore. 'It's not as easy as that,

377

Mum,' I tell her carefully. 'I need to see a change. I need you to stop trying to control us or manipulate us. We're grown-ups and need to make our own choices without being undermined by what you've decided is better for us. I love you, but I need you to try and be better.'

She takes a deep breath, looking determined. 'OK.' She regards me now, her expression softening. 'You *are* a grown-up,' she says now. 'And I'm really proud of you. You're such a smart, capable, beautiful woman.' She pauses. 'And you have strength, which I'm so glad about. I wasn't sure.'

I breathe in her compliments, my chest filling with pride. I do feel stronger. I feel like I'm making decisions for myself, instead of for others. I've been putting myself first and standing up for myself when it's required.

'I'm sorry about earlier,' she says quietly.

I cock my head. 'Upstairs?' I ask and she shakes her head.

'I mean earlier, in the store. When you asked again about the engagement concierge role.' She looks intensely vulnerable as she continues, 'I got insecure, I think. You are so brilliant and clever—'

'I'm not clever,' I interrupt automatically and she regards me askance.

'Of course you are!' She sounds like she means it. 'Darling, you're so clever. And you have all this emotional intelligence, which is far harder to come by than book smarts. You can read people and help people. Your empathy could fill a swimming pool.'

My eyes dampen. 'Thank you,' I whisper.

'Anyway,' she says, dabbing at her own eyes, 'I definitely think we should launch the store's very first engagement concierge. I spoke to my publicist on the way over here and she loved it. She's putting together a press release right now.'

I stand up. 'You're serious?'

She nods. 'Of course. It will actually be a great distraction from that godawful *Love Island* range.' She rolls her eyes. 'What was I *thinking*? Another area where I should've listened to you.' She sighs. 'Anyway, let's try the engagement concierge concept, which, by the way' — she winks at me — 'comes with a pay rise, of course!' We grin at each other across the kitchen table. 'I'm also going to speak to Zach and say sorry. See if he'll come back to work with us. You were a good team. We'll try it all,' she says. 'And *I* will try.'

'Thanks, Mum,' I say softly and reach for her hand. We stay there for another minute, holding hands and smiling at one another.

CHAPTER FORTY-THREE

'Oh darling, don't worry about it!' Celeste is saying into her phone. 'Not a second thought, I insist! It's not a problem *at all*. You are an angel with diamond wings who can do no wrong as far as I'm concerned, my sweet!' She pauses. 'Darling, let me put you on hold, I just need to make a note of something.' She jabs a finger at her phone and then turns to face the room where me, Myfanwy and Sonali are sprawled around the living room in various states of undress, enjoying a celebratory sleepover in honour of their big engagement news.

'What a CUNT!' Celeste is wild-eyed as she waves her mobile at us. 'This stupid prick on the phone has sent out our engagement concierge press release with a huge typo! It was his job to proof it before it went out. He had one job, the stupid twat! I'm going to have him fired so hard. I'm not just going to have him fired from his job, I'm going to have him loaded into a fucking cannon and fired at the sun. So he can burn to death knowing he's been fired twice. What a complete tosser.'

She pauses for only half a second but it is long enough for a small, tinny voice to pipe up from her phone.

'Er, Celeste, I think you might've put me on loudspeaker instead of on hold.'

Celeste jabs at her phone again, returning it to her ear. 'Oh no, not *you* my darling,' she tinkles smoothly. 'Of course not you, I'd never talk about you like that, you're my delicious peach melba with extra raspberry sauce.' Turning to our group again, she points at the phone in her hand and slow-motion mouths, 'CUNT.'

She stomps out of the room, still pouring confusing sweet nothings into this man's ear, and we all glance at each other, delighted at her outrageous ability to get away with anything. In the corner, Myfanwy flicks through the early morning channels, finding nothing and landing on *BBC Breakfast* weather.

'Carol Kirkwood is my sexuality,' Sonali announces, moving closer to the screen where the Scottish weather presenter beams her daily winning smile to the nation.

'Oi,' Myfanwy shouts across the room, lobbing a cushion. 'You're engaged now, Sonali, no perving at other women.'

'Try not to wreck my mum's house,' I faux-scold, then add with a huge grin, 'Especially just as I'm moving out . . .' There is excited murmuring and they both turn to me with interest. 'Well, soon anyway,' I explain, embarrassed by my premature grand announcement. 'As you know, Mum's given me a new job at the store and with the extra money I'm earning, I've worked out I can *just about* afford to get somewhere.

And the most exciting part is' – I try not to squeal – 'I've decided I'm going to live alone!'

The funny thing is, until a few days ago, I'd literally in my life never once considered living on my own. Which is so strange given how much I love being alone. I always thought I'd be too scared or too lonely, but I've never been more scared and lonely at points in this last year, and I've been living in a house with two other people! So much has happened and I've realized that I'm much braver than I thought I could be.

Myfanwy and Sonali cheer as I continue, 'I don't care how cheesy it sounds – I'm a strong, independent woman, who can enjoy her own company. I don't need a boyfriend to *protect* me or give me, like, permission to get out there and live my life.' I roll my eyes. 'And it's not like I'll be alone-*alone*. I have you brilliant pair who will no doubt turn up uninvited regularly.' I pause. 'And sure, I will probably end up in huge debt, living off payday loans and stealing diamonds from my workplace but still, I'm SO excited about it!'

Myfanwy lets out a big, 'You go, gurl!'

I beam, thinking how excited I am about this huge new adventure. I've done so much and changed how I see myself. I know I can do this.

From out in the hallway, the front door slams with dramatic flourish as Toni bounces into the room. 'It's over!' she shouts happily. 'It's OVER!'

'YES!' I yell back as she joins us, as pink-cheeked and more full of the joys than I've seen her in ages. Since before

Shawn actually. 'You did it?' I ask, trying to get out of the beanbag so I can hug her.

'Yes, and it was awful but it's OVER!' She can't stop smiling. 'I'm so relieved. He tried to explain to me so many times why I was wrong and how I'm being foolish, but thankfully I stayed strong.' I pull her in for a hug and I can feel how exhausted she is.

'Come sit down.' I lead her across to the sofa, where Sonali shuffles over to make room for Toni's tiny bum. 'We're objectifying weather legend Carol Kirkwood.'

She collapses down, adopting a thousand-yard stare. 'It's really over,' she whispers, mostly to herself now.

I bring my beanbag across to the sofa and lean my head against her arm as we all fall silent, hypnotized by the TV's low hum.

After a few minutes Toni turns to me, 'Hey Ginny,' she says thoughtfully. 'I actually did see one really nice flat when I was looking at places with Shawn.'

'Uh oh, you're not regretting dumping him already?' Myfanwy leans closer, the horror plain on her face.

Toni giggles. 'Definitely not! No, I ...' She glances at me hopefully. 'I wondered if maybe we could rent it together, Gin?'

All eyes turn to me, waiting for me to give that speech from earlier about wanting to be independent and all that guff.

'YES PLEASE!' I scream instead and we both stand up jumping up and down and shrieking.

Because sod it.

Yes, of course it's good to be a strong, powerful, independent woman, but you can still be all that while living with someone you love. It's OK to need people and to lean on people. I love my sister and we're simpatico introverted souls. We will make great housemates – we already have for a long time – and it might be some reassurance to Celeste, knowing we're looking after each other.

'Check it out,' Toni says excitedly, showing me photos on her phone of a small but bright two-bed flat on a leafy, tree-lined road. It looks amazing. The windows are large, the ceilings high, and there are two tiny but sweet bedrooms. Obviously, it's extortionately expensive, like everything in London, but I know between us, we can just about afford it.

'I love it!' I breathe, meaning it.

'Yay!' she squeaks. We both leap up excitedly, dancing around the room as we show everyone our – hopefully – new home.

This is the start of a new adventure for both of us, and I can't wait.

CHAPTER FORTY-FOUR

'OK, OK, hear me out.' I put up both hands in a surrender position. 'What if we put the ring . . .' I take the most dramatic pause of my life before the reveal ' . . .inside an *LOL Surprise!*?'

He sits up straight, eyes wide. 'Oh my god, yes. I could get four normal *LOLs* for the girls, and one special one for Cynthia. They all open them together and bam, I'm down on one knee!'

'Yes!' I squeal. 'It's easy enough to get hold of an empty *LOL Surprise!* plastic egg, and I have a handy guy who can rewrap it in plastic, so it looks unopened and brand new.'

I have a lot of *handy guys* now. Helium balloon specialists who can spell out all kinds of sweet messages, a fairy lights hire company that can completely dress a garden gazebo in under ten minutes, tent hire people who do everything from teepees to multi-room marquees, calligraphers who will deliver me a gorgeous, hand-painted *Marry Me* sign to hang around any number of dog necks – I have them all on my speed dial these days.

That is, if speed dial were still a thing.

I make some quick notes about our next steps as across the desk from me, my client goes quiet. Glancing up, I realize he is close to tears. Nigel here has been with his lovely partner, Cynthia, for nine years. They have four daughters, all close in age and all obsessed with dolls. He said right from the beginning of the meeting that he wanted them there, with him and Cynthia for the proposal, and after much discussion and brainstorming, we've landed on Nigel proposing via their favourite toy: *LOL Surprise!*

They're basically a kind of doll, each individually wrapped up in a plastic egg that is perfect for hiding a simple solitaire engagement ring.

'She's going to love it,' I tell him softly and he looks up at me gratefully.

'I know she will,' he replies, eyes shining.

It's been a few weeks since we launched the engagement concierge service and there's really no point trying to deny it – it's been an absolute hit. I am so booked up with appointments, it's a little overwhelming. Not to mention all the interview requests and magazine features we've appeared in. The public and media have even, thankfully, completely forgotten about Celeste's Stones' brief foray into those terrible accessories.

After Nigel and I finish up, I have two more appointments today. One is with a woman who's planning a proposal in a cave because she and her partner met spelunking five years ago. After that, I have a man who wants to do 'something around *Game of Thrones'* and would like to chat through some ideas. I hope he doesn't want me to sort something out with a dragon – I don't have a handy guy for that.

I promise to get chasing on the *LOL Surprise!* plan and Nigel makes a follow-up appointment for next week. We say our goodbyes and I feel a thrill of excitement race through me as I glance at my packed diary. This job is better than I ever could've anticipated. I love helping people like Nigel so much! I even love helping steer those men – because it is, sadly, always men – who want to do something terrible and attention-seeking. In just a short few weeks, I've already tact-fully moved one guy away from proposing in the middle of his sister's wedding and another who wanted to do it during his girlfriend's university graduation ceremony.

Last week I managed to talk down a guy whose girlfriend is an actress, about to star in her first-ever play. He wanted to interrupt her *first night* of performing the show, climb up on stage and pop the question there and then, if you can imagine.

And then there are those with just plain bad ideas. I got an email the other day from a bloke who wanted to know what I thought about him pretending to dump his girlfriend and then doing the whole 'Hey, JK!' thing, before getting down on one knee. Someone else asked me if he should hide the ring in his own dirty underwear, so his girlfriend would find it when she did his washing.

Shudder.

But even those chats are entertaining and I am bouncing into work every day, full of excitement.

It's also been the perfect antidote to working with my family. I have my own separate office that no one bothers me in. It means I can go see the rest of them in the main store if I *choose* to, but I also have a private space where I can work uninterrupted. No more micro-managing from Celeste.

To be fair to my mother, she's been a lot better in the last few weeks, since our big talk. She occasionally slips up and demands to know what I'm doing and where I'm going, but then you can see her pulling herself up – self-correcting. She's working on it, and I have more sympathy for her, knowing the context.

And it's definitely been easier since last weekend, when Toni and I moved out. We *love* our new flat. Really, really. It's been so lovely having someone to chat to in the evenings, but we both also totally get it when one of us wants to just head into our own bedroom for alone time.

Toni's been doing a bit of dating, but she's also taking some time to explore her asexuality. She's met some amazing people through a support group and though she says she's not ready to identify as Ace yet, she seems happy being on her path and taking her time figuring it all out. No more Shawns have passed through and I think she's more than happy to stay single indefinitely.

So am I, actually. I've lived through ten whole months of having my destiny written for me. Everything was pre-ordained and decided half a lifetime ago. So much of this period has made me feel like I didn't have any agency or choices of my own. I'm finally feeling like I have control back over my life now. And it feels good. It's only two months left until my thirty-third birthday and OK, I didn't meet my soulmate after all, but, without wanting to sound cheesy, I think I kinda did find my soulmate in myself.

And that is not a masturbation reference, whatever Myfanwy says.

I check my phone; I have half an hour until my cave diver arrives so I head into the main store to say hi to Toni. She's busy with a customer, who has his back to me, so I dawdle by the vintage range.

Because it's like ghostly Aunt Diane said, a soulmate doesn't have to be a partner, does it? I have multiple soulmates in my friends, Sonali and Myfanwy, and in my sister Toni. They are all jigsaw pieces that help form the whole picture of me.

'Oh, there she is!' Toni says from across the room, noticing me at last. 'Sorry Ginny, I thought you were still with a client. There's someone here to see you.'

I notice too late the twinkle in her eye, as in slow motion he turns to face me, all gorgeously tousled hair and tattoos.

Zach.

'Ginny,' he says in his familiar voice, adding simply, 'It's you.'

I swallow hard.

Despite everything, I haven't stopped thinking about him. I haven't stopped hoping I might hear from him. I haven't stopped dreaming about him.

'Are you . . .' I swallow. 'Has Celeste asked you to come back? Are you going to be back in the store?'

He nods slowly, as he crosses the room towards me. I watch him, my heart beating faster and faster. He's so handsome – but more than that, he is a good person. Fun and kind and sweet. And I am my best version of me around him.

After what feels like an eternity, he stands in front of me, and I can see now that he's breathing hard. We stand there, looking at one another for a full minute, his eyes searching mine.

'Ginny,' he says again and with that one word, his pupils dilate to black. He grins and clears his throat. 'So . . .' He raises his eyebrows and I put up a hand to stop him.

'Wait,' I say and his face drops with consternation. I know what he's going to say, and I want to do it. I want to be the brave one. I want to be the one being open and honest and real about my emotions. After all, I've only come on to this man three times – it's high time I tried again, right?

'Zach,' I begin seriously and he looks suddenly afraid. 'Even though you're not a TV star and you're definitely not Steve Buscemi, I do think you're the most beautiful man I've ever seen, and I'd like to take you on a date.'

His gorgeous face breaks out into a huge, dazzling grin as I echo his note back to him. 'You stole my line!' he accuses, throwing back his head in a bear laugh.

'I know,' I say proudly, standing tall. 'But I also really mean it. I like you a lot, Zach. And I know it's been complicated and weird and stupid, but it's also been amazing, hasn't it?'

He steps closer, holding his breath. I'm holding my breath, too.

'It's been fucking amazing,' he says in a whisper. 'You're fucking amazing and this could be fucking amazing.' He moves a tiny step closer, reaching a hand to my face and leaning in to kiss me. And he's right, it *is* fucking amazing.

When he finally pulls away, both of us now breathless, I take him in properly. 'Your hands are cold.'

He laughs. 'Sorry.' He smiles that devastating smile. 'I ran out of the house without my coat.'

I feel like my feet are no longer touching the floor as I ask in a faraway voice, 'What took you so long?'

He shakes his head. 'Flo.' He rolls his eyes. 'She only *just* told me you weren't dating anyone. I saw her for lunch today. We've both been working like fiends, and then—'

'Why did you think I was dating someone?' I ask, shaking my head in puzzlement.

'Well, I wasn't sure,' he admits, cocking his head. 'But I saw you hugging your ex, Daniel, at the funeral. Then you were wearing a wedding ring and someone told me you went on your honeymoon?!' Then it seemed like you were dating that guy Mikey, but Daniel was also still around?' He pauses. 'Basically, you had a guy with you pretty much every time I saw you! Honestly, I thought you had a situation going on like your Aunt Diane.'

I burst out laughing at this. Then look down at my hands, covered in a variety of rings. 'I work in a jewellery store, Zach!' I laugh. 'And OK, technically I went on my honeymoon, but with Myfanwy and Toni, not Daniel.' I nod. 'Mikey was just some idiot distraction, and Daniel and I had some unresolved stuff to sort out.'

Zach studies my face. 'Is it resolved now?'

I smile. 'Big time.'

He smiles back, 'OK, good, because—' This time I can't stop myself and I cut him off with another kiss. He tastes so good and somehow exactly like I thought he would. When we come up for air, he smiles again, dopily. 'God, I've thought about doing that for ages.' He pauses, looking sad. 'When Flo told me you were single, she mentioned it so casually. Like I wouldn't even care.' He hesitates again. 'But I really do care, Ginny.' He swallows hard, tracing a cold finger along my jawline as he studies my face. 'I haven't been able to stop thinking about you.'

'Same,' I admit, my skin tingling where he's touched it. 'But I'm not saying you're my soulmate,' I add with importance. 'I *have* a soulmate, and it's me, OK?'

He raises an eyebrow. 'Er, good?' He bites his lip. 'Can I kiss your soulmate?'

'Yes,' I tell him and he pulls me close again.

And it's the most amazing thing.

EPILOGUE

Two Months Later

I can't believe we're really here.

The lights dim and a sign over our heads instructs us to applaud. We oblige – enthusiastically.

It's my thirty-third birthday tomorrow and as part of my gift, Celeste has arranged for the whole lot of us to be in the audience for Crystal Ball's show. Sonali and Myfanwy are on one side of me, while Celeste, Toni and Zach sit on the other. Plus . . . Emily. Our old uni friend. A couple of months ago, I decided to reach out to her separately on WhatsApp. We had a big, honest chat – one I never would've dared have a year ago – about the distance between us. She admitted she'd felt pushed out over the years, and gradually involved herself less and less in our group. It made me sad that she'd held so much inside for so long. Since then, she's starting messaging us all more on the Uni Dicks Whatsapp group, and we've met up a few times. It's been so brilliant to reconnect and we're all so happy to have her back in our lives. We've been pretty much inseparable ever since. In fact, I'm pretty sure she was actually prediction number five – the person I thought lost forever. I'd assumed it was Flo, but, amazing as it was to resolve that awfulness between us, we only really see her when Zach and I are at family events.

The lanyard guy we met during our last visit was in reception to greet us, leading us to our special seats in the middle of the packed audience. It's apparently the perfect spot – *acoustically* – according to my mother.

Zach gives my hand a little squeeze and I glance at him appreciatively. He gives me a flash of his smile, his teeth lit up by the studio lights.

God he's gorgeous.

This is his first experience of Crystal Ball and I know he's going to love her. Even though, as he keeps reminding me, he's not really into this stuff. But neither was I, I remind him, and now I love it. I've become much more open this last year. I've downloaded an astrology app, and I've been learning about rising signs, moons, houses – all of that stuff. I'm letting a bit of magic and mysticism into my life and I like it. Oh! *And* I went wild swimming with Myfanwy and Sonali at the summer solstice the other day. I'm not saying I believe in everything, but I think it's good to try new things. And it's fun!

I did end up telling Zach about the six predictions, and he was intrigued, but he didn't really buy into it. To be honest, open as I am to my spiritual side these days, I'm still not totally convinced.

So many odd things have happened in this last year. I had so many inexplicable experiences, but does that mean there really are bigger things out there? Does the moon actually have any say in how I feel? Do the lines on my palm tell me my destiny? Does the day I was born mean something for what I choose to do with my life tomorrow?

I glance over at Zach. Is he my soulmate?

Sure, it might feel like he is right now, but that's chemicals, orgasms and hormones, not my nakshatras, surely?

Either way, I think I've come to the conclusion that . . . I don't know. I don't know anything, that's what I've realized. And that's probably a good thing. It's hard knowing what's coming. I was on high alert for so much of this past year, waiting and fearing; trying to second-guess the choices I didn't feel that I had much choice in.

'You OK?' Zach asks in a whisper and I nod, excitedly.

This is just one of the things I'm into when it comes to Zach: he checks in with me a lot. When we're out together as a group, he isn't glued to my side. He chats to everyone but he will always return to see how I'm doing. It sounds like such a small thing, but it's these little acts showing he cares that make me happy.

He's also an introvert like me and I can't emphasize enough how much easier that is. After those group outings, we both need recovery days. But I feel increasingly that I can recover with him by my side; he doesn't drain me in the same way other people usually do. In fact, he recharges me in a way no partner ever has before.

Lanyard guy shouts across the audience's murmurs. 'OK, we're going to start filming any second now, so get ready to applaud again – as loudly as you can please, folks! – when Crystal arrives on stage.'

I nod unnecessarily in the low light and he scuttles off backstage.

And there she is. The audience collectively gasps and then breaks out into spontaneous, thunderous clapping at the sight of her. She beams out at us, waving, though she likely can't see much beyond the first row thanks to those stage lights.

Crystal quickly launches into her opening monologue, speaking to the camera like it's the only person in the universe, before turning her sights – first and second sights – on the audience.

'Here we go . . .' Myfanwy breathes out beside me.

Half an hour in, multiple takes later, and the lanyard guy is back.

'WE'RE JUST HAVING A SHORT BREAK,' he shouts at all of us in his distinctively nasal voice. 'THERE'S TEA AND COFFEE BEING HANDED OUT, JUST SIT TIGHT. PLEASE DO NOT GO ANYWHERE. I MEAN IT, PLEASE STAY SEATED.'

The entire audience ignores him, standing up en masse to shuffle off and out of their seats, heading for the loo or outside for a cigarette break. For a moment, it looks like lanyard guy will yell at everyone again to return to their seats but I watch defeat enter his eyes as he lets out an exaggerated sigh and slumps back off the stage.

Only our group remains seated.

'She's really very good,' Celeste announces. 'Maybe I will get her on my show after all. There must be some psychic angle we haven't explored in the jewellery-making process.' She looks thoughtful and pulls out her phone to note something down.

'How did you avoid giving up your mobile?' Emily leans over, intrigued. The rest of us had to hand over our devices to put into a plastic bag with a cloakroom tag.

Celeste gives her a withering stare. 'I'm a celebrity,' she says as if no other explanation is required. Emily nods, accepting this and sitting back, engaging Sonali on the other side of her in conversation instead.

'Crystal's *brilliant*,' Myfanwy breathes, happily.

'It's great fun!' Zach says generously.

'I love her,' I declare, looking around. 'This is the best birthday present ever, thank you so much everyone.'

Sonali eyeballs me. 'Maybe if she zeroes in on us, you'll get a new set of predictions for your thirty-third year,' she suggests excitedly and I grimace.

'Sorry, but I really hope not. This has been the most dramatic, bizarre, telenovel-y year of my life. I want my next year to be quiet and peaceful, thank you.'

'But you *do* believe now, right?' Myfanwy quizzes me, frowning. 'You do believe in the predictions she gave you?'

'Hmm,' I begin, unsure how to explain how I feel about the whole thing.

'Oh my god,' she cries, 'You *have* to, surely!

'She doesn't have to!' Emily interjects as Sonali adds in a murmur, 'And don't call her Shirley.'

Emily leans in. 'Much of what happened can be attributed to coincidence,' she points out. 'Or, indeed, seeing what suited you. It's called confirmation bias. You see what you want to see and then everything else appears to be proof of what you already believe.'

'You are newly back in the fold,' Myfanwy tells her archly, but with a smile. 'You weren't here for any of the shit that went down.' She shakes her head determinedly. 'It was all too much. Too real. You can't deny it. You had the three losses: a break-up, a death and your flat.' She counts them off on her fingers.

'Aren't you a science teacher?' Zach raises a single eyebrow quizzically, and she snorts.

'Are you saying that just because I believe in evolution and know the periodic table, I can't also believe in the mystical universe?' She adds playfully, 'What a joyless life you must endure, Zach.'

'It is *horribly* joyless,' he says, grinning at me.

Myfanwy continues, ignoring her detractors. 'Then you had your three gains. You had your life-changing trip with the mushrooms, when you realized you were never getting back with Daniel,' she throws Zach an apologetic glance at the mention of my ex before moving smoothly on, 'and then you had the return of someone you thought you'd lost forever.' She nods at Emily, who rolls her eyes. 'And then you also found your soulmate! Duh!'

I duck my head, mortified at the mention of this one.

Zach and I have said we love each other and are having the most amazing time together, but *soulmates* is still a terrifying concept. Plus, how, like humiliating if he thinks I've been telling Myfanwy he's The One or whatever.

'How can you still be denying the truth?' Myfanwy sounds exasperated. 'And if you didn't think Crystal was on the level, why did we even go searching for her? Why are we here today?'

'I'm not saying I don't believe it . . .' I begin slowly. 'And I don't know why I wanted to find her. I think I just wanted answers, I wanted certainty. I thought she could reassure me.'

The truth is, ultimately, I think what I wanted from Crystal Ball wasn't anything to do with my predictions, really. I think the real, honest – too honest – truth of it is that I wanted to know everything was going to be OK. That's all. I wanted her to tell me my life was going to work out. That I would be happy and make others happy. I just wanted to know I would be all right.

But none of us can really know that. Life is full of bad and good. Whether there is such a thing as fate or destiny, we have to ride the weird train. If we try to second-guess what's coming, we'll never get anywhere because we'll be too afraid to take the steps we have to take.

'Well, I think you're a bunch of cynics,' Myfanwy declares, folding her arms crossly and slumping in her seat.

Sonali snuggles in. 'I believe,' she tells her loyally and my insides turn to lovely mush as I watch them smile at each other in their special way.

They've set a wedding date for next summer. I'm the best man. The best *person*.

Oh! And I'm getting a dog! All by myself!

I'm picking Kirstie the Cavapoo up in a few weeks and I can't wait.

Maybe down the road, if Zach and I end up living together or whatever, we can get Phil, too. But I have a feeling Kirstie's going to realize she doesn't need Phil and that she's perfectly complete and happy without him. I guess we'll see. You never know what the future holds. Right?

A figure appears beside us and I start to move my legs so they can get past, when I realize who it is.

'Oh my god, *Dad!*' I squeal. I leap up to wrap my arms around him and he laughs.

'Not too tight!' he says, sounding a bit squeezed. 'I'm very jetlagged.'

'How did you . . .? Where did you come from?' I ask, confused and glancing around. Everyone else looks smug, which means they knew he was coming along to surprise me.

'Happy birthday, darling!' he ruffles my hair annoyingly and I giggle.

'I can't believe you came!'

Myfanwy and the rest all shuffle down one seat as Dad greets Celeste, kissing her on the lips. Their mutual affection is clear to see.

'Of course, Ginny,' he smiles fondly at me. 'And I'm going to be home a lot more from here on out.' He glances at Celeste. 'We've decided it's time to take the plunge with lab-grown diamonds here in the UK!'

I squeal at this. It's something I've been pitching to them for a while now and I can't believe they're finally doing it. Dad nods. 'I know, I know, you've been telling us for ages it's the best way to ethically produce stones, so we're formally investing in a London lab. We've got more money to play with since we shut down the new store.'

Celeste leans in. 'I took a leaf out of your book, Ginny, and told Daddy the truth about how lonely I've been without him.' She looks at me pointedly. 'And there's money rolling in thanks to the huge success of our new engagement concierge!'

Dad beams happily. 'So I won't have to travel nearly so much going forward.'

'That's brilliant!' I say, feeling emotional.

'It *is* brilliant,' he confirms, glancing at Celeste with big, loving eyes before glancing back at the stage. 'So anyway, what have I missed?' he asks, as the audience starts to file back in around us. I spot the lanyard guy watching everyone return, relief on his face.

'COUPLE OF MINUTES, FOLKS!' he yells, and people start moving a little faster.

'Oh, Dad, the first half was awesome. Crystal Ball is amazing,' I enthuse, waving at the stage. 'They took a break from filming so we were just chatting about how, er, *mad* my thirty-second year has been!' I laugh and Myfanwy leans into my dad.

'We were talking about her six predictions, y'know? The psychic predictions from when Ginny was a teenager?' She narrows her eyes at me. 'And how they were *definitely* true and real.'

Dad looks surprised. 'God, I'd totally forgotten about that!' He glances at me. 'Do you remember I was with you that day at the funfair?'

Around us, people are finally seated and the lights get lower.

'You were?' I ask, shocked, trying to place him in my memories of that day.

'You've forgotten,' he laughs. 'I took you to the fair and then thought I'd have a wander about with you.' He laughs again. 'You were *very* embarrassed. But then you were seventeen, so that's fair enough.'

'Sixteen,' I correct him.

'QUIETEN DOWN NOW EVERYONE, PLEASE!' Lanyard guy shouts desperately as the voices around us become whispers.

In a lowered voice, Dad answers. 'No, you were definitely seventeen, Gin. I remember because I was teaching you to drive at the time. We did a lesson on the way to the funfair.' He pauses. 'I think you're confusing your age with how long the fortune teller said it would be before the predictions came true.'

I frown. 'What do you mean?' I whisper as around us everyone falls silent.

In the near-darkness he leans closer. 'Don't you remember?

She said it would be sixteen years until the six predictions came true. She said that a few times, I remember that *very* well. She said they'd begin after your birthday.'

The lanyard guy cues us and the room erupts again into applause as Crystal Ball retakes the stage.

'But that would mean . . .' My frown deepens, my mind whizzing as I process what he's saying. Have I? I couldn't have . . . ? Surely not? But if he was there with me, as an adult . . . and he remembers so clearly . . .

Dad leans in. 'No wonder you've all been talking about those predictions tonight, given it's your birthday tomorrow, Gin! I can't believe you're turning thirty-three – the year it's all meant to come true! You must be very excited.'

I stare at him in pure dismay. I'm too far gone, too astonished by his words, so I don't notice Crystal Ball until she's upon us.

'YOU,' she shouts, pointing directly at me.

'Oh god no,' I whisper as every head in the room turns in my direction. 'Not again . . .'

Acknowledgements

Hello! Don't mind me, I'm feeling a little wobbly, and not just because I'm writing acknowledgements for my SIXTH NOVEL (don't, I'll cry). My wobbledom is thanks to my brother, who's just been by with his partner to show me the 12-week scan of their first baby, due about a month before this book-baby hits shelves. So that's really nice, isn't it? I don't want babies myself (I like sleep and I don't like snot or poo), but I do LOVE being an aunt, and this will be my 10th niece or nephew!!! Isn't that mad and cool? But that's not what I'm here for, is it? Sorry about the tangent. I'm here in these back pages, to say a massive thank you to YOU. Thank you to you lovely, brilliant person, for buying and reading *Date With Destiny*. It blows my mind that real human beings are out there right now, reading words I typed out, like, a year and a half ago?! Strange, right? You are the best, and I hope DWD made you laugh and feel good things.

I had a lot of fun writing this one, and really enjoyed exploring my woo-woo-curious side – but it was also pretty hellish at times, as these things are. So I have to say the biggest thank you to my beautiful, kind and clever editor, Molly Crawford, who saw me through those tougher times so patiently. She has been wonderful throughout this whole process – as have the whole team at Simon & Schuster – and I can't thank all of you enough. Sabah, oh my god, Sabah. How do I love thee? I lits cannot count the ways. You have been so supportive and generous and calm when I have been an anxious mess. Thank you SO MUCH for all you've done and all you continue to do. Thank you brilliant Amy, for your marketing magic, and to SJV for singlehandedly changing the industry for the better with your #RespectRomFic movement. Thank you hugely to Clare, to Pip, to Jess, to Harriett, to Mina, and OBVIOUSLY a huge mega-thanks to the legendary rights team, Amy, Ben and Maud, who have made me some nice money. Thanks guys. I like money. Very much up for more money, if possible, ta.

I am unbelievably grateful to my beloved Diana, and the whole Marjacq gang – Guy, Leah – thanks to all of you.

One of my favourite things about writing books is the new world of boundless human kindness it has opened up to me. Women's fiction writers have to be among the most generous out there, and I can't thank you all enough. LOVE YOU Daisy Buchanan, Lauren Bravo, Beth O'Leary, Holly Bourne, Caroline Corcoran, Lindsey Kelk, Paige Toon, Ayisha Malik, Isabelle Broom, Rosie Walsh, Cesca Major, Kate Riordan, Caroline Hulse, Sukh Ojla, Marian Keyes, Milly Johnson (JOHNNYYYYYY), Mhairi McFarlane,

Salma El-Wardany, Laura Jane Williams, Louise O'Neill, Lia Louis, Justin Myers, Lizzy Dent, Beth Reekles, Hannah Doyle, Oenone Forbat, Poorna Bell, Sophie Cousens, Kate Weston, Olivia Beirne, Elena Armas – and so many more I've definitely forgotten, sorry.

And to my friends and family: fuck you all, you were useless. JK! Although it is true, you were mostly useless. Despite that, I really love you. Thank you for putting up with my weirdness, my introversion, and my self-hating endless moaning about procrastinating. Special thanks to Abi Doyle, who kinda inspired this story after making me go see my first psychic. Oh, and cheers David, I love you or whatever.